The Adventures of Neldon Broadbuckle:
Volume I

THE KINGBLADE CHRONICLES

The Adventures of Neldon Broadbuckle: Volume I

by Jarrett Skaddisson

Other Books by Jarrett Skaddisson:

The Kingblade Chronicles

Saga 1: Tarnadins of the Elder Forest
Book 1: Call of the Danna
Book 2: The Road to Anganor
Book 3: The Sign of the Sengara

This Work Is Dedicated
to
all those who have taught me
the tremendous value and virtue
of Humor

ACKNOWLEDGEMENTS

Here I wish to heartily thank those who have helped bring this book from my head to your hands with their various skills and talents: Max Garrison for editing and consulting, Ferdinand D. Ladera for cover art, Blaine Morehead for font and cover design, Cornelia Yoder for maps, Charlie Haas (CharlieHaas-Artwork.com) for character and concept art for thekingbladechronicles.com, Dawn Allman for text layout and design, Shang Tea for countless cups of refreshing and inspirational tea, and all my family and friends for inspiration and encouragement.

Table of Contents

———•◦•———

The Eleventh Annual Siloa Snow War

———•◦•———

Captain of the Koobachinky

———•◦•———

Pandemonium at the Prandingars' Pageant

Appendices

Maps

Preface

hen I first visited the world of Orona (and that was several years ago now), I did not realize how large of a place it really was. Indeed, it has many realms, vast and wild, seen and unseen, of which I yet have no knowledge. However, there are certain locations there that I know exceedingly well and would feel fully qualified to act as a guide in, should anyone from our world choose to visit them.

One of these is the village of Siloa. This village, of course, is the home of Aradis Kingblade and Girion Ringmark, with whom the readers of Saga 1 of the Kingblade Chronicles will be quite familiar. Oft have I wandered down Siloa's wide thoroughfares and in the woods, fields and farms nearby, under both sun and moon and in the full round of the seasons. I have heard many stories in my time there, but there was little space to tell them among the adventures of Aradis and Girion in the Elder Forest, beyond providing glimpses of them here and there. To rectify this, I have composed this volume, for herein reside some of the stories of Siloa, enriching those other adventures and yet not interfering with them. And although neither Aradis nor Girion is the principal focus of these stories, they do come into them as the companions of their primary player, the exceedingly oafish Neldon Broadbuckle.

There is certainly a place (and a very important one at that) in the human mind and heart for tales of faraway lands, great dangers and perils, terrifying darkness rent by glorious light, fear and courage, deeds that shake kingdoms and heroes who ride the waves of destiny. But there is also a place (a very dear one) for stories of home and hearth, of mirth, fellowship and family, of bright summer days and cool winter nights in places both comfortable and kind. The heart of man yearns, in one way or another, for both the trackless wilds of afar and the familiar ruts of a path leading to his own cottage, as it were.

This volume is offered in the hopes of treading those familiar ruts and presenting in writing the depth and breadth of Siloa that it has long possessed. In *Call of the Danna*, it is remarked that Aradis had many joyous memories in Siloa in times past, before the troubles of the year 717 began. Herein the reader may partake of some of these and hopefully be refreshed by them as he treads the byways of his own adventures.

Sincerely Yours,
Jarrett J. Skaddisson

How to Read This Book

A Note on Introductory Material and the Sequence of the Stories

The reader may, in truth, read this book however he wishes, including upside down, although that may prove quite troublesome and is not recommended. If the book is the reader's first entrance into the world of Orona, for the sake of getting his bearings, he may benefit from reading the introductory sections: *A Sketch of Siloa: Notes on a Velarisian Village and Its Relation to the World of Orona* and *Lazing and Lollies, Bungling and Buffoonery: An Introduction to the Humorous Histories of Neldonicus Broadbuckle and His Associates.*

I must confess that I am an absolute fiend for lore, and so far, no physician has been able to cure me of that. However, I am by no means under the delusion that others are also necessarily afflicted by such a condition. Nonetheless, there are some who do have a taste for such things, and it is for them, as well as for any curious new arrivals to Orona, that I have included the introductory sections that follow. The rest might well be pleased to know they may read the three main stories in this volume and follow them quite satisfactorily without consulting the introductory sections. They do provide more detail to the backdrop of the tales but are certainly not a prerequisite to the enjoyment or comprehension of them.

The aforementioned three main stories are *The Eleventh Annual Siloa Snow War*, *Captain of the Koobuchinky* and *Pandemonium at the Prandingars' Pageant*. These are arranged in chronological order (a configuration that seemed quite sensible to the author) but need not be read in that sequence to be fully intelligible, so the reader may begin with any one he likes. The first is about a great snowball fight and the second about a journey by raft. The third concerns a village pageant which goes terribly awry. They all feature a great deal of Neldonry and thus some very high-grade buffoonery and numerous comical antics.

It is hoped that the reader will enjoy these tales as much as Neldon Broadbuckle himself relishes one of his mother's summer plum cakes drizzled with torlinberry syrup. And if you've never had one of those before, I do recommend making a trip to Siloa, if only just to try one. But if this is unmanageable at present, hopefully this volume will suffice as a worthy (if not somewhat lesser) substitute.

A Sketch of Siloa

Notes on a Velarisian Village and Its Relation to the World of Orona

The stories contained in this volume are set in and around a village known as Siloa. For those readers who have not had any prior acquaintance with the world of Orona, the following explanation may prove helpful in illuminating something of how Siloa fits into that world. It will also give them a notion of the village's various facets: its climate, governance, economy, culture and so forth. And even those who have been to Orona before may learn a fair amount of new information in the following survey.

The World of Orona and the Kingdom of Velaris

Orona is an exceedingly large place, just like our own world, with sundering seas and majestic mountains, ancient forests and impenetrable jungles, sprawling deserts, some of sand and others of ice, thronging cities, quaint hamlets and much more besides. It is populated by various groups of people known as Narthanna. These include such familiar beings as Elves, Gnomes, Dwarves, Leprechauns and Menfolk (humans), as well as less familiar ones like Farga and Ingans. Any and all of these intelligent inhabitants of Orona are referred to as Barada; that is, an individual Gnome may be called a Barada, but a group of Gnomes, Elves and Menfolk may likewise be denoted as Barada, in this case without a preceding article.

In Orona, there are nine Neathmarda, which are the most populated landmasses of that world (although one of them is technically a group of landmasses, since it is a chain of islands). Siloa is located on the Neathmarda of Quarana, which is in the southern half of Orona. It is a small Mannish community (that is, a community of Menfolk or humans) in a kingdom known as Velaris, which lies on Quarana's eastern seaboard. Velaris is actually an Elven kingdom, and its chief administrators are all Plains-Elves, who have considerable disdain for the likes of Menfolk and thus are prone to mistreat them in various ways, both in word and in deed. Fortunately for the Siloans, however, there are not a great many Plains-

Elves in their area, so their dealings with them are rather minimal – a situation generally to the liking of both parties.

An Overview of Siloa

Siloa stands on the very western edge of a region known as Agleri, which is largely occupied by vast prairies, known quite sensibly as the Plains of Agleri. Only a short distance to the west of Siloa lies the Rimwold region, which is covered by Rimwold Forest. This forest contains a mixture of deciduous trees and evergreens, with evergreens becoming generally more dominant the farther west one goes.

Siloa itself is primarily a farming community, having somewhat more than four hundred persons in the town proper and several hundred more on homesteads surrounding it. Some of its population works in the forest to the west, others in the fields and orchards to the east, north and south, some in town at trade shops and others as hired hands on nearby farms or in settlements several miles up the road.

The Site Before Siloa

In the spot where Siloa now stands, there was once a settlement of Harvest-Gnomes known as Burradig. The Harvest-Gnomes were a group of Barada that lived in the Plains of Agleri before more recent settlers arrived, but they (including the inhabitants of Burradig) largely deserted the area during and after a war known as the Branding of Agleri, which occurred in 239-251 of the Latter Epoch, the fifth and current age of Orona. Remnants of Burradig are still uncovered by Siloans every now and then, including artifacts, bones and even lodgings.

As for whether there were any occupants of the site before the time of the Harvest-Gnomes, there have been discoveries that seem to indicate a Trollish presence there at one time. Dwarven and Goblin artifacts have been found in the vicinity as well, with the Goblin items appearing to be of the greatest antiquity.

The Founding of Siloa

Siloa has been in existence under that name since the late spring of the year 463 of the Latter Epoch, the current age of Orona. (Just as a point of reference, Neldon Broadbuckle, the hero of our stories, was born in LE

699.) At that time, thirty-five Mannish persons spread throughout eleven families, including men, women and children, came to the spot, journeying from the northeast, and decided it was an excellent place from which to access the gifts of both field and forest, since it lay right on the cusp of both Agleri and Rimwold. Immediately, some of them set to felling timber in the forest, while the others continued to tend the livestock they had brought with them and began to plant such crops as they could in that season.

These eleven families (known locally as "The Eleveners") are as follows: the Applecots, Barleycrofts, Beamstanders, Berrydores, Boughplucks, Broadbuckles, Harrowdells, Lamplers, Micklemares, Rushwicks and Woodhews. (Incidentally, all of these names can still be found among the inhabitants of Siloa today, and the families are still generally well-respected.) Their leader was a very resourceful, intelligent, determined and charismatic man known as Langman Lampler, a skilled lampwright whose name has been memorialized in several prominent locations in Siloa and its environs, including Lampler's Lane, the main street of the village, and Langman's Bridge, which crosses a watercourse called Bardlin Creek a short distance north of Siloa.

Not long after the arrival of these settlers, Langman himself carved the names of each of them into a specially selected rock taken from nearby Sarmallen Hill in Rimwold Forest. Above their names were etched the village code, "Noble Deeds Are a Crown to Both King and Commoner," the village proverb, "Against Righteous Resolve No Barrier Can Stand" and the village motto, "Honest Labor Is the Road to the Stars." Also emblazoned upon the rock, down at the bottom, was the recently chosen village emblem, which consisted of a standing evergreen on the left, a winding line running from top to bottom in the middle (a representation of Bardlin Creek) and a sheaf of grain on the right. This much-treasured stone was dubbed Founders' Rock and currently stands just north of town on the main road leading out of Siloa, which is known as the Eavesway, called thus because it runs for many miles along the very edge of Rimwold Forest.

Inhabitants and Language – Menfolk and Daiga

As was noted above, all of Siloa's inhabitants are Mannish; that is, they are Menfolk or humans. An individual male of the Menfolk is called a Manfellow, and an individual female is referred to as a Maena. All the Manfellows and Maenas of Siloa speak a language called Daiga, which was originally an Elven language from northern Orona, but in the past few hundred years, it has become the common tongue of many Oronic populations, though naturally not of those who are isolated or culturally resistant.

Siloan Seasons

The village of Siloa is located at a mid-latitude and consequently has a temperate climate with four distinct seasons. However, as it is more than two hundred miles inland, it does not experience as many of the mitigating effects of the sea as the coastal regions. Its climate is thus rather "continental," hosting the corresponding flora and fauna of mid-latitude eastern Quarana. Siloan summers are usually hot and humid but only occasionally blisteringly hot, and Siloan winters are cold and snowy but only occasionally bitterly cold. Springs and autumns there are generally mild and pleasant.

However, depending on the year, springtime can be rather volatile, as cyclones sometimes spawn on the Plains of Agleri, and ferocious thunderstorms may pass through the area as well. Siloa receives an average amount of rain through most of the year, with somewhat more in the spring, particularly early on. This comes in the form of increased winds and showers, which may be quite strong, from the Brines of Ferassi (the ocean to the east), a phenomenon which is referred to as the Brineblasts, the Bresslini or the Bresslings by the people of Velaris (with the Bresslini being the preferred Plains-Elven name and the Bresslings being commonly employed by Gnomes, Dwarves and Menfolk).

Government – The Dolnario and the Denossa

The only governmental positions that Siloa has are that of the Dolnario and the Denossa. (These words are both of Plains-Elven origin.) Both of these are appointed by higher officials in the Velarisian government. The Dolnario is a post somewhat akin to that of a mayor that was instituted by the Plains-Elves to promote and preserve order in more remote settlements. He is responsible for organizing community events, for maintaining an accurate census (primarily for tax-collecting purposes) and for acting as the town's representative in matters related to the barolla where it is located, if such a need should ever arise. For those who are curious, a barolla is a district of Velaris. The barolla in which Siloa is situated is called Feldryn, and its capital is Tellig.

In smaller communities like Siloa, the Dolnario is also responsible to some extent for keeping the peace, serving as a chief constable, a judge and even a jailor (if necessary) when misdemeanors are committed. For more serious transgressions, the Dolnario is required to summon and defer to an officer of the Sardolia, which is the authorized constabulary force of the Ruphani, the title for the ruler of all Velaris. In the days in which the tales in this volume occur, a Plains-Elf named Malvardo is the reigning Ruphani.

The Denossa acts as a deputy to the Dolnario, assisting him in his duties and most especially in the job of peacekeeping. Both the Dolnario and the Denossa receive a stipend from the Velarisian government for their work. However, generally speaking, both of them have additional occupations, as these civic posts are only substantial enough to consume a modest portion of their time.

The Dolnario of Siloa, a fellow by the name of Fennadris Barleycroft, has held the position for quite some time and is well-respected by the community. He is an amiable chap and for the most part genuinely does his best to serve both the government of Velaris and his fellow Siloans. The Denossa of Siloa, Cobbanick Wrastlebuck, is somewhat less well-liked, as he has something of a disagreeable and aggressive personality. Nonetheless, the prospect of being confronted or chased down by the likes of Mr. Wrastlebuck has given many a Siloan youth second thoughts about committing some prank or petty crime that might incur his wrath.

Education and Knowledge of "Other Parts"

Siloa has nothing to offer in the way of formal education, other than study of a particular trade or occupation with a craftsman or master; for in Velaris, that is a luxury primarily restricted to larger cities. Consequently, nearly everyone in Siloa (including the Dolnario) is illiterate and has only a rudimentary understanding of things such as history and the sciences, although craftsmen are of course privy to whatever processes are involved in their particular work. And even though Siloans have no awareness of the higher forms of mathematics, they are generally adept at arithmetic operations of a basic sort and are quite skilled with such things as rapid counting, measurements, calculations involving dates and figures needed for construction. They also have impressive memories, as is often the case among the illiterate. But regarding geography of the wider world, their competence is usually rather minimal.

Still, there is some knowledge among Siloa's populace of the larger world of Orona, even if it is rather hazy. They know of other Narthanna (i.e. other types of Barada) and a little of other Neathmarda, as well as some of the more famous happenings, locations, phenomena and so forth in the world. All of this information is disseminated either from visiting travelers or simply from common knowledge among the villagers that is passed down informally to their young ones.

Knowledge among Siloans of Velaris is much better, for travelers pass through on a regular basis and bring accounts of what is going on in the kingdom. Folk from Siloa do not often travel far afield in the kingdom, but if they do, upon their return, they are viewed as valuable sources of information regarding happenings in "other parts," which is what Siloans call anywhere beyond a few miles away. When it comes to local geography, though, particularly of places within five to ten miles away, most Siloans are thoroughly competent, especially because many of them must travel several miles to reach their place of employment.

Craftsmen and Apprenticeships

Although Siloa may not be renowned for its book-learning or academics, it does boast a number of very capable, skilled craftsmen who supply all of the villagers' basic needs. The trades of wagonwright, glazier, weaver, cooper, baker, blacksmith, carpenter, chandler, tanner, cobbler, tailor and many more besides are all represented.

Siloan youths, depending on their inclinations and their parents' wishes, may pursue either a vocation in some kind of agriculture or in a trade. All children are expected to help with basic chores on a farm, in the forest or in a tradesman's shop from a very young age, although some parents are not as diligent as others about making their children participate in these tasks.

Boys and girls alike are encouraged to begin study of a trade by the age of ten if that is to be their path. Ordinarily, this apprenticeship occurs under their parents' tutelage, but if their parents have no skill in a trade or if they desire for their children to pursue a different trade than their own, the children may work with a relative or someone from another family who is proficient in the trade they wish to master. Usually, apprentices are considered to have obtained enough mastery of their trade by the age of nineteen to be able to operate independently. Frequently, though, they will assist in their parents' or masters' endeavors for several years past this to become more established in the eyes of the community. Then, typically in their early twenties, youths start to ply their trade on their own to help meet the needs of Siloa's populace.

Economy

Siloa is largely structured around agricultural work (and has been from its inception) but of course includes all the trades that help sustain that kind of work, plus some others. There is also a segment of the population that works in the forest, either in cutting timber, hunting or gathering herbs for both culinary and medicinal purposes.

Those who obtain yields from field and forest usually bring their products into town to sell them. To facilitate the ease of transactions between those who live outside of town and those dwelling in the village proper, a farmer's market of sorts is set up on many days in a spacious lawn northeast of town called Harvesters' Green. The transactions held there, along with those held in shops and so forth, can take the form either of bartering or of simply using Velaris' designated coinage.

The monetary divisions of Velaris run from the tarion, a small bronze coin, up to the orgella, a medium-sized gold one. A complete list of the coin divisions and their respective worths is as follows: four bronze tarions make a copper gerrin, four gerrins make a bronze grandig, two grandigs make a silver byrna, eight byrnas make a silver skranna, eight skrannas make a silver taldryn and eight taldryns make a gold orgella.

There is some level of economic diversity among Siloans, but nothing as substantial as one might find in Velaris' larger cities. The poorest are often farming families that have smaller plots of land and who, for one reason or another, have difficulty consistently producing a good yield. The wealthiest are usually capable and diligent merchants whose goods or services require much study and finesse. Due to their higher income, these persons often reside in larger houses and have more niceties available to them.

Most Siloan goods and services stay within the community, but there are instances when they find their way beyond its borders, such as when Siloans have dealings with roving merchants or when surplus yields are sold to neighboring villages. Also, those who have skills in a particular trade may occasionally be called upon to ply them in or for settlements nearby. And, of course, there are occasions when travelers coming down the Eavesway pass through Siloa and purchase items or services during their sojourn there.

Agriculture

Siloa is, as was noted above, a settlement originally based around farming, and that continues to be its primary emphasis, for a significant portion of Siloa's populace is still involved in agricultural work. This is especially the case with Siloan youth, who often serve as laborers on the farms of their immediate families or those of close relatives and also as hired hands of others in the community or of villages nearby. Even those youth who are pursuing a trade generally have some kind of agricultural experience, whether it be with crops or with livestock, which usually comes through aiding friends or relatives with farm work in their spare time or during harvest season. Depending on the arrangement, youths may or may not receive wages for their labor.

A number of different crops are cultivated in the fields around Siloa. Wheat is most predominant, followed by barley, rye, holgum (an indigenous grain), oats and hay, but there are all kinds of vegetables, herbs and roots as well: carrots, rutabagas, turnips, radishes, onions, cabbages, parsley, mint, etc. and the ubiquitous cullet, a root which is a staple in the diet of Agleri dwellers. In addition, some of the houses in Siloa have small, family gardens adjacent to them which feature many of these same edibles, especially the herbs and the hardier root vegetables.

There is an assortment of orchards and berry patches near Siloa also, and these boast a respectable variety of nuts, fruits and berries. The nut orchards feature tarmins (which are reminiscent of almonds in flavor), banlogs (which are large, oblong nuts native to Rimwold Forest), chestnuts, walnuts and several other kinds, though these latter ones are grown in much smaller quantities. Siloan fruit orchards produce luscious plums, cherries and apples, along with a few other varieties (also in much smaller numbers).

It is the berry patches, however, which are the most diverse and for which Siloans most thoroughly pride themselves. (This is excluding their wheat production, of course, which is considered preeminent, since, as the Velarisian adage goes, "In Agleri, wheat rules without rival."). Within Siloa's berry patches, one will find torlinberries (which are magnificently sweet and juicy), strawberries, raspberries, dellumberries (which have something of a citrusy flavor), elderberries, blackberries, currants and more. Several villagers in town even have a berry bush or two just outside their homes.

Livestock that can be found around Siloa include cows (used for both milk and meat), pigs, chickens, geese, ducks, wratchens (a type of plump, flightless bird), sheep, goats and hindrogs, which are somewhat like rabbits. There are also horses and donkeys, but these are used only for transportation and labor.

Also, a handful of beekeepers reside in the area, and these keep Siloa well-supplied with honey. This honey comes from hives of both Rimwold Duzzledrones and Agleri Hallockhummers, which are the respective bee species of their namesake regions. Honey from Rimwold Duzzledrones is a bit on the darker side and has a tinge of nuttiness, and that from Agleri Hallockhummers possesses a milder, floral flavor.

Siloan Table Fare

Although Siloa is by no means a wealthy community, at least by Velarisian standards, it is generally a well-fed one, since it hosts so much agriculture. Farming families are, of course, able to dine upon their own yield, and families built more around a trade or something else can readily purchase food from local farmers.

When Siloa was first founded, the Menfolk there only consumed two meals a day, one in the late morning and the other (which was more extensive) well into the evening, as has been the custom of Menfolk for millennia. However, after a number of years, they adopted the Elven routine of three meals per day, and this continues to be observed in Siloa. Breakfast comes around dawn or a little before and is generally quite light. Lunch falls at noon and can last quite a bit longer, as it gives laborers a rest from the heat of the day. Supper is certainly more substantial than breakfast, but often less so than lunch, and is usually taken after nightfall.

Due to the great variety of foods available locally, the assortment of victuals found on Siloan tables can be considerable. Vegetables are featured heavily in Siloan cuisine, and fruit and berries are almost always to be had, either fresh or dried (when they are out of season). A decent store of nuts is practically assured in every Siloan household. Bread and grains are always in good supply, but in the case of dairy and eggs, the supply can vary considerably. Meat is available from both hunters and farmers but is more costly than other items and thus may only be included in one meal per day or even once every other day or more for those who are less well-off. Seasonings are mild and usually made from herbs grown in family gardens or purchased from local farmers. Also, mushrooms and wild herbs can be obtained from nearby Rimwold Forest by and from those who have the proper knowledge to gather them. More foreign commodities, such as tea and sugar, can be procured from traveling traders or from merchants in town who keep such things in stock.

Original Siloan recipes for standard dishes of Agleri are numerous and are passed down within families, with some being much more closely guarded than others. Also, in the Siloan consciousness, there is a general association between particular groups of food and particular seasons. In this thinking, vegetables go with autumn, meat with winter, grains with spring and fruit with the summer. In fact, there is a Siloan saying which encapsulates what the villagers consider to be classic local cuisine for each of the seasons:

Autumn roast for leaves of gold; winter stew for ice and cold.
Golden grain for winds and showers; berry feast for summer's flowers.

Trade and Tavenndi

To obtain more exotic items or ones simply not available in their own community, Siloans must await the arrival of traveling traders known as tavenndi (or tavenndo in the singular). These come through the village every now and then with wares from other parts of the kingdom, usually either from deep Rimwold or, more often, from Velaris' port cities. They customarily set up their wagons at the edge of town in a grassy space known as Tavenndi Lawn for a day or so and then move on to the next village. In exchange for their wares, they will accept either coinage or a trade. But regardless of which form of payment is chosen, these dealings are often quite lively, for the tavenndi are shrewd bargainers and some of the villagers are rather decent at haggling as well.

As each tavenndo's merchandise is different, those villagers who are looking for a certain item must be particularly diligent in paying a visit to Tavenndi Lawn each time the traders are there to see whether any of them have what they are looking for. Fortunately for those who may have missed a recent camp of tavenndi, there is also a merchant in town, Hillarnia Peddlepot, who functions somewhat like a resident tavenndo, as she regularly makes trades with and purchases from the tavenndi and keeps a supply of many of the random items they carry in her shop, Peddlepot Emporium. There is also a dry goods store, Quintessentials, run by Quinty Broadbuckle and his wife Halinda, that carries certain foodstuffs, textiles and other items commonly sold by the tavenndi.

Many of the tavenndi – or at least the ones that come through Siloa – are Mannish, but there are also some Elves and Dwarves among them, with the Elves almost always hailing from regions closer to the shores of the Brines of Ferassi, namely the Marlassi Coast and Cape Loresso, and the Dwarves quite often coming from the Rimwold region.

Life in Siloa:
Interactions with Outsiders, Activities and Leisure

For many in Siloa, the visits of the tavenndi are practically the only occasions when they interact with the outside world. Tax collectors make periodic trips to Siloa, of course, and travelers pass through not infrequently, but none of them stay long. Siloa does have a very well-kept tavern known as the Ploughman's Shanty, which also doubles as an inn, and if wayfarers do come through, that is the only place Siloans are likely to meet with them. And Siloans generally like things that way. Many of them are of the opinion that what goes on in "other parts" is mostly bad and bothersome and would prefer that such troubles left them well enough alone.

Indeed, the Menfolk of Siloa are quite content to ignore the outside world, for they have plenty to keep them occupied in their own village. They pride themselves on being self-sustaining, and, as a rule, are very industrious. They work hard at their labors, be they in field or forest or in some kind of tradesman's shop. And after a long day, many of them are accustomed to going to the Ploughman's Shanty to converse with friends or relatives before going home to their immediate families.

Nightly gatherings with friends at the Ploughman's Shanty or elsewhere, followed by a supper at home with family, constitute substantial enough leisure for many Siloans that they seek little else. There are, however, other activities in which folk engage in their spare time (although this commodity is rather limited, since there is often a great deal of work to be done). Some go fishing in nearby Bardlin Creek, and others go walking in Rimwold Forest. Many enjoy whittling, straw weaving, embroidery (many of the ladyfolk are quite adept at this) or some other type of handicraft. The honing of various physical skills, such as axe-throwing or juggling, may occupy folks' time as well. There are some who fill their leisure hours with creating poetry (ranging from excellent to abominable, depending on the individual) and others who fill them with telling stories to anyone who will listen, often crafting tales of their own, but also drawing from stock ones of both recent and age-old provenance. And there are quite a few who take to music for personal development as well.

Siloan children are not so easily satisfied as the adults and thus engage in a broader range of activities, including both harmless pursuits, like climbing trees and playing games out in the fields, and more troublesome ones, like juvenile pranks and general mischief-making.

Music and Dance

Nearly everyone in Siloa has a large repository of songs for all occasions stored in his memory. And, even though the villagers rarely have any formal training in music, simple exposure to Siloan culture aids in producing a satisfactory singing voice and a good sense of both pitch and rhythm. There are a few Siloans who can play instruments – simple flutes, fretted stringed instruments and the like – but most people's abilities are restricted to the vocal realm.

Music functions not only as an outlet for leisure and as an essential for celebrations, but is woven into nearly every other aspect of Siloan life as well. There are walking songs, working songs, songs of sorrow and songs of mirth, songs of allegiance to Velaris and also to the heritage of the Menfolk. Some folk are much more likely to burst spontaneously into song than others, but almost every Siloan does it on occasion, and music is nearly always in the air at least somewhere in Siloa during any given day.

Dance plays a role in Siloan life as well, but not one as prominent as that of music. Most Siloans can dance passably well, and some can do so quite skillfully. There are a number of communal dances that everyone learns from a young age, since they are performed at festivals throughout the year. Some of these are very somber dances from Siloa's ancient Mannish heritage, which often bear a quasi-ceremonial function, while others are inspired more by lively folk traditions of Velaris. And, of course, there is a fair amount of dancing that goes on in various gatherings at the local tavern, the Ploughman's Shanty. And there is always a good deal of dancing around harvest time, both in outdoor celebrations involving the whole village and in individual homes.

Marriage and Family

Marriage traditions in Siloa are a fascinating blend of ancient Mannish practices and more modern Elven ones, although the Elven elements have begun to eclipse the Mannish ones in more recent years. Siloans generally marry between the ages of sixteen and twenty-four, although the average is around nineteen. Wedding ceremonies and celebrations are largely structured around Elven traditions, but betrothals and preparation for marriage draw more heavily from Mannish roots.

Arranged marriages (a practice the Elves of Velaris largely view as outmoded) were normative in Siloa around the time of its founding, but nowadays there are much fewer of them. Nonetheless, they are still viewed as being perfectly viable and appropriate by Siloans. In cases in which the marriage is not set up by the parents, the prospective groom must approach the prospective bride's parents to ask for her hand in marriage. If permission is denied, that is simply the end of the matter, and if granted, the marriage is practically inevitable. This is because betrothal is viewed nearly as seriously as marriage itself, and thus, engagements are only ever broken off in the most extreme of circumstances. But regardless of whether a marriage is arranged or not, the aspiring groom is usually expected to pay a bridewealth to the parents of the prospective bride, with the objective of showing that he is fully capable of financially sustaining a wife.

Newly married couples, if they are well-off, may be able to move into their own house and operate independently of their parents. But as a rule, this is not quite feasible, so couples often reside with one of their sets of parents for a year or two before relocating to a home of their own.

Children invariably live with their parents until they get married (and even beyond that sometimes, as we have just noted). And when parents grow elderly and are less capable of sustaining themselves through their own work, they frequently move in with one of their children, with the expectation that he or she will now care for them. Indeed, as there is no sort of welfare to be had in Velaris, this is practically the only option for many aging individuals during their laborless years. Overall, the system works quite well, as parents provide for their children when they are unable to do so for themselves, and children return the favor when the situation is reversed.

Siloan Celebrations

Throughout the year, Siloans observe a number of different festivals and holidays, a few of which are ancient and Mannish in origin, but most of which are from what is known as "pan-Elven culture," which is the culture of certain groups of Elves from the northern half of Orona that has been disseminated throughout the whole of Orona in the last few centuries. Several of these festivals are celebrated in a green field known as Midsummer Meadow that lies in-between Siloa and the eaves of Rimwold Forest. Others are celebrated in individual families' homes, and still others take place in Lampler's Lane, the main street that runs through Siloa. Yet another much-beloved location is Harvesters' Green, a wide lawn lying just northeast of town.

Traditions of the Tessnah in Siloa

The vast majority of Menfolk around the world share something of a common culture and set of traditions that reflect their origins in southern Tassaru, which is a Neathmarda in the northern half of Orona. This collection of common culture and traditions is referred to as the Tessnah. Some groups of Menfolk have retained a great deal of it; Siloa has kept only a little, but elements of the Tessnah are nonetheless clearly present there.

Siloans still celebrate a few of the festivals of the Tessnah, and they quote semi-frequently from a work it holds in very high esteem known as the Sayings of the Sages. Few, if any, Siloans have ever read it, of course, but memory of many of its maxims is strong among the villagers, as they have been passed down from generation to generation.

The Tessnah holds that there is a realm known as the Haedra that is veiled from mortal sight, yet is interwoven or connected in some mysterious way with the world of Orona, although it extends far beyond it. The Haedra, it is believed, is populated by beings known as the Hadathi, who are more powerful than even the greatest of mortals. Siloans have a vague notion that these Hadathi are benevolent beings, but there are some who are persuaded that, although this may be true for some of the Hadathi, there are also a number of them that are wicked and conniving. All are agreed, though, that Hadathi are mighty in magic and may pass between their own realm and Orona if they wish. As the Haedra is the Hadathi's natural domain, their presence there is no great cause for concern, but most Siloans feel that an encounter with a Hadathi in Orona would be rather a different story.

Also, according to the Tessnah, there is a remote being known as the Danna, who is the ruler of a blissful land called Erdion, which is a dominion within the Haedra. It is thought that the Danna has tremendous knowledge of goings-on in Orona and that he may interfere with various happenings there in diverse ways. Depending on which Siloan one asks, one may hear that all of the Hadathi are in the Danna's employ as servants and messengers or that only some of them are. The Tessnah itself has rather a lot to say about the Danna, but knowledge of this subject has mostly been lost among the folk of Siloa over the centuries. The most that many Siloans will say with any certainty about him is that he is the most powerful and knowledgeable Haedran ruler, that he had a critical role in the founding of Orona itself and that it is best to speak well of him, for his reach is long. However, some talk favorably of him because they believe him to be essentially good, and others do thus more so because they are concerned with what might happen if they do not.

It is believed by many Siloans that, upon death, the remaining essence of a deceased mortal passes into the Haedra and there is comforted, provided he has made a decent effort at performing good deeds during his life (Although, an exact definition of what constitutes "good deeds" is something the vast majority are eager to make rather nebulous.) Most prefer not to speculate about what may become of those who are wicked.

The Tessnah also speaks of a bygone epoch commencing with Orona's founding and ending in the distant past, an age of heroes, monsters and magic, when the experience of mortals was far more mystical, as the veil between the Haedra and Orona was reputedly thinner. This age is known as the Forgotten Days, and for the Siloans, the name is apt, for memory of most happenings in that time has utterly vanished from among them. Mannish convictions about the Forgotten Days elicit no small amount of mockery from the Elves of Velaris, who regard belief in this period as a silly superstition. They themselves refer to the age stretching from the far past back to the origins of Orona as the Mists of Old, a period which has rather different characteristics than the Mannish Forgotten Days.

In any event, a few names and occurrences from the Forgotten Days have survived among the Siloans, and storytellers still remind folk of them periodically. Increasingly, Siloans themselves have come to regard these events and personages as tainted by fiction, but there are yet stalwarts who hold all of them to be real. This sometimes gives rise to lively arguments about the proper history of the world among the villagers, although these are never satisfactorily resolved, as there is no adequate source of authority for either side to appeal to in order to refute the other.

There is, however, a strongly united sentiment among the Menfolk of Siloa regarding one particular aspect of the Tessnah: all are well aware that they possess only a fraction of it, and all are grieved by this fact and wish they could regain what has been lost, for it is the very essence of their Mannish heritage. And many have a sneaking suspicion that it would behoove them to know a good deal more about the Hadathi and the Danna, especially if these entities have a good deal of influence on what really lies beyond death for mortals. A relevant proverb from the Saying the Sages which is from time to time repeated among Siloans (often in uncomfortable tones) is this: "Knowledge of this hither world may keep a man content all the days of his life, but he will wish for but a mite of understanding of what lies beyond when the hour of his passing draws nigh."

———•◦•◦•———

An Imperfect Vessel

The sketch of Siloa provided above is just that – a sketch. It is certainly not complete nor is the author fully at ease vouching for its absolute accuracy. It is difficult to take a place, a people and all that passes between and among them and convey it in the form of words to others without losing or marring some of the thing in the transference. However, words are perhaps one of the best mediums that we have for this endeavor, and for our purposes, they might well be satisfactory.

However, for those who wish to know Siloa better still after reading through this material, there is yet further understanding to be gained. If one wishes to study a place from afar, he may read about it and, in so doing, learn widely. If he wishes to set foot there without actually journeying thither, he may read a story about it and, in so doing, learn deeply. And fortunately, in the pages that follow, there is not only one story about Siloa, but three.

For those wishing to journey to that distant village, these stories may be an imperfect vessel for the trip, but a vessel nonetheless. And if the recorder of these adventures has done his work properly, it is hoped that readers will come away from these tales feeling that they really *have* set foot in Siloa after all.

Lazing and Lollies, Bungling and Buffoonery

An Introduction to the Humorous Histories of
Neldonicus Broadbuckle and His Associates

In the village of Siloa, there are a number of persons who may, at one time or another, be regarded as dunces, jesters, idlers or gluttons. But there is only one who is practically synonymous with those designations – a lad by the name of Neldon Broadbuckle. In fact, Neldon excels so magnificently at representing these traits that there is not a single Siloan who is unaware of his unenviable reputation. Now, it may be fairly debated whether or not the lad is famous, but it is an uncontestable fact that he is dismally infamous.

The stories contained in this volume are centered around the activity of the aforementioned Neldon Broadbuckle. Therefore, in the interest of those who would like to know a little something about the lad before they delve into a set of tales about him and his disastrous doings, the author thought it appropriate to provide a brief description of his personage and of those friends and family members who are rather closely affiliated with him.

NB: the following abridged biographies of Neldon and his associates are written from the perspective of the year LE 717.

A Basic Biography of Neldon Broadbuckle

Neldon Broadbuckle was born on the 26th of Ferenos in the year 699 of the Latter Epoch (Orona's current age) to Drampadus and Flinnadred Broadbuckle at Broadbuckle Bungalow (his house) in the village of Siloa. His full name is Neldonicus Pattermanny Broadbuckle, but hardly anyone besides his mother calls him that. It is actually somewhat uncommon for Menfolk to have middle names, and even those who do normally don't use them much. However, Neldon was given the middle name of Pattermanny in honor of his mildly famous ancestor, Pattermanny Ludwick Broadbuckle, whose chief renown came from rescuing a caravan of tavenndi (traveling merchants) passing through Siloa from a bear. This he did by playing a variety of trumpet called a murglesnop, which has an extremely jarring tone. Allegedly, the bear was so disturbed by the blasting of Pattermanny's murglesnop that it swiftly bounded off into the forest. (Incidentally, this very same murglesnop has been passed down through multiple generations and is now proudly on display over the fireplace in Broadbuckle Bungalow.)

Neldon has lived in Siloa his entire life and thus has received the typical natural education and experience acquired from growing up in that community. Initially, his parents guided him toward following in his father's footsteps by pursuing the lucrative trade of milling, but after a particularly unfortunate incident at the mill, they decided it might be better for him to learn the trade of a baker from his mother. This has not been without its difficulties, and so, through the years, Neldon has pursued various other apprenticeships and occupations, including working at his older brother Quinty's dry goods store, though he has returned to baking time and time again. If nothing else, this has proved convenient, since Broadbuckle Bakery, where his mother works, is actually connected to their abode by a short hallway. Thus, Neldon need only walk a handful of steps each morning in order to engage in his training.

Neldon's family is decently well-off, so it has not been as pressing for him to settle down in a particular line of work as it might be for other Siloan children. Also, though Neldon's mother does push him to be active in the bakery, it often requires far more effort than it is worth for her to motivate him to help her. So, out of sheer frustration and defeat, she will often simply exempt him from any chores in the bakery for the day. Consequently, he has been able to idle a lot of time away with his friends. For although they are all much more industrious than him, they are still inclined to spend time with each other whenever they can. And it is chiefly when Neldon is engaged in shenanigans with his friends that his less desirable traits of bungling and buffoonery are put on full display.

As for Neldon's appearance, he is a little taller than average and has sandy blond hair that is simultaneously curly and shaggy and is most often styled in a bowl cut. His eyes are a misty blue, and his skin is quite smooth and pasty, which unfortunately leads to him getting sunburnt rather easily. However, in roundness he rather exceeds the average. In fact, there are many parts of Neldon's anatomy that are rather round. This is most noticeable with his belly, but is also the case with many of the features of his plump face.

A Survey of Various Aspects of Neldon's Personality

Though Neldon Broadbuckle may be rightly classified simply as the village oaf or resident buffoon, his personality is quite complex and has a number of different aspects, which we will endeavor to detail here.

1) Paradoxical Work Ethic

Generally speaking, Neldon is quite lazy, and it takes a great deal to convince him to get off his indolent behind and make something of his day. He often operates at a rather slow pace even when he is asked to do something and must be constantly hounded to keep at it in order to make decent progress. And if he's not looking for an excuse to take a nap, he's often trying to find other ways to get out of whatever task it is that he's supposed to be engaged in. He sleeps late into the morning if his mother will let him and will slip off for an afternoon snooze almost any chance he gets.

However, even though idleness is the norm for Neldon, there are instances when he works practically harder than anyone else in Siloa. If the task before him, even if required, is something that he finds inspiring or stimulating, he will work at it with sincere fervor, frequently to the neglect of all else. It is this somewhat paradoxical, even outright contradictory, approach to labor which makes Neldon so unpredictable when work is assigned to him: one never knows what version of the lad one will get.

2) The Food Dimension

It would be by no means inaccurate to say that one of Neldon's greatest and enduring passions is for food. Indeed, his character cannot be properly understood without including this dimension. And, although he has a particular inclination toward sweets, he is enthralled to some degree with all kinds of edibles. Fruits, vegetables, grains, dairy, meat and much more are regularly consumed in great quantities by the lad. But his devouring of all manner of treats, sweets, lollies, cakes, cookies and pies is nothing short of legendary. Folk from neighboring villages, upon hearing how many pies or cookies Neldon ate in a single sitting, have more often than not labeled such reports as sheer exaggeration. But exaggeration they are not.

Neldon's parents have hoped for years that his appetite might be curbed at some point, even minimally so, but this has not occurred. His practically insatiable and nearly perpetual craving of munchables has continued unabated. Of course, this has resulted in something of a rotund shape for the lad's belly. Thus, according to Neldon's own words, he is "comfortably plump," although it should be noted that this is something of an understatement.

Like a goat, Neldon will not necessarily eat virtually anything put before him, but he'll certainly try it and may go through with eating it as well. In fact, it is well-known by Siloan children that if there is a dare involving whether so-and-so would be crazy enough to eat such-and-such, then whatever the such-and-such is, Neldon will almost certainly be the so-and-so.

3) Ineptitude Unparalleled

As Siloans have seen time and time again, once Neldon is brought into an affair, it is only a matter of time before he will bungle it badly in one way or another. Frequently, this is a consequence of his significant and unfortunate lack of ability in some area, such as physical coordination. Indeed, physical clumsiness is a persistent blight with the lad. He is notorious for spilling drinks, dropping breakable objects, tripping over his own feet, inadvertently causing injury to other people and many other like transgressions. But on many occasions, it is his intellectual clumsiness, as it were, that brings about disaster.

It is often the case that Neldon adopts some notion as an excellent idea but doesn't much bother to think it through. And even if he does, his judgment is so poor that ideas with disastrous consequences are heartily given his mental stamp of approval. Oblivious to many things that others consider self-evident and therefore requiring no explanation whatsoever, the lad botches most endeavors he is involved in. After the fact, when his errors are pointed out to him, he often sees the sense of others' analysis, but in the moment, his high esteem of his own abilities and decisions leads to catastrophe after catastrophe. Fortunately, most of these only have a minor effect, but the bigger the affair Neldon is involved in, the more wide-ranging the ruinous results will likely be.

Everyone who engages Neldon in a task thus does so with great risk. But most pity the lad and so continue to give him opportunities to redeem himself. He is very earnest in his attempts to do the right thing and very apologetic when things go awry, and this makes him quite endearing. He almost never fouls things up on purpose, and this may be partially why Neldon himself assumes that much of the cause for debacles he is associated with must lie in some way with his bad fortune rather than his own clumsiness and cluelessness.

4) Oaf Extraordinaire

Perhaps Neldon's most prominent characteristic is his complete and matchless buffoonery. While his ineptitude can be regarded as a lack in particular domains, this buffoonery is a unique *addition* to the brew of Neldon's persona. Just when you think he can't do anything more ridiculous or foolish, he'll go one step further. This, more than anything else, is the ingredient that has placed Neldon at the center of so many notorious incidents in Siloa. It is the special potency which takes him beyond being a mere bumbler to being a positive scourge; it is that which catapults him from being a problematic pest to being a catastrophe walking around on two lumpy legs. And this is made all the more picturesque by the fact that Neldon has no clue just how doltish he is. Indeed, to hear Neldon himself talk, one might come away with the impression that he is a fully viable candidate for Siloa's greatest unrecognized genius. Actually, there are many skills and attributes in which Neldon has appraised himself at a much higher level than their genuine status.

In its milder forms, Neldon's witlessness may manifest simply as him asking dumb questions, which elicit much annoyance. In its more severe forms, it may result in him doing idiotic things on impulse that lead to terrible results. Also, and perhaps even more unfortunately, Neldon's ignorance can be (and often is) preyed upon by other Siloan children (particularly his friend Corim Timberfall) for their own ends. Since Neldon is so gullible, he can be put up to do others' dirty work without realizing that such is what is going on. In this manner, blame for any mishaps that come out of the situation can be pinned on Neldon, while those who have manipulated him remain unsoiled.

5) Distinguished Oddball

Neldon has a tendency for very odd behaviors, not generally disturbing ones but odd ones nonetheless. One of the most prominent of these is his tendency to converse with inanimate objects or animals. Invariably, Neldon provides the narration in some comical (to others, not to Neldon) voice for whatever object or animal he is talking to. In his bedroom, he even has a sort of puppet made out of a stick, which he has dubbed Yankaboo, and he consults this Yankaboo for advice on a regular basis. It may be that Neldon engages in this practice of talking to objects simply to help himself think more clearly, but no one, including Neldon himself, is sure of the real reason. Whatever the case, Neldon doesn't believe the habit to be strange or perplexing and is actually curious why others don't have it as well.

Neldon also has the peculiar practice of sleeping with food in his bed, a custom that is perhaps easier to explain due to his great affinity for edibles. Along with this, he has a host of other odd quirks, like his obsession with his favorite orange vest, his constant failed attempts at being an acrobat and his spontaneous coining of new words, which he then tries to convince the rest of the villagers to adopt.

6) Earnest Friend to All

From all the previous categories, the reader may well get the impression that Neldon's personality only includes lamentable, laughable and unfavorable attributes. However, this is simply not the case. Neldon does indeed have several redeeming qualities, and they are quite strong. One of them is his generally kind heart toward everybody (or at least, nearly everybody). If it were wholly dependent on him, Neldon would almost certainly get along with everyone. He doesn't hold grudges, virtually always thinks the best of people and is very eager to be as friendly as possible.

Also, as all of his close friends know quite well, he is extremely loyal and sincere. He sticks by others through thick and thin, constantly looking for ways to cheer them up. And one never need speculate about whether he's being facetious or not, because sarcasm is simply not a component of any of his communication.

Though Neldon may be a disaster waiting to happen, proverbially put, he is also a fountain of enthusiasm and goodwill, and if he reaches out to encourage or befriend others, they can be assured that the gesture is genuine. And that is a rare and wonderful trait indeed.

Neldon's Close Relatives

Neldon is the second son of Drampadus and Flinnadred Broadbuckle, who are more commonly known as Drampo and Flinny, as folk in Siloa have something of an aversion to long and pretentious names. Drampo, his father, is the master miller at Hildenrill Mill, which stands near Bard-lin Creek in Rimwold Forest, just a few miles from Siloa. And Flinny, his mother, is the proprietor of Broadbuckle Bakery, which lies nigh to the north end of Siloa, on the east side of Lampler's Lane, the village's main street. The bakery is connected by a short hallway to their residence, Broadbuckle Bungalow, which lies just to the north. The entire Broad-buckle family is actually decently respected (with the exception of Neldon) and well-to-do, as Drampo and Flinny, along with their son Quinty, are competent and hard-working.

Neldon only has a single sibling: an older brother, Quinty, who lives next-door, just to the north, where he runs a dry goods store cleverly dubbed Quintessentials. He is more than a decade older than Neldon, and he and his wife Halinda have two children, a young boy, Milbert, and a little girl, Kebley (known often by the nickname of Kebbles). Quinty is very intelligent, perceptive and caring, and he has faithfully supported Neldon through the years, often giving him sound advice and encourage-ment, both before and after he gets himself into various predicaments. Quinty's full name (which is hardly ever used, even by his mother) is Quintavium Linderquanning Broadbuckle. The moniker of Linderquan-ning came from Linderquanning Elbaniggs Broadbuckle, his esteemed forefather, who was the patriarch of the Broadbuckles at the time they first settled in Siloa.

On Neldon's father's side, his grandparents are Hobbalin (Hobbsy) and Magdellium Broadbuckle, who have a very prosperous cottage in-dustry in town. Hobbalin is a joiner and makes excellent, sturdy articles of furniture out of wood, while his wife, Magdellium, is a quilter and embroiderer of considerable prowess. Both also work part-time as bar-bers. In Siloa and even in neighboring settlements, folk speak highly of them for their perfectionism in all of their crafts and their admirable dedication to their work.

Neldon's maternal grandparents, Talliford and Rengaletta Stickytub, are also quite well regarded. Talliford is primarily a cheesemaker and is even the inventor of the locally famous Stickytub Cheese, but he also works as a toymaker in his spare time. Toys are something of an extrava-gance in Siloa, but folk are willing to spend on Talliford's creations, as they are really quite amusing. Rengaletta is a candy and pastry maker (and the creator of the much-beloved Stickytub Taffy), and although such delights as she produces are also luxuries in Siloa, Siloans still purchase such things on occasion, for Rengaletta's culinary creations are second to none. Indeed, she is an all-around excellent cook and has a sort of catering business that services special events in Siloa, such as weddings, birthday feasts and the like. And when she isn't catering or making candies or pastries of her own, she assists her daughter (Neldon's mother) in Broadbuckle Bakery.

The Hemmigan Hideaway Gang

Like many other boys, Neldon has a group of steady, close friends with whom he spends much of his free time. These friends have been instrumental in many episodes of his life, and, though they frequently give the blundering Neldon a hard time, they genuinely do enjoy spending time with him (to an extent) and are concerned for his welfare.

Neldon's principal companions are five in number, and they (along with Neldon) may be grouped under the title of the Hemmigan Hideaway Gang, a name they imparted to themselves due to their longtime practice of meeting at a fort that they built up in Rimwold Forest in their younger years. This structure lies in the roots of a hemmigan tree and thus has been dubbed Hemmigan Hideaway. The original group consisted of Neldon, Tallis Pestleman, Darmon Barnwain, Aradis Kingblade and Corim Timberfall, but not long after Girion Ringmark moved to Siloa from Velaris' capital, Aragest, in the spring of LE 711 (i.e., the year 711 of the Latter Epoch), he was annexed to the band due to his close and fast friendship with Aradis Kingblade.

Below are brief biographical examinations of each of the members of the Hemmigan Hideaway Gang (save Neldon, who has already received a fair amount of description), included here since these individuals have been heavily involved in so many of Neldon's adventures. The order in which Neldon's friends are listed has nothing to do with their prominence in the group nor the strength of their relationship to Neldon, but rather is based on how closely they reside to Broadbuckle Bungalow. In fact, this is likely the sequence Neldon himself would use were he to compile a document of this nature. (Although, of course, this is only hypothetical, since Neldon can neither read nor write.) This is because he, like other Siloans, routinely categorizes things by geography as a memory aid.

Tallis Pestleman

Tallis was born on Serona 12, LE 698 at Pestleman Place (his house) in Siloa. He is Neldon's next-door neighbor, residing in the house just to the south of Broadbuckle Bungalow. Since he dwells in such close proximity to Neldon, he got to know him rather well early on as a child. In truth, Tallis found Neldon to be rather obnoxious for a time and dreaded the inevitable ruination that he brought to whatever activities in which they were both involved. However, he eventually came to see Neldon's finer qualities, so they ended up spending more and more time together.

Tallis has six brothers; one of them is his identical twin, Dallis, and the others, in descending order of age, are Edlimar, Tornigus, Bollicot, Leddaric and Pinnadore. His parents are Murraden and Melbyn. Murraden is a healer and herbalist and frequently enlists his sons' aid when searching for herbs in Rimwold Forest. Melbyn is a maid at the Ploughman's Shanty and assists both with serving food and drinks and tending to the sleeping rooms behind the counter.

In temperament, Tallis is rather reserved and intellectual. He is also given to criticism and is something of a pessimist and a naysayer. He doesn't like change, is distrustful of strangers and is an unfailing creature of habit. Before the exceptionally brilliant Girion Ringmark moved to Siloa, Tallis was considered one of the premier authorities on local geography and a great many other matters, but Girion has since eclipsed him in this regard, which has led to a degree of envy and competitiveness on Tallis' part.

However, while Tallis certainly is a source of criticism and negativity, he is also very industrious and helps to inspire others to work hard as well. In addition, he is an excellent drinking companion, as he loves few things more than a chat with friends and a fine mug of ale.

Moreover, he is very close to his family and enjoys taking care of his siblings. When his friends are faced with decisions, he is always ready to offer solid advice with their best interests in mind, even if it is delivered in a somewhat negative way, invariably prefaced with his classic "If I were you …"

He is quite creative and thoroughly enjoys coming up with little rhymes, which he refers to as "ditties." These are often of a comical and slightly insulting nature. He is also a superb forager and survivalist and knows a great deal about the plants and animals of the area, particularly of Rimwold Forest. And if one needs a tree climbed, Tallis is one of the best candidates around for such a task. In fact, he's quite good at climbing practically anything – not just trees – as he has spent a fair amount of time clambering around on the steeper rocks of Sarmallen Hill in Rimwold Forest.

In appearance, Tallis is both lean and tall, taller than all of his friends, in fact, and has straight, dark brown hair that curls up a bit where it falls at the back of his neck. His face is rather long, and he has a pronounced chin and cool brown eyes.

Darmon Barnwain

Darmon was born on Tannaril 29, LE 699 at Barnwain Stead (his house) in Siloa. He resides on the west side of Lampler's Lane about midway down the street. A longtime friend of Tallis due to shared interests and compatible temperaments, Darmon initially came to know Neldon more personally through time spent with Tallis when Neldon would accompany them, usually uninvited. Like Tallis, Darmon took a liking to Neldon's sincerity, transparency and innocence, but unlike his companion, he additionally rather enjoyed the humor value of Neldon getting into various messes.

Darmon has three siblings; the oldest of the Barnwain children is his brother, Fellaren, followed by another brother, Hobbo, and a sister, Sindagil, who sometimes goes by Sindy. Darmon is the youngest of the set. His parents are Brannic and Cornella. Brannic is a repairman and builder specializing in fixing and building fences and wagons, although he is also quite capable of constructing houses, barns, sheds and the like. However, his skills are more often called upon for mending than for construction. Cornella is an able seamstress and a skilled chandler as well. However, as the Barnwain family doesn't have its own chandlery, she assists in the making of candles at the Tapertrim Chandlery, which lies just two houses to the north.

Although sometimes giving the appearance of being extroverted, Darmon is actually quite introverted and keeps many of his true emotions and thoughts to himself. He is intelligent and witty, and his sense of humor is sophisticated and sometimes quite sarcastic. In a given conversation, he can usually be counted on to provide a continuous stream of good-natured jokes, and for this reason, he is often misunderstood to be frivolous. But those who know him well recognize that this is simply his way of maintaining a jovial atmosphere. Even though he is perhaps the least noticeable of the Hemmigan Hideaway Gang in an outright sense during one of their chats or in their various shenanigans, he in fact often provides the prevailing mood for whatever is going on. He feels no need to be the center of attention, but if he is placed there, he can certainly hold his own.

At home, he is both responsible and respectful, though when he is with his companions, he may be quite a bit more mischievous. He can be rather pensive at times, though not usually melancholy, and he seeks out time to be alone. Consequently, many of his interests and hobbies lie in solitary activities. Fishing in Bardlin Creek and nearby Trollig Lake is one of his favorite pastimes, and he has a special, private spot up in Rimwold Forest where he likes to go to think, especially when faced with troublesome decisions or situations. In his hours alone, Darmon also likes to whittle and juggle, and he is quite skilled in both of these pursuits. Additionally, he enjoys tinkering and inventing clever little devices and toys with his father's tools.

Notably, out of the friend group, Darmon is the only one who has had (and still has) a steady girlfriend, a very pretty, polite and resourceful girl named Ryaleth Beamstander who lives on the west side of Rimwold Row (the street west of Lampler's Lane), just a short distance to the south from his own abode. The two of them chiefly enjoy long walks and conversations, and Darmon has instilled a love for fishing in her over the years. Since Darmon's friends either have relatively little interest in girls (This is the case with Tallis and definitely with Neldon.) or else haven't had tremendous success in their relationships with them (which is particularly the case with Corim), they often give him a hard time about his tranquil relationship with Ryaleth.

In appearance, Darmon is about average height and is just a bit stocky. His eyes are a winsome hazel, and his wavy hair varies in length depending on the season, since he gets it cut only once a year. This annual trimming occurs at the beginning of the summer, and Darmon defends this somewhat unusual practice by claiming that it is "both astute and sensible" since it helps his head remain cooler in the summer and warmer in the winter.

Corim Timberfall

Corim was born in Timberfall Hall (his house) in Siloa on Bellin 4, LE 700 and is therefore the youngest member of the Hemmigan Hideaway Gang. He lives toward the south end of Siloa, on the east side of Lampler's Lane. And his relationship with Neldon has arguably the most complex of origins of the friend group, since it came about through the greatest number of connections. Corim had been friends with Aradis Kingblade since they were both very young, and Aradis had long been friends with Darmon Barnwain. Darmon, in turn, was friends with Tallis Pestleman, who was friends with Neldon. At some point, Corim started joining Aradis in spending time with Darmon, and Darmon often invited the two of them to do things with himself, Tallis and Neldon. Corim was greatly annoyed by Neldon even before he knew him well, and for a time, his annoyance only increased after this became the case. However, Corim eventually settled down to the idea of enjoying Neldon's company, and since he naturally was inclined to seek out people he could be competitive with and over whom he could demonstrate his superiority, he later came to relish Neldon's company even more. But despite this less-than-savory motive, it must be made clear that Corim really does have a soft spot in his heart for Neldon, although he doesn't very often show it outwardly.

Corim has seven siblings, and he is the fifth of the eight Timberfall children. The oldest three are girls; in descending order, they are Hendra, Mylis and Furdie. The fourth Timberfall is Branko, a boy. Corim's younger siblings are, also in descending order, Tedge, a brother, and Leena and Traysia, sisters. Corim's parents are Trambo and Lonnaren. Trambo is a lumberjack and is widely considered one of the best, a fact which he is unashamed to frequently broadcast to his wife and children. Lonnaren is a nanny; since she already has so many children of her own to mind, she regularly watches the children of families in which both the husband and wife must be out working in the fields and woods. Often, she receives some measure of financial compensation for this service.

Generally speaking, Corim is a very polarizing individual; people either think he's fantastic or find him practically intolerable. He is quite brash, loud and egotistical but is also a superb athlete, a strong leader and altogether charismatic. Indeed, he can be quite charming when he wants to be, and no one would argue that excitement didn't follow him like a shadow, since he never stops talking and is always stirring things up. But quite understandably, this is one of the very reasons many people can't stand him. Even in small doses, he can be exhausting to spend time with. Moreover, he is perpetually gossiping and sticking his nose in other peoples' business, and besides all this, he is defiant and manipulative and delights in opportunities to make fun of others. He has been described (quite accurately, one might add) as being downright mean on occasion, and he is infamous for holding grudges, even for years. Also, he is almost thoroughly devoid of tact and can be exceedingly blunt and rude. And in addition to all these undesirable traits, he has the bearing of a know-it-all, as he considers himself to be the foremost authority on virtually every subject or at least tries to convince other people that he is.

However, though his negative qualities are numerous, he has a number of admirable traits as well. He has thoroughly mastered the art of fun, and it is next to impossible not to be caught up in the contagious nature of his ongoing reveling. Also, he's quick-thinking and downright hilarious, and even when people of the respectable sort want to ignore or frown upon his endless stream of clever quips and comical remarks, they often find it difficult not to break into laughter or, at the very least, a stifled chuckle. In addition, Corim is really quite inspiring and can often persuade people to do things they wouldn't normally do on their own. He is very loyal to his friends in an absolute sense, although he will not hesitate to sacrifice them or their reputations for his own well-being if such is being threatened. This tendency, however, does have its limits, and if it comes down to it, Corim will work to help his companions, even if it means lying or doing something else unscrupulous to protect them. (Incidentally, it should be noted that Corim is an excellent liar.)

Corim's bubbling, exuberant exterior is apparent to all, but he also has a softer, sappier side. He is, without a doubt, a hopeless romantic, and this drives him to constantly be in pursuit of female affection. Unfortunately, his more disruptive, aggressive behaviors usually lead to the termination of his relationships. And no sooner is he out of one relationship than he begins seeking another. This sorry cycle has brought about much heckling from the Hemmigan Hideaway Gang. But in spite of this perpetual ribbing, Corim is always trying to enlist their assistance in helping him establish inroads with his next female prospect.

Although Corim is normally quite peppy and outgoing, he is also given to mood swings, which are obvious to everyone, since day in and day out, practically every emotion he has is displayed for all to see. He also has something of a nervous streak and is constantly running his hands through his hair or tapping on a table or whatever is nearby when he's worried about something. His friends have thus often advised him to pursue some sort of personal development or hobby to alleviate his anxiety. He does find a degree of relief in athletic pursuits, but he is so addicted to interaction with others that he can only manage doing things by himself for short stints of time.

In appearance, Corim is tall and good-looking, and he has a very winning face and smile. His frame is lean and lithe, yet muscular, and his head is topped with shortish, stylishly unkempt blond hair. His eyes are a flashy blue, and he has one of the best sets of teeth in Siloa.

Aradis Kingblade

Aradis was born on Derrig 19, LE 698 at Kingblade Cottage (his house) in Siloa. His home is just a short distance from the south end of Siloa, on the west side of Lampler's Lane. Like most everyone else in Siloa, he had long been aware of Neldon's reputation as a bumbler. But they did not get to know each other in earnest until their mutual friend Darmon Barnwain encouraged them all to do things together. Aradis then came to realize that, though Neldon was indeed as much of a bumbler as folk claimed (if not more so), he was also very kindhearted and friendly. This is, in fact, what prompted him to persuade his own friend, Corim Timberfall, to become better acquainted with Neldon.

Aradis is the eldest child in his family and has two siblings, a younger brother, Teric, and a little sister, Mellora, the youngest of the Kingblade children. His parents are Darion and Eribeth. Darion is an accomplished blacksmith; most of the time, his skills are employed in forging and fixing various farm implements, but he is also fully qualified to forge swords and other weaponry and is able to make intricate, decorative works of iron as well. Eribeth is a wool-spinner, a weaver and a seamstress, all trades much in demand in Siloa. She thus divides her time between these three occupations, apportioning the greatest number of hours to whichever one happens to be the most profitable at a given time.

Since childhood, Aradis has been an extremely hard worker. Whatever tasks his mother or father set before him, he performs them with great gusto and efficiency. He is very dedicated and passionate about whatever he's doing and is in some respects quite ambitious. Also, he has a very strong sense of right and wrong, and he tries to follow his own code of duty as best as he can. Consequently, he does not much appreciate it when others violate or interfere with this code.

This does not mean, however, that he always disapproves of mischief or antics or that he is never given to them himself. On his own, he wouldn't normally engage in such things, but his friend Corim certainly has influenced him on numerous occasions to do things that would be frowned upon by more upstanding folk. Generally speaking, the sentiment that Corim has tried to instill in him is that as long as the humor value of something outweighs the negative repercussions, it's all right. (This concept has been pretentiously dubbed the "Timberfall Principle" by none other than Corim himself.) Aradis hasn't fully bought into this idea, but it nonetheless overrides his better sensibilities every now and again.

When he feels someone is acting out of line, especially when that someone is his brother Teric, Aradis can demonstrate an explosive temper. Given to fighting both verbally and physically, he has been in more than a few brawls with other children in town. Whenever he is affronted or sees what he deems to be injustice, his blood begins to boil, and he impulsively lashes out, a behavior which has gotten him into no small amount of trouble. And sometimes, even when he isn't particularly angry, he can come across as aggressive and tactless. He is also something of a complainer and can be rather moody at times. Still, there is a side of him that is very appealing to many, as he is incredibly sincere and often quite idealistic in an admirable way. Also, there have been many situations in which he has exhibited boldness and raw courage. He is incredibly protective of his family and particularly of his little sister and will do almost anything for his friends, as he is tremendously loyal to them.

Although Aradis spends the vast majority of his time working and being as productive as possible, he relishes his free hours as well. In his spare time, he greatly enjoys talking with his friends and going out into the forests and fields with them for adventures. And he loves athletic activities of all kinds. He is both strong and swift, although his strength is greater than his speed, and he is quite good at tasks involving a high level of physical coordination. Competitions excite him, and he is always very exhilarated about festivals and events when he can contend with other youths.

In his quieter moods, Aradis is given to taking walks up in Midsummer Meadow and Rimwold Forest, and he loves looking up at the stars on clear nights. Aradis is arguably the most philosophical of the Hemmigan Hideaway Gang, or at least he was, until Girion Ringmark moved to Siloa. For this reason, he and Girion often have conversations about the deeper meaning of things, which the others, with the exception of Darmon and sometimes Tallis, find to be a little too abstract and probing for their liking.

In appearance, Aradis is tall and handsome, with coarse, shoulder-length, dirty-blond hair and determined green eyes. His build is simultaneously slender and muscular, with a predominance of the latter. The results of his constant wielding of a blacksmith's hammer under his father's direction are displayed noticeably in his arms, but his legs are quite solid also, as he spends a fair amount of time walking, particularly to and from Ringmark Farm to see his friend Girion.

Girion Ringmark

Girion was born on Galrim 9, LE 697 and is therefore the oldest member of the Hemmigan Hideaway Gang. Notably, unlike the rest of his friends, he was neither born nor bred in Siloa. In fact, he was born in the birthing ward of the Cavelli Point Dispensary in the port city of Belestro, which lies in the barolla (province) of Eldrasso in northeastern Velaris. He resided in Belestro for about two years before his parents moved with him to Velaris' capital city of Aragest. There his parents established themselves as profitable artisans and merchants, and Girion attended a private school, Lavrassi Academy, for a number of years. He was actually admitted to the school at a younger age than normal, since he demonstrated such remarkable aptitude.

However, persecution of Menfolk became heightened in Aragest in ensuing years, and his parents decided that it would be prudent for them to relocate before things got worse. Unfortunately, their home was robbed and their workshops ransacked shortly before they had planned to depart, and much of the money that his parents had hoped to use to reestablish themselves was stolen. Thus, in great haste, they bid their friends and relations farewell, purchased a wagon, two horses and some supplies with much of their remaining funds (some of which had been donated to them by relatives) and set out to the southwest. This was in the early spring of LE 711. Their aim was to go deep into Mannish territory, for they hoped they might receive better treatment from their fellow Menfolk than they had from the other Narthanna of Aragest, particularly the Plains-Elves and the Druids.

The Ringmarks' journey (which had a profound effect on Girion, we should note) took them diagonally across Cape Loresso down to the city of Telzuri. They followed the coast from there through Jacanno and on to Tarwyn. After a brief stay there, they traveled on up the River Tarino to the city of Rondo, then took a route known as the Couriers' Trace through Demryn and on to Tellig. Girion's father considered settling in Tellig, but as there was a Plains-Elven presence there (though not a significant one), he thought better of it, and the family journeyed on southwest across the barolla of Feldryn, in which lies Siloa. They eventually came to an east-west road known as the Parellian Plainsline, and this they took all the way west to Siloa, where it has its western terminus.

By the time they reached Siloa, they had nearly run out of money and supplies, but fortunately, they were now in a village that was wholly populated by Menfolk who were quite friendly to them. As a matter of fact, on the very evening Girion's family arrived, they encountered Aradis Kingblade's father, Darion, who, upon hearing their story, invited them to lodge at his home until they could determine what they would be doing from that point on. Within just a few days, Girion's parents decided that they would settle in Siloa.

With assistance from Aradis' family, they were soon able to take up residence in a small homestead (which they dubbed Ringmark Farm) two miles to the east of the village as tenants of a kindly landowner, Weslin Furrowmead, who needed laborers to aid him with his bountiful wheat harvest that spring. In the months that followed, Girion's parents, in addition to farming the adjacent fields for Mr. Furrowmead, began plying their respective trades again. And eventually, several years later, they were able to actually purchase their homestead and some farming land from him.

Girion came to know Neldon and the rest of the Hemmigan Hideaway Gang not long after moving to Siloa, as he was introduced to them via Aradis. The friend group welcomed him warmly and was generally fascinated by his life story and experiences and his knowledge of the wider world. They also thoroughly enjoyed explaining the ways and world of Siloa to him, and he was eager to learn everything they would teach him.

Girion is an only child, and his parents are Dugamar and Anella. Dugamar is a first-rate cooper, and his products were always very sought after in Aragest, as they still are in Siloa, where it is said, "A Ringmark barrel is hard to beat." Also, since his time in Siloa, he has become a thoroughly proficient wheat farmer. Anella is both a magnificent artist and a superb potter, although her skills in the former area are not in much demand in Siloa, though they certainly were in Aragest, where she was even commissioned to paint a mural on the Civic Records Hall of Storvossi, a borough in the capital district.

Anyone who spends even a modest amount of time with Girion quickly comes to realize that he has both a prodigious intellect and a great thirst for learning. His expertise and knowledge cover a dazzling array of subjects, and he is almost always making insightful observations or analyses. However, for all of his brilliance, he is still extremely humble and personable. In fact, he is one of the very best conversationalists in Siloa and is earnestly interested in others' lives and concerns. Ever seeking to compliment and encourage others, he wins the hearts of most everyone he talks to. He is also an excellent mediator, since he is often able to smooth over disputes and de-escalate hostility with remarkable tact and finesse. Frequently, when placed in the middle of difficult positions, he can contrive clever and well-received compromises, since he recognizes that both sides of a conflict usually have valid points.

As a worker, Girion is exceedingly diligent, careful and dependable. His mother has trained him to be a skillful artist and potter, and his father has brought him up well in the work of a cooper. In addition, he has tremendous knowledge of geography and history and is quite adept at mathematics at well. Also, he, along with his parents and Tas Wedgenware, a potter in town, are the only ones in Siloa who can read. Since there are so few books available in the area, Girion has read the few that he has over and over again, to the point that he has practically memorized them. And, to augment his collection, he buys new books from tavenndi (traveling merchants) whenever he can.

Girion has many skills, talents and interests, some of which are more valued than others by Siloans. His academic skills, such as writing, are seen as interesting and unique by many villagers, but not as terribly useful. This, however, has not deterred the lad from continuing to develop them. He has a great love for maps and also a knack for acting, as he was an acclaimed thespian during his time at Lavrassi Academy at Aragest. Girion is also a marvelous musician, and in his spare time, he enjoys singing and playing his kindarra, which is a five-stringed, fretted instrument he brought with him from Aragest. Besides the kindarra, he also plays the crannylig, a six-holed fipple flute, and the hallsdocken, a sort of concertina. In addition, he is an amazing thrower and can hurl stones and other small objects farther and more accurately than practically anyone in Siloa.

In appearance, Girion is a little above average height and has curly, black hair. Also, he is decently well-built, as he often engages in farm labor. His eyes are an introspective brown, and his face overall gives an impression of great maturity.

———•◦•◦•———

Beyond Introductions

The preceding material is, of course, only intended to serve as an introduction to Neldon, his family and his friends. It is hoped that the reader, after having become acquainted with them in brief, will seek to know them better. This end can be most readily achieved by reading the main tales that follow in this volume, which one and all are now invited to do.

And to those who have gone through the whole of the introductory material in this text (which is presumably the case if you are reading this segment), a warm congratulations is extended. You are now well on your way to becoming an able initiate in the lore of Siloa and its inhabitants.

Orona

Murnia
Tassaru
Estereth
Jassuna
The Bushbelt
The Eldritch Isles
Byram
Quarana
Fenrost
75°N
60°N
45°N
30°N
15°N
0°
15°S
30°S
45°S
60°S
75°S
180°W
150°W
120°W
90°W
60°W
30°W
0°
30°E
60°E
90°E
120°E
150°E
180°E

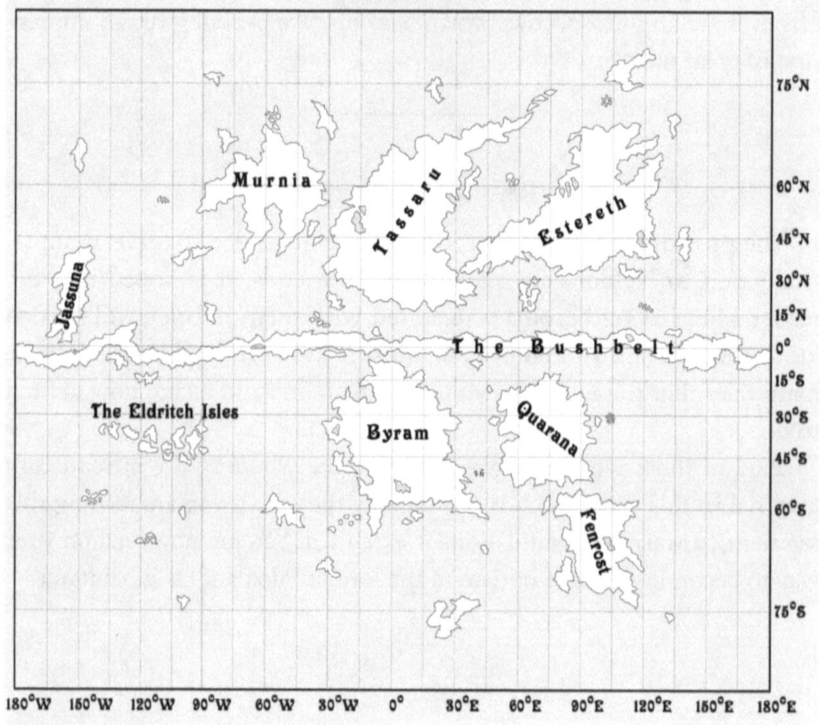

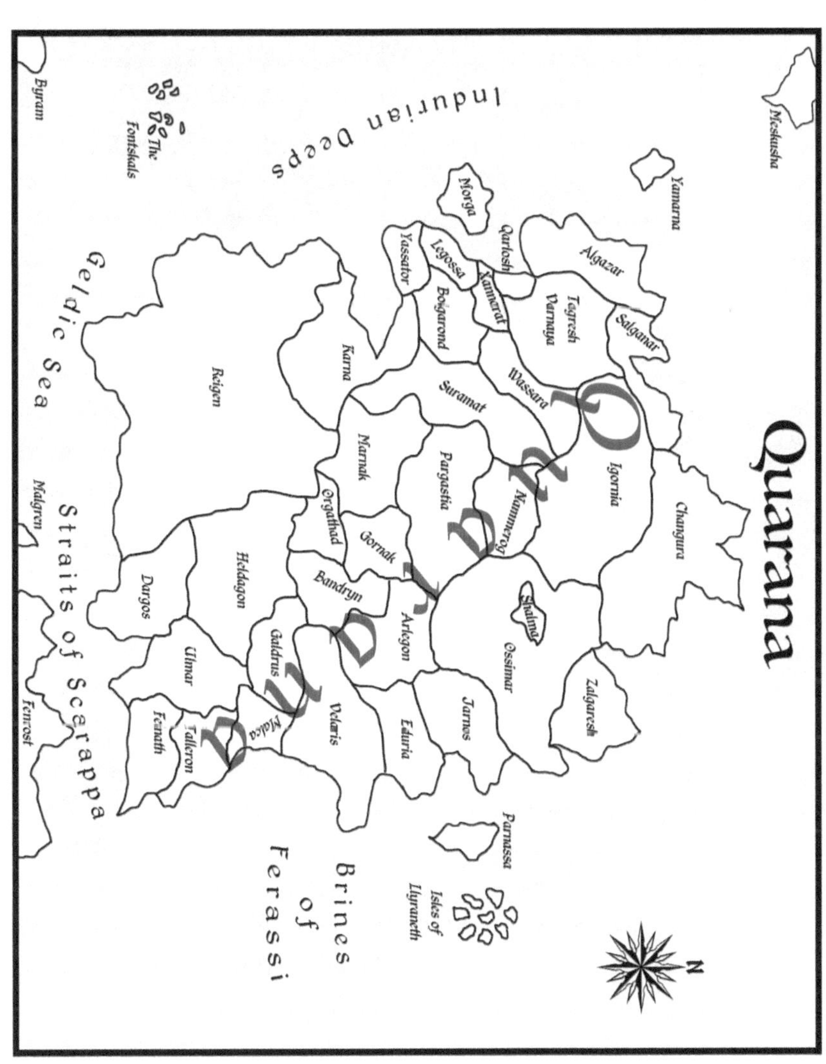

Quarana
Byram
Meskusha
The Fontskals
Indurian Deeps
Yamarna
Morga
Qarlosh
Algazar
Yassator
Legossa
Kamerat
Tegresh
Varnaya
Salganar
Boigarond
Wassara
Karna
Suramat
Geldic Sea
Reigen
Marnak
Pargastia
Nammarog
Igornia
Changura
Orgathad
Gornak
Thalmar
Ossimar
Zalgaresh
Malgren
Heldagon
Bandryn
Arkegon
Eduria
Jarnes
Dargos
Straits of Scearppa
Ulmar
Galdrus
Velaris
Fenatth
Talleron
Malaca
Fencost
Parnassa
Isles of Lluraneth
Brines of Ferassi
N

The Kingdom of
Velaris
(West)
N
Parlaedian Mountains
The Kingdom of Arlegon
River Tarins
The Kingdom of Eduria
Aldric
Tarnim
Londi
Urnig
Durman
The Kingdom of Bandryn
Osgaria
Meregon
Gallig
Trommendall
Rimwold Forest
Ardol
Forlig
Baldis
River Algo
The Far Forest
Donrast
Talgryn
Rellig
Geldin
River Algo
Marlig
Hagrum
The Kingdom of Galdrus

Legend
Town, City or Village
Bridge or Ferry
Road
Barolla Capital
Regional Capital
National Capital
Miles
0   50   100   150

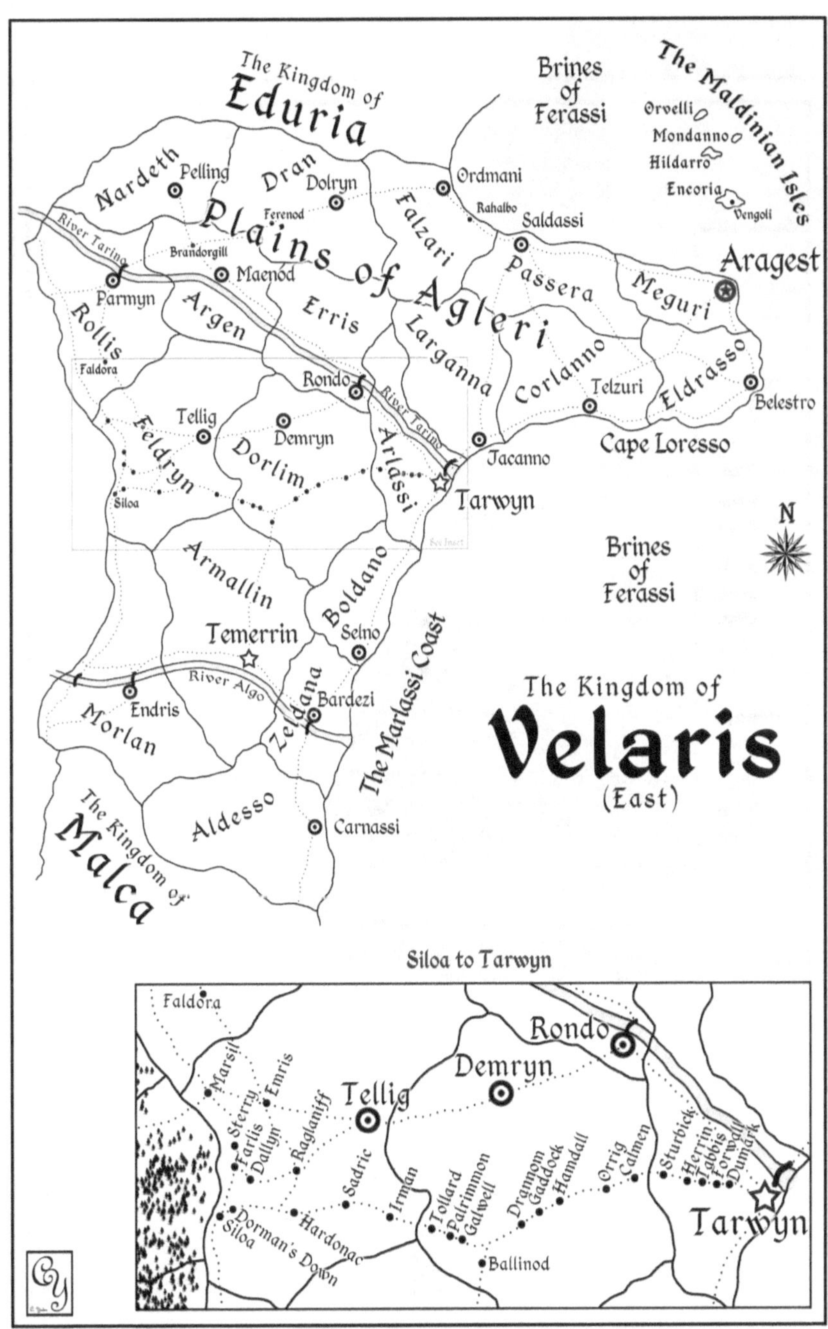

The Kingdom of
Eduria
Brines of Ferassi
The Maldinian Isles
Orvelli
Mondanno
Hildarro
Encoria
Vengoli
Nardeth
Pelling
Dran
Dolryn
Ordmani
Rahalbo
Saldassi
Aragest
Ferenod
Plains of Agleri
Falzari
Passera
Meguri
Brandorgill
Maenod
Erris
Larganna
Corlanno
Eldrasso
River Tarina
Parmyn
Argen
Telzuri
Belestro
Rollis
Faldora
Rondo
River Tarina
Cape Loresso
Tellig
Demryn
Arlassi
Jacanno
Feldryn
Dorlim
Tarwyn
Siloa
See Inset
Brines of Ferassi
Armallin
Boldano
N
Temerrin
Selno
The Marlassi Coast
The Kingdom of
Velaris
(East)
River Algo
Endris
Zeldana
Bardezi
Morlan
The Kingdom of
Malca
Aldesso
Carnassi
Siloa to Tarwyn
Faldora
Rondo
Marsili
Demryn
Sterry
Emris
Tellig
Farlis
Raglaniff
Sturbick
Dallyn
Herrin
Labbis
Sadric
Orrig
Torwald
Caimen
Dumark
Irman
Drannon
Dorman's Down
Tollard
Gaddock
Hamdall
Hardonac
Palrimmon
Galwell
Tarwyn
Siloa
Ballinod

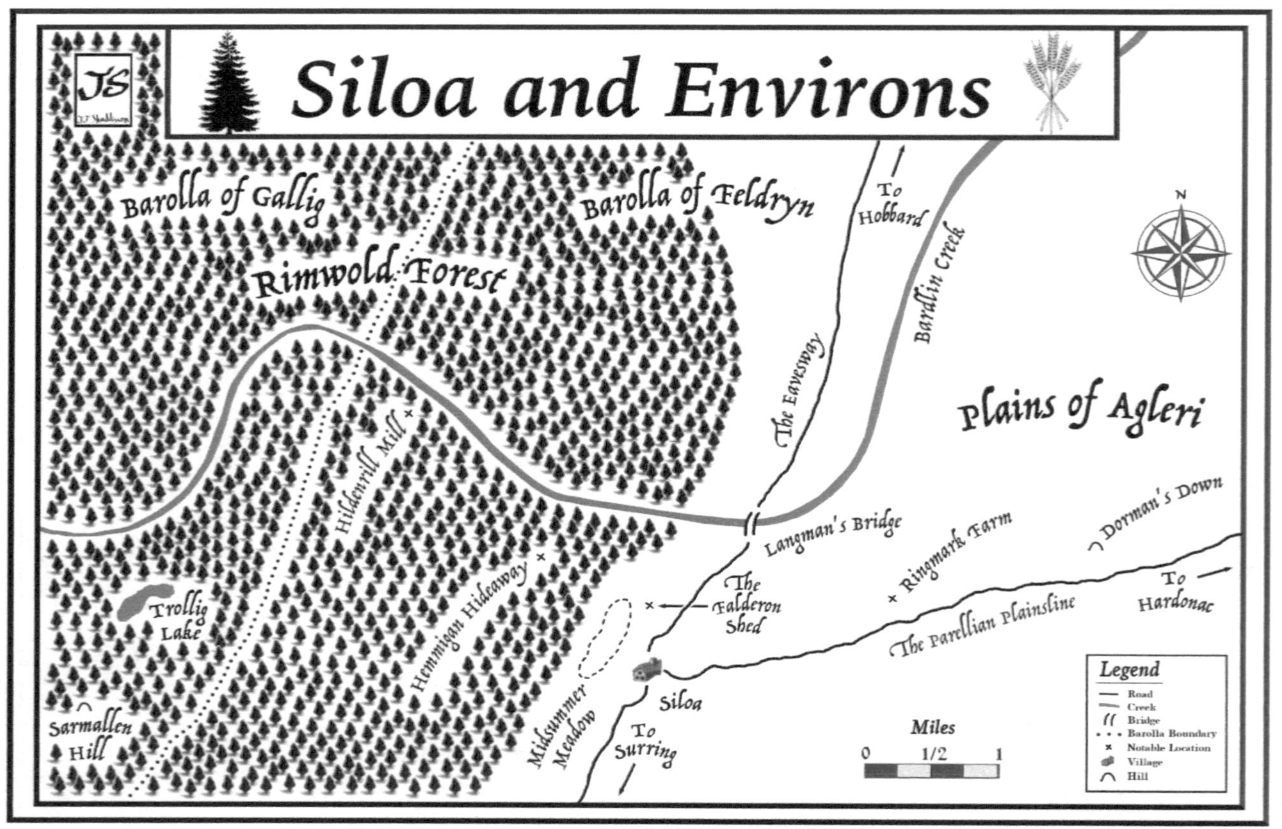

Siloa and Environs
JS
Barolla of Gallig
Barolla of Feldryn
Rimwold Forest
To Hobbard
Bardlin Creek
The Eavesway
Plains of Agleri
N
Hildenvill Mill
Langman's Bridge
Ringmark Farm
Dorman's Down
To Hardonac
The Falderon Shed
The Parellian Plainsline
Trollig Lake
Hemmigan Hideaway
Sarmallen Hill
Midsummer Meadow
Siloa
To Surring
Miles
0   1/2   1
Legend
Road
Creek
Bridge
Barolla Boundary
Notable Location
Village
Hill

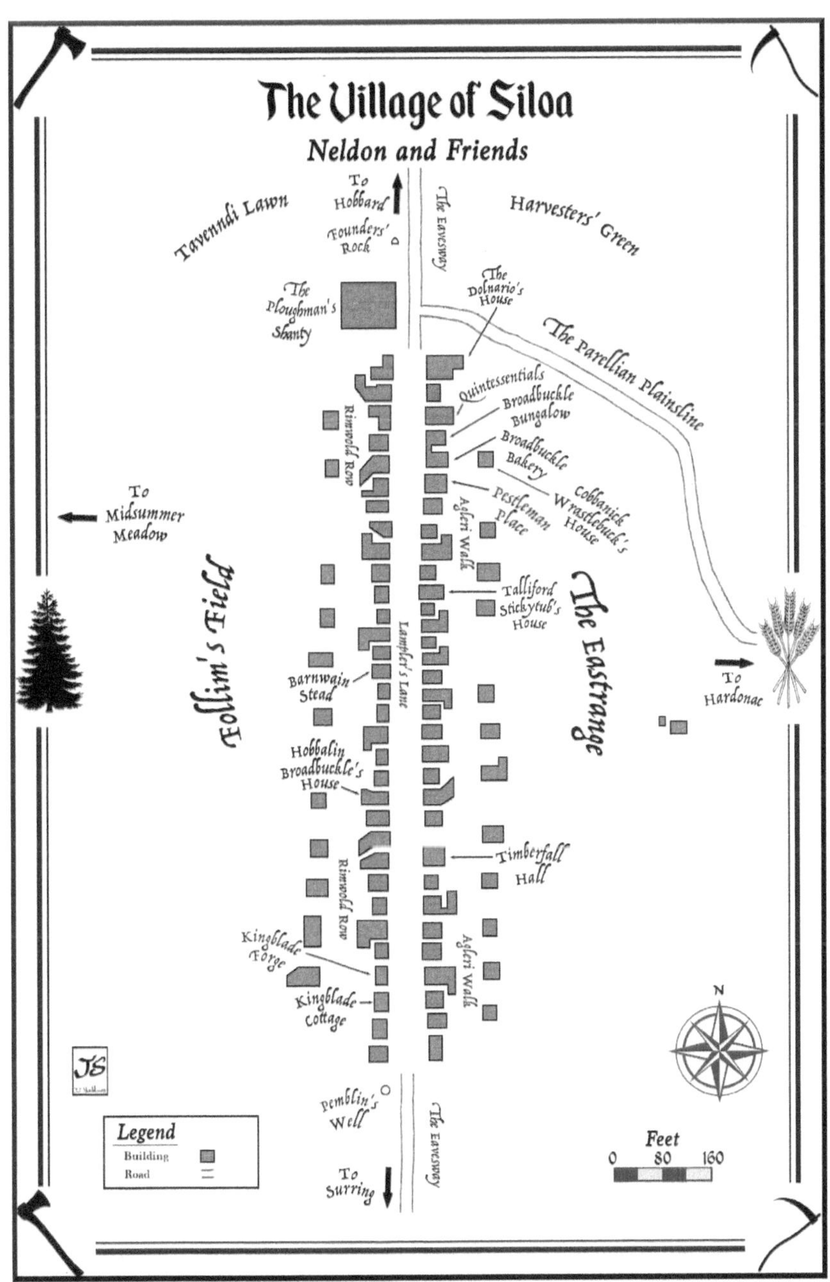

The Village of Siloa
Neldon and Friends
Tavenndi Lawn
To Hobbard
Founders' Rock
The Eavsway
Harvesters' Green
The Dolnario's House
The Parellian Plainsline
The Ploughman's Shanty
Quintessentials
Broadbuckle Bungalow
Broadbuckle Bakery
Cobbanick Wrasslebuck's House
Rimwold Row
Agleri Walk
Pestleman Place
To Midsummer Meadow
Talliford Stickytub's House
Follim's Field
The Eastrange
Lampfer's Lane
Barnwain Stead
To Hardonac
Hobbalin Broadbuckle's House
Rimwold Row
Timberfall Hall
Kingblade Forge
Agleri Walk
Kingblade Cottage
N
Pemblin's Well
The Eavsway
To Surring
Feet
0   80   160
Legend
Building
Road
JS

The Adventures of Neldon Broadbuckle: Volume I

The Eleventh Annual Siloa Snow War

Captain of the Koobachinky

Pandemonium at the Prandingars' Pageant

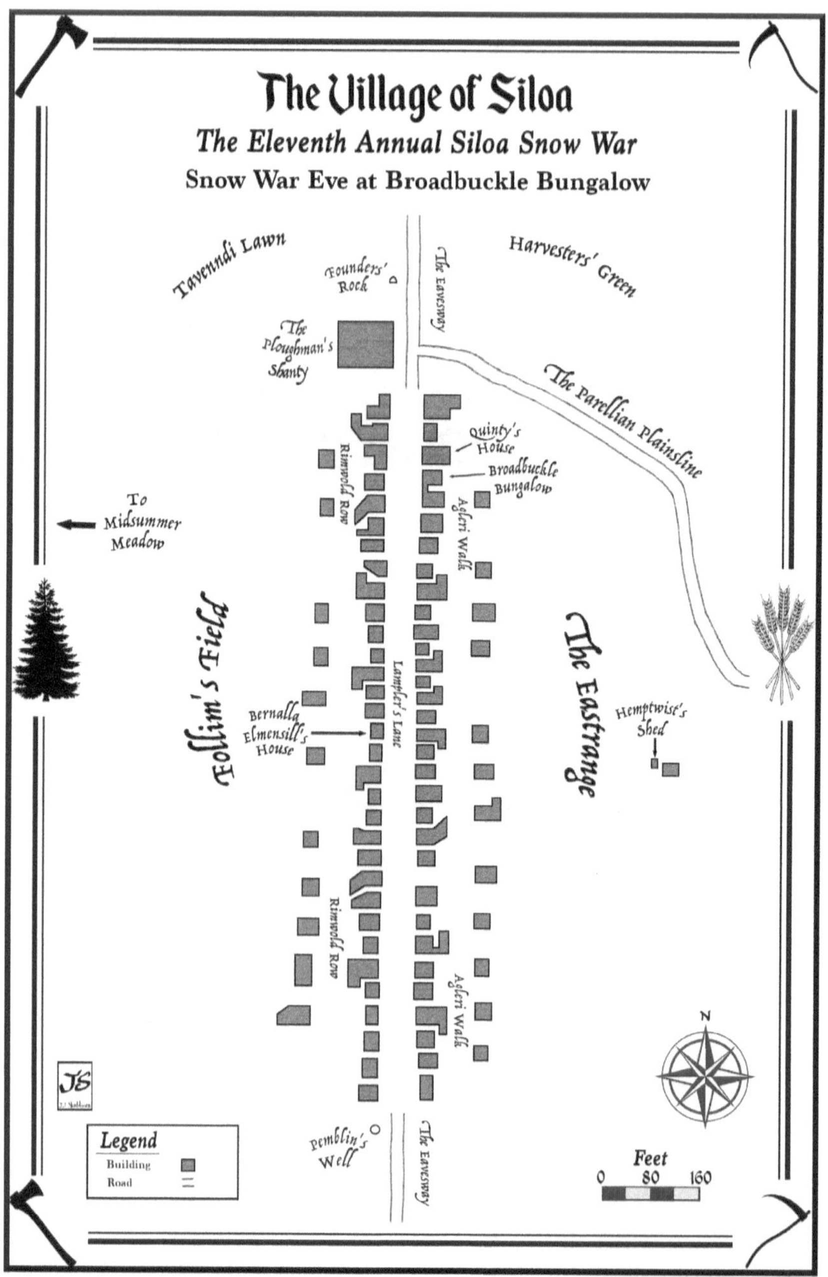

The Village of Siloa
The Eleventh Annual Siloa Snow War
Snow War Eve at Broadbuckle Bungalow
Tavenndi Lawn
Founders' Rock
The Eavesway
Harvesters' Green
The Ploughman's Shanty
Quinty's House
Broadbuckle Bungalow
The Parellian Plainsline
Rimwold Row
Agleri Walk
To Midsummer Meadow
Tollim's Field
Lampler's Lane
Bernalla Elmensill's House
The Eastrange
Hemptwise's Shed
Rimwold Row
Agleri Walk
Pemblin's Well
The Eavesway
N
JS
Legend
Building
Road
Feet
0   80   160

The Eleventh Annual
Siloa Snow War

CHAPTER ONE

Snow War Eve at Broadbuckle Bungalow

"Oh, cratchenmanks! Is that what I think it is?" gasped Bernalla Elmensill. She had been sitting by the fire in her cottage, knitting away on this chilly evening in late Alareth. But now she rose from her chair and hastened over to a window looking out on the main street of the village of Siloa.

"Bogglesnop!" she hissed, frowning. "It is indeed. The first snow!"

Outside, glinting snowflakes were falling gently from the cloudy night sky, and the ground already sparkled with them in the moonlight.

"Dreadful. Ever so dreadful," Bernalla clucked. "On the morrow, all those pesky Siloan ne'er-do-wells will be out running around, hooting and shrieking and making a general ruckus, throwing snowballs at each other like a bunch of maniacs and damaging village property, like as not. Ah, ah, but not if *I* have anything to say about it!"

The elderly woman hurried over to a peg by the door where hung her gray bonnet. She quickly tied it on, cinched the knot and stamped her foot resolutely. Then she opened her front door, stomped out into the street and flung the door shut behind her.

Meanwhile, on the opposite side of the street and down toward the north end, the Broadbuckle family was in their bungalow sitting at dinner, which was salted pork, rutabaga stew and rye rolls with strawberry jam. Neldon Broadbuckle was eating much too quickly, as usual, and his mother Flinny scolded him, "Your food isn't going anywhere, Neldon, and there's plenty more stew on the fire anyhow. Slow down, please. Eating too fast will only lead to indigestion, as I've already told you four times tonight."

"My, my!" said Neldon's father Drampo, who had glanced out the window. "I do believe it's snowing."

"It is?" asked Neldon, looking up from his dinner. "How do you know?"

"Because I looked out the window," Drampo answered flatly.

"Oh, yes, the window," said Neldon, who was so focused on his meal he had forgotten they had several of these. The lad promptly set his spoon down, sloshing rutabaga stew on the table, and rushed to the front window, pressing his face against it.

"It *is* snowing," he said with great delight. "Whooee!" he hollered.

Neldon turned to his parents. "May I please be excused from dinner just a little bit early?" he asked eagerly.

"Whatever for?" his father inquired, mystified. Neldon was so very fond of food that he had only made a request such as this a handful of times in his life. Therefore, Drampo suspected that something rather serious was afoot.

"To go to bed of course, so I can be well-rested and get up early tomorrow for the Siloa Snow War," Neldon replied.

"Ah," his father said. "I see. It does look as if there will be enough snow accumulated by the morning to warrant it, eh?"

"I thought you said you were starving," said Neldon's mother. "Besides, it's still rather early in the evening."

"I know," Neldon said. "But I think I'm full now, and I'm pretty tired, too." He yawned as authentically as he could to reinforce this point.

"All right, then. Go on to bed," Drampo laughed.

"Thank you," Neldon sang, as he hurried off to his room and tunneled under his covers quicker than you could say Noddington, Yawnbury and Dozedale.

Neldon's parents continued to eat their dinner, chuckling and conversing about their son's passion for the annual Siloa Snow War. Then, a short while later, they heard a knock at the door.

"That'll be Bernalla Elmensill, I'll wager," sighed Drampo. "She'll have come to tell us not to let Neldon take part in the Snow War tomorrow."

He went to the door and opened it, and sure enough, there stood the old woman in the snowy street with a scowl as sour as a bushel of balcumberries (which are extraordinarily sour, in case you are wondering).

"Is your Neldon about, Drampadus?" she asked brusquely.

"No, I'm afraid he's already in bed," Drampo replied.

"No matter. You'll do just as well," Miss Elmensill returned. "Now, hear me well. You'd best advise him not to participate in the roistering and rumpus that is almost certain to take place tomorrow. There are already plenty of hoodlums in this town that will be scuttling about. We certainly don't need another one."

"I suppose you're referring to the children who compete in the Snow War, the game they all play on the first snowfall," Neldon's mother said, as she went to join her husband at the door.

"Game indeed!" said Miss Elmensill sharply. "That event is nothing but an excuse for children to toss their good sense and respectability in the rubbish heap and gallivant about like a pack of savage lunatics. But it certainly *will* be a war if my person or any of my property gets damaged. And should anyone go running through my turnip patch, you can be assured I'll see to it that he gets what's coming to him," she concluded ominously.

"We'll make sure to pass your message along to Neldon, Miss Elmensill," Flinny said, smiling cordially.

"I'm glad to hear that, Flinnadred, as your lad doesn't exactly have the cleanest record, does he? And we wouldn't want him getting any more corrupted than he already is from running around with that wretched Timberfall boy, that pest of a Pestleman, the Barnwain runt and their naughty Kingblade companion, now would we?" With that, Miss Elmensill turned on her heel and marched on to the next house to the south.

This final suite of remarks was intended to be a not-so-subtle reminder to the Broadbuckles that Neldon and his friends had had a number of negative run-ins with Miss Elmensill in the past. However, Drampo disregarded this smear and called out after Bernalla, "Have a pleasant evening, Miss Elmensill." Then, after briefly looking up and down the snowy street, he closed the door.

Drampo pursed his lips and then shook his head, saying, "You would think that after all this time she would just give up. She's certainly dedicated, that one, traipsing about in the cold every single year to practically every house in town and receiving a response far less civil than ours at most of them. But you can't stop Siloan children from playing in the first snow any more than you can stop the first snow from falling."

"No, indeed," agreed Flinny. "They do enjoy the Snow War so. Neldon especially seems to look forward to it, as we've been discussing. And besides, there's no harm in it, unless you consider it a grave offense, as Miss Elmensill does, for you or your house to be hit by a snowball or two."

"It might do old Bernalla some good to be hit by some snowballs," Drampo remarked. "It seems she's always hot and bothered about one thing or another. Perhaps it'd help cool her off a bit."

"Perhaps it would at that," chuckled Flinny.

The couple now returned to the table. Then Drampo, regarding it with considerable puzzlement, exclaimed, "I say, where's the jam gotten off to?"

"That's a very good question," returned Flinny. "I'm certain it was here at dinner, and I'm quite positive I didn't move it off the table. Did you?"

"No, indeed," said Drampo.

"Then perhaps Neldon took it and put it back in the pantry before he went to bed," mused Flinny, "although I don't remember him doing so."

"No matter. It will turn up, I expect," said Drampo, as he sat down in his chair. "Now, let's finish our dinner, plumkins, and not trouble about the jam anymore at the moment."

And so the couple continued eating their portions of stew, pork and bread.

———•◦•———

Now, the reader ought to know that Flinny's guess about the jam was partially correct. Neldon had indeed taken it, but he hadn't returned it to the pantry. While Miss Elmensill and Neldon's parents had been speaking, Neldon had gotten out of bed with the intention of going back to the table and getting more rolls and jam to eat before he went to sleep. Although he himself was the one who had asked to leave dinner early, he had realized after he had lain down that he was still hungry.

However, since he was rather afraid of Miss Elmensill and was especially disconcerted at overhearing her threats against any who might cross her, he had wanted to avoid being seen by her at all costs. Thus, he had crouched and waddled as speedily as he could to the table, grabbed a handful of rolls, the jam and a knife and then scurried back to his room. Remarkably, Miss Elmensill had not spied him doing this, for she was so intently focused on delivering her diatribe about Neldon and his friends to his parents (who, incidentally, were somewhat blocking her view of the dining area).

After Neldon had returned from his successful mission, he had sat up in his bed under the warm covers, happily spreading jam on his rolls and then munching away at them. In this manner, he had heedlessly left a great many crumbs and a number of jam smears on his sheets.

Now, as Neldon was going about this business, he was jolted by a distant, but sharp knock at the front door of his house. "The Elmensill!" he whispered in terror.

Fearing she might be returning, perhaps with a demand to speak to him personally, he pulled his covers over his head and listened carefully. He heard his parents get up and go to the door, and a few moments later, he heard it swing open. Then he breathed a great sigh of relief, for he caught strains of a very pleasant and familiar voice, that of his older brother Quinty, who lived in the house next door, just to the north.

Quinty and Neldon's parents conversed for a minute or so, though Neldon could not make out what they were talking about. Then, suddenly, Neldon heard footsteps approaching his room. Just in case one or both of his parents came in and caught him eating in bed – a practice they firmly disapproved of – he threw the covers off his head, shoved the jam and rolls far under his sheets, closed his eyes and started snoring.

The door to his room creaked open, and Quinty's familiar face appeared. Quinty smiled, tiptoed into the room, closed the door, observed his brother for a few moments and then whispered, "Neldon, I know you're awake. You can't fool me with that fake snoring business," he chuckled, as he sat down on the bed. "Hey, why is your quilt all sticky?" he asked, as soon as he set his hand on Neldon's comforter.

Neldon stopped snoring and cracked one eye open, as he whispered, "All right, so I'm only pretending to sleep. And I've been having a bit of jam and bread in here. That's where the stickiness has come from. But please don't tell Mums and Pappers or they'll be quite annoyed at me."

"Don't worry." Quinty winked. "Your secret's safe with me."

"What are you doing over here so late?" Neldon asked.

"I had to bring Mums some sugar from my shop that she'll need in the bakery early tomorrow morning," he said. Then, nodding toward the solitary window in Neldon's room, he added, "And speaking of tomorrow morning – you should be having the Snow War tomorrow at the rate those flakes are coming down, eh?"

"I certainly hope so!" replied Neldon. The lad took a substantial bite of a roll now that he was confident Quinty wouldn't tell on him. Then, with his mouth stuffed and spewing crumbs every which where, he explained,

"That'sh why I wen' to bed sho early. I wunt to be up at sunrise tomorrow sho I can work on a shecru' projec' to help ush take dow' thoze rashcally Rimwold Thunders."

The Rimwold Thunders was the Snow War team composed of all the youths from ages seven to fifteen in the village of Siloa proper who lived west of its main street, the side that was closest to Rimwold Forest. And their mortal enemies, the Agleri Whirlwinds (the team to which Neldon belonged), was made up of youths in the same age bracket on the east side of Siloa's main street, which was closest to the Plains of Agleri.

"Ah, I see," Quinty said. "And what is this project?"

"It's so secret, I can't even tell *you*," Neldon returned, his face growing very grave.

"Oh, my!" returned Quinty. "It must be very secret indeed then. I'll bet you told Yankaboo about it though."

Neldon nodded, as he smiled at the aforementioned Yankaboo, a three-pronged stick, about nine inches in length, that was sitting atop his dresser, leaning against the wall. Yankaboo was clad in a miniature tunic of sorts, so that the prongs on the left and right of the stick served as his arms and the middle one as his neck. On top of the middle prong was a lumpy, gray pincushion, upon which Neldon had painted a stupid grin and large, googly eyes.

"Did Yankaboo have any advice for you about your plan?" Quinty inquired after a few moments.

"No," Neldon replied dolefully.

"Well, if you'd like some advice from an old veteran, I've got some to offer. I was in the very first Snow War ever and did quite well for myself, you know," Quinty said proudly.

"Oh, yes, of course," Neldon returned. He took another bite of roll and, haphazardly spitting more crumbs, asked "How munee yurz ago wuz tha'?"

"Eleven," said Quinty.

"That's *ancient* history now," Neldon said in awe, "because I was only a baby then. But what's your advice, anyway?"

"I know you're not one of your team's leaders," Quinty said, "but if you get a chance to put a word in to them, this tidbit may help. If you're on offense, attacks with a whole bunch of groups of about six or seven people work best. If you try to attack by yourself, you'll almost certainly get hit unless you're fantastic at dodging, and if you run with a huge group, there are so many targets, the other team won't have any difficulty hitting at least some of you. Even with medium-sized squads that can be an issue. But with the right size of group, especially if you launch a number of groups at once, it'll be difficult for the defenders to repel you. Now, if you're on defense –"

"The Agleri Whirlwinds haven't been on defense for the past three years, except at the very beginning of the war three years ago," Neldon cut in.

"What?" said Quinty, astonished. "You mean to tell me that the Rimwold Thunders have beat you for three years running and you haven't gotten the Topaz Turnip from them even once?"

Neldon nodded ashamedly.

"Has it really been that long?" Quinty asked, still incredulous. "I thought it'd only been two years, which is already bad enough. Yes, you and the rest of the Agleri Whirlwinds need to make sure to have the Turnip at sundown this year to put an end to the Thunders' victory streak."

"Don't you worry," Neldon assured. "If my plan works, I may single-handedly turn the tide for us."

"That's a hefty claim, mister," Quinty laughed, as he rose. "But it'd be splendid if things really did turn out that well for you tomorrow." He now walked over to the door and whispered, "Good to chat with you, Neldon. I've got to go now, though; it's time I was getting back over to Halinda and the babies. Best of luck to you and the rest of the Whirlwinds."

Just before he opened the door, Quinty turned and said, "Oh, and one more piece of advice that you can use regardless of whether you're on offense or defense – aim high. Since a strike with a snowball only counts if it hits at the waist or above, unless they've changed the rule, that is, it's always better to aim too high than too low."

With that, Quinty slipped out of the room and left Neldon alone with his contraband rolls and jam and a few snippets of advice.

Only a minute or two after Quinty left, Neldon heard a brief rapping at his window. He looked over and saw a face pressed against it. It was that of Cromnic Barleycroft, the fifteen-year-old son of the Dolnario of Siloa (an office essentially akin to that of a mayor). Cromnic had been appointed one of the official leaders (a captain, in fact) of the Agleri Whirlwinds this year based on discussions that had taken place among the team members in the past month or so.

"Hey, Neldon!" Cromnic said, waving his hand rapidly in front of the window. "Are you in there?"

Neldon climbed out of his bed, rushed to the window, opened it and said, "What's afoot, Cromnic?"

"All of us Whirlwinds are meeting at Hemptwist's Shed just after first light tomorrow morning to talk about our first attack," Cromnic replied. "Make sure you're there on time! And don't forget to bring a satchel for snowballs," he said, then rushed on to the next house to the south.

Neldon promptly closed his window, got back in bed, looked at Yankaboo and ordered, "Make sure to get me up in time for that meeting tomorrow."

"You can always count on me, Neldon," Neldon replied to himself in a high, wobbly voice.

The lad now set about eating his rolls and jam in earnest once more. Not too long afterward, he finished appeasing his appetite, so he put the lid back on the jam and then held it and a half-eaten roll close to his chest, as he rolled over and went to sleep.

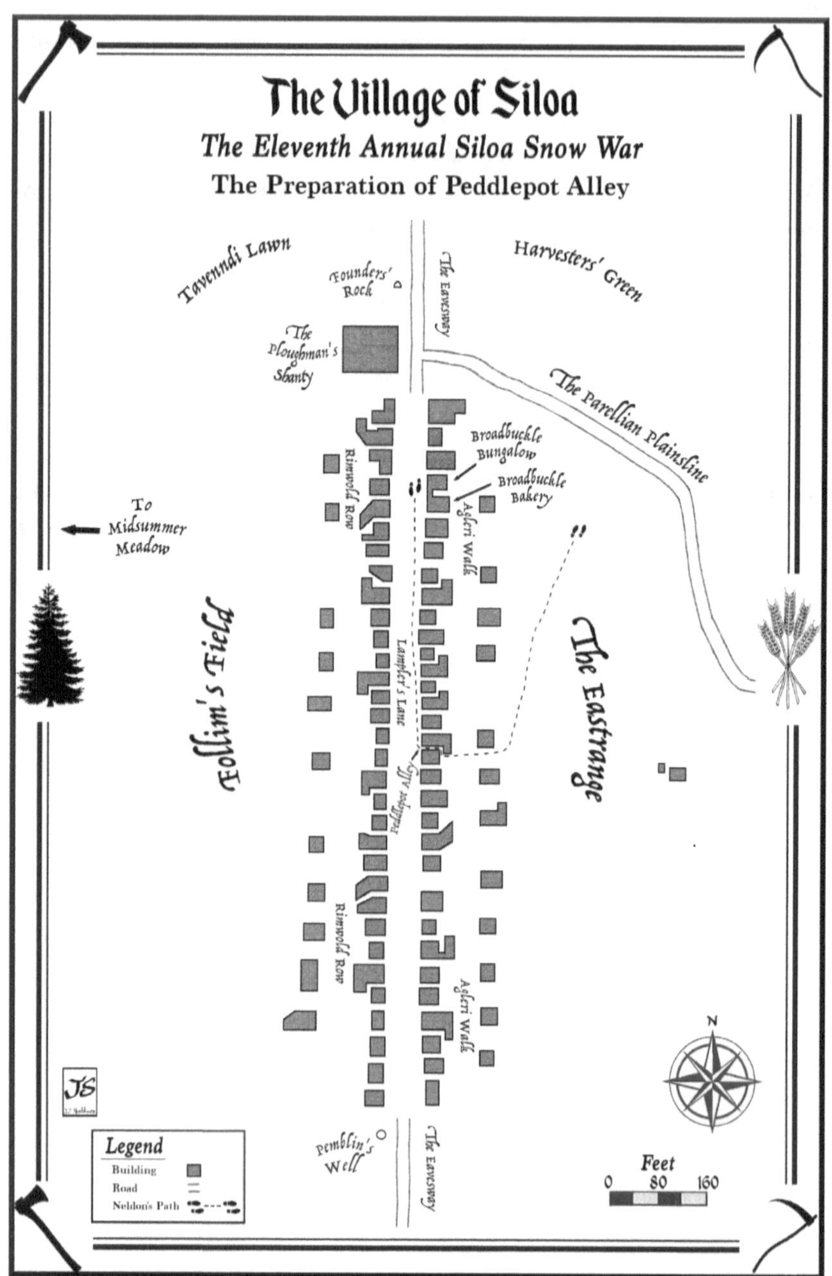

The Village of Siloa
The Eleventh Annual Siloa Snow War
The Preparation of Peddlepot Alley
Tavenndi Lawn
Founders' Rock
The Earysway
Harvesters' Green
The Ploughman's Shanty
The Parellian Plainsline
Broadbuckle Bungalow
Broadbuckle Bakery
Rimwold Row
Agleri Walk
To Midsummer Meadow
Follim's Field
Lampfer's Lane
Peddlepot Alley
The Eastrange
Rimwold Row
Agleri Walk
Pemblin's Well
The Earysway
N
Feet
0   80   160
Legend
Building
Road
Neldon's Path
JS

The Preparation of
Peddlepot Alley

Just as Marda was rising the next morning, Neldon rolled over, awakened and noted that he was still holding a partially eaten roll and the jar of jam. He dug around under his sheets for the knife until he found it. Then he opened the jam, spread some of it on the roll and hastily consumed this remnant of last night's dinner. All of a sudden, he remembered that it had been snowing the previous evening, so he popped out of bed and raced to his window.

"Oh, yes! Today is going to be terrific," he exclaimed. Turning to Yankaboo, he said, "You know, Yankaboo, I just have that yumscious feeling in my belly that something magnifulous is coming our way. This year our side will win for sure."

"And your name will forever be hallowed among the Agleri Whirlwinds!" he responded to himself in his high, obnoxious Yankaboo voice.

It wasn't snowing anymore, but outside there was a thick blanket of clean, crisp snow. Glistening in the almost magical light of clear dawn, this pristine landscape beckoned for Neldon to enter it as speedily as possible.

Without delay, Neldon gathered his warm winter garments. He was so giddy with excitement that he looked almost frantic putting them on. As soon as he was properly attired, Neldon raced to the table and found that his mother had placed a loaf of bread and an apple tart there for breakfast, for she was already at work in Broadbuckle Bakery, which was connected to their house by a short hallway. Neldon tore off half the loaf and more than half of the apple tart and began scarfing them down as he raced out into Siloa's main street, which was formally known as Lampler's Lane, but more commonly as Main Lane.

Several other lads and lasses emerged from their houses at the same time Neldon did, and there were quite a few trails of footprints showing that a great many youths had left even earlier than them.

The air was cold, but not tremendously so; it was almost the ideal temperature, in fact, for playing outside all day and not feeling too frigid but still being able to enjoy the delights of winter. Neldon dropped his bread and tart, bent down, put his hands in the snow and found that it was the perfect sort for making snowballs. Happy as could be at this finding, he quickly formed a snowy sphere and blindly hurled it into the street. He heard a thud and a cough and then looked up, immediately realizing that he had just hit Tas Wedgenware the potter, one of his neighbors from across the street.

"Oops. Sorry, Mister Wedgenware," Neldon apologized sheepishly.

"No harm done," Tas assured, brushing himself off. "But it doesn't look like the Snow War's actually commenced yet, Neldon. You'll want to save your best throws for then. Don't use them all up now." And with that, he walked off north down the street.

Suddenly, Neldon remembered that he was supposed to be at the meeting Cromnic had told him about. "Fannymash and fudbuddles. I think I might be late for that meeting already," he said worriedly. But then, after looking up and down the street, a realization came to him. "Actually, since all the Whirlwinds will be occupied at Hemptwist's Shed, this would be a perfect time for me to work on my project."

And so, he picked up his breakfast, dashed down the street to the south and turned east into a rather narrow alleyway. This was known informally as Peddlepot Alley, called thus because it lay just south of the shop belonging to Hillarnia Peddlepot, the so-called "Merchantess of Miscellany" (a title earned from the fact that her store offered a truly random assortment of articles).

Neldon had what he thought to be an absolutely brilliant construction to undertake here in Peddlepot Alley that he was sure would help his side achieve victory in the Snow War. And he wanted to work on it all by himself and not tell anyone else until the time was right, so that it might be a wonderful surprise for them, an unexpected boon in the midst of what was bound to be a very difficult fight. This, of course, was the secret project he had mentioned to Quinty and the details of which he had confided to none but Yankaboo.

Neldon set the remainder of his bread and apple tart in the snow in the alley. He then raced behind Hillarnia's shop to a bush where he had secretly been piling sizable rocks over the last month or so in anticipation of the winter's first snow, when he could carry out his plan. He now began carting them back to the alleyway and burying them under little drifts of snow in a haphazard fashion, so that anyone passing through the alleyway would be almost certain to trip on one of the stones, mistaking the small drifts where they were hidden for soft, innocent mounds of snow.

When Neldon had finished this task, he decided to see how effective the traps he had made really were, so he began running through the alley.

"Ooh! Ouch! Ah!" he cried, as he stumbled over a hidden stone and landed smack on his face in the snow. Standing up, he brushed himself off and said, "Good job, Mister Trap. You should work very fine in tripping up any Rimwold Thunders who try to break into our territory through this route. Ah, yes, it really looks like you're going to be of great assistance to our team today."

"I certainly hope so, Neldon," he answered in a nasally voice, which was supposed to be his trap replying. "I try my best, you know. But you were the one who made me, so you should get all the credit."

"That's very kind of you, Mister Trap," Neldon replied to himself, bowing and beaming.

Neldon tried to run through the alley again and injured himself several more times. However, he eventually figured out where all the rocks he had buried were. After that, he practiced navigating the alley several times more to make sure he could pass through it quickly, going either direction without tripping on his own obstacles. Soon, he was satisfied that he could manage it (although he regretted that he had left footprints in the correct path to take) and sat down to finish his bread and apple tart.

Neldon hurriedly devoured the rest of his breakfast, wanting to waste as little time as possible, and then raced off to the snow drifts just to the east of town, which were in a wide field known as the Eastrange. There his fellow Whirlwinds were readying defenses against the enemy. Even though the Agleri Whirlwinds were actually starting on offense that year, since the Rimwold Thunders still had the coveted Topaz Turnip, they were nonetheless building up defenses in hopes that they would actually get the Turnip back and have need of them.

The Topaz Turnip was a block of wood whittled to look like a turnip by an individual named Fargalin Chipperchop, who was regarded as the Snow War's founding father due to his pivotal involvement in launching the first one as a lusty and boisterous lad. (Nowadays he was a respectable adult and a carpenter in town.) In any event, whichever of the two teams had the Turnip at sundown on the day of the Snow War was declared to be the victor. Also, the winning team would retain the Turnip for the commencement of the Snow War the following year. The Turnip had, in fact, been named in honor of Siloa's resident killjoy, the crotchety Bernalla Elmensill. This was because she had a critical role in unwittingly transforming the first Siloa Snow War into an annual tradition through her fierce protection of, and obsession with, her turnip patch behind her house. But that tale is told in more detail elsewhere, and we need not trouble ourselves with it now.

In any event, the children preparing defenses in the Eastrange regarded the Snow War as serious business and were none too pleased that Neldon had showed up so late to help them. But they were downright irate that he had missed the meeting at Hemptwist's Shed.

In response to their berating Neldon for missing the meeting, he did little more than make excuses about oversleeping and partaking of a lengthy breakfast, which the others found quite plausible (as these were very Neldonish things to do), although these deflections did nothing to cool their annoyance toward him. The reason he didn't divulge what he had actually been up to was, as mentioned previously, that he wished to reveal the Trip Maze of Peddlepot Alley (as he had dubbed his creation in his mind) as a delightful surprise at an opportune moment.

And so Neldon, still resolved to fill the role of an unforeseen hero in turning the tide against the Thunders, tried to hold this vision before himself, as he did his very best to ignore all this murmuring and railing against him.

"After all," he said to himself, "the day has only just begun, and my team needs me. I can't very well let my spirits be dampened so early on, now can I?"

"No, indeed!" he replied mentally in the voice of Yankaboo.

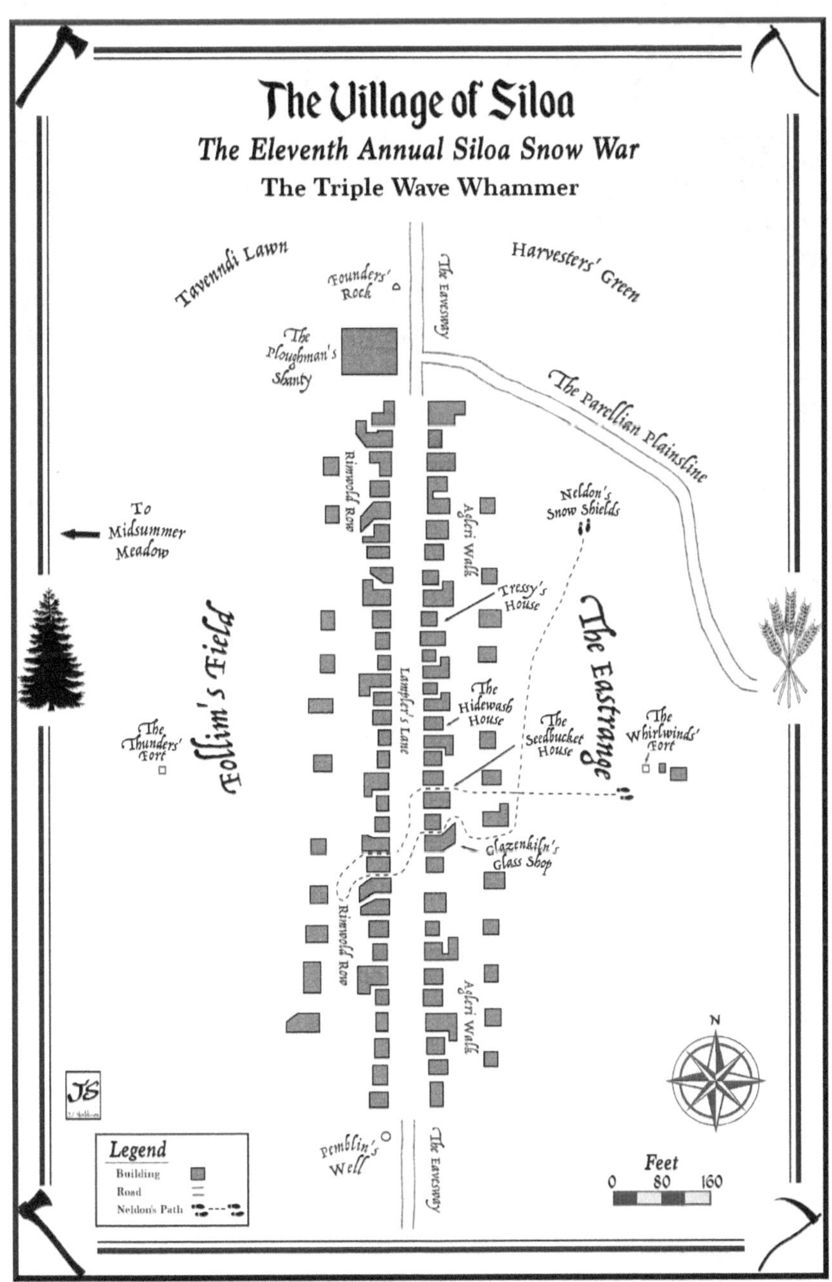
The Village of Siloa
The Eleventh Annual Siloa Snow War
The Triple Wave Whammer
Tavenndi Lawn
Founders' Rock
Harvesters' Green
The Eavesway
The Ploughman's Shanty
The Parellian Plainsline
Rimwold Row
Asferi Walk
Neldon's Snow Shields
To Midsummer Meadow
Tressy's House
The Eastrange
Follim's Field
Lampfer's Lane
The Hidewash House
The Seedbucket House
The Whirlwinds' Fort
The Thunders' Fort
Glazenkiln's Glass Shop
Rimwold Row
Asferi Walk
JS
Pemblin's Well
The Eavesway
Legend
Building
Road
Neldon's Path
Feet
0   80   160
N

The Triple Wave Whammer

hile the children near Neldon continued to complain about how poor of a teammate he was for missing their opening meeting, Neldon bent down in the snow fields east of town and started molding little convex bulwarks of a very modest height. He had made four of these when a boy some five months his junior, with messy blond hair and a rather athletic build, ran past him. It was his friend, Corim Timberfall, who also happened to be one of the Whirlwinds' five team leaders this year.

"Neldon Broadbuckle, what in all Orona are you doing?" Corim said exasperatedly, as he stopped and turned to more closely examine Neldon's constructions.

"I'm building snow shields," said Neldon, blinking. "If we get the Turnip back this year, then we can hide behind these."

"A gopher could barely hide behind one of those stupid shields of yours," Corim scoffed. "I really hope these pathetic things aren't all you have to show for your work so far this morning. Whatever the case, though, we're about to take down those filthy Rimwold Thunders with the Triple Wave Whammer."

"The what?" Neldon asked, thoroughly confused.

"The Triple Wave Whammer," Corim repeated, even more annoyed now. "Come on, Neldon. We've been talking about this maneuver for about three months now."

"We have?" Neldon said incredulously.

"On a regular basis, muffinhead! And what's more, Cromnic Barleycroft and my sister Hendra just explained it to everybody at the meeting at Hemptwist's Shed just a few – wait, you didn't miss the meeting, did you?"

Neldon drew his lower lip between his teeth and looked away guiltily.

"Unbelievable," Corim muttered. "Well, I'm not going to explain the whole thing to you now. No time for that. And anyway, in just a minute, I'm giving a short debriefing behind Glazenkiln's glass shop to the group

I'm leading to make sure everyone knows exactly what to do, so you can hear the basics then. We divvied up who was going to be in which group at the meeting at Hemptwist's Shed, but of course you weren't there. I guess I was paying too close attention to notice. Well, I suppose you can be in my group," he sighed. "Now, leave off with these dumb shields of yours and hustle on over to Glazenkiln's, Chubkins! Every minute we spend dawdling around is more time the Thunders have to get their defenses ready." And with that, Corim raced off.

Neldon patted his most recent snow shield and whispered, "Don't worry, Mister Snow Shield. I'll use you, even if anyone else won't." Then he ran off after Corim.

Corim was now standing behind the workshop of Garridan Glazenkiln the glassblower, surrounded by a number of other youths.

"All right," Corim was saying, as Neldon jogged up to join the group. "Here's the plan, Whirlwinds. Like Cromnic and Hendra said at our huddle just a bit ago, we've got to strike hard and fast before those blasted Rimwold Thunders finish setting up their defenses. Since we have no idea who has the Topaz Turnip, we'll have to make a mass assault and freeze as many of them as possible so we can search them for it. Remember, our goal with this Triple Wave Whammer is to confuse them with the first wave, to freeze them with the second and to do a search for the Turnip with the third. As we're part of the second wave, we need to focus all our energies on hitting as many Thunders as possible, so they're frozen when the final wave comes through."

"Who's in the first wave?" Neldon asked.

"The Stickytubs," Corim answered curtly, rather irked that Neldon had interrupted his debriefing. "They're doing a suicide charge from the alley immediately south of the Hidewash house to distract the Thunders so that the second wave can do more damage."

The Stickytubs – Bingleton, Hapworth and Mozzalyn, two boys and a girl – were Neldon's cousins on his mother's side and were quite broad in girth, even more so than Neldon, who was himself somewhat rotund. Unfortunately, none of them were very fast runners (or even decent throwers). They were, in fact, more of a liability than anything else in the Snow War, but Cromnic Barleycroft and Corim's older sister Hendra, the Whirlwinds' two designated captains, had thought a suicide charge would be a good way to put them to use.

"And as for how the setup for the second wave will go," Corim went on, "we've got two squads – this one and Tressy Axleman's. I'll be leading our group through the alley north of Glazenkiln's shop here, and Tressy will be taking her group through the alley just south of her house. Then we'll wait. As soon as the Stickytubs have either been hit or have made it across the street, both of our groups will launch at the same time. At that point, we've got one job and one job alone: hit all the Thunders we can and push as far westward as we can into the heart of their territory."

"Are there any Thunders we need to particularly watch out for?" asked a younger girl named Daniseth Tillwater. This was her first year playing.

"All of them, actually," Corim laughed, "but yes, there are a few you need to be especially careful of and really try to take out if you can. Their five leaders this year are Rannion Rillspan, Stayla Beamstander, Branlum Harrowdell, Aradis Kingblade and Carrayna Nockshaft. I wouldn't be a bit surprised if one of that lot has the Turnip, as a matter of fact. But if you do happen to hit one of those people I just mentioned, just keep on moving, because the third wave will be coming right behind us to search them."

Corim now clapped his hands, and said, "Is all of that clear? Are we ready for this?"

Neldon raised his hand and coughed.

"What, Neldon?" Corim groaned.

"What if we haven't made any snowballs yet?" Neldon asked.

Corim rolled his eyes, and sighed, "If by 'we,' you're referring to yourself, then you'd better make a few as fast as you can or else just come along as an expendable target, since I don't want to waste any more time. Besides, Tressy just signaled that she and her crew are ready to go."

"Oh," said Neldon, who hastily began forming a snowball, which he dropped into what he thought was his satchel. However, his snowball just plopped sadly to the ground. Just then, he realized he had regrettably forgotten to bring a satchel for snowballs, despite the fact that Cromnic had reminded him to do so last night. Quickly, he made another snowball and held it tightly in his hand.

"Too bad I'll only be carrying one of these," Neldon muttered. "But who knows? Maybe this little snowball will hit the Thunder who has the Turnip."

Corim now issued one final word of instruction before his squad moved to its launching point. "We'll run in a mass until we get to the middle of Main Lane and then spread to go into as many different alleys as possible. Anyone who gets through one of the alleys needs to rejoin on the other side. From there, we'll try to break into Follim's Field and even get as far as the Thunders' fort if we can. Got it?"

Everyone nodded, and the group began moving stealthily down the alleyway north of Glazenkiln's shop, with Corim leading the way. When Corim reached the west end of the alley, he looked up and down Main Lane to see if he could spot anyone lurking in the alleyways on the far side. However, not a single Thunder was to be seen.

"Get your snowballs in hand," Corim whispered, and all but Neldon reached into their satchels, each of them grasping a snowball to have at the ready. Meanwhile, Neldon firmly clutched his single piece of ammunition, hoping it might find a sure target.

Suddenly, there was a great deal of wild shouting and hollering to the north, as well as an obnoxious tooting of horns. The three Stickytubs, who were responsible for this racket, had emerged from their designated alley, carrying makeshift, rudimentary trumpets and running as quickly as their stout legs would carry them (which was not terribly fast) toward the west side of the street. Before they reached it, however, each of them was hit by snowballs launched from various alleyways by opponents concealed there. Now, per the regulations of the Snow War, the unfortunate Stickytubs would have to walk all the way back to the Whirlwinds' snow fort by Hemptwist's Shed before they could make any further moves against the Rimwold Thunders.

"Go!" Corim whispered, just as the Stickytubs were being hit, and he dashed out into the street, with his troops following right behind him. Simultaneously, Tressy Axleman led her group out into Main Lane to the north of the Stickytubs.

When Corim's band was about halfway across Main Lane, a few Thunders stuck their heads out from around the corners of alleyways and struck three Agleri Whirlwinds soundly with snowballs. However, when Corim's group scattered and attempted to enter a host of different alleyways, this made things much more difficult for the defenders. Several of the Thunders were hit by the Whirlwinds and, according to the rules of the Snow War, had to remain frozen until their mates touched them – that was the fate of anyone on defense who was hit by a snowball. A number of those in the alleyways retreated at the onslaught of the Whirlwinds' snowballs, but others were able to repel the attackers.

Corim nailed two defenders who were blocking the alley he had chosen and roared triumphantly as he raced past them, since they had to remain motionless and mute until some other Thunder came to their aid. As for Neldon, he happened to pick an alleyway in which there were no defenders, so he continued unscathed to the west side of the row of buildings, entering the next lane over, which was known as Rimwold Row.

The squad of Whirlwinds that regrouped in Rimwold Row was about half the size of that which had begun the assault, as there were now only six of them. Neldon glanced to the north and saw that Tressy's group had fared about like Corim's.

"Watch out!" Corim cried, as a snowball from an alley behind them hit a girl in his group. Corim's younger brother Tedge struck the Thunder who had hurled it, and he was forced to remain frozen where he was. However, the Whirlwind girl, Pelania Tarmintree, had to begin walking back to the fort at the back of Whirlwind territory.

"All right, let's get on into Follim's Field and see if we can reach their fort before more of them show up," Corim said. The fort in question lay at the far side of the aforementioned field, which was just west of town. In accordance with the regulations of the Snow War, the Thunders' fort had to be built on the western border of the permissible area of play, which coincided with the western edge of Follim's Field at the base of a slope leading up to a large, open area called Midsummer Meadow.

"Yeah, I wonder where all those pesky Thunders are," Neldon said, looking around.

"Here's one of them, Neldonicus!" yelled a voice, as a Thunder lad leapt from behind a barrel and pegged Corim dead-on in the shoulder. The Thunder in question was Neldon's good friend Aradis Kingblade. However, their friendship in no way hindered either of them from enthusiastically opposing the other during the Snow War.

"Aha!" cried Neldon. "Now you're done for!" He loosed his single snowball toward Aradis, but his aim was so poor and hasty that the snowball hit the back of his own teammate Belgo Strapstitch's head. Belgo was just about to throw a snowball at Aradis, but Neldon's blunder caused his aim to falter, so that his own snowball only barely missed its target.

"Whoops," mumbled Neldon.

"Neldon, you dolt!" Belgo yelled, fuming.

A moment later, Aradis' younger brother Teric appeared from behind a building farther to the south and hit Neldon with a snowball. "Ha ha! Got ya!" he cried. "Now who's done for?"

Now the rest of Corim's group tried to overwhelm Aradis with a flurry of snowballs, but he simply sprang back behind the barrel. Meanwhile, a small pack of Thunders came running from behind buildings to the north. Corim's folk were badly outnumbered now, and soon they had all been hit.

"Too bad," sang Aradis. "You'll all have to go back to your fort now."

"Just you wait, Aradis Kingblade," Corim seethed, as he trudged off. He, like Neldon, was also good friends with Aradis, but the two of them were transformed into bitter enemies during the annual Snow War. "We'll be back, and then you'll be sorry, or my name isn't Corim Timberfall. You can bet your very last tarion we're getting the Turnip back this year."

"That would mean you'd have to figure out who has it," called Aradis.

"If we freeze every one of you stupid Thunders, that won't be a problem," Corim retorted.

"Like that will ever happen!" Aradis laughed. "You're all blow and no show. So blow on back to Hemptwist's Shed, you bunch of weakling, windbag Whirlwinds."

"Trust me, your gloating will be short-lived," Corim yelled over his shoulder.

"Yeah," Neldon shouted, "because the third wave is about to come and search everyone we've frozen for the Turnip!"

"Shut up, ding-dong!" Corim hissed, as he slapped the back of Neldon's head.

"Oho!" Aradis crowed. "We may have to acknowledge Neldon Broadbuckle as the most tremendous asset the Thunders have this year. He's just done us a great service indeed, and I expect he'll do us many more."

Then, calling to a number of Thunders nearby, he ordered, "Oy, lads, get in the alleyways to prepare for this third wave, and unfreeze as many of our players as you can before the enemy can get to them."

———◆◦◆◦◆———

Meanwhile, Corim and his companions continued walking back toward their fort. "Neldon, if you do or say something that stupid again at any point today, I swear I'll knock you halfway to the Dark Meridian," Corim bellowed.

"I don't even know where that is," Neldon meekly replied.

"Good," said Corim. "Then you won't be able to find your way back."

Just then, Corim saw one of the two squadrons of the third wave, the one led by his sister Hendra, getting ready to run across Main Lane, and he shouted, "Don't bother, Hendra. Neldon already opened his fat mouth and let the Thunders know you lot are coming, so now they're all rushing to guard the alleyways and unfreeze everyone we hit."

"Neldon!" Hendra said exasperatedly. "Why did you do that?"

"I dunno." Neldon shrugged. "It was an accident, I guess. I'm sure sorry about it, though."

"At least Cromnic's group should still be able to carry out their mission," Hendra sighed, shaking her head and looking north up the street. Then, motioning to her group, she said, "Come on, let's strike at the very south edge of town; they surely won't have as many defenders there." And with that, she ran off back behind the row of buildings on the east side of the street, with her squad right behind her.

As soon as Hendra and her group were gone, Corim continued raging against Neldon. But as they were walking down Main Lane, he found a new subject upon which to vent his wrath. He looked at a particular house on the east side of the street and said, "Blast those Seedbuckets. They never participate in the Snow War because they're just too *proper*. You know, we could use the extra numbers, even if we only deploy them as expendables. The Thunders have forty-two this year, and we only have a measly thirty-six."

Corim reached into his satchel, took out an especially large snowball and chucked it at the side of the house. "Come on, Seedbuckets!"

he yelled. "I know you're awake! You're really letting us down. We need more numbers!"

A few moments later, the door of the house opened, and the elder Seedbucket girl, Dretchina, stuck her head out and said disdainfully, "I'll have you know that none of us appreciate you throwing snowballs at our house, Corim Timberfall. And we won't be taking part in your uncouth Snow War either. For, as perhaps the only civilized children in this village, we have a certain level of dignity to maintain." With that, she slammed the door.

"That's really too bad." Neldon shook his head. "They could have given us a nice boost, since there are three of them that could play this year."

"Ah, we don't want them around anyway, fouling things up with their attitude," said Corim. "Crommenblatt is an absolute sourball and a stuffed shirt besides. And so are Dretchina and Mergatha. And even if Hammygrob were old enough to play, he'd probably be useless. Besides, we really do have some good Whirlwinds this year."

"Yeah, isn't this the only year you and all your siblings will be able to participate?" asked Neldon.

"Yep," answered Corim.

Corim and his siblings were all about one year apart, and there were eight Timberfall children in all, most of them athletically inclined; Corim was the fifth in the lineup. The oldest was Hendra, a fiery young woman and one of the Whirlwinds' two captains this year, followed by another sister, Mylis, the quietest of the Timberfalls. Then came a third sister, Furdie, who was known for getting into frequent spats with Hendra (and almost everyone else, for that matter). Branko, Corim's older brother, was next, and he was almost as feisty (and bossy) as Corim. After Corim came another brother, Tedge, a bundle of energy and sass, and then a sister, Leena, the family jester. Traysia was the youngest, and even though she was only seven years old (but almost eight), she was quite precocious for her age.

The Whirlwinds, in addition to hosting an army of Timberfalls, had several other very capable players. Cromnic Barleycroft, the Dolnario's son, was one of the captains and a force to be reckoned with. His younger sister Saneldra was also of good service to the team. And Tressy Axleman (one of the five leaders) and her younger brother Mannidor (who went by Mando or Manny) were both highly valuable assets. Ossner Boltsnip, a splendid dodger and one of the team leaders, was also quite skilled, as was his good friend Tambris Turnsoil. Besides these, the Whirlwinds had twenty-two others who, though not champions, could at least aid their team in some capacity, some of them to a greater extent than others, of course (like the Stickytubs, for instance).

But the Rimwold Thunders had such luminaries as those Corim had already warned his troop about: Rannion Rillspan, Stayla Beamstander, Branlum Harrowdell, Aradis Kingblade and Carrayna Nockshaft, all of whom were exceedingly formidable snow warriors. And in addition to these, they had quite a few other players who were almost as skilled as the Whirlwinds' champions. Plus, they had six more players than their opponents, as Corim had been lamenting. All things considered, the Whirlwinds did not appear to have the best chances of surfacing as victors this year. And unfortunately, thus far, Neldon had only succeeded in bringing those chances down.

Although Neldon had started the day with great aspirations of leading his team to triumph, he was rather disheartened that everything he had done so far seemed to have been of little or no help to his team. And what's more, in his most recent escapade, he had even accidentally sabotaged the Whirlwinds. Still, Neldon, being an optimistic fellow, held out hope that things would turn around for him soon.

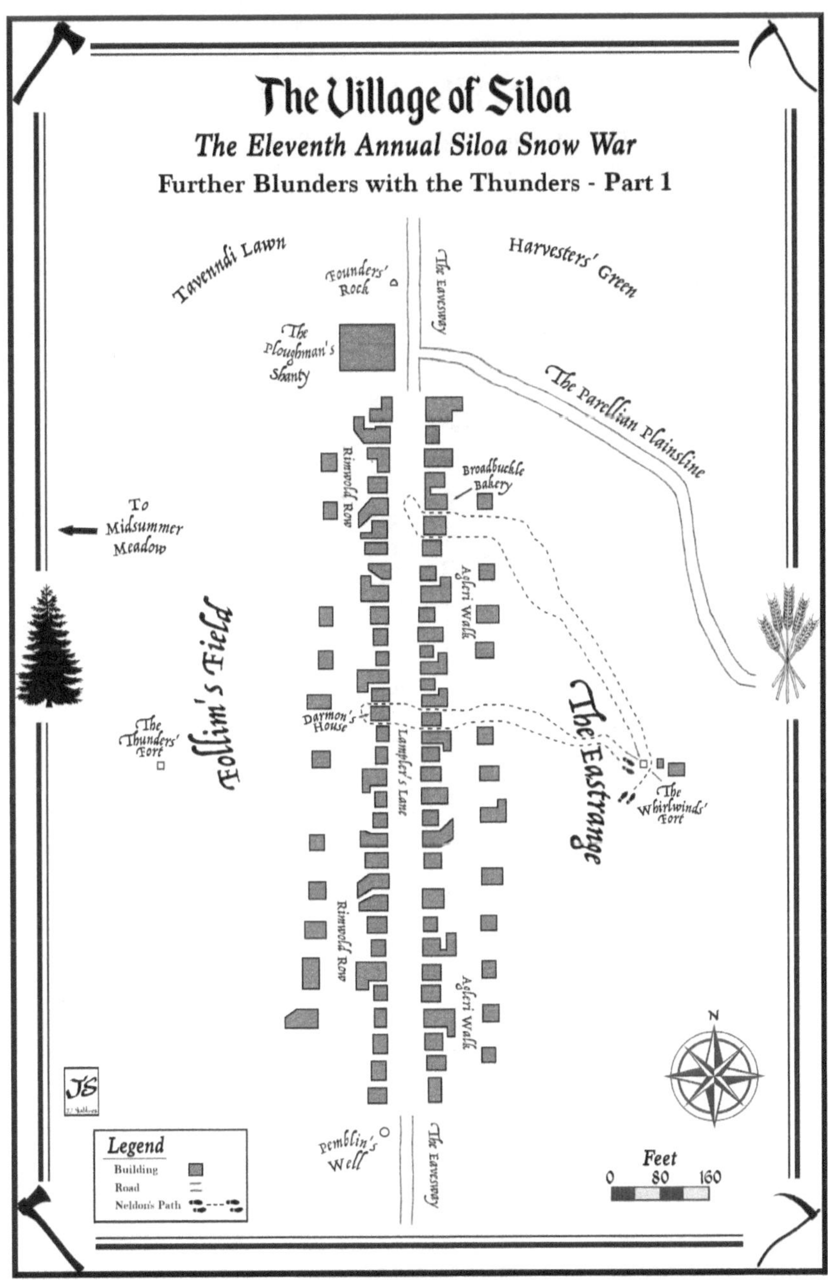

The Village of Siloa
The Eleventh Annual Siloa Snow War
Further Blunders with the Thunders - Part 1
Tavenndi Lawn
Founders' Rock
The Eavesway
Harvesters' Green
The Ploughman's Shanty
The Parellian Plainsline
Broadbuckle Bakery
Rimwold Row
To Midsummer Meadow
Agleri Walk
Follim's Field
The Thunders' Fort
Darmon's House
Lampler's Lane
The Eastrange
The Whirlwinds' Fort
Rimwold Row
Agleri Walk
N
Pemblin's Well
The Eavesway
Feet
0   80   160
JS
Legend
Building
Road
Neldon's Path

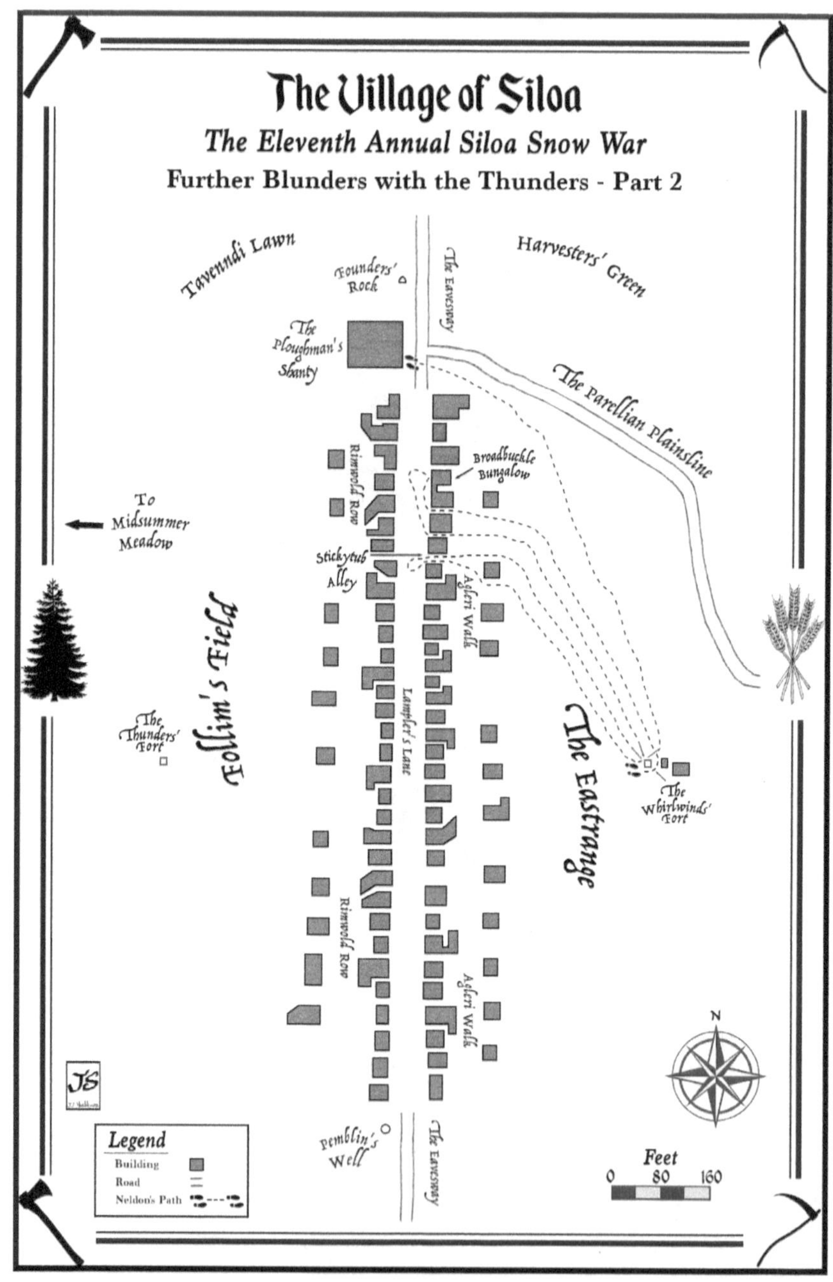
The Village of Siloa
The Eleventh Annual Siloa Snow War
Further Blunders with the Thunders - Part 2
Tavenndi Lawn
Founders' Rock
The Eavesway
Harvesters' Green
The Ploughman's Shanty
The Parellian Plainsline
Broadbuckle Bungalow
Rimwold Row
To Midsummer Meadow
Stickytub Alley
Agleri Walk
Follim's Field
Lampler's Lane
The Thunders' Fort
The Eastrange
The Whirlwinds' Fort
Rimwold Row
Agleri Walk
Pemblin's Well
The Eavesway
N
Legend
Building
Road
Neldon's Path
Feet
0   80   160

Further Blunders with the Thunders

hile Corim and Neldon were discussing their teams' rosters and what their next set of maneuvers was going to be, they continued heading back to their fort, which was essentially a square compound with snow banks for walls that were stacked up as high as the available snow allowed. This fort only had a single opening, which was in the east wall, although it also featured a mound of snow on the inside that would enable any Whirlwinds hiding therein to peer over the west wall and hurl artillery at approaching enemies.

After the boys had tagged the fort, as the rules mandated, Corim said to a group of Whirlwinds that was glumly arriving there after being hit, "Hey, do you want to run up to the north end of town and see if we can help Cromnic's group? I haven't seen any of them come back yet, so they must be doing all right."

The others were amenable to this, so they, along with Neldon, hurried after Corim to the north end of town, which was actually the area where Neldon's house was. After conducting some brief reconnaissance, Corim led the group out into Main Lane.

Suddenly, there was the sound of a door opening, and a voice called, "Neldonicus Pattermanny Broadbuckle! Stop right there. I need a word with you." It was Neldon's mother.

Neldon turned around and saw her standing in the door of Broadbuckle Bakery, her hands on her hips.

"What's the matter, Mums?" he asked.

"Your bedsheets, that's what," she returned. "They've got jam stains and bread crumbs all over them."

Just then, Neldon felt a snowball strike the back of his head. He turned around and saw that Corim and the Whirlwinds with him had already reached the alleyways on the other side of the street, leaving him behind. However, there was a lone, young Thunder girl, Faysa Berrydore, standing just inside one of the alleys. She was presently taking great delight in the fact that Neldon had been such an easy target and giggling at the embarrassing conversation he was having with his mother.

"Ah, now I have to walk all the way back to the fort," Neldon moaned, turning again to his mother.

"Well, I'm sorry you got hit," said Neldon's mother, "but you can't very well expect to get away with sullying your sheets so badly without my noticing. Besides, you know how strongly your father and I disapprove of your slovenly practice of eating in bed. Now, when can I expect you to clean them?"

"Can I do it tomorrow?" pleaded Neldon. "Please? The Snow War only happens once a year."

"Oh, I suppose," his mother answered. "But you'd better take care of it first thing in the morning. Anyway, good luck in the rest of your Snow War!" She blew him a kiss and then retreated into the bakery, shutting the door behind her.

Sighing deeply, Neldon started the trek back to the Whirlwinds' fort. As soon as he had tagged it, an idea sprang into his head.

"Hody hody hoo! I know what I'll do!" he crowed excitedly. "I don't believe anyone's ever tried this idea before, but it's absolutely brilliant. If this works – and it's almost bound to – I could get quite far into the Thunders' territory and maybe even find out which of them has the Topaz Turnip before they realize what I'm up to!"

The ecstatic Neldon launched himself with a little, exuberant hop, then ran back up to Main Lane. After checking the area for enemies as best as he could, he bolted across the street into the alleyway to the north of his friend Darmon Barnwain's house.

Darmon and four other Thunders were standing behind the house, but they were facing away from Neldon and did not hear his approach, since they were talking intently among themselves.

"Hey, can you lot tell me the best spot to station myself in order to protect us against the Whirlwinds' next attack?" Neldon asked loudly.

The group of Thunders turned around and were quite startled to see Neldon standing there, not even attempting to conceal himself.

Darmon shook his head, laughing, and declared, "Neldon, if you actually make it to our side of the street, you really shouldn't go out of your way to make yourself so easy to hit."

One of the Thunder boys, Wellis Brackenlay, raised a snowball to throw at Neldon.

"Wait, don't attack!" Neldon said in a ridiculously chesty voice. "I'm not Neldon, whoever he is. And besides, I'm on your side."

Wellis was in such incredulity of this response and of the absurd voice Neldon was using that he actually didn't throw his snowball, but instead guffawed, "All right, if you're not Neldon Broadbuckle, then who are you?"

"Umm …" Neldon's mouth dropped open, as he fumbled for an answer. Then he cleared his throat and said, "I'm Yankaboo Foodcooker. I'm new in town."

"You have the same name as Neldon's stick friend?" Darmon asked.

"Stick friend?" the other four asked. They, unlike Darmon, had never heard tell of this personage, or else if they had, they had forgotten.

"I have no idea what you're talking about," Neldon asserted, still quite chestily. "All I know is that I live on the west side of Main Lane, and somebody told me that means I'm a member of the Rimwold Thunders. Now, with that being the case, I'd like to know who has the Topaz Turnip, so I can help protect him."

The whole group of Thunders erupted into riotous laughter.

"Neldon, do you really expect to convince us that you're not yourself with that outrageous voice?" Darmon chortled.

Neldon frowned, as it dawned upon him that his scheme really wasn't getting a whole lot of traction. "Okay, fine. I am Neldon Broadbuckle," he admitted in his normal voice. "But I just moved across the street a few weeks ago, so I actually am a Rimwold Thunder now."

"Hobnoggets," said Wellis, as he hit Neldon in the chest with a snowball. "Now, get out of here and stop wasting our time. Maybe you can go set up a stage by Hemptwist's Shed and perform your comedy act back there to boost your team's morale. I really think they're going to need it if the best Cromnic and Hendra can do is send clowns like you over here."

Neldon sighed loudly, buzzed his lips and then walked back to Hemptwist's Shed once again, growing increasingly disheartened with every step by his repeated failures so far this morning. This was simply not how he had envisioned the day going.

When Neldon arrived at the Whirlwinds' fort, the only ones around were his Stickytub cousins.

"Hey, Nelders, do you want to do an assault with us?" Bingleton, the oldest, asked.

"Sure," Neldon replied. "Nothing else I've done today has gone terribly well. Maybe this will be different."

"Hey where's your satchel for snowballs?" asked Mozzalyn, the youngest.

"Oh, that reminds me. I need to go get one from home," said Neldon.

"Okay, we'll just wait here while you get it," said Hapworth. "I think we need a breather anyway. After all, we've already made two full charges this morning."

Neldon ran off to his house, grabbed a satchel, made several snowballs to put in it and then rejoined the Stickytubs. After that, the four of them walked off to the alley just south of the Stickytubs' house, which was widely referred to as Stickytub Alley. It was actually wider than nearly all the alleys in town and might more appropriately be called a street, except that Siloa had no official east-west streets. Every year during the Snow War, the Stickytubs stationed themselves in this spot and used it as the launching point for all of their attacks.

The Stickytubs' idea of an assault was to run across the street in the exact same spot every single time, but in various random configurations, in hopes that these would keep them from getting hit. However, they had only made it to the far side of the street a handful of times in the past few years with this method. Unfazed, they never bothered to modify their strategy, as critical thinking wasn't really one of their strong suits.

"All right, here we go." Hapworth grinned, as he and his siblings, along with Neldon, began running what the Thunders had dubbed a "Stickytub Sortie." But before the four of them got even halfway across the street, four Thunders pegged them with snowballs.

"We were so close," groaned Mozzalyn. "Almost made it to the other side."

Dejected, the foursome walked back to the fort and then returned for another assault. They actually made eight of these (with each of them failing miserably, and with Stickytub "breathers" in-between) before Neldon decided he was going to go try something else. The Stickytubs were somewhat disappointed to lose their cousin's aid but bravely resolved to continue their attacks regardless.

As Neldon parted ways from his cousins, he said to himself, "Well, I guess I can add attacks with the Stickytubs to my tally of flops for today. My goodness, I suppose I've had quite a few blunders with the Thunders this morning. Whatever am I going to do? Let's see. So far, I've been rather short on luck. Perhaps I just need to sleep my bad fortune off. That's probably what Yankaboo would say about the matter."

Neldon, who had always been rather given to superstition, had long ago convinced himself that napping was a powerful antidote to bad luck. This belief had never been verified with any hard evidence, but it had received much hearty endorsement from his natural inclination toward laziness. And Yankaboo was often called in as a witness to buttress Neldon's completely unsubstantiated theory.

As Neldon walked on, he mused, "Also, I could certainly benefit from restocking my stomach. It's off to the Shanty, then!" he concluded, as he began walking toward the Ploughman's Shanty, a large building at the north end of town that functioned as both a tavern and an inn.

Each Snow War from the second annual Snow War onward, Orinn Berthaway, the generous proprietor of the Shanty, had opened up his tavern as a rest station for both the Whirlwinds and the Thunders. He always provided free cider and edibles and let the troops sit by the fire to warm up before going out to fight again. Neldon fully intended to take advantage of all of these services.

When Neldon entered the Ploughman's Shanty, there were only a few Thunders there. They were leaning against the counter and casually talking with Orinn Berthaway about how the Snow War was going. Neldon went up to the counter, thanked Mr. Berthaway for his provisions this year and immediately helped himself to a mug of cider, as well as several little fried sugar cakes, some prunes and a few handfuls of nuts. Then he went and sat down near the hearth against the south wall and started into his cider and snacks. When he had finished, he crawled under a table so as to be out of anyone and everyone's way. Removing his satchel, he put it under his head for a pillow and soon nodded off to sleep, confident that when he awoke, all of his bad luck would be over with and he would be able to achieve his vision of bringing about the downfall of the Thunders, to the joyful acclaim of all his teammates.

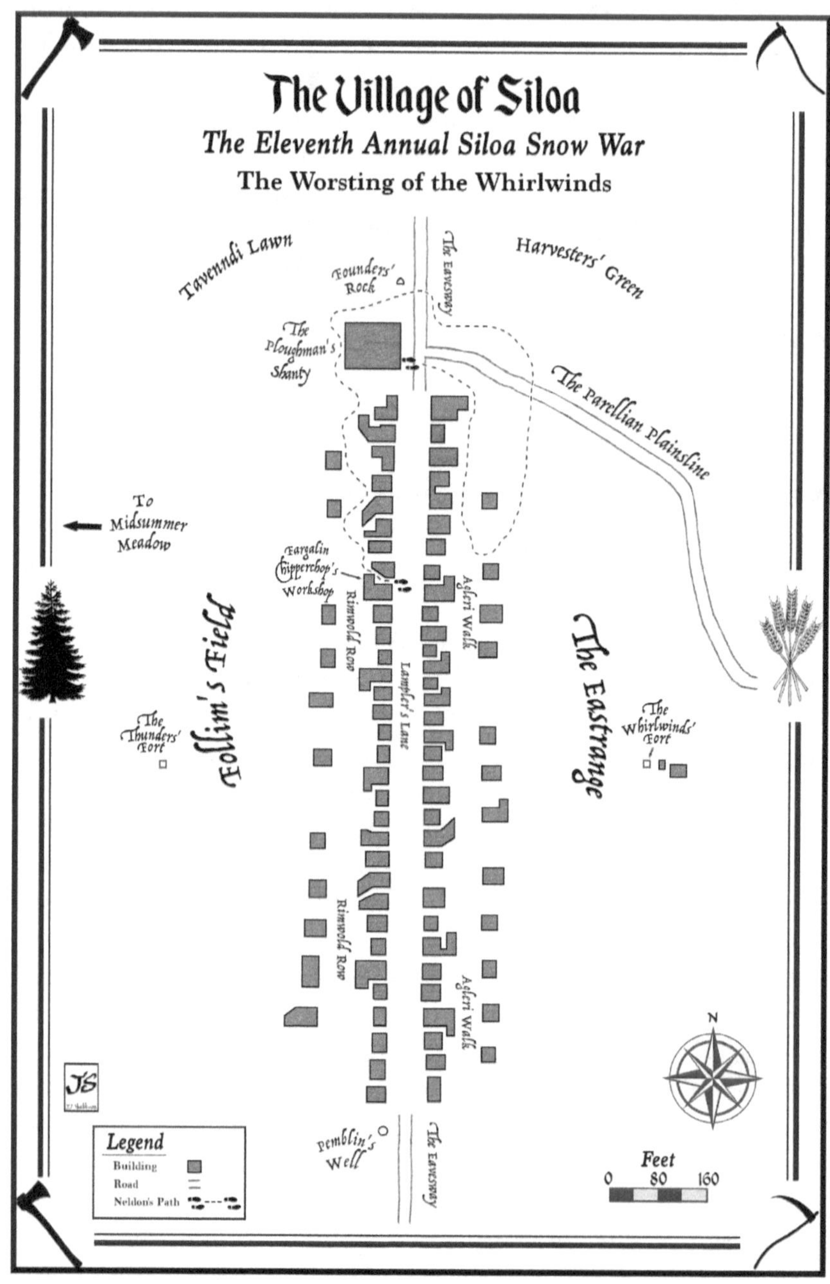

The Village of Siloa
The Eleventh Annual Siloa Snow War
The Worsting of the Whirlwinds
Tavenndi Lawn
Founders' Rock
The Eavesway
Harvesters' Green
The Ploughman's Shanty
The Parellian Plainsline
To Midsummer Meadow
Fargalin Chipperchop's Workshop
Rimwold Row
Aeleri Walk
Lampler's Lane
Follim's Field
The Eastrange
The Thunders' Fort
The Whirlwinds' Fort
Rimwold Row
Aeleri Walk
N
Pemblin's Well
The Eavesway
JS
Legend
Building
Road
Neldon's Path
Feet
0   80   160

The Worsting of the Whirlwinds

A while later, Neldon awoke, and when he sat up, he bumped his head on the table above him.

"Ouchers!" he cried.

Several Whirlwinds and a Thunder who were up at the counter getting refreshments looked over in surprise as they saw Neldon crawl out from under the table. Neldon grinned awkwardly at them and then hurried over to the door of the Shanty. He wasn't sure how long he had slept but hoped that he hadn't missed lunch, both because he was looking forward to more food and because he wanted to conduct at least a few more assaults against the Thunders before noon.

As he stepped outside, he immediately noticed that it was snowing. And from the looks of it, it may have been snowing for a while, for there were fresh accumulations all over the place.

After catching a few snowflakes with his tongue, Neldon headed for Agleri Walk, which was the street that ran parallel to Main Lane and was just to the east of it. It was essentially the eastern counterpart of Rimwold Row, and it was there that Neldon hoped to find some fellow Whirlwinds that he could join for an attack.

As it turned out, there was a squad of six Whirlwinds toward the north end of Agleri Walk preparing to cross over into the Thunders' territory momentarily. Leading the group was Tressy Axleman, one of the Whirlwinds' better players. With her were Tallis Pestleman, one of Neldon's good friends, and a boy a year younger than Neldon named Condrig Brakesnare who was quite decent at both throwing and dodging.

"Well, looky look who it is!" said Condrig. "Neldon Broadbuckle! I've hardly seen you all morning. Where have you been, eh?"

"I was just in the Shanty resting for a few minutes," said Neldon. "I haven't missed lunch, have I?"

"Ha," laughed Tallis. "You can hardly have been in the Shanty only a few minutes if you don't even know whether lunch has happened or not. But just so you know, it will be time for lunch rather soon."

"Okay, so I must have been in there for a while," Neldon said. "But before that, I was with my cousins for quite some time."

"How did things go with them?" Tressy asked politely.

"Not so great," Neldon returned, sighing. "We didn't break through even once. How have the rest of the Whirlwinds been doing?"

"We still haven't got ahold of the Turnip," said Tressy's younger brother Mando. "And unfortunately, we lost two of our players a while ago."

"What do you mean you *lost* two players?" asked Neldon, thoroughly perplexed.

"Ossner Boltsnip and Handora Swiftsaw injured their ankles and had to go home to lie down," explained Tallis. "It seems some joker put a bunch of rocks in Peddlepot Alley and covered them up with snow. Haven't figured out who it was yet though because no one will fess up to it. Poor Ossner and Handora both took a bad tumble on the rocks, so they'll probably be out the rest of the day. It's a real shame because Ossner was one of our leaders, so of course one of our better players, and Handora wasn't too bad either."

"That's rotten luck for sure," said Neldon. He twitched nervously, as he realized that his Trip Maze was responsible for this misfortune. Evidently, the fresh snow had covered up the tracks he had left in the safe route through the alley. He had, of course, intended for the Trip Maze to give the Thunders some trouble, but he hadn't intended to hurt anybody. And it hadn't even crossed his mind that his obstacle course might end up putting some of his own teammates out of commission.

"Perhaps my nap wasn't long enough to cure all my bad luck," he said to himself.

As Neldon was ruing the unfortunate mishap that had come about because of his Trip Maze, Tressy bent down and made a snowball to add to her satchel. As she stood up, she said, "Cromnic and Hendra were furious about the business with Ossner and Handora, but they thought it'd be best to leave the rocks be, on account of the fact that they might do some Thunders in. All Whirlwinds have been advised to steer clear of the place, though, so no more of us get put out of play."

"I'll try to remember to stay out of there," mumbled Neldon, hoping no one would notice how uncomfortable he was during this conversation.

"Hey, we'd better quit jawing, Tressy, and get this attack underway," said Mando. "Aren't we planning to meet up with Corim's squad in Rimwold Row in just a few minutes?"

"We are," Tressy replied. "And you're right, Manny. It's time for us to head out." Then, turning to Neldon, she said, "I haven't got time to explain everything, so just follow me and the others and do as we do. Basically, we're trying to find and take down Damrig Brightcup because we think he might have the Turnip. Someone spied Alnasyn Wrastlebuck giving it to him earlier."

"Okay," said Neldon, and he placed himself at the rear of the group.

Tressy's squad made its way stealthily northward toward an open area known as Harvesters' Green, which was northeast of town. Crouching down and darting from one mound of snow to another, the group reached the designated northern boundary of the Snow War, which ran through Founders' Rock, an engraved stone just north of the Ploughman's Shanty. Here they planned to cross the road that ran north from Siloa and get over into the Thunders' territory undetected.

As the group was skulking along, Neldon realized he had left his satchel in the Ploughman's Shanty and that he didn't have any snowballs to throw. So, periodically, he bent down and grabbed some snow, which he then formed into snowballs and inserted in various places in his garments, seeing as he didn't have a bag to put his ammunition in.

The group soon successfully crossed over into the Thunders' area and then made their way back south to Rimwold Row, which had a number of Thunders posted as sentries. Like true professionals, Tressy, Mando and Condrig (the most skilled members of the squad) worked together to freeze the Thunders' guards, one by one, without being detected. The other three members of the group Neldon had joined then searched the frozen sentries for the Turnip.

However, Neldon was of no help at all during this operation because he had to dig around in his clothes for a snowball every time he wanted to throw one. By the time he found one, there was no need for it anymore. Also, he was too preoccupied with his own miserable condition to aid in frisking for the Turnip, for the snow he had shoved in his garments was beginning to melt, and now even the inner layers of his clothes were wet and cold. He quivered and shivered as he followed the others from alley to alley along Rimwold Row, and it was the most he could do just to keep an eye out for enemies approaching.

After they had frozen and searched seven Thunders, they encountered a squad of Whirlwinds led by Corim Timberfall in an alleyway north of Fargalin Chipperchop's workshop.

"Good work, Tressy!" Corim said, as soon as he spotted her. "Your group made it to the rendezvous point! Did you find Damrig?"

"No," lamented Tressy. "He's got to either be farther south or back west of town somewhere."

Suddenly, Corim launched a snowball with great force at a target behind Tressy's squad, out in Rimwold Row. Almost immediately, there was the sound of a little girl crying out.

Neldon whirled around and saw that Corim had just nailed Aradis Kingblade's little sister Mellora dead-on in the face with his snowball.

"Thought you'd sneak up on us, did you!" laughed Corim. "You've got to be more careful than that if you want to outwit Corim Timberfall."

Suddenly, eight Thunders led by an older boy named Rannion Rillspan raced around the corner and deluged all the Whirlwinds gathered in the alleyway with a torrent of snowballs. Many of them were hit almost instantly. Corim and Tressy expertly evaded most of the missiles, but both of them were ultimately taken down by Rannion himself. Amazingly enough, no one hit Neldon, mostly because they assumed somebody else had and weren't paying close enough attention to notice that he hadn't been hit.

Among the group of Thunders was Aradis Kingblade, who went to unfreeze his sister by touching her. As he did so, he berated Corim, "You should be ashamed of yourself, Corim, picking on a little girl like that. Besides, it's her first game! You know, you've been a perfect beast to her all day. There's no need to take out your annoyance toward me on her. And you know what? If you don't put a stop to it, I'm going to make you pay for it."

"How is hitting her with a snowball picking on her?" Corim retorted. "That's what people do in the Snow War – hit each other with snowballs."

"Well, you don't have to hit people in the face so hard like that to freeze them," Mellora said indignantly.

"Come now, let's not squabble about petty affairs of this sort when there's a war on," cut in Rannion condescendingly. Then, turning to the defeated Whirlwinds, he said, "And speaking of that war, it's time you tramps started walking back to your lair so you can reformulate a better strategy – one that might actually work. However, I must admit your most recent attempt wasn't half bad, Whirlwinds," he laughed mockingly. "You actually took out quite a few of us before your reign of terror came to an end. It's a downright shame you've got no Turnip to show for it and that all your hard work in freezing our mates is about to be unraveled. Too bad you don't have any backup left to stop us."

"Technically, I could still stop you," said Neldon boldly. "I haven't actually been hit yet."

"We can fix that quite easily," said Rannion, as he lobbed a snowball casually toward Neldon, which hit him in the belly.

"Neldon, you idiot!" yelled Corim. "You could still have done some good over here spying or something if you hadn't opened up your big mouth."

Neldon's expression sank, as he realized it hadn't been the most clever move to inform the Thunders that he was still technically at large in their territory.

"Come on, everybody, let's get back to the fort before Neldon does something even stupider," said Condrig resignedly. "I'm sure he will, of course, because he just seems to get worse every year, but I'd rather not be around to watch it. It's just too embarrassing."

The other Whirlwinds all immediately chimed in that they were in full agreement with his assessment. The Thunders laughed and began to disperse, while Neldon gulped and stood there stupidly. Then the Whirlwinds turned to go.

As the Whirlwinds were walking off, Corim turned to him and stormed, "Neldon, you are completely worthless!"

"I've only been trying to help," Neldon said timidly. "I just –"

"Well, you've been anything *but* helpful, you bumbling jughead," Corim angrily cut him off. "In all honesty, Hammygrob Seedbucket would probably be a greater asset to the Whirlwinds than you are. I would even go so far as to say that, without a doubt, you're the very worst of the Whirlwinds. And with virtually no assistance, you've brought about the *worsting* of the Whirlwinds, time and time again. Absolutely everything you've done today has just been a preposterous parade of nincompoopery. You missed the meeting this morning, you forgot to bring a satchel for snowballs, you wasted your time for building defenses by shoving a few snowflakes together and calling them 'snow shields,' you hit Belgo Strapstitch's head when he was about to hit Aradis, you gave away the final stroke of a plan we've been talking about for three months that probably would have helped us get the Turnip back hours ago – what else? Oh, and you just threw away a perfect opportunity to spy and find out who has the Turnip. And those are only the things I know about. I'm sure there are many more. You might as well just join the Thunders at this point."

"I already tried," Neldon sighed.

"What?" said Corim, outraged.

"Well, I didn't *really* try to join them," Neldon explained. "I just tried to trick them into thinking I was on their team."

Corim just shook his head, then marched swiftly off toward the Whirl-winds' fort.

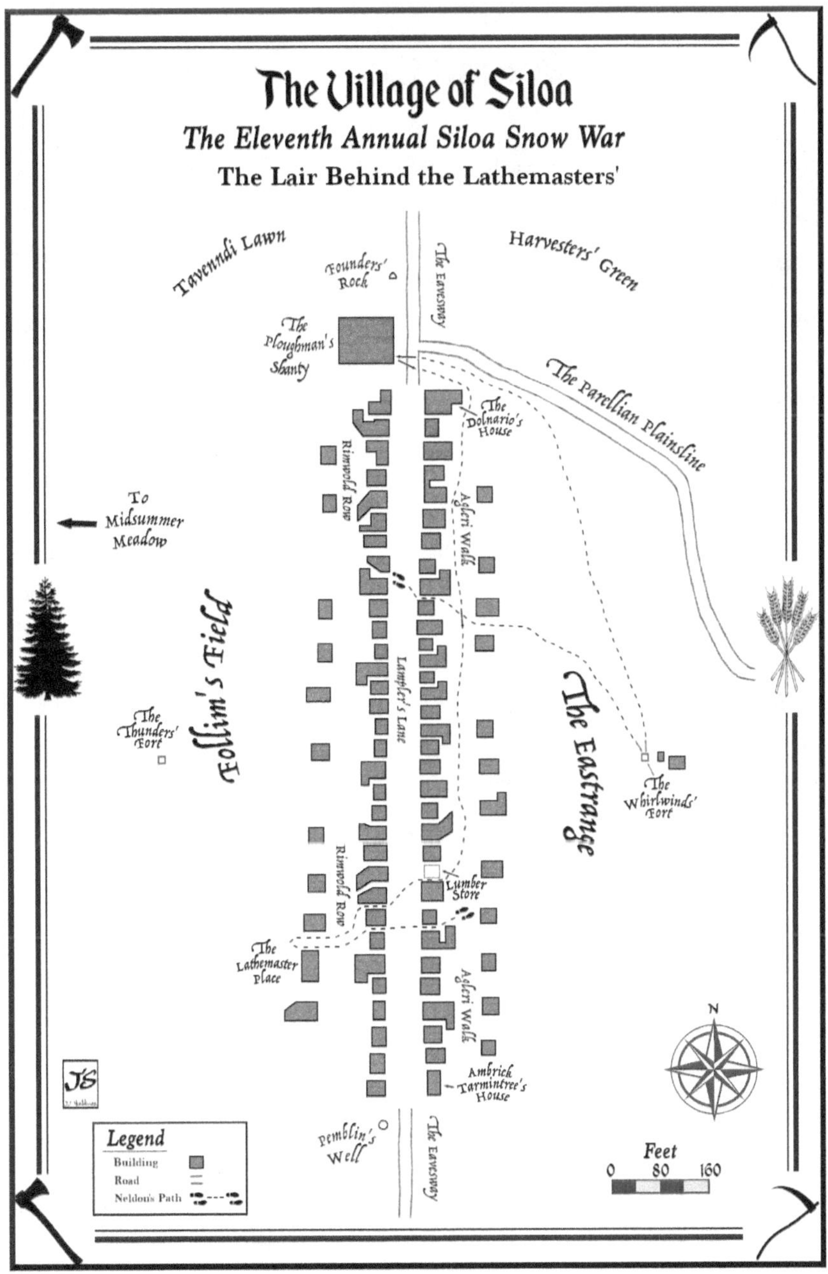

The Village of Siloa
The Eleventh Annual Siloa Snow War
The Lair Behind the Lathemasters'
Tavenndi Lawn
Founders' Rock
The Eavesway
Harvesters' Green
The Ploughman's Shanty
The Parellian Plainsline
The Dolnario's House
Rimwold Row
Asleri Walk
To Midsummer Meadow
Follim's Field
Lampler's Lane
The Eastrange
The Thunders' Fort
The Whirlwinds' Fort
Rimwold Row
Lumber Store
The Lathemaster Place
Asleri Walk
Ambrick Tarmintree's House
Pemblin's Well
The Eavesway
N
Feet
0   80   160
JS
Legend
Building
Road
Neldon's Path

The Lair Behind the Lathemasters'

eldon sadly watched Corim go until he disappeared into an alley on the opposite side of Main Lane, then started walking slowly after him. However, he began to drag more and more with each step. His mounting blunders throughout the day were weighing quite heavily on him. In fact, so despondent was his mood that he even considered going home and just removing himself from the Snow War so that he didn't have a chance to louse anything else up.

"I can't even count how many of my efforts have gone awry today," Neldon sighed. "This is a truly rotten bit of luck. Things can hardly get any worse than this, I suppose." Abruptly, he stopped, and his face brightened, as he epiphanized, "If that's true – and things really can't get any worse, then that means they can only get better. Yes, they can only improve from here! Victory is mine for sure."

All it took for Neldon's mood to be completely reversed were these few moments of slipshod analysis. Now, with a merry spring in his step, he resolutely marched back to the Whirlwinds' fort, ready to take on the entirety of the Thunders at once, if need be.

As soon as Neldon reached the fort, however, he recalled that he had left his satchel at the Shanty, so he hurried back there to get it. No one was in the main room of the tavern when he arrived, not even Orinn Berthaway, who was presumably in one of the rooms or the hallway behind the counter. After eating a few more sugar cakes, Neldon crawled under the table beneath which he had previously been napping and located his satchel.

Just then, two Thunders walked in: Aradis Kingblade and Rannion Rillspan by the sound of their voices. They walked over to the counter for some refreshments, and Rannion said quietly but just loud enough that Neldon could hear, "There's no one else in here, is there?"

"Not that I can see," came Aradis' reply. "Not even ol' Berthaway's around."

"Good," said Rannion. "This is the perfect opportunity, then."

"For what?" Aradis asked.

"Me to give you the Turnip," Rannion said.

"Ah," Aradis returned.

Neldon held his breath, trying not to make a single sound.

"Damrig Brightcup just gave me the Turnip because apparently some Whirlwinds figured out he had it," Rannion explained. "But if they get a chance to search Damrig and find out he doesn't have it, they'll probably come after me next, since I always have quite a few guards with me. Anyway, I think you should take it and stay hidden rather out of the way for a while, maybe at some place it will be hard for the Whirlwinds to get to because it's deeper into our territory – a good spot might be that cluster of snow walls behind the Lathemaster place."

"Excellent idea," said Aradis. "Because even if someone does get through, those walls make such great defenses, I should definitely be able to hit them before they hit me. Plus, if they're expending most of their forces going after you or Damrig, there'd be no good reason for them to waste troops on a raid deep into a tricky area."

"My thoughts exactly," said Rannion. "I'll use Damrig as a decoy, surround him with a whole bunch of guards and put him somewhere far away from you. We can still put a few guards in your area just in case, though. Here, now take the Turnip, and let's get back outside."

Neldon heard a bit of shuffling, which he took to be Aradis stuffing the Turnip somewhere in his clothes. He remained hunkered down while the Thunders finished their conversation, ate a few snacks and then finally left.

Releasing a huge sigh of both relief and exhilaration, Neldon got up, shouldered his satchel and waited a minute or so until he thought that Aradis and Rannion wouldn't be around to see him coming out of the Shanty. Then he dashed out the tavern door and bolted for Agleri Walk to try and find someone to whom he could report his tidings.

As it so happened, the first person he encountered was Corim. A more reflective person than Neldon would have been extremely hesitant to engage with Corim after their parting not long ago for fear of being the victim of an immediate torrent of vitriol, but Neldon was so overcome with excitement about his findings that all he could think about was proclaiming them.

"Corim, Corim, Corim!" Neldon yammered. "I've got the most amazing news! I found out who has the Turnip!"

Corim made an enormous eyeroll. "Oh, really? Did Yankaboo tell you who had it? Or did one of the Thunders just feel terribly sorry for you and slip you that information?"

"Neither," Neldon replied breathlessly. "I was in the Ploughman's Shanty under a table, and I overheard Rannion giving it to Aradis. They didn't know I was there, so I even overheard exactly where Aradis is going to be hiding. He's going to be behind a bunch of snow walls back behind the Lathemaster place."

"Are you making this up just so you can feel better about yourself, Neldon?" Corim asked.

"No, I promise it's the truth!" Neldon insisted. "Please believe me. Please, please, please, pleasy please, please – "

"Okay, just stop," Corim said, holding up his hand. "Fine. I'll go tell Cromnic or Hendra and see if they can organize an assault to go after Aradis. But if you're making this up just so – "

"I swear I really overheard all this!" Neldon maintained.

"Okay." Corim shrugged. "But we don't have much time before the lunch bell rings, so we'll have to work fast."

From the very first Siloa Snow War on, a jovial, elderly gentleman named Pappy Greengrove had served as the bell-ringer for the event. He was something of a practical jokester, could almost always be counted on to brighten up one's day and was much beloved by all the children, who had issued a special invitation for him to serve in this role. Also, he lived just north of town and had no close relatives participating in the Snow War and was thus seen as being quite impartial in the competition.

When it was time for lunch, Pappy would ring the bell outside the Dolnario's house, which was at the north end of Main Lane on the east side of the street. As soon as the bell rang, the Snow War was officially on hold until he rang the bell again to signal the end of lunch. Also, and even more importantly, Pappy rang the bell at sunset to signal that the Snow War was over, so whichever team had the Turnip at the first evening bell-stroke was declared the winner for the year.

Corim, armed with Neldon's findings in the Shanty, raced southward down Agleri Walk, with Neldon running along behind. About halfway down the street, the pair found Cromnic Barleycroft with a cluster of older children gathered around him. Corim promptly told him Neldon's news. Cromnic then questioned Neldon further about it and immediately decided that they would try to launch a massive attack with the vast majority of the Whirlwinds as a decoy of their own to draw away all the Thunders' best players. While this was going on, he would go after Aradis with just a few assistants as backup in case he were hit or else to protect him while he searched Aradis for the Turnip.

In short order, all the Whirlwinds had amassed by the town lumber store, which was rather toward the southern end of Main Lane. Just to the south of the main group, Cromnic gathered around him his sister Saneldra, Tambris Turnsoil, Hendra Timberfall and Belgo Strapstitch to aid him in the raid on Aradis' lair behind the Lathemasters'. Corim and Neldon were also allowed to be in his elite squad since they brought him the news about Aradis.

"It's a good thing the Thunders can't go past the streetfront on their side while they're on defense," said Cromnic, "so they have no idea what we're plotting over here right now." He glanced across the street and laughed, "This is going to be so great!"

"What's the exact plan for our group, Cromnic?" asked Tambris.

"I'm going to try and get across the street alone," Cromnic said, "and hope that no one notices me because they'll be too preoccupied with the big attack. Also, if I go across alone before the rest of you six, we can hopefully find out how many guards there are and where they're hiding if they pop out to attack. If I get hit, the rest of you need to rush over and take out the guards and then carry on the mission toward Aradis. But if Neldon's report is accurate, there shouldn't be that many defenders in this area. Also, even if I don't get hit, I want you to follow behind me as soon as I've crossed the street because I'll want backup in case things go wrong with Aradis. He won't expect me coming, though, so I have a good chance of getting to the snow walls without being stopped."

Now Tressy Axleman, who was to lead the big charge, came over and talked to Cromnic for a minute to make sure she knew exactly what to do in the event of a number of different scenarios. When they were finished discussing these, Tressy ran off to lead the rally.

Not long afterward, Cromnic gave the signal, and Tressy's huge group of Whirlwinds burst out into Main Lane, heading northwest and immediately drawing the attention of the Thunders. Quite a few Whirlwinds were hit, but there were so many of them overall that the greater part managed to burst through into Rimwold Row. Meanwhile, Cromnic darted into Main Lane, heading south.

Now it just so happened that none other than Bernalla Elmensill was walking north down Main Lane at this exact same time. She was returning to her house from a visit to the home of Ambrick Tarmintree, where she had purchased a sack of tarmins, which were a tasty nut and a favorite snack of Siloans in both winter and summer. Adults did go about their business during the day of the Siloa Snow War but were mindful of the fact that the children would not hesitate to throw snowballs at them in jest. Miss Elmensill, however, as we have learned, took this as anything but jest. In addition, she was determined to carry about her daily business in defiance of the "uncouth hooliganry" of the Snow War.

As Cromnic was dashing down the street, Rannion Rillspan leapt out from an alleyway and tried to take him down. Rannion's snowball only barely missed Cromnic, who, seeing Miss Elmensill just a short distance ahead, decided to use her as a shield. Swiftly, he ducked behind her, which put Rannion in the very unpleasant position of having to let his quarry go or risking the raging and wrath of Bernalla Elmensill.

"What in the Ruphani's sausage pantry do you think you're doing, young man?" shrieked Miss Elmensill, as she sought to shove the crouching Cromnic away from her. "How dare you harass an old woman when she's on her way to her cottage! If you don't stop this nonsense immediately, I'm going to tell your father about this incident."

"I'd rather you do that than me be hit by a snowball right now," Cromnic hastily replied.

Just then, Rannion decided that protecting the Turnip was a loftier goal than self-preservation, so he hurled a hefty snowball at Cromnic. However, since he was positioned so precisely behind Miss Elmensill, it slammed into her arm instead, the one that was carrying the sack of tarmins, which she dropped in surprise.

"You can be fully assured, young man, that I'll be informing *your* father of this immediately!" she screamed at Rannion.

As she was yelling this, Cromnic bolted off south, waving to his elite squad to follow him as he did so. They burst out into the street, and Rannion managed to hit Hendra as she ran past. The rest followed after Cromnic, who darted into an alleyway and then made his way on toward Rimwold Row.

The only guards nearby were Branlum Harrowdell, Donnemig Berthaway, Mallany Applecot and Jalanna and Orris Boughpluck. Cromnic spectacularly dodged snowballs hurled by all of them and ran along the north side of the Lathemaster place, which was on the west side of Rimwold Row. The guards sought to follow him, but several of them were hit by his elite squad, which had arrived in Rimwold Row not long after him. An intense battle ensued between Cromnic's squad and Aradis' guards. However, as this was going on, Rannion raced past to try and get Cromnic from behind.

Cromnic reached the cluster of snow walls behind the Lathemaster place and saw Aradis poke his head up to see who was coming, as he had heard snow crunching swiftly. That was all it took for Cromnic to know where to aim. Aradis immediately tried to disappear behind the snow wall, but it was too late. Cromnic flung a snowball with lightning speed and accuracy, and it struck the top of Aradis' head.

At that very moment, Rannion arrived. Cromnic heard his approach, so he whirled around to face him. The two then engaged in a frantic snowball duel, but only a half-minute or so in, Rannion felt a snowball hit his back.

He turned around to see who had hit him, roaring, "Now who – " But he stopped short when he saw a goofily grinning Neldon Broadbuckle.

"That's my first hit of the day, and it was one of the Thunder's captains," Neldon sang jubilantly. "I always knew I had it in me."

Rannion made an ugly face at Neldon and shook his head. He certainly would have done more but was not permitted to speak until another Thunder tagged him or else his team switched to offense, which would happen as soon as the Whirlwinds claimed the Turnip from them. In the meantime, Rannion watched helplessly as Cromnic's squad defeated all of the nearby Thunder guards, with the exception of Orris Boughpluck, who ran off to get reinforcements. And with still greater dismay, he looked on as Cromnic searched Aradis for the Turnip and then extracted it. And no sooner had he taken it than he took off running to the east.

Since the Thunders were now instantly turned to offense, both Aradis and Rannion made desperate, but vain, attempts to hit the fleeing Cromnic with snowballs. However, the Whirlwinds were in luck, for Cromnic and his squad could now hear the distant, welcome ringing of the bell outside the Dolnario's house. Now there was nothing the Thunders could do to regain the Turnip until after lunch.

Throwing his fist in the air with a mighty "Hurrah!" Cromnic burst forward to rejoin his squad.

"We've got the Turnip!" he exulted. His troop let up a collective cheer, and then they raced back across Main Lane to Whirlwind territory.

When they reached it, Cromnic and his squad cheered again, and then they ran to their fort to break the news of their victory to all the Whirlwinds who were returning from the massive attack led by Tressy.

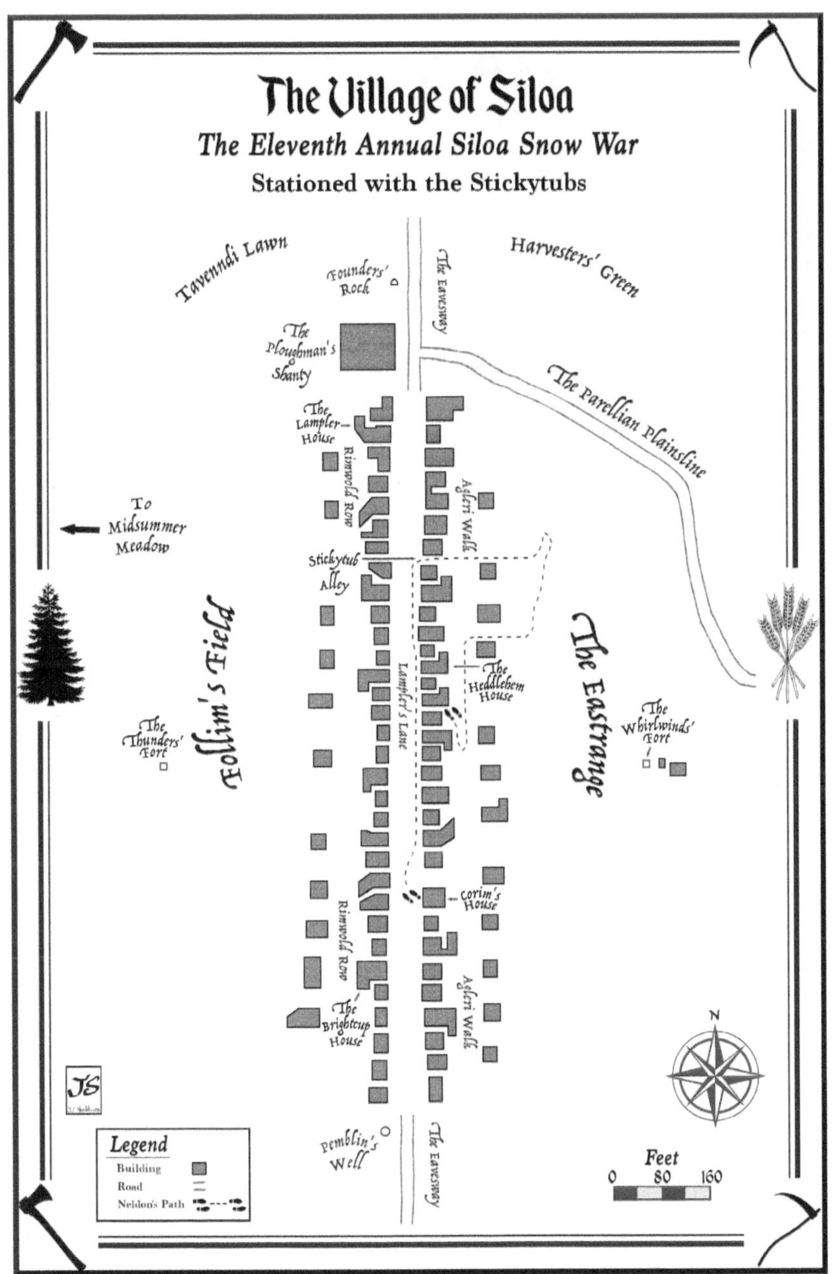

The Village of Siloa
The Eleventh Annual Siloa Snow War
Stationed with the Stickytubs
Tavenndi Lawn
Founders' Rock
Harvesters' Green
The Eavesway
The Ploughman's Shanty
The Parellian Plainsline
The Lampler House
Rimwold Row
Agleri Walk
To Midsummer Meadow
Stickytub Alley
Follim's Field
Lampler's Lane
The Heddlehem House
The Eastrange
The Thunders' Fort
The Whirlwinds' Fort
Rimwold Row
Corim's House
Agleri Walk
The Brightcup House
Pemblin's Well
The Eavesway
N
Legend
Building
Road
Neldon's Path
Feet
0   80   160
JS

CHAPTER SEVEN

Stationed with the Stickytubs

s it was now officially lunchtime, everyone from both the Thunders and the Whirlwinds went to one of four designated host houses to eat, chat and play games for a while before the second half of the Snow War commenced. Corim's parents were thoroughly invested in the success of the Whirlwinds. After all, no less than eight of their children were on the team this year, so they had offered their home as one of these host houses. The other Whirlwind house was that of Idaline Heddlehem, one of the older girls. The two Thunder houses were the Brightcups' and the Lamplers'. Whoever hosted had to make enough food for about twenty youths, but the Timberfalls were quite used to preparing multiple meals a day for a number of growing lads and lasses, so this wasn't anything too out of the ordinary for them.

Neldon decided to go to the Timberfall house, both because he was friends with Corim but also (and perhaps more importantly) because he liked Mrs. Timberfall's cooking better than that of Mr. and Mrs. Heddlehem. Also, the Stickytubs had gone to the Heddlehem house, and Neldon didn't want to have to compete with them for the limited supply of food.

During lunch, there was no end to the amount of gloating among the Whirlwinds that they had finally gotten the Turnip. Neldon's role in all of this was widely discussed, and he became something of an instant celebrity. Between bouts of devouring massive amounts of the Timberfalls' lovely spread of dishes, Neldon made a circuit among different groups of children, embellishing his part in the capture of the Turnip with each new telling of his exploits. However, Corim was always quick to correct Neldon's numerous inaccuracies.

Children would often migrate from one host house to another during lunch, and partway through the meal, Cromnic came over from the Heddlehem house to report with great relish that Bernalla Elmensill had gone to the Rillspan house to advise Rannion's parents to punish him for hitting her with a snowball. This had resulted in a stalemate between Rannion's father and Miss Elmensill, which had then escalated into a shouting match, as they had drastically differing views of whether what Rannion had done constituted a serious misbehavior or not. Eventually, however, she abandoned her attempt to bring justice down upon Rannion when she perceived that his parents were nothing but "unreasoning bullies and opponents of common decency."

Boiling after her failure with Rannion's father, she went to Cromnic's father, the Dolnario, and tried to get the Snow War terminated and also get Cromnic in trouble for using her as a shield. However, Cromnic was happy to relate that his father refused to put a stop to the Snow War and that he also said he wouldn't punish Cromnic unless his actions resulted in injury of another person or damage to someone's property. Miss Elmensill had then stormed off to her house in an even greater fury, vowing she'd find some way to make sure that justice was served even if she had to involve the Ruphani, the ruler of all Velaris, in the matter. (Velaris is, of course, the kingdom where Siloa lies.)

Since Neldon had told everyone about his grand achievement at least twice and because the youths were now beginning to discuss their strategy for defending the Turnip after lunch, a topic which didn't terribly interest him at the moment, he decided to go curl up in the corner and take another nap. As was typical for him, he fell asleep in only a minute or two. This was because Neldon had perfected the art of sleeping even through a great racket, even when he wasn't particularly tired. It was a hibernation practice of sorts that he had honed over the years to supplement his natural laziness.

⸺⸱⸱⸻

Neldon was wakened not terribly long afterward by Corim shaking him.

"Hey, get up, Neldon! The bell's just rung, and lunch is over," Corim said.

"Already?" Neldon yawned. "Does Cromnic still have the Turnip?"

"No, he gave it to the Stickytubs," Corim said. "He thinks – and everyone else agrees – that the Thunders would never expect us to give it to them, especially with this being the first time we've gotten it in years. I mean, honestly, the only person worse than them to give it to would be you."

"Nuh uh," Neldon shot back. "I'm one of the best players on our team. I actually was the one who got the Turnip before lunch."

"No, you weren't," Corim returned adamantly. "Cromnic was. You did tell us that Aradis had the Turnip and where he would be hiding, but Cromnic was the one who planned the attack and executed it, and he's the one who actually hit Aradis and got the Turnip from him."

"Well, I hit Rannion," said Neldon.

"Yes, because you were behind him and at rather close range. Plus, he was too occupied to notice you approaching."

"Whatever." Neldon waved dismissively. "You're just envious that I'm so good."

"You keep telling yourself that, Neldon," Corim snorted. "Now, here's a great idea. If you're such a fantastic player, why don't you go chum around with those bumbadoodle cousins of yours in Stickytub Alley? Then we can make it even more implausible to the Thunders that that's where the Turnip will be hiding."

"Okay, I'd be glad to help them out," agreed Neldon hastily, failing to recognize the backhanded insult in Corim's statement. And so, grabbing his satchel, he rushed out the door and hurried off to Stickytub Alley to join his cousins. And as soon as he stepped outside, he noticed it had stopped snowing. The sky was now clear and bright.

————•◆•————

Neldon found his cousins sitting down and playing a game called pinglybop (which is not unlike tiddlywinks) behind a large wagon in the alley. They were using Bingleton's relatively new pinglybop set, which he had purchased from a tavenndo, a traveling merchant, only a few months ago. Initially, the Stickytubs were somewhat annoyed that Neldon had showed up since they feared their games would be spoiled, as Neldon's pinglybop skills were quite formidable. However, he promised them that he would refrain from unleashing the full extent of his abilities. After this assurance, they were very glad to have Neldon's company because they were merely going to be hiding out while the rest of the Whirlwinds worked hard to make sure the Thunders availed themselves elsewhere. The whole idea was to bait the Thunders into thinking various persons besides the Stickytubs had the Turnip and then expending all their physical and mental energy trying to get them.

This turned out to be a magnificent stratagem, as, for a large portion of the afternoon, the Thunders were fully occupied with assaulting well-protected areas and wearing themselves out by chasing the fastest Whirlwinds through various series of obstacles. Meanwhile, Neldon and his cousins were glad to have a rest from having to run around. Plus, they had a grand old time playing pinglybop, and it somehow made it even more enjoyable to play it in the midst of a high-stakes snow battle.

Neldon stayed with the Stickytubs for several hours all told, although he left them every so often to go to the Ploughman's Shanty and partake of snacks and cider. These goodies had always been one of Neldon's favorite parts of the Snow War, but this year, since he spent so much time sitting around with the Stickytubs, he made more trips to the Shanty than he ever had before. Mr. Berthaway had always been a little peeved at the large amount of snacks and cider that Neldon consumed, but that afternoon, the lad's visits became so frequent that Mr. Berthaway suggested rather bluntly that he consider leaving some goodies for others to enjoy. Neldon didn't quite get the hint, so the next time he returned, Mr. Berthaway informed him that, only a few minutes ago, he had instituted a limit on how many refreshments a given youth could have to make sure they would last through the day. What's more, he said, Neldon had actually surpassed this unspecified limit. Neldon was greatly disappointed by this news but said that he understood Mr. Berthaway's position.

Rubbing his stomach and thinking longingly of sugar cakes and cider, Neldon returned to his cousins, and the four of them played several more games of pinglybop. By this point in the afternoon, Neldon was beginning to feel as if he needed another nap – or really anything that would enliven him. He had rather worn himself out that morning and did not feel as if his snoozes in the Shanty or the Timberfall house had been sufficient to restore him to full Neldonry.

Gently massaging his eyes, Neldon yawned, "I'm sorry, dear cousins, but I'm getting rather drowsy. Do you think we could do something requiring a little more activity? Something besides pinglybop? Don't get me wrong. I love the game. But I think I just need to get up and move around a little bit."

"I wouldn't be at all opposed to doing something else," said Hapworth eagerly. He hadn't won a game in over an hour and was quite tired of the others (and particularly Neldon) bopping more pinglies than him.

"All right, then," said Bingleton. "How about a game of catch or something?"

"What'll we use?" Mozzalyn asked. "Snowballs will be too cold."

"Agreed," Hapworth said.

Neldon thought for a moment. "Oh, I know!" he said, his face lighting up. "How about we use the Turnip?"

"Ah, that's a splendid idea. It's just the right size and everything," said Bingleton, who dug around for it in his coat and then excitedly pulled it out.

"Don't we need to worry about the Thunders seeing us with it?" asked Mozzalyn hesitantly.

"Nah," Hapworth said dismissively. "We'll just have to make sure we keep out of sight behind this wagon."

Momentarily, the four of them were tossing the Turnip lightly to each other behind the wagon, chuckling quietly at their own audacity in using the object the Thunders were so desperately seeking for such a trivial purpose.

"Oh, the Thunders would be so furious if only they knew what the Turnip was up to right now," laughed Bingleton.

"We'll certainly have to tell them how clever we were after sunset, when we've already won," giggled Mozzalyn.

The foursome continued their game for a few minutes, laughing giddily all the while. However, they soon decided that the area behind the wagon was too cramped for a proper game of catch, so Neldon suggested moving out into the middle of Stickytub Alley.

Mozzalyn promptly raised several concerns about this idea, but Neldon airily brushed them aside. "There's nothing to fear from those dimwitted Thunders. They haven't got a clue we have the Turnip. Besides, it will be quite easy for us to keep an eye out for them while we're playing. And if anyone does come by, we'll just stop our game immediately and then hit them with snowballs."

"I think we can manage all that just fine, Nelders," said Bingleton confidently.

And so Neldon and his cousins, despite Mozzalyn's misgivings, relocated their game of catch out into the middle of the alley.

⸺◆⸺

Now, when Cromnic and Hendra had determined to give the Turnip to the Stickytubs, they agreed it would be necessary to post several guards near the alley just in case the Thunders did try to pass through it and happened to see the Stickytubs hiding. As Neldon and his cousins would almost assuredly be overwhelmed, perhaps even by a single Thunder, these guards were instructed to hit any approaching Thunders with snowballs, regardless of whether they tried to come in through the west end of the alley or sneak around to the east entrance. Once hit, they would, of course, have to walk all the way back to their fort before attempting anything else.

However, Cromnic and Hendra didn't want to make it too obvious that the Whirlwinds were protecting Stickytub Alley in particular, so they had only left this task of shielding the Turnip to a few individuals: Tallis Pestleman and his identical twin brother Dallis, along with Sharessa Woodhew, Talaysia Cantlecraft and Branko Timberfall, Corim's older brother. These Whirlwinds had strict instructions to keep an eye on both entrances of the alley from nearby, but not to enter it unless a Thunder did, so as to simultaneously keep it secure without arousing suspicion.

It was due to these very instructions that none of the guards realized the very foolish thing that Neldon and his cousins were up to, for they could see either end of the alleyway, but not the area in which the game of catch was being played. They were, however, just about ready to go investigate what was going on, for the Turnip-keepers were making a considerable racket.

"Ooh, ooh, look at me," chortled Neldon, spinning around just after he had caught the Turnip. "I'm Rannion Rillspan," he said in a husky voice. "And I'm the best Thunder ever. You'll never get the Turnip away from me, you wimpy Whirlwinds." He laughed loudly at what he thought was a superb impression of Rannion but was actually just a lower and more thuggish version of his own voice.

Just then, a little Thunder girl, Erranet Brightcup (who usually just went by Netty), ran by on the far side of Main Lane. In an instant, she spotted Neldon and the Stickytubs in the middle of the alley and came to a sudden halt.

"Uh oh," Neldon gulped. "I think she's noticed we have the Turnip."

"What are we going to do?" whispered Hapworth.

"I know exactly what we can do to fix this situation," said Neldon boldly, as Netty continued to stare at them.

Quite dramatically, he put the Turnip up to his mouth and pretended to take a bite out of it. Then, pretending to chew, he loudly declared, "Mmm, Bingles, this turnip is deeee-licious. I'm so glad I brought it as an extra snack today."

"Oh, I wish there was enough for me to try some too," said Bingleton wistfully, winking at Neldon.

Netty's mouth dropped open, and then she dashed off into an alley leading to Rimwold Row.

"She's gone," said Neldon, wiping his brow. "I think my trick worked."

"Sure looks like it," agreed Hapworth.

"Quick, let's get back behind the wagon anyway," said Mozzalyn.

The four children rushed behind the wagon just as the Whirlwind guards that had been assigned to them entered the alley.

Tallis, who was one of them, asked with tremendous irritation, "Who exactly was responsible for inciting all that buffoonery I just heard? Are you all out of your minds?"

"You were supposed to stay in hiding and keep quiet," hissed Dallis, Tallis' brother.

"We were just having a bit of fun with the Turnip," explained Bingleton. "Playing a little, harmless game of catch with it, you know." Seeing how greatly the others disapproved of this, he hastily added, "It was actually Neldon's idea to use the Turnip."

"We might have known you'd be the ultimate source of all this stupidity," stormed Sharessa, glaring at Neldon, who smiled awkwardly in return.

"Do you realize Netty Brightcup was just running by?" raged Talaysia Cantlecraft.

"Don't worry, we fooled her quite convincingly, so she still doesn't know we have the Turnip," Neldon assured, as he proudly held it out for all to see.

"Oh, is that so?" snorted Branko. "Come off it, Neldon. We heard your dunderheaded 'ruse' quite well. Probably everyone in Main Lane heard it, you were talking so loud."

"Oh no!" cried Sharessa sharply. "The Thunders are coming! Run for it!"

Everyone looked up and saw a whole slew of Thunders racing across the street toward them, with Netty Brightcup among them. Evidently, she had taken her report quite swiftly, and there had been enough Thunders nearby to hastily assemble an attack squad.

"Get that thing out of sight!" hissed Branko to Neldon, who frantically stuffed the Turnip into one of his coat pockets.

Now Neldon and the Stickytubs, flanked by Sharessa and Tallis, raced off into the Eastrange, the field east of town, deeper into Whirlwind territory, while Dallis, Branko and Talaysia bravely stood their ground, trying to hit as many Thunders as they could to buy the fugitives time. They did manage to peg four Thunders – Olligon Furrowmead, Rayela Rushwick, Fanella Berthaway and Haldren Wedgeneware – but they themselves were soon frozen by snowballs hurled from the Thunders' ranks.

Although Sharessa and Tallis did their best to call for aid and reach other Whirlwinds who could help them, the Stickytubs ran so slowly that the Thunders were able to gain on them quite rapidly. Thus, any assistance that might come would undoubtedly be too late. Realizing this, they turned and waited for Neldon and his cousins to pass them, so that they could act as a barrier between them and the approaching Thunders, while simultaneously giving the Turnip-bearer more time to get away.

"I wonder if the Thunders actually know who has the Turnip," Sharessa whispered to Tallis.

"Don't know," Tallis replied. Just then, a clever idea came to him. "Hey, Stickytubs! Hey, Neldon!" he yelled over his shoulder. "Split up!"

The fleeing foursome stopped running, then turned and looked at Tallis with very puzzled expressions. A moment later, it registered what he had asked them to do, and Bingleton ran northeast, while Hapworth raced straight east. Neldon, who was a good deal more panicked than the others since he was currently in possession of the Turnip, started to run north, then thought better of it and wheeled back around to race southward, hollering hysterically as he did so. Mozzalyn had already started running to the south, but Neldon quickly overtook her.

Meanwhile, a few of the Thunders stuck around to engage with Tallis and Sharessa, but the rest broke up and ran off after the Stickytubs and Neldon. Fortunately, Sharessa was able to take out two of the

Thunders who were running after Neldon and Mozzalyn, leaving only one to pursue them, an older girl named Carrayna Nockshaft. Simultaneously, Tallis faced off with three Thunders, Brammiston Lathemaster, Hobbo Barnwain and Mellinor Rushwick, keeping them occupied just long enough that Sharessa was able to make her throws.

Neldon, who was nearly overwhelmed with alarm, noted Carrayna's approach over his shoulder and veered to the west. As he did so, he shouted, "Don't worry, Mozzles! I'll get help before the Thunders can take the Turnip from you." Although his previous ruse had been a complete failure, this did not stop him from trying to concoct a new one.

"I thought you had the Turnip, Nelders!" Mozzalyn called, nearly out of breath.

"No, I definitely gave it to you!" Neldon yelled back, as he tore across a swath of open ground leading to Agleri Walk.

A few moments later, he reached the far side of the swath and swerved south on Agleri Walk. Then, after he had run a fair number of yards, he reached down to check that the Turnip was still in his pocket. But, to his enormous consternation, he felt only the padding of his coat and not the firm form of the Turnip. "Oh, curdnuggets!" he exclaimed, as he looked over his shoulder. Some sixty feet back, he spotted the Topaz Turnip lying in the snow some distance south of the west entrance of the swath through which he had just passed.

Just then, to his utter dismay, Carrayna Nockshaft sprinted out of the swath and turned sharply south, sighting both him and the Turnip. Frantically, Neldon began to race back toward the Turnip, but almost immediately tripped over his own feet and went sprawling headlong into the snow. This blunder gave Carrayna just the edge she needed. By the time the now spluttering and wailing Neldon had picked himself up, she had already scooped up the treasured Turnip and was on her way to the west side of Agleri Walk.

Neldon was completely beside himself. He grabbed a snowball out of his satchel and threw it wildly at Carrayna. However, she dodged it and then raced into an alleyway leading back to Main Lane. Neldon ran after her but soon fell behind. He chucked one more snowball at her, but she was out of range by that point.

Smiling, she waved and called, "Thank you ever so much, Neldon Broadbuckle. I'm very glad you helped the Turnip back to its proper place. You've truly been a blessing to the Thunders today." Then she swiftly disappeared into an alleyway on the west side of Main Lane. The Turnip was now firmly back in Thunder hands.

Not long afterward, Tallis and Sharessa, who had managed to avoid being hit by any Thunders, ran up to Neldon. They came to a halt and then gave him a long, hard look.

At length, Tallis sighed, "I really can't believe you, Neldon. All you and those strawhead cousins of yours had to do was sit in Stickytub Alley and do absolutely nothing, and we would have won the Snow War this year. I'm sure of it."

"But no," fumed Sharessa. "That was just too difficult for you lot. And all because of your ninnyish antics the Turnip is gone, just like that. It will probably be another three years before we get it back again. You know, you could have chased after Carrayna. You didn't have to just let her get away. As soon as the Turnip is in enemy hands, our team reverts to offense."

"I did try to hit her as she was running off, but I forgot I could chase her across the street now," said Neldon numbly. "I guess I just didn't think of it."

"You don't do a whole lot of thinking, do you?" said Tallis scathingly. "Well, maybe it's time others did your thinking for you. I think – and I'm sure everyone else would agree if they knew what you'd just done – you need to just stay out of the way for the rest of the Snow War. You've apparently done your one useful deed for our team before lunch, so we can't very well expect any more."

Then, turning to go, Tallis said, "Come on, Sharessa, let's go find Cromnic and tell him what's happened before the Thunders have any more time to strategize."

Tallis and Sharessa briskly walked off, leaving Neldon standing in the alleyway. He had felt terrible when Corim had walked off on him before lunch, but now he felt ever so much worse. For earlier, his teammates' disgust was directed at him because he had on a number of occasions kept them from getting the Turnip, but this time he had actually lost it. And he feared it would be almost impossible to get it back now, for the Thunders would be on their guard more than ever before.

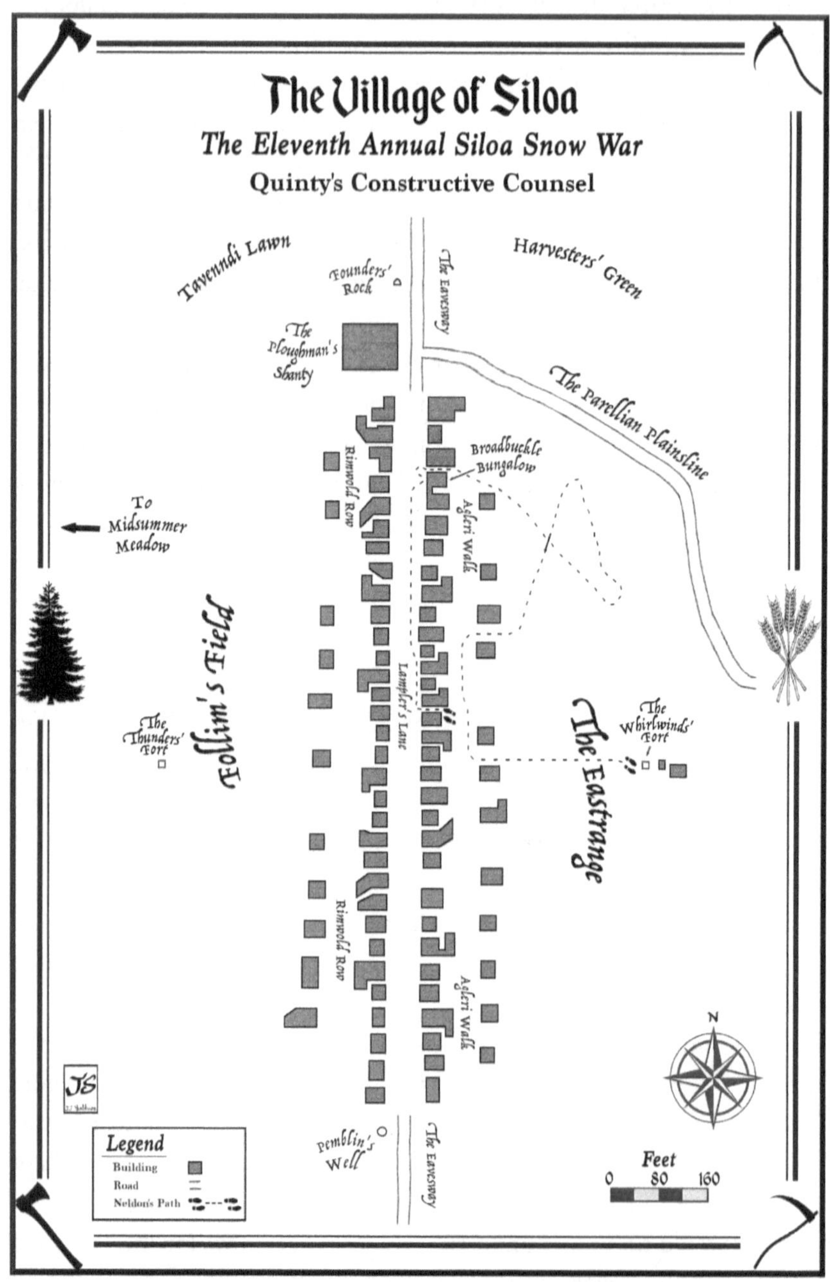

The Village of Siloa
The Eleventh Annual Siloa Snow War
Quinty's Constructive Counsel
Tavenndi Lawn
Founders' Rock
Harvesters' Green
The Eavesway
The Ploughman's Shanty
The Parellian Plainsline
Broadbuckle Bungalow
Rimwold Row
Asferi Walk
To Midsummer Meadow
Follim's Field
Lampfer's Lane
The Thunders' Fort
The Whirlwinds' Fort
The Eastrange
Rimwold Row
Asferi Walk
N
JS
Legend
Building
Road
Neldon's Path
Pemblin's Well
The Eavesway
Feet
0   80   160

Quinty's Constructive Counsel

fter Tallis and Sharessa had gone, Neldon sighed loudly and set out for his house, where he hoped to sit and warm up for a bit and also get some refreshments, since he wasn't allowed to eat any more at the Shanty. When he was about halfway there, a cloud drifted across the sun, and snow began gently falling.

"This is simply dreadful," said Neldon mournfully. "I was supposed to be the team's best player. How could everything have gone so terribly wrong? Maybe Tallis is right. Maybe I should just drop out for the rest of the day."

Neldon only grew more confirmed in this conviction as he drew closer to his abode, for he had set to mentally wandering down the trail of his many mistakes from dawn onward. Consequently, by the time he reached his front door, he was quite persuaded that he should remove himself from the Snow War. He slowly opened the door and then, with his head hanging shamefully, he plodded toward his room. He was so downcast by this point that he decided to even forego sitting by the fire and partaking of a snack.

Neldon suddenly heard a voice calling to him. "Neldon, dear, is something the matter?" It was his mother. She had just come from the bakery into the house proper to get some items from the pantry.

"Not at all," Neldon lied solemnly, but quite unconvincingly. "I'm just going to go and have a little chat with Yankaboo about something."

"I see," his mother said, giving him a skeptical look as she walked over to the pantry.

Neldon went into his room and closed the door behind him. Then he sighed, frowned and flopped on his bed. After a few moments of staring at the ceiling, he said, "I'm afraid I've really let the Whirlwinds down this year, Yankaboo. And now they're all going to be quite furious with me, at least for the rest of the day and probably for months afterward."

"Why is that?" he inquired in his wobbly Yankaboo voice.

"Well, the Stickytubs and I actually had the Turnip, and we lost it. I'd rather not go into the details."

"Tsk, tsk, that is unfortunate indeed," clucked Neldon in his Yankaboo persona.

"Yes, and I've decided that to avoid further botching things for the Whirlwinds, I'm going to remain in bed for the rest of the day. If you need me for anything, I'll just be under my quilt."

After Neldon said this, he proceeded to nestle himself into his warm bed and pull his sheets and quilt over his head. Quite often, he was blissfully unaware of his shortcomings and errors, but this time they were so glaring that even he was mindful of them. So he lay there, ruefully considering his sorrowful lot for nearly half an hour.

Suddenly, Neldon's cheerless reflections were interrupted by a knock at the door to his room.

Neldon peeped out from under his covers, as his brother Quinty walked in, looking quite concerned. "I beg your pardon, Neldon," Quinty said, "but what exactly are you doing lying in bed while the Snow War is still raging outside?"

Neldon quietly cleared his throat, then said, "I have decided to remove myself from the Agleri Whirlwinds for the remainder of the day so as not to cause them any more trouble than I already have."

Quinty shook his head, then sat down on Neldon's bed. "You really think you're doing the Whirlwinds more good hiding in your room than you would be running around outside?" he asked.

"I sure do," Neldon replied quite honestly. "What are you doing over here, anyway?"

"Mums hopped over to my place and told me you went into your room looking rather down," Quinty explained, "so I thought I'd come investigate. I'd have come earlier, but I had to finish some things up first. Now, did you really foul things up so badly as to warrant burrowing in your bed instead of aiding your comrades?"

"You don't understand, Quinters," Neldon said adamantly. "I've been lousing things up the entire day, and just a few minutes ago, I lost the Turnip to the Thunders – in a very embarrassing way, I suppose I should add. And now it's too late to get it back."

"No, it isn't," Quinty returned matter-of-factly. "You've got until sunset to reclaim it. And sure, you may have lost the Turnip; you can't change that now. And you may have been making a fine mess of things all day; you can't change that either. But you *can* change how this year's Snow War ends, although you can't do so by hiding out here in your bed. For good or for ill, you're an Agleri Whirlwind, so you've got to go do what you can. Just because you've been bungling everything up to this point doesn't necessarily mean that trend will continue, but you'll never know unless you try."

Neldon lay there, his head propped up on his pillow, as he considered all that Quinty had said. Then, at length, he declared, "That all sounds very sensible. I would still like to give things a go and help the Whirlwinds if I can. I'm just not sure exactly what to do to get the Turnip back. And I'm afraid the rest of my teammates will not want me around."

"As for the latter matter, even if they don't want you around, they're stuck with you," Quinty said firmly. "And as for the former, did you tell any of your chief players about the strategy I mentioned yesterday?"

"Why, no!" exclaimed Neldon. "I totally forgot about it. What was it again?"

Quinty sighed, "Oh, Nelders. Come now. I told you about it only last night. Anyway, make sure not to forgot it this time. Now, it's quite simple. Since you're on offense, you ought to send out a whole slew of parties numbering some six or seven persons each. And they've got to be sent all at once. The Thunders should find such groups rather difficult to fend off, especially if you make certain there are at least several decent players in each group. Skilled throwers are especially important to distribute evenly. Trust me; this strategy is highly effective. It's not foolproof of course, but it should at least give you a fighting chance of reclaiming the Turnip."

"I've got it this time," Neldon said enthusiastically. "And I'm going to go find one of our captains right away and repeat it all before I forget it."

"Good." Quinty smiled. "Now, if you get all melancholy like this again before sunset, stop by my place before retreating to your room, will you?" He stood up now, winking good-naturedly at his brother.

"I sure will," said Neldon, as he climbed out of bed and followed Quinty out of the room.

Crossing the main room of the bungalow, Quinty raised his hand for a brief farewell. Then, just as he was about to exit through the front door, Neldon asked, "Hey, Quinters, were you really one of the best Whirlwinds of your time?"

Quinty nodded. "One of the very best. Ask anyone you like from my age and they'll tell you the same."

Neldon smiled. "Maybe I'll be one of the best someday too."

"Maybe you will," returned Quinty brightly. He opened the front door and walked outside. Then, right before he closed it behind him, he looked at Neldon and said, "Oh, and don't forget – aim high."

"Right," Neldon said, as the door shut.

As soon as Quinty had gone, Neldon rushed to the pantry and pulled out a wedge of cheese, several handfuls of nuts and three carrots, all of which he stuffed into his pockets. Then he dashed outside, where it was still snowing, to look for Hendra or Cromnic, so that he might share his brother's strategy with one of them.

———•◆•———

Not long afterward, Neldon spied Hendra from afar in the Eastrange. She was on her way back to the Whirlwinds' fort, for she had been hit by a Thunder snowball while trying to enter Rimwold Row.

"Hendra, Hendra!" Neldon panted excitedly, as he ran toward her. "I've got the very best idea ever of how we can beat the Thunders. You just have to hear it!"

Hendra stopped, turned and glared at him with supreme annoyance, even disgust. "Oh, I'm sure you do, Neldon. I bet it's as amazing as all your other ideas today, like telling the Thunders about the third wave of our Triple Wave Whammer or using the Topaz Turnip in a game of catch."

"You heard about that, huh?" Neldon asked dejectedly.

"Of course I did!" Hendra snapped. "All the Whirlwinds have heard about it, and I'm sure every Thunder has too. It's one of the most ridiculous and asinine things that's ever been done in the history of the Siloa Snow War. Now, I've really no desire whatsoever to waste my time listening to one of your dumb ideas." Shaking her head, she continued walking toward the Whirlwinds' fort.

"But this technically isn't my idea," Neldon said, walking swiftly to catch up with her. "It came from my brother, Quinty. He was one of the very best Whirlwinds back in his day, you know. Ask anyone you like from around his age and they'll tell you the same."

Hendra stopped and turned to face him, then said, much to Neldon's surprise, "I don't need anyone to vouch for Quinty. I was one of the youngest Whirlwinds when he was one of the oldest ones. He was actually one of the captains during my first year. So I know he was good."

"Really?" Neldon asked, astounded.

"Yes, now please hurry up and tell me the idea because I need to try to get another attack squad together as quickly as possible. Also, I just want you to know that the only reason I'm listening to you at all is because this idea came from someone other than you."

Neldon, elated that Hendra had given him an audience, quickly related his brother's stratagem.

Hendra pondered the plan he had offered for a few moments, then said, "You know, that strategy doesn't sound half bad. And that tells me for sure that you didn't come up with it."

Neldon scrunched up his face a little, as he tried to figure out whether this was a compliment or not.

"I'm going to go and talk to Cromnic about this," Hendra said. "Time is running out to get the Turnip back, and I think it's at least worth giving this thing a try."

Abruptly, she ran off toward the fort, as she said, "Thanks, Neldon."

"Anytime," Neldon called after her.

—•◆•—

Neldon now scratched his head, as he pondered what he ought to do while waiting for Hendra to confer with Cromnic about his suggestion. After a few moments, he decided he would go have a look at what was happening in Main Lane, so he set off in that direction.

However, before he reached this destination, he saw his cousin Hapworth standing still and looking miserable as could be some distance farther north in the Eastrange.

"Hullo there, Happles," Neldon said, as he approached. "Whatever are you doing standing like that in the middle of this field?"

"I can't move until someone touches me," Hapworth whispered hoarsely.

"Oh, we're on offense now," Neldon explained, "so you only have to walk back to the fort if you get hit. And anyway, as soon as the team reverts to offense, you don't have to stay frozen anymore."

"We lost the Turnip?" Hapworth said, astonished. "Last thing I knew, you had it. What happened? I thought you would be able to get away."

"I did get away, actually," Neldon said proudly, "although I dropped the Turnip while doing so. Anyway, Carrayna Nockshaft took it and raced off to Thunder-town."

"Ah, that's a rotten turn of things," lamented Hapworth.

"It sure is," agreed Neldon. "So, um, have you been standing here for a while, then?"

"Yes, now will you just hurry up and touch me?" Hapworth said irritably, still failing to grasp that he was free to move at any time. "Everyone else on our team has just walked by and ignored me."

"That's very unfortunate," said Neldon, as he walked up to Hapworth and tapped him. "Now, where are Bingles and Mozzles?" he asked.

"Bingles is over there," Hapworth pointed to his brother, who was equally as miserable and standing rigidly behind a tree to the north. "I'm not sure where Mozzles is."

Together, Neldon and Hapworth went and touched Bingleton, who was very grateful to be released from his condition, although very downcast to hear that the Turnip had been taken. Then the three of them hunted around for Mozzalyn and found her likewise stationary (and miserable) a ways farther south and west in the Eastrange. They touched her so she would be able to move again (even though the three boys should have realized the needlessness of this entire business, since they already knew the Turnip had been taken and their team was thus on offense.)

Neldon and his cousins now held council for a minute or two, and Neldon explained that he had shared an excellent strategy of Quinty's with Hendra, who had said she was going to talk to Cromnic about it. The Stickytubs thought this was very fine and were excited about the prospect of participating in a charge with others besides themselves. However, since they had remained immobile for quite some time, they were now rather cold and wished to go to the Ploughman's Shanty and warm up. And, of course, they planned to consume a fair amount of nuts, sugar cakes and cider. Neldon dolefully informed them that he wouldn't be joining them, since he had exceeded Mr. Berthaway's limit of how many snacks a given youth could eat in the day. And, as he saw it, partaking of goodies was the primary purpose for visiting the Shanty.

"There's a limit to the number of goodies you can have?" Bingleton said, quite distressed. "I didn't have any idea. I sure hope I haven't passed it!"

"If Mr. Berthaway's started setting limits on how many snacks a body can have, that might be because he's running out of them," gasped Hapworth.

"We'd better hurry over to the Shanty, then, before they're all gone," urged Mozzalyn.

Bidding a hasty farewell to Neldon, the Stickytubs rushed off toward the village tavern. And so eager were they to get their hands on Mr. Berthaway's sugar cakes that they ran a good deal faster than they did during the majority of their Stickytub Sorties.

———•◆•———

Now that Neldon's cousins had departed, he decided to see if he could find Cromnic and Hendra. To begin his search, he headed to Agleri Walk and started walking southward. However, he had not gone terribly far when he heard voices coming from one of the open swaths that led eastward, as two individuals approached. Right away, he knew them to be Corim and Tallis.

"Say, who do you think unfroze the Stickytubs?" asked Corim. "None of them are in their spots anymore. I thought we had all agreed to let them stay where they were. Did someone tell them we were on offense?"

"I haven't any idea who would do such a terrible thing," replied Tallis, "but I can tell you one thing: it wasn't me."

Just then, the two lads entered Agleri Walk and spotted Neldon.

"Oh no," groaned Tallis, as Neldon turned to greet them. "What are you doing out here again? Somebody said they saw you going into your house, and we all thought you were bowing out for the rest of the day."

"I was going to bow out," replied Neldon, "but then I ... I changed my mind. Anyway, you're stuck with me, and there's nothing you can do about it." He grinned broadly.

"Oh yeah?" Corim shot back. "We'll just see about that."

"Uh, Corim," Tallis said, "Neldon is actually right this time. We *are* stuck with him, unfortunately."

"Now, listen here, Neldon Broadbuckle," Corim fumed. "We may be stuck with you, but that doesn't mean we have to like it. This year alone, you have almost singlehandedly done more damage to our cause than the Thunders have done for the past three years combined. I mean, we had the

Turnip in our custody for multiple hours, and if you and your blockhead cousins hadn't had the brilliant idea to use the Turnip in a game of catch, we'd still have it."

"Nothing can be done about that now." Neldon shrugged. "But as we speak, your sister Hendra is talking to Cromnic about a new strategy I proposed." He smiled confidently.

"Oh, sure she is," Tallis scoffed.

"Because you're the very first person Cromnic and Hendra would go seeking advice from," Corim laughed loudly.

Then, all of a sudden, the boys heard a voice calling to them. It was that of Ambril Boughpluck, a youngish Whirlwind girl. "Hey, Corim! Neldon! Tallis! All of you need to hurry to our fort. Cromnic and Hendra just called a meeting."

"Ah, I guess they decided to use my idea," Neldon said, with great satisfaction.

Corim and Tallis both rolled their eyes, then jogged off toward Hemptwist's Shed.

"Hey, wait for me!" cried Neldon, as he ran after them.

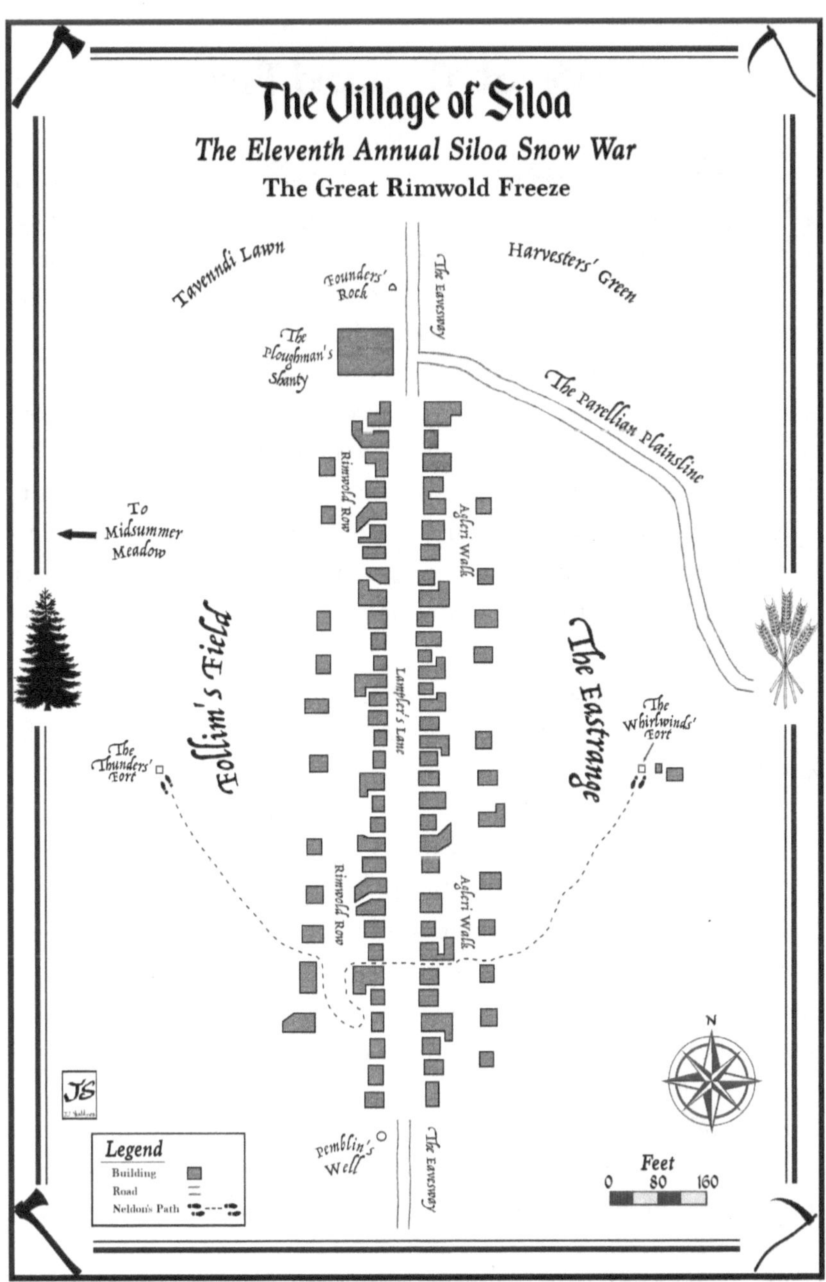

The Village of Siloa
The Eleventh Annual Siloa Snow War
The Great Rimwold Freeze
Tavenndi Lawn
Founders' Rock
Harvesters' Green
The Eavesway
The Ploughman's Shanty
The Parellian Plainsline
Rimwold Row
Agleri Walk
To Midsummer Meadow
Follim's Field
The Eastrange
Lampfer's Lane
The Whirlwinds' Fort
The Thunders' Fort
Rimwold Row
Agleri Walk
JS
J. Salkers
Legend
Building
Road
Neldon's Path
Pemblin's Well
The Eavesway
N
Feet
0   80   160

CHAPTER NINE

The Great Rimwold Freeze

ome ten minutes after Neldon and his friends had been summoned to the meeting, every single Whirlwind (including the Stickytubs, who were none too pleased to be pulled away from their sugar cakes and cider) was gathered by the fort next to Hemptwist's Shed.

Cromnic stood up on a small mound of snow and announced, "Time is getting short for us, Whirlwinds. Sunset's probably less than an hour off, and the Thunders have only tightened up their security since they got the Turnip back. But that certainly doesn't mean it's impossible for us to seize it again. Quite to the contrary. As a matter of fact, we've come across an excellent means of attempting to get it back. You see, an idea has been presented to Hendra that was formulated by a veteran player from former years who –"

"My brother Quinty," Neldon interrupted loudly. Several children glared at him, and the rest tried to pretend they didn't even know he was there.

"So it wasn't your idea after all," whispered Corim. "I knew it!"

Neldon protested, "Well, I was still the one who –"

"Shut up and listen!" snapped Tallis.

Cromnic did his best to ignore this brief banter and continued, " – a veteran player who said it was highly effective. I don't recall this strategy ever being used by either side in any of the Snow Wars I've been in, but it sounds like it really might help us to break through the Thunders' defenses, so I'm willing to give it a run. Here's how it will look." He turned to Hendra and nodded.

Hendra explained, "We're going to have every last Whirlwind charge the Thunders all at once, but with our ranks spread down the entire length of Main Lane."

"And we're going to be partitioned out into squads of six or seven people," said Cromnic.

"Our decent players need to be distributed evenly through all of the squads," said Hendra. "It'd be preferable to have at least two good throwers in every group."

"And our goal is not merely to break through the Thunders' defenses," said Cromnic. "If we're going to do this strategy, I say we should get all we can out of it."

Hendra continued, "On the way across Main Lane, everyone should of course try to avoid getting hit, but similar to what we had in mind with the Triple Wave Whammer, we want to make hitting all the Thunders we can a tremendous priority, even at the expense of dodging."

"Only this time," said Cromnic, "there won't be a third wave to check all the frozen Thunders for the Turnip. What we're going to attempt with this run is no less than to freeze *every single Thunder*. And then we'll go back and search all of them. That way we'll get the Turnip for sure."

"That's impossible!" blurted out a boy named Egliston Doughbury.

"Maybe," Cromnic returned. "But I'm up for attempting it, anyhow. And if we succeed, we can call it the Great Rimwold Freeze. Think of it; children years from now may be talking about this. Now, let's break up into our groups. You can try to place yourselves strategically first, and then Hendra and I will rearrange things as needed."

⸻ ◆ ⸻

Murmuring with excitement about the daring strategy that had just been presented, the Whirlwinds separated into five squads, with four of them being composed of seven persons and the last one of six. Cromnic and Hendra then moved players around until they were quite satisfied. After that, they explained a few more details about how they would begin the charge and what exactly they were going to do once they reached the other side of Main Lane. Not much later, the squads were marching off to their designated starting points for the charge. And as they were sojourning there, the gentle snowfall that had begun some time ago ceased, and the clouds overhead began to drift away.

Neldon rubbed his hands together in delight as he walked along through the snow, thoroughly elated at the prospect of redeeming himself from his former errors. He was in the single group of six, which was dispatched to the very south end of Main Lane. His squad mates were Tambris Turnsoil,

Nemmadib Strapstitch, Sanny Tillwater and Furdie and Branko Timber-fall. Hendra had said that there would preferably be two skilled throwers in every group, and Neldon was priding himself on being one of them, since he imagined that he and Tambris were the designated two from this squad. Of course, as the reader can probably guess, this was simply not the case. In fact, the throwers Cromnic and Hendra had in mind were Tambris and Branko. But Neldon, who was deluded far more often than not when it came to self-assessment, was experiencing a marked inflation of both his assurance and sense of importance on the basis of his delusion.

Once Neldon's squad was in place and all the other squads were as well, there was a tremendous sense of anticipation and tension that descended upon the Whirlwinds. Their time was growing short, and if this strategy didn't work, no other promising ideas remained to them. Everyone knew that this might very well be their last decent shot at getting the Turnip back and ending their miserable three-year-long streak of defeat. So they waited with bated breath for Cromnic to begin his assault from near the center of Main Lane, for this was to be the signal that the others must commence their charges as well.

Fortunately for all of their nerves, they didn't have to wait long. For all of a sudden and with a mighty cry, Cromnic and his group bolted forward into the street, hurling snowballs furiously at the Thunders who sought to halt their advance. All of the other squads, including Neldon's, followed suit. Neldon was near the back of his group, but he nonetheless threw snowball after snowball as forcefully as he could toward the Thunders who appeared in the alley they were making for. However, this proved to be unnecessary, for the three Thunders that attempted to block them were promptly pegged by Branko, Tambris and Furdie. As Neldon ran past these vanquished foes, he chortled giddily, "They'll be no stopping us this time, you picklepants pack of Thunderdunders!"

The three Thunders, Tombro Brackenlay, Nammalyn Bevelbrick and Farbis Berrydore, stared at the departing Neldon with severe annoyance, not so much at the insult, but rather from the fact that it was Neldon who had issued it and who undoubtedly thought himself very clever for doing so.

Several minutes of continuous, ferocious warfare followed, and all up and down Rimwold Row, cries of both Thunders and Whirlwinds could be heard as they sought to best their mortal enemies. But gradually, the cries began to lessen, and soon there were hardly any at all. The size of groups that Quinty had recommended, combined with the placement of the various squads and the determination and suddenness of the Whirlwinds' attack, had brought a severe blow to the Thunders' defensive positions in Rimwold Row.

Under the advice of Rannion Rillspan and Stayla Beamstander, the Thunders' captains, the Thunders had distributed their forces thinly and widely, since they were expecting one of three maneuvers to be employed against them: a stealth approach with adept throwers seeking to pick them off and search them individually, numerous attacks by groups of two or three, which they could have readily repelled, or else a mass assault by all the Whirlwinds at once. To combat this third potentiality, they had prepared several counters. But the Whirlwinds had done something thoroughly unanticipated, and none of the Thunders' contingency plans could be easily repurposed to deal with it. Consequently, the majority of their less-skilled players were rapidly overcome during the Whirlwinds' initial onslaught, and a fair number of their better players were forced into hectic snowball duels or else into hiding behind buildings, barrels and the like in order to retain some kind of presence in Rimwold Row.

Neldon's squad in particular had done quite well for itself during the attack. The six of them worked quickly to freeze all of the Thunders in their area, and in this endeavor, they had largely succeeded, hitting a number of players from the opposing team: Pallamen Barleycroft (Cromnic's cousin), Stecko Wealdwalker, Ryaleth Beamstander, Rannarom Woodhew and Mallimo Lampler. However, Aradis Kingblade was concealed nearby, and he managed to hit Tambris and Sanny from Neldon's squad, forcing them to hike all the way back to the Whirlwinds' fort. As for Aradis himself, who was now sorely outnumbered, he fled back into Follim's Field before any of the other Whirlwinds could get him.

The various Whirlwind squads spent several more minutes driving out the remaining Thunders from Rimwold Row, and although a few of these were hit, most were able to retreat to the system of bulwarks in Follim's Field, just as Aradis had. In the process though, they wholly abandoned a huge and critical swath of their territory: for now, the field was the only area they had left.

Although the Whirlwinds had incurred substantial casualties in their assault, they had been massively successful nonetheless, and those who had been hit could return to swell their comrades' ranks as soon as they tagged their fort. The Thunders were not so fortunate. They could, of course, only recoup their losses by tagging their teammates, but they were cut off from these by the watchful Whirlwinds, who had been ordered to stalwartly guard their defeated opponents. Furthermore, the Thunders who were left were mostly isolated from each other and so were unable to mount a coordinated attack against their foes.

⬦

Cromnic and Hendra conferred briefly about how to retain their tremendous advantage and make sure they got every single remaining Thunder. Hendra suggested they count up how many of the enemy had already been frozen and thus discern how many were still on the loose. This would give them a better idea of how dense the Thunder defenses might be in Follim's Field. Cromnic said he thought this was a splendid idea, and several of the more reliable boys and girls were dispatched to see to this task.

"What's all this wiggy-wagging about?" Neldon asked Branko, as he scratched his head and looked on in perplexity at Cromnic, Hendra and those to whom they were quietly giving orders.

Branko gave him a rather disturbed look and said, "Wiggy-wagging? What's that supposed to mean?"

"Just wasting time and diddle-dawdling," Neldon explained. "We've gotten nearly all the Thunders by now; why don't we just go into the field and finish them off? Bing! Bang! Bongle!" Neldon clumsily hurled a snowball toward a snow bulwark in Follim's Field to illustrate his idea of binging, banging and bongling.

Branko shook his head and sighed, "Because Cromnic and my sister – unlike you, Neldon – know that we have the upper hand now and almost certainly won't get it again. So they don't want to lose it by rushing into a maze of snow banks where all the Thunders' best players are skulking about. Besides, we can afford to take our time at this point, at least for a little bit," he remarked, as he glanced up at the sky.

"Well, if I were one of the chief strategizers of our team," Neldon harrumphed, "I wouldn't be letting a few weaselly little Thunders scare me off from just plowing through their stupid snow walls."

"It's a good thing you aren't one of our chief strategizers, then," Branko's sister Furdie cuttingly chimed in.

"Yeah, I wouldn't appoint you as chief strategizer of a moldy handkerchief," Branko mocked.

Neldon, who was more confused than offended by this comment, opened his mouth to reply, but could think of nothing to say, so he just pulled out one of the carrots he had brought from home and started munching on it.

Branko and Furdie looked at each other, shook their heads and then walked off to converse with their brother Corim, who was not far off.

While Neldon consumed his carrot and complained to others about what he saw as a needless delay, the boys and girls assigned to tally the frozen Thunders did so. After several minutes, they returned to Cromnic and Hendra and reported that were precisely twenty-seven Thunders out of commission. The more mathematically inclined among the Whirlwinds deduced that this meant there were only fifteen Thunders left to conquer.

Cromnic and Hendra, who were of course incredibly pleased by these circumstances, made sure that every Whirlwind who had been hit had by now returned from tagging their fort. Then they sent delegates to each squad to personally explain what they had in mind for their next step. Cromnic's proposition was that since they had so many expendable troops, they should send out scouts to figure out exactly where all the active Thunders had hidden themselves. If the scouts were hit, they could be restored, but any Thunder who hit them would give his position away. And because there were so many Whirlwinds, they could easily overwhelm a Thunder as soon as they knew where he was.

Soon this procedure was implemented, and it worked fantastically. The Thunders, once discovered, had no choice but to throw or be thrown at. And so they were rooted out, one by one, by the scouts. There was nowhere else for them to retreat to, since the western edge of Follim's Field was the western edge of their territory. Nine of the Thunders soon fell to the throng of Whirlwinds, just as Cromnic and Hendra had designed, but the fearsome fivesome of Rannion, Aradis, Stayla, Carrayna and Branlum did give them some trouble, as once they realized what the Whirlwinds were up to, they gathered together and made a final stand at the Thunders' fort. This was of very similar design to that of the Whirlwinds, only this fort had its sole entrance on the west, rather than the east. However, even these five eventually succumbed to the Whirlwinds' attacks, with Aradis being the last to be frozen. As soon as he was hit, a great and mighty cheer went up from the Whirlwinds, and many of the boys and girls began jumping up and down, hooting and hollering.

"I don't believe it!" Tambris gasped to his squad. "We really did it. We froze every single Thunder. Something like this has never happened before! The strategy really worked."

"Of course it worked," said Neldon smugly. "It was my brother Quinty's strategy after all – although I'm surprised I didn't think of it myself."

"Can't say anyone else is," muttered Furdie.

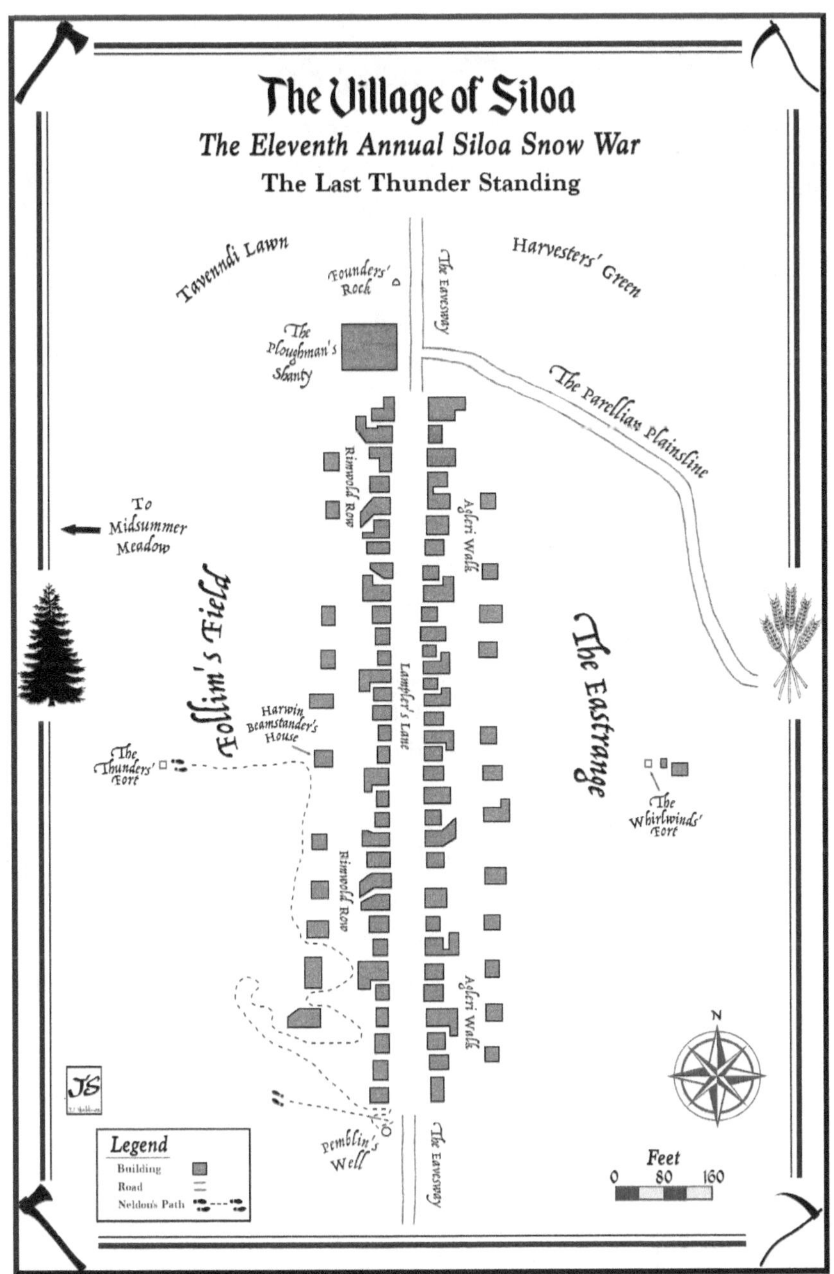

The Village of Siloa
The Eleventh Annual Siloa Snow War
The Last Thunder Standing
Tavenndi Lawn
Founders' Rock
Harvesters' Green
The Eavesway
The Ploughman's Shanty
The Parellian Plainsline
To Midsummer Meadow
Rimwold Row
Ashri Walk
Follin's Field
Lampfer's Lane
The Eastrange
Harwin Beamstander's House
The Thunders' Fort
The Whirlwinds' Fort
Rimwold Row
Ashri Walk
Pemblin's Well
The Eavesway
N
Feet
0   80   160
Legend
Building
Road
Neldou's Path
JS

CHAPTER TEN

The Last Thunder Standing

romnic whistled loudly and waved for everyone to calm their celebration so he could be heard. Once the Whirlwinds had quieted down, he proudly exclaimed, "Great job, Whirlwinds. Absolutely marvelous. But remember, we haven't won yet, and we don't have that much time before sunset. It's time to search everybody for the Turnip. Let's be quick about it, but thorough nonetheless."

"Start with these five," Hendra ordered.

And so the Whirlwinds eagerly patted down the five Thunders in the fort. Branlum Harrowdell smirked when they were frisking him, so they searched him with extra thoroughness.

"What's so funny, eh, Branlum?" asked Tallis Pestleman, who was feeling up and down Branlum's coat sleeves.

Branlum shrugged. According to the rules of the Snow War, he wasn't allowed to talk while frozen, and he was especially enjoying this fact at the moment, since the Whirlwinds would have loved to pry information from him if they could.

After the Whirlwinds had finished searching the five Thunders in the fort, they realized, to their great disappointment, that none of them had the Turnip.

"That's really too bad," said Cromnic. "I thought for sure one of them would have had it. It would certainly have saved us the trouble of searching everyone else if they had. Oh well, let's get on with it."

And so the Whirlwinds set about searching every single Thunder they had frozen. Some minutes later, they all gathered to the west of Harwin Beamstander's house, at the eastern edge of Follim's Field.

"Did no one find the Turnip?" asked Hendra, looking about in dismay.

The Whirlwinds shook their heads sorrowfully.

"You're all sure you searched thoroughly?" Cromnic pressed.

"Aye," the Whirlwinds replied in unison.

"How can this be?" said Hendra, growing greatly agitated.

"Maybe someone accidentally ate it," suggested Neldon during the uncomfortable silence that followed. At this, many of the Whirlwinds sighed collectively.

"This is no time for jokes, Neldon," Tallis' younger brother Edlimar said reprovingly.

"I wasn't joking," Neldon said defensively.

Suddenly, there was the sound of a boy loudly clearing his throat. It was Egliston Doughbury. Everyone turned to look at him.

"Excuse me, everyone, but I've been doing some calculations," announced Egliston. This revelation caused everyone to pay much closer attention, for Egliston had more prowess in arithmetic than virtually any other child in Siloa.

"What sort of calculations?" asked Cromnic earnestly.

"Well, we know there are forty-two Thunders total this year. And before we started freezing the Thunders in Follim's Field, we tallied twenty-seven that we had already hit. I just walked around the field and counted nine that are frozen in the field proper, and then there are five in the Thunders' fort. If you combine all those numbers, you get – "

"Forty-two!" shouted Neldon excitedly.

"Shut up, Neldon!" shouted a great many of the Whirlwinds at once. They had had more than enough of him for the day – or for the month, for that matter.

Egliston glared at Neldon, cleared his throat again, and patronizingly said, "No. You get *forty-one.*"

The group fell silent.

"So someone's missing," said Tallis. "That must be why Branlum Harrowdell was looking so smug."

"Yep, one of them must be hiding somewhere," said Cromnic.

"Let's spread out and find whoever it is right away," said Hendra, looking nervously up at the sky. "We really are almost out of time now."

Indeed, the quality of the sunlight was changing in a way that made the Whirlwinds rather uncomfortable. Pappy Greengrove might well be ringing the evening bell in as little as half an hour or perhaps even a third of an hour.

———•◦•———

Hurriedly, the Whirlwinds disbanded and began combing the entirety of the Thunders' territory for the missing player.

Neldon offered his services to several other children to assist in this endeavor, but they all told him they could work much faster without him and didn't want him constantly cracking jokes while they were trying to take advantage of the narrow window of opportunity that remained to them.

After Neldon had been turned down no less than five times (and had five times adamantly insisted that he hadn't been joking earlier), he sighed and decided to go search solo.

At first he wandered around several of the buildings at the south end of Rimwold Row. Finding no one, he paced around the southeast area of Follim's Field. He didn't find anyone there either, so he thought he might now go scrutinize the snow banks near the Thunders' fort. However, right before he turned to go in that direction, he happened to glance to the southeast and spied Pemblin's Well, a picturesque, circular stone well with a small, pointed red roof over it. Besides being a source of water for the village of Siloa, this well bore significance as the marker for the southern boundary of the viable play area for the Siloa Snow War.

"Hm," said Neldon aloud. "I wonder if anyone's looked by Pemblin's Well. It is technically within the Thunders' territory, I believe."

Resolutely, Neldon marched toward the well. There was no one visible on the west side of it, so Neldon walked eastward so that he might see the opposite side clearly.

But he didn't even have to see the east side in its entirety before he spotted a little girl crouched down next to it. After squinting a bit, he realized exactly who she was. At this particular moment, the girl was looking straight to the east, so she didn't notice Neldon. Hastily, he withdrew a number of feet to the west so as to be out of her sight.

Now Neldon gasped and started shaking, so overcome was he with excitement. "I found her!" he whispered. "I found the final Thunder. And that means that I found the Turnip."

Then, gaining a measure of composure over himself, he chuckled, "And it's just little old Quinnia Greyloam. I can easily take care of her. She's only nine, after all." Neldon, who was eleven, was fully convinced that the two years he had on her constituted a significant advantage.

As stealthily as he could, Neldon began creeping toward the well. His plan was to get right up next to it and then surprise Quinnia, snowballing her in the face at close range. With each step he took, he made every effort to crunch the snow as little as possible, always keeping his eyes fixed on where Quinnia might pop her head out if she heard him approaching. But her head did not appear, and so Neldon continued on until he was standing just west of the well. There he got on his hands and knees and started to inch his way around to the well's north side. Then he got an even better idea, as he reckoned it, than the one he had had originally.

"I'll get her from above," he said to himself. "Yes, that's what I'll do. I'll toss a snowball right on top of her Thunderdunder head and say 'Boo!' at the same time."

So, reaching ever so quietly into his satchel, he drew out his finest snowball and prepared to lob it over the rim of the well to its east side.

"Boo!" he shouted at the top of his lungs and launched the snowball into the air.

Unfortunately, his snowball didn't make it to the other side of the well, but merely fell down into the well itself. And as soon as he yelled, "Boo!" Quinnia screamed, nearly scared out of her skin, and shot forward like a rabbit, her heart racing furiously. Realizing that someone was right next to the well, she sprang to her feet, pulled a snowball out of her satchel and whirled around. Suddenly, she saw Neldon's grinning face appear over the north rim of the well.

"Gotcha!" he crowed gleefully. Instantly, he realized with great consternation that he had not gotched Quinnia at all. Indeed, she was about to gotch him. His mouth fell open in dismay.

Quinnia hurled a snowball directly at Neldon's face, but it failed to strike its target, as Neldon, who was crouching, lost his balance in his fright and fell backwards. Quinnia seized this opportunity to make a mad dash to escape to the west. Neldon scrambled up as she was passing and tried to hit her in the back with a snowball, but missed.

"Rabid Thunder! Rabid Thunder!" yelled Neldon in a panic, as he ran after her. "Turnip-carrying Thunder on the loose!"

Now, at that time, Tressy Axleman happened to be not far off, as she was searching for the final Thunder in the southeast corner of Follim's Field. Quinnia knew that Tressy had a formidable aim, but the raving Neldon was not far behind her, and she thought the snow bulwarks scattered throughout the field provided her best chance of survival, so she continued running westward, even though that would take her dangerously close to Tressy. She thought about trying to vanquish Tressy in a snowball duel but decided it would be better to just concentrate on running away and avoiding enemy fire at this point.

Quinnia was a rather good dodger, but Tressy was a better thrower. As soon as her quarry was in range, Tressy flung two speeding snowballs at her in rapid succession. Quinnia just barely dodged the first one, but the second one hit her in the arm. With a cry of both mourning and exasperation, she froze and hung her head.

"The Turnip is ours!" Neldon exclaimed, as he ran up to Quinnia and started patting down her coat pockets.

Tressy raced over to assist, but Neldon found the Turnip before she even got there.

"Oh ho!" he cried, pulling the treasured Topaz Turnip from one of Quinnia's larger coat pockets. "Never try to escape from the great Neldon Broadbuckle. You'll be absolutely certain to fail!"

"Quit running your mouth and run with your legs, Neldon!" Tressy yelled sharply. "As soon as our team has the Turnip, the Thunders revert to offense!"

"Yeah, and there's no way we're letting you take that Turnip back over to your side," snarled Quinnia, as she made a grab for it. Neldon only just managed to pull it out of her reach.

Suddenly, Neldon realized how perilous their situation really was, for all of the Thunders who were frozen were now free to move, and there were a number of them nearby who had just seen him claim the Turnip. But a matter of even greater concern was that there were no other Whirlwinds close enough to come to his and Tressy's aid.

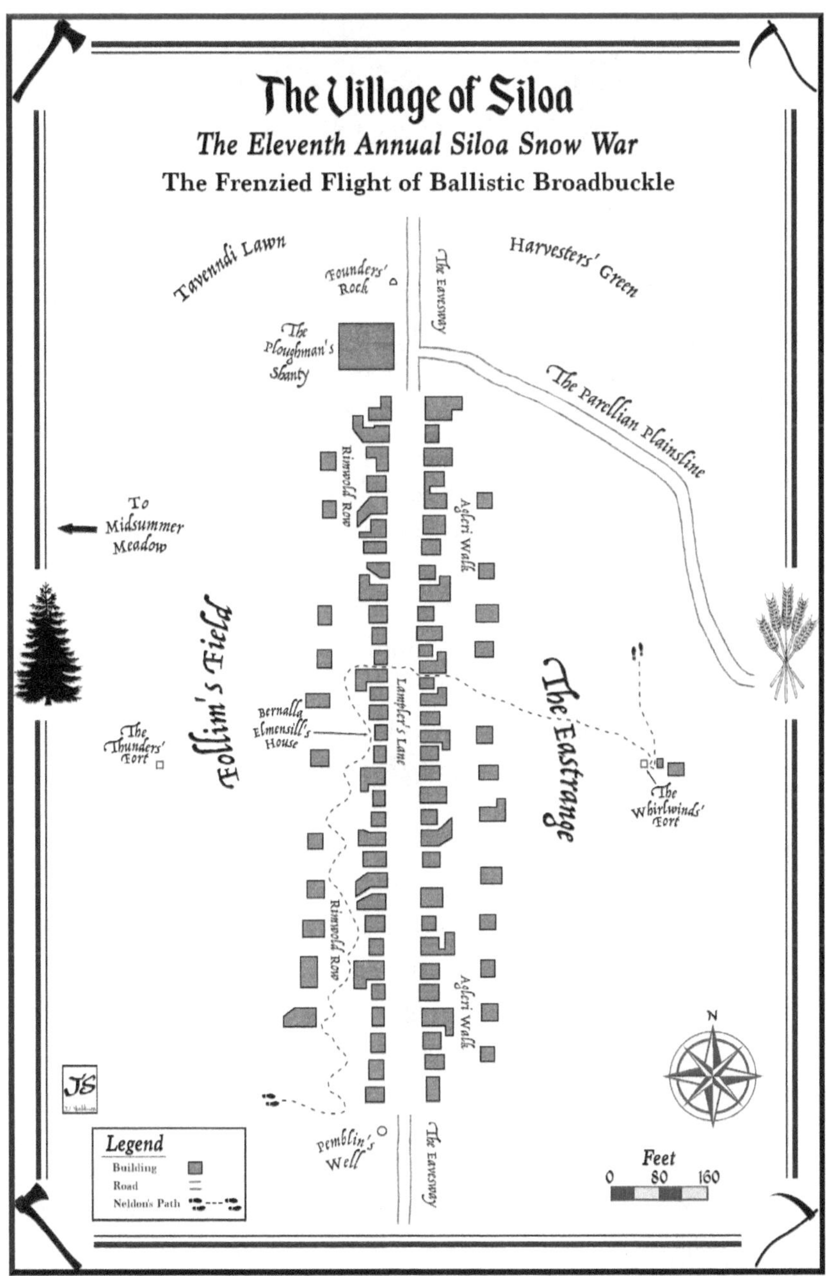

The Village of Siloa
The Eleventh Annual Siloa Snow War
The Frenzied Flight of Ballistic Broadbuckle
Tavenndi Lawn
Founders' Rock
Harvesters' Green
The Eavesway
The Ploughman's Shanty
The Parellian Plainsline
Rimwold Row
Asleri Walk
To Midsummer Meadow
Follim's Field
The Eastrange
Bernalla Elmensill's House
Lampler's Lane
The Thunders' Fort
The Whirlwinds' Fort
Rimwold Row
Asleri Walk
Pemblin's Well
The Eavesway
N
Legend
Building
Road
Neldon's Path
Feet
0   80   160

CHAPTER ELEVEN

The Frenzied Flight of Ballistic Broadbuckle

creaming like a madman, Neldon instantly tore off toward Main Lane with Quinnia not far behind him, chucking snowballs and only just missing him each time. However, he was soon forced to wheel around, for Mallimo Lampler, whom Neldon's squad had frozen earlier, had raced south from Rimwold Row to cut him off, and he was eager for revenge.

"Go north down Rimwold Row," called Tressy, who was some distance back, "and then try to charge through an alley to the east as soon as you can!"

Neldon immediately heeded this advice (or at least the first part of it) and veered north, as snowballs from Mallimo and Quinnia hurtled toward him. Luckily, they both narrowly failed to strike their mark. But now there were even more formidable attacks to be overcome, for up ahead, there were more four more Thunders, and all of them realized what had happened, if nothing else because Neldon was clutching the Turnip in plain sight.

Rapidly assessing the situation, Mallimo decided he might be of better service running along the western edge of Main Lane than continuing to chase Neldon down Rimwold Row, since he could attempt to block any of the alleys Neldon might escape through. So he dashed to Main Lane and then turned north, trying to keep apprised of where Neldon was so that he could move to thwart him if necessary. This proved to not be very difficult, since Neldon was hollering all the way down the street.

To Neldon, it seemed like veritable hordes of Thunders were rising out of the snow before him and that every Thunder had a deadly glint in his eye and was throwing scores upon scores of snowballs at him. As a matter of fact, there were a decent number of Thunders seeking to waylay him, and they were hurling quite a few snowballs, but Neldon's panic had distorted the situation so as to be far more dire than it actually was. As a result, he went into something of a manic mode.

The Thunders who stood in Neldon's path were taken aback by multiple aspects of his transformation that followed. For one thing, they had not thought him capable of running as fast as he was, even under the most extreme of circumstances. His legs were moving so quickly and he was kicking up so much snow that they half-imagined the lower part of his body was merely a whirlwind of flying white powder. And he was yelling so loud that it made their eardrums hurt. Also, he was holding the Turnip in front of him like some kind of talisman, and they half-expected magical energy or the like to shoot out of it toward them. And, despite their best efforts, they were unable to hit this speeding, broadbuckled lunatic. Remarkably, every single one of their snowballs was missing him. This was not so much because Neldon was dodging them, per se, but because he was running in such an erratic manner that no one could quite predict his trajectory.

Speaking of Neldon's trajectory, he had actually run nearly halfway up Rimwold Row by this point, having thoroughly forgotten Tressy's advice for him to escape into Main Lane through one of the alleys. Also, a number of Whirlwinds were now aware of the fact that Neldon had the Turnip and were in close enough proximity that they could do something to help him. Their assistance mostly came in the form of them attacking various Thunders and in calling out advice, although Neldon completely ignored all of this.

"Watch out for Ballistic Broadbuckle!" yelled a youngish Thunder girl named Laysaree Lyelather, as Neldon nearly plowed into her while she was hurriedly trying to make a snowball, since she was fresh out of them. She tried to hit him in the back with the snowball when she completed it, but he was careening so crazily that her missile simply flew past him.

Now, as Neldon was so utterly overrun by his fit of terror, he failed to notice that he was headed straight for a plot of ground which every Siloan child (and adult, for that matter) knew better than to set foot in. And that spot was Bernalla Elmensill's turnip patch.

Heedless of the doom he might bring upon himself, Neldon vaulted over the low fence surrounding the turnip patch and trampled through it, swerving right and left as he had been doing all down Rimwold Row. All the watching warriors, both Whirlwinds and Thunders, gasped as they witnessed Neldon commit this grave folly. Tallibot Tapertrim, a young

Thunder boy, and Sullaryn Nimbletack, a little Thunder girl, were so aghast at Neldon's deed that they nearly fainted.

At once, from inside the house just east of the turnip patch, there came a terrible shriek. "Aha! Aha! I knew it would come to this!" a high voice cried.

If Neldon had not been completely consumed by his temporary lunacy, this voice would have curdled his blood and made him quiver from highest hair to lowest toe. But as it was, it didn't even register, since all Neldon could hear was the wobbly voice of Yankaboo in his ears yelling, "Flee! Flee! Flee for your life, Neldon! If you die, the Turnip dies too! The Whirlwinds need you!"

Neldon leapt over the fence on the opposite side of the turnip patch and ran a number of yards more. An especially sizable group of Thunders was just ahead now, and in Neldon's crazed state, he let out a shriek to rival that of Miss Elmensill and then swerved eastward into an alleyway leading to Main Lane.

Mallimo Lampler was south of Neldon when he emerged into Siloa's main street and was close enough that he could have hit him with a snowball had Neldon not been in the condition he was. As it was, Mallimo made a good attempt, but it was in vain, for the careening Neldon evaded no less than three of Mallimo's snowballs before disappearing through an alleyway on the east side of the street.

———•·•◆•·•———

By this time, all of the Whirlwinds and Thunders knew that something serious was afoot, even if they had been far out in Follim's Field and unable to see what was going on. (Indeed, even the adults of Siloa could discern this from inside their shops and homes, since there was so much racket.) Tressy had run to several key Whirlwinds and very briefly explained that Neldon had gotten the Turnip and that the Thunders were now on offense. These then spread the news to others, and the Whirlwinds started pouring back toward their own territory.

Meanwhile, several Thunders who had been nearby when Neldon got the Turnip ran out to their frozen teammates in Follim's Field and told them what had transpired. When the news of these events reached the five top players, who were standing in the Thunders' fort wondering what in all Orona was going on, these five players immediately charged out and started suggesting various plans for getting the Turnip back. However, within a very short amount of time and with practically no deliberation, they landed on a plan offered by Rannion. As soon as it was approved, Rannion called out loudly to any Thunder within earshot that they must all do a mass sortie across Main Lane, since the Whirlwinds would hardly have time to arrange themselves properly for defense. But it mattered little what Rannion or any of the others said at this point, since most of the Thunders had already engaged in a mass sortie anyway.

⸻ ✦ ⸻

As for Neldon, he didn't stop running until he had reached the Whirlwinds' fort. When he got there, he snapped out of his mania and panted like a wild bull, dropping the Turnip to the ground and putting his hands on his knees.

"I got the Turnip," he gasped. "It'll be safe here, won't it? No, it won't, because the Thunders are on offense now. That means they can come all the way over here. But there aren't any other Whirlwinds to help me. Where are they all anyway?"

Not long after Neldon uttered this query, four Whirlwinds dashed into the fort and looked at him in amazement. One of them, a little girl named Verraliss Peddlepot, said, "That was incredible, Neldon. I've never seen anything like it."

"Yeah," said her friend Lempeera Boltsnip. "I'm not even sure what just happened."

"Are you okay, Neldon?" asked Tornigus, one of Tallis' younger brothers.

"Sure," said Neldon, still heaving desperately for air. "We've got the Turnip now. That means everything's okay."

"Do you realize you ran through Bernalla Elmensill's turnip patch?" asked Tedge Timberfall.

Neldon's eyes grew enormous. "I did? Surely not. There's no way I would have done that. That'd be insane."

"Well, you *were* acting pretty crazy," said Verraliss.

"Did she see me?" asked Neldon, who was now shaking a bit.

"Yes, but I don't think she knew it was you," said Tedge. "I got in a short duel with Mallimo Lampler when we were running across the street – a duel which I won, by the way – and during the duel, I heard the Elmensill yelling 'Who ran through my turnip patch? What vile urchin was that? Somebody had better fess up!'" Of course, his quoting of Bernalla Elmensill occurred in an obligatory impression of her voice, which practically all the youth of Siloa could do, though some could do it much better than others.

Neldon breathed a huge sigh of relief and said, "I can't believe I ran through her turnip patch. I don't know what came over me. But I'm sure glad she didn't realize it was me."

"Yet. . ." added Tedge ominously.

"Hey, one of us had better take a look outside," said Lempeera abruptly. "There might be Thunders coming."

Tedge hopped up on the snow pile that had been formed to allow one to peer over the west wall of the fort and said, "No Thunders yet, but there are some of our own jolly Whirlwinds blowing in."

A few moments later, several more Whirlwinds rushed into the fort, and one of them, Belgo Strapstitch, announced, "There's an absolutely wild battle going on up by Main Lane and Agleri Walk right now. The Thunders basically just rushed across the street, trying to get back here to the Eastrange before we did. Fortunately, we had enough folk nearby that we were able to keep them from overrunning the place. But we've got to figure out how we're going to protect the Turnip because if even a small group of the Thunders gets through, they'll probably come looking here first."

"Well, what should we do?" asked Neldon.

"I don't know, but hopefully one of our leaders can get back here soon and figure something out," Belgo answered. "In the meantime, I'm going to go outside and keep watch."

With that, Belgo ran out and stood by the snow fort's north wall. But it was not long before he uttered a cry of alarm, as he witnessed Hendra Timberfall racing at a breakneck speed toward him from the northwest, yelling, "They've broken through! The Thunders have broken through!"

Behind her, Cromnic was leading a desperate retreat of some dozen Whirlwinds. And there was an angry swarm of around twenty-five Thunders led by Rannion Rillspan and Branlum Harrowdell not terribly far behind them, lobbing an unceasing torrent of snowballs.

Momentarily, Hendra bounded into the fort, crying "Where's the Turnip? And where's Neldon?"

"Here and here," said Neldon, holding the Turnip up.

"We're not going to be able to defend this fort for long," Hendra panted, speaking at a frantic pace, "and we only have to hold on to the Turnip for a few more minutes until sunset. But I don't think it should stay here. We just need to give it to our fastest runners and do something like a relay, with each runner passing it off to the next. Honestly, at this point, we just need to keep the Turnip moving faster than the Thunders."

Hendra looked at the Whirlwinds gathered there, then nodded at Mando Axleman. "You're fast, Manny. Take the Turnip and run wherever the Thunders aren't. We'll send someone else to meet up with you. And we'll try to keep the Thunders away from you. Not all of them are accounted for, so watch out for any stray individuals or squads roaming around. Hide if you can; run if you can't. Really, all you have to do is not get hit or caught."

"Got it," said Mando. He snatched the Turnip from Neldon, shoved it in his coat pocket, and then bolted off to the south.

"My Turnip!" cried Neldon, who was quite displeased to have it torn away from him so unceremoniously.

"*Our* Turnip," corrected Condrig Brakesnare.

Belgo, who had still been keeping watch outside the door, popped his head into the fort and said, "Cromnic turned our forces around and has been able to stall the Thunders a bit, but whatever you're going to do, you need to do it fast. I don't think he can hold out much longer."

"The Turnip's already gone," said Hendra. "Manny's running south with it. But, you know. . ." she paused, thinking.

Then, suddenly, she said, "Neldon, you need to run to the north."

"Why is that?" asked Neldon, who had just started eating the wedge of cheese he had stuffed into one of his pockets.

"Oh, I see. Maybe they'll think he has the Turnip," said Talaysia Cantlecraft.

"How about this? Even better – do whatever that crazy thing was you were doing before," suggested Belgo. "That will probably make it more convincing."

"I shall gladly bear the Turnip longer, even if Manny's the one who has the real thing." Neldon nodded. Standing erect and saluting, he bounded out of the fort, then took off running northward, hollering as he went.

The Thunders took the bait. When Rannion saw Neldon race out of the fort, waving his arms, he noted that he was clutching something in his left hand. This Rannion assumed to be the Turnip, but it was actually Neldon's wedge of cheese. Rannion ordered his followers to cease the engagement with Cromnic and the others and run down Neldon. With a terrible, savage roar, they began pouring across the field toward the speeding Neldon.

Cromnic, who was unaware that Neldon did not in fact presently have the Turnip, instantly ordered his own troops to pursue the Thunders who were chasing Neldon.

Neldon was now being chased by about forty youths, some of whom were trying to protect him, but most of whom were hoping to pound him with a snowball. But none of them knew that they were simply chasing a lunatic with a piece of cheese.

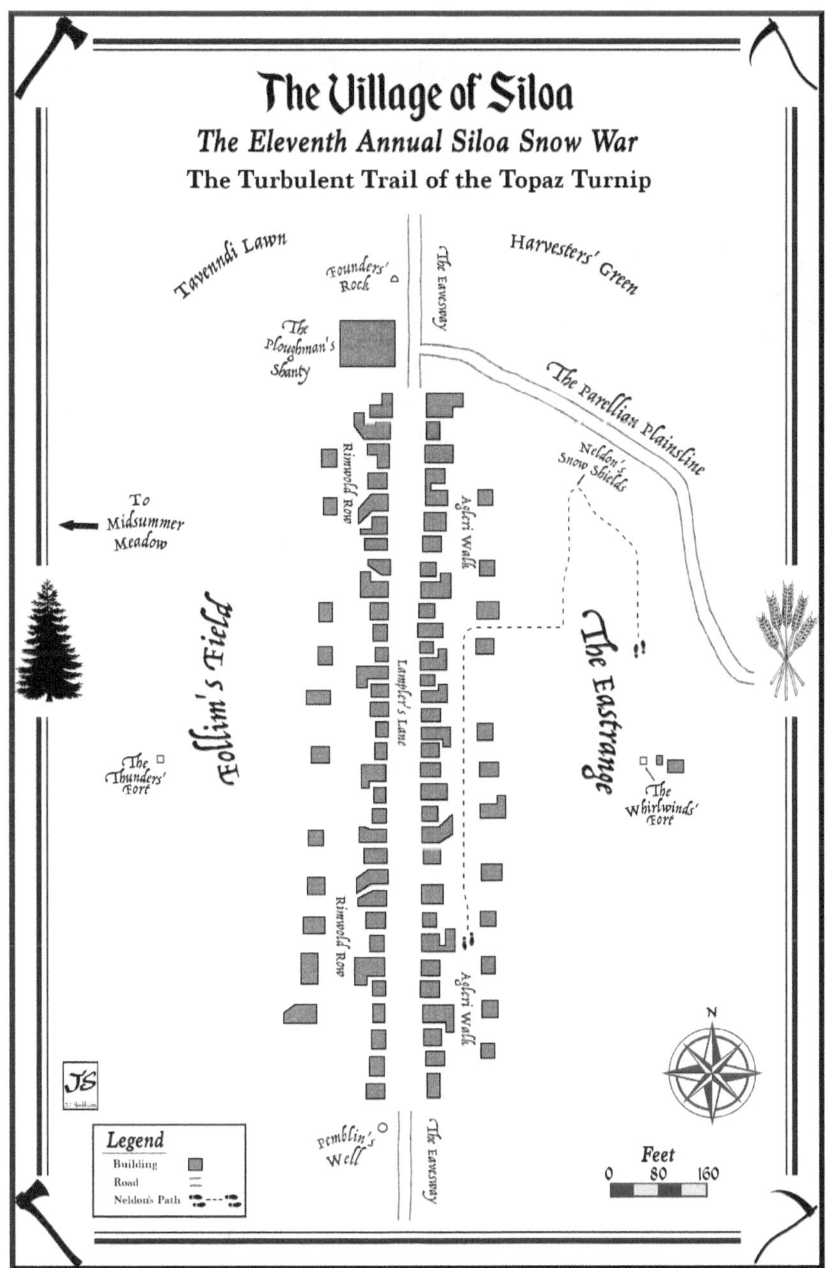

The Village of Siloa
The Eleventh Annual Siloa Snow War
The Turbulent Trail of the Topaz Turnip
Tavenndi Lawn
Founders' Rock
The Eavesway
Harvesters' Green
The Ploughman's Shanty
The Parellian Plainsline
Neldon' Snow Shields
Rimvold Row
Aslcri Walk
To Midsummer Meadow
Follim's Field
Lampler's Lane
The Eastrange
The Thunders' Fort
The Whirlwinds' Fort
Rimvold Row
Aslcri Walk
Pemblin's Well
The Eavesway
N
Legend
Building
Road
Neldon's Path
Feet
0   80   160
JS

The Turbulent Trail of the Topaz Turnip

ow, as Neldon ran ahead of these forty youths, he was running quite swiftly, but not more so than the swiftest Thunders in the pack behind him, who were slowly gaining on him. Neldon wheeled to the northwest and started running in the direction of the Ploughman's Shanty, hoping to make it to the buildings on the east side of Agleri Walk before his pursuers could reach him. However, things did not look hopeful, and Neldon was beginning to panic again.

Seizing any measure he could to rescue himself, he shouted, "Please don't hit me! I don't have the Turnip! I swear! I'm just a decoy. They actually made me give it to the Stickytubs." Neldon had no idea where the Stickytubs were or what they were doing, but he assumed they didn't have the Turnip, since it had been given to Mando. He didn't wish any particular ill on the Stickytubs; they were just the first ones that popped into his mind.

Now, if anyone but Neldon had made this claim, the Thunders would have ignored it altogether. But Neldon was just loony enough that they thought he might actually be telling the truth just so he wouldn't get hit and because he didn't realize in the heat of the moment that he was outright betraying his own team.

So in response to this, Rannion yelled, "Five of you, go look for the Stickytubs. The rest keep running after Broadbuckle."

Immediately, five Thunders ran off to the west to search for the Stickytubs in Agleri Walk, which was the last place anyone had seen them.

Neldon had so hoped that his con would cause all of the Thunders to abandon pursuit, but this, of course, was not to be. He should have been ecstatic that he was able to get rid of any of them, but as it was, he was beside himself that there were yet close to a score of them on his tail. Now on the verge of manic mode again, he began squealing like a piglet which has just had its tail cut off.

So terrified was he that his pace was boosted just enough to match that of his fastest pursuers. He wove around the numerous snow bulwarks the Whirlwinds had constructed, wailing all the while, and occasionally dodging a snowball from behind.

Then, suddenly, he saw something that greatly brightened his prospects and even caused him to stop hollering. Up ahead, Corim, Tressy and five other Whirlwinds ran out from behind a building on the east side of Agleri Walk. Seeing Neldon racing toward them, they ran toward him and began yelling pointed threats at the Thunders that were chasing him.

But then his heart sank, for there were eight Thunders bounding along not far behind Corim and Tressy's group. Both he and they were caught between two clouds of Thunders, and the only intervention they could expect would come from Cromnic and those following him. But this might come just a little too late. And even when it did, the Whirlwinds would still be outnumbered. It looked like it might turn into a massacre. But at least, as far as Neldon knew, Mando still had the Turnip.

"Protect yourself at all costs," Tressy shouted, as she and the others drew nigh to Neldon. "Get behind a barrier, and we'll keep you safe as long as we can."

"And don't do anything stupid," added Corim.

Neldon spotted some little mounds of snow nearby, and he darted toward them, then flung himself behind one of them.

"I do believe these are my snow shields from this morning," he said, swelling with pride.

No sooner had he gotten behind the shields than three snowballs crashed into them. The bulwark had just barely kept him from being frozen.

"My snow shields, Corim! My snow shields saved my life!" Neldon yelled excitedly.

"That's only because Tedge and I made them higher while we were on defense earlier today, when you were playing pinglybop with those idiot Stickytubs," Corim yelled back, as he hit one of the Thunders in Rannion's group, which was nearly upon them now.

"He can never just accept my genius for what it is," Neldon muttered. Then, seeing that several Thunders were about to pound him with snowballs, he tried to do a backward somersault to get out of the way. He did manage the somer part, but couldn't pull off the sault, so he ended up falling on his back after failing to get his legs over his head. And on account of this, the Thunders, who had aimed where his somersault would have finished had he completed it, just missed him.

There was at that very instant a tremendous uproar, as all the groups of Thunders and Whirlwinds collided practically at once. It was absolute mayhem, with Thunders accidentally hitting Thunders and Whirlwinds accidentally hitting Whirlwinds, along with people hitting those they were supposed to be hitting. However, as there was so much chaos, most of the children didn't know whether they'd been hit by enemies or allies. So, honorable though they were, the Whirlwinds didn't freeze unless they absolutely knew they'd been hit by a Thunder, and the Thunders didn't start running toward their fort unless they absolutely knew they'd been hit by a Whirlwind. What this amounted to was very few doing anything at all except continuing to scream and throw snowballs every which way.

⸻◆⸻

During all this hullabaloo, Neldon had scuttled out of the battle untouched, which had been possible only because everybody was too busy dodging and trying to take out their opponents to notice. As soon as Neldon got to the edge of this snow-flinging circus, he took off running southward across the Eastrange.

It was then that he noticed Condrig Brakesnare racing toward him. And hot on his heels was a squad of seven Thunders led by Aradis Kingblade.

"Somebody! Anybody!" yelled Condrig.

Neldon stopped and waved to him.

But meanwhile, across the Eastrange, coming from the direction of the fort, was Tedge Timberfall, who hailed Condrig, calling, "Toss it here!"

Condrig yanked the Topaz Turnip out of one of his pockets and hurled it with all of his might toward Tedge. It didn't quite make it to the latter, but Tedge quickly scooped it up and started running toward the Whirlwinds' fort, where his sister Hendra was standing next to the west wall.

"Throw it to me, Tedge!" she cried, and he promptly did so. It didn't make it all the way to her either, but she quickly grabbed it and took off running to the south.

"Hey!" yelled a Thunder girl named Harlia Harrowdell; she was Branlum's little sister, who was currently enmeshed in the brouhaha where all the Thunders and Whirlwinds were still pelting each other like mad with snowballs. "Neldon's gotten away with the Turnip!" She pointed at the now extremely alarmed Neldon.

In an instant of what may be considered quick (but not necessarily clever) thinking for the frantic Neldon, he cried, "I don't have the Turnip; this is just a piece of cheese!" He swiftly held up his wedge of cheese so that any who were looking might verify his assertion.

"Yeah, Neldon is right for once. He really doesn't have it!" shouted a voice to the south. It was Aradis.

"Hendra Timberfall's got it!" yelled Mayvelyn Rushwick, an older Thunder girl in Aradis' squad, who was pointing vigorously at Hendra.

Though initially only two Thunders in the frenzied snow battle heard this, these loudly proclaimed it to the rest. Once the thing had registered, all the Thunders rapidly charged after Hendra, except for eight individuals Rannion advised to linger in the area in case things swung back around in this direction. That way the Thunders would be able to attack from two directions instead of just one.

That Hendra, not Neldon, was the current Turnip-bearer was news not only to the Thunders, but to all of the Whirlwinds in the battle as well, and they took off after the departing Thunders en masse as soon as they realized what was going on. However, under Cromnic's orders, some of them separated from the group and ran off to the west, as Cromnic had told them to try to meet up with Hendra near the south end of Agleri Walk, since he suspected she might end up running toward that spot. This rapidly appointed squadron consisted of his sister Saneldra, Tallis and Dallis Pestleman, Tambris Turnsoil, Tressy Axleman and Corim and Branko Timberfall.

Since Neldon no longer had anyone pursuing him, he thought for a moment about what he ought to do. The sun was getting very low in the sky indeed, and Pappy Greengrove would almost certainly be ringing the village bell within the next five to ten minutes or so. "Hm, since there's so little time left, I need to do something brave and bold to leave my mark even deeper than it already is upon this Snow War, something that will be remembered for generations. I think I'll go with Corim and them," he decided. "It looks like they're going off to do something important, and naturally, I should be helping them." He was not near enough to hear what Cromnic had instructed them to do, but he had noted that he had pulled them aside individually and thus presumed he had issued them a mission of some consequence.

Cromnic's special squadron had run over into Agleri Walk, then turned south, and Neldon followed suit, falling in behind them. They had started their run farther north than him, but his moments of deliberation made it so that they were already south of him by the time he reached Agleri Walk.

Now, as the squadron was running down the street, a boy rushed to join them from an alley leading to Main Lane. It was Mando.

"Where have you been, brother mine? asked Tressy, as he jogged up alongside her.

"I've been hiding ever since the Thunders saw me pass off the Turnip to Condrig," said Mando. "Incidentally, who has the Turnip now?"

"Hendra," Tambris answered. "We're hoping to meet up with her at the south end of Agleri Walk."

"You know what I think we should do?" Mando said, as they ran along.

"What?" Neldon asked from the back of the group, much more out of breath than the others.

"Butt out of this, Broadbuckle," said Branko, glancing over his shoulder. "What are you doing over here, anyway?"

"Well, I – " Neldon started.

"What's your idea, Manny?" asked Corim, cutting him off.

"Let's spread out down the whole south length of Agleri Walk, and if and when Hendra shows up, she can throw it to the person farthest south, and then we can just throw it all the way up the street. The Turnip will travel faster that way than with any of us carrying it."

"That's brilliant," exclaimed Saneldra. "Let's do it!"

And so, as they got closer to the end of Agleri Walk, they stopped, one by one, at intervals of less than a Turnip's throw.

Not long after Dallis, who was the farthest south, reached the end of Agleri Walk, Hendra came bounding around the corner from the east, just as Cromnic had surmised she might.

"Throw the Turnip here, Hendra!" called Dallis.

Hastily, Hendra chucked the Turnip toward him. This was only just in time because she was hit by a snowball from behind as soon as the Turnip left her outstretched hand.

Dallis mightily threw the Turnip to Tallis, who threw it to Tambris, who threw it to Saneldra. She then flung it to Branko, who passed it on to Neldon. Though Branko's throw was excellent, Neldon failed to catch the Turnip, much to Branko's annoyance. And then, after Neldon picked it up, he clumsily dropped it. This fumble elicited angry shouts from both Corim and Branko. Quickly, Neldon grabbed the Turnip once more and threw it to Corim, who threw it to Mando.

The Thunders who stormed around the corner after Hendra were furious at this stratagem, for in very short order, the Turnip had traveled a great distance up the street, finally landing in the hands of Tressy Axleman.

"Get that girl!" yelled Rannion, who was at the vanguard of the Thunder swarm.

Those who had participated in the relay, including Neldon, were now in grave danger, for they couldn't travel anywhere near as fast as the Turnip, and the Thunders were out for blood. Additionally, the Thunders' range was extended to as far as they could hurl snowballs, which was, for some of them, quite far.

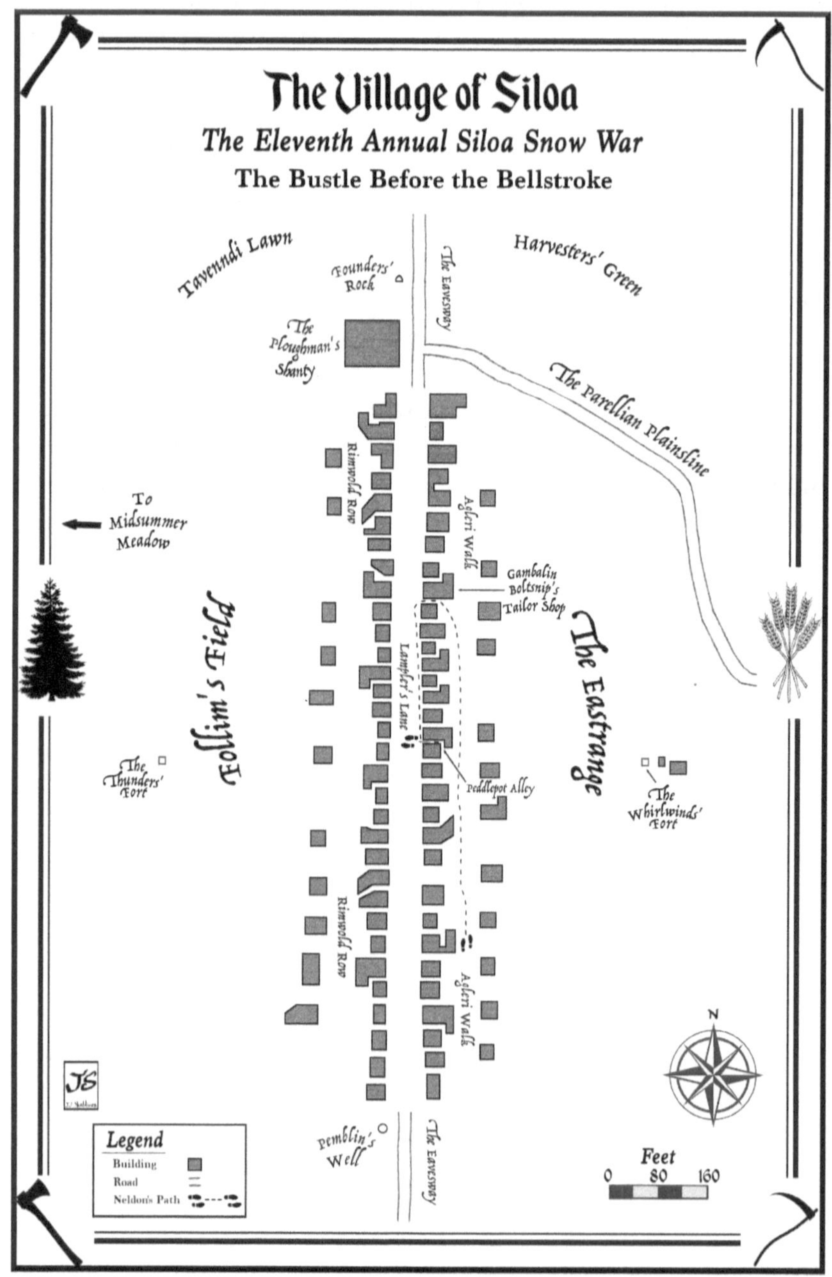

The Village of Siloa
The Eleventh Annual Siloa Snow War
The Bustle Before the Bellstroke
Tavenndi Lawn
Founders' Rock
The Eavesway
Harvesters' Green
The Ploughman's Shanty
The Parellian Plainsline
Rimwold Row
Agleri Walk
To Midsummer Meadow
Gambalin Boltsnip's Tailor Shop
Follim's Field
Lamplet's Lane
The Eastrange
The Thunders' Fort
Peddlepot Alley
The Whirlwinds' Fort
Rimwold Row
Agleri Walk
JS
L. Selleen
N
Legend
Building
Road
Neldon's Path
Pemblin's Well
The Eavesway
Feet
0   80   160

CHAPTER THIRTEEN

The Bustle Before the Bellstroke

As one, the Thunders charged down Agleri Walk. Both Dallis and Tallis were hit before long, despite their desperate flight, and Saneldra was hit as well. Tambris and Branko fled to the east, hoping to go north in the Eastrange and come to Tressy's assistance if need be. Corim was far enough up Agleri Walk that he was out of the Thunders' snowball range and was able to run north to try and catch up with Mando and Tressy. However, he was soon forced to abandon this course, as six of the eight Thunders Rannion had left stationed at the site of the great snow-flinging rumpus earlier ran straight into Agleri Walk from the east, thwarting his advance. Now there were Thunders both before him and behind him, although the ones behind him were much farther distant. Desperately, he whirled around and began running south, hoping to find a way to cut west toward Main Lane, then run north, coming to Tressy's aid that way should she require it. Or even better, he might be able to hide and hit some of the Thunders when they ran by before going on to help Tressy.

Corim then happened to be not far north of old Gambalin Boltsnip's tailor shop, so he raced behind it so as to be out of the Thunders' sight and then darted into the alleyway just south of it that lead out to Main Lane. This he was able to manage without being seen by Thunders from either direction, since the view of the alley's entrance from the south was blocked by other buildings from the sight of Rannion and his troops, who were still a ways down Agleri Walk anyhow.

All of a sudden, Neldon, to Corim's great aggravation, rushed into the same alleyway, seeking to remove himself from the Thunder's line of fire.

"You'd better not have given me away," Corim said irritably.

"I'm pretty sure those silly Thunders – "

"Shut up and get between these crates!" hissed Corim. "They'll be here any second now. I want to take some of them out as soon as they appear, if possible."

Hastily, Corim grabbed Neldon by his coat collar and shoved him down between two large crates resting against the north wall of the alley. Then he immediately ducked down himself, and the two of them tried to be as still and quiet as possible, as they pressed their backs against the wall.

Now if Corim had been out in Agleri Walk but a few moments longer, he would have seen that both Tressy and Mando had run into some trouble. Initially, since they had been farther north in Agleri Walk than any of the others, they had been able to run northward unimpeded. But as they neared the north end of the street, the six Thunders who attacked Corim had emerged just south of them, and when Corim had run around the corner to hide, these six had started after Tressy and Mando. Simultaneously, seven other Thunders had attacked them from the northeast; five of these were those who had gone off a few minutes ago to look for the Stickytubs, and the other two were from Rannion's recent dispatch of eight.

Fearing she might be hit, Tressy threw the Turnip to Mando. He tried to escape to the south but realized this would be impossible with six Thunders blocking his path, so he called to Tressy to retreat to an alley running west to Main Lane. Then he threw the Turnip over there for her to get it, thinking that if only one of them survived, whoever it was could retrieve it. But if he were hit while still holding the Turnip, all would be lost.

Only a moment later, Mando was snowballed by Falgren Timberfall, Corim's cousin, so his tossing the Turnip proved to have been a prudent move. Tressy just barely managed to evade being hit by a snowball from Sindagil Barnwain, Darmon's older sister, then turned and dashed to the alleyway, where she grabbed the Turnip and ran on to Main Lane.

⸺•◆•⸺

Now, back in the alley with Corim and Neldon, things had turned into something of a waiting game. Thunders did not come running around the corner from the north, as Corim had expected, but the boys did hear a considerable amount of shouting in that direction, which they took to be related to Tressy and Mando, since they were the only Whirlwinds up that way. There was also a good bit of hollering to the south, but most of it seemed to be coming from Agleri Walk. Taking all this into consideration, Corim told Neldon they should attempt to sneak out the west entrance of the alley. However, just as they were about to make a move to do so, Neldon whispered, "Oh no! There's someone coming from the south. Listen to the footsteps out in Main Lane."

The boys froze and tried not to make a single sound, as the crunching footsteps came nearer and nearer. When they were practically at the very entrance of the alleyway, Neldon took out a snowball and then, with considerable force, he flung at it the individual who appeared only a moment later.

"No, you'll – " Corim protested, but it was too late.

Neldon's snowball slammed into the fellow's face. It was his Grandfather Stickytub.

"Sorry, Grampers," Neldon laughed meekly, as his elderly relative wiped the snow from his frowning visage.

"You're only supposed to throw those at other children, Neldon," his grandfather chided.

"I know," Neldon said. "It was just a mistake, honest."

"Ahem, well, see that you're more careful from now on. Now, I'll leave you to your game, as I've got to be getting down to the Shanty." With that, he tramped off northward.

Corim and Neldon now grew terribly tense, for this boded that the bell to end the Snow War would be ringing at just about any time now. This was because Siloan adults always began pouring into the Ploughman's Shanty precisely at sunset on the day of the Siloa Snow War, right as the battle was ending. Orinn Berthaway, the owner of the Shanty, had many years ago started the tradition of hosting a celebration for adults that commenced as soon as the Snow War concluded. It was a time for them to converse, sup, drink, dance and enjoy themselves as much as the youths did pegging each other with speeding orbs of snow.

But even apart from the migration of adults down to the Ploughman's Shanty, the hue of the sky indicated that sunset was very nearly upon them, if it had not, in fact, already arrived.

Now, Corim and Neldon would have emerged from the alley at this point, but Thunders were running northward past it both to the east and to the west. The lads listened carefully and heard Thunder shouts of, "There she is! She looped back around! Get her!"

"They've found Tressy!" Neldon whispered.

Corim bit his lip.

Then there was a sharp rise in the Thunder rage, with cries of, "Don't let her get away! She broke out into Agleri Walk!"

They heard the rapid movement of feet coming toward them, and not long afterward, Tressy bounded around the corner holding the Turnip. Corim raised his hand so that she could see him down the alleyway, and, instinctively, she threw it to him. Corim expertly caught it, as Tressy continued running to the south. This was none too soon, for a rabid pack of Thunders came pouring around the corner only a short distance behind her. They charged after their prey, but she still had a bit of a lead on them and was able to successfully dodge all the snowballs they hurled at her.

Based on the sounds of continued pursuit, Corim and Neldon deduced that Tressy had not yet been captured.

Neldon could no longer contain his excitement. "We're going to win, Corim! The Thunders don't have a clue that you've got the Turnip, and the bell is going to clang at any second now!" he said giddily, putting his hands on Corim's shoulders and shaking him a bit, so joyful was he.

"Shut your yapper, Knucklebuckle!" Corim growled. "Otherwise they'll hear us. And that'll end your celebration really quick."

Just then, both of the boys noticed that someone was watching them from Agleri Walk. It was Rannion Rillspan, who had just run around the corner from the north.

Neldon felt the need to scream, and so scream he did. He and Corim sprang up and raced to the west with all their might, swerving south and running down the eastern edge of Main Lane. Rannion was not far behind them, although the two Whirlwinds were moving faster than he was, since they had been sitting still for a bit and he had barely stopped running since he first led the charge after Hendra.

"Go! Go! Go!" yelled Corim.

"I am! I am! I am!" Neldon yelled back.

As they tore down the street, all of the adults heading down to the Shanty looked on in astonishment at the surprisingly swift pace of the young Broadbuckle. Before long, Neldon actually pulled a little ahead of Corim, and as he did so, an idea suddenly struck him. They were not far from Peddlepot Alley, and all of Neldon's traps were still there. "At last, they can serve the purpose they were made for!" he thought.

"Follow me!" Neldon said, bounding into the alley as soon as they reached it. He paused for a moment just inside the entrance.

Corim raced in right after Neldon, and immediately realized where they were. "Neldon, this is Peddlepot Alley. This is where all the hidden rocks are!" he protested.

"Right – the Trip Maze of Peddlepot Alley," said Neldon gleefully. "But don't worry. Rannion won't know where the rocks are, but I do, since I put them there," Neldon assured.

"What?!"

"Come on. Do as I do," Neldon urged, as he nimbly sprang forward. Expertly, he danced down the alleyway, not hitting his foot on a single rock. It was quite possibly his finest moment of the entire day.

Corim, who was still reeling from the revelation that Neldon was the one who had set all these traps up, shook his head and began to follow his companion.

———◆———

Now, Rannion had actually been delayed a bit in Main Lane because Cromnic had charged out of an alleyway and blocked his path. However, Rannion was able to hit him soon enough that he didn't lose sight of where Corim and Neldon had gone. So, as soon as he had dispensed with Cromnic, he raced on to the entrance of Peddlepot Alley, calling for aid as he went.

Aradis Kingblade, along with his brother Teric and sister Mellora, plus Vahlia Lampler and little Tamyra Berthaway, who were all toward the south end of Agleri Walk, heard Rannion's distant cries and started running turned the sound of his voice, though they were uncertain exactly where he was. Most of the other Thunders were so intent on chasing Tressy Axleman that they paid Rannion's shouts little heed.

Neldon had reached the far end of the alley by this point, where a wall of Hillarnia's Peddlepot's shop forced one to turn southward to exit into Agleri Walk. He looked back and saw that Corim was only halfway through the alley, hopping to the spots where Neldon had hopped. He also noticed that Rannion had arrived at the alley's west end.

"Oh no, Corim, watch out for Rannion!" Neldon yelled.

Corim instantly looked over his shoulder so he could dodge any incoming snowballs. But he leapt forward as he did so, and his foot struck a largish rock hidden under a short, snowy mound. Howling with hurt, he crashed down into the snow.

Of course, the prostrate Corim was now an easy target for Rannion, who promptly hurled a snowball at him, which pounded into his back.

"Noooo!" Corim wailed, as he lifted his head out of the snow.

Rannion raced forward to claim the Turnip from Corim, and as he did so, Neldon started hollering and frantically throwing snowballs at him. Rannion successfully avoided all of these, but ended up stubbing his toe on three of Neldon's rocks in the process. He cried out in pain each time but never lost his balance. After dodging one final snowball from Neldon, which happened to be the very last one Neldon had in his satchel, he proceeded to swipe the Turnip from Corim's hand. Corim tried to grab it back as soon as it left his fingers, but Rannion was too quick. With a mocking laugh, the latter dashed out of the alleyway, using the depressions in the snow where he had already stepped in order to expedite his escape.

Now that the Whirlwinds had reverted to offense, Corim leapt up, gritted his teeth and swore, "Neldon, you big blob of stupid! This is all your fault!"

"We might still get the Turnip back," Neldon offered hopefully. "After all, the bell hasn't rung yet."

No sooner had he said this than the clear, ringing peal of the village bell rang out over the rooftops of Siloa from the north.

"Blast it! Blast it! Blast it!" Corim yelled, punching the north wall of the alley. Angrily, he ran to the alley's west exit. Neldon trotted meekly after him.

Rannion was now in the middle of Main Lane, laughing, "Ha ha ha! We won! We won! The Thunders triumphed again! Take that, Whirl- winds! Ha ha ha!"

Aradis and those with him had arrived in Main Lane now, and though they were still some ways to the south, it was clear that the Thunders were victorious, so they began to gloat as well.

Corim's rage burned even more fiercely now, particularly at Rannion. Stooping down, he grabbed one of Neldon's rocks from the snow and started forming a snowball around it. Neldon failed to notice exactly what Corim was doing, since his head was practically spinning from all the intensity of what had just happened.

"I'm sure sorry, Corim," Neldon gulped. "I didn't mean – "

"It's not over yet," Corim said menacingly.

"What do you mean? I thought it was over as soon as the bell rang."

"It's not *officially* over until the bell *stops* ringing," lied Corim, as the clanging of the bell continued to sound throughout the whole village.

"Really? I thought it was when it first – "

"Well, you thought wrong, as usual. Here, take this," Corim shoved the snowball he had just made into Neldon's hand.

"What's this for?" asked Neldon, hefting it. "And why is it so heavy?"

"Never mind about that," Corim hurriedly replied. "And it's for Rannion."

"Why'd you give it to me?"

"Will you stop asking stupid questions and throw it already!" Corim raged. "I gave it to you because you're the best thrower the Whirlwinds have and we've only got one shot. If you hit Rannion, I'll run and get the Turnip from him, and we can still win."

"Okay," said Neldon hesitantly, as he looked out into the street at Rannion, who was now much closer to the other side and was jumping up and down with the Turnip in his hand, whooping in sheer rapture and exultation.

Just then, he very distinctly heard Quinty's voice in his head saying, "Don't forget: aim high."

"Oh, yes," Neldon silently agreed.

Taking a deep breath, Neldon drew the unusually heavy snowball back behind his head and then, aiming high, flung it toward Rannion with every last ounce of his strength. The snowball zoomed through the air, arcing high over the street, passing only a few feet from its intended target – and then, to Neldon's horror, hurtled into a window, which shattered with a loud crash. His high aim had helped carry the snowball far indeed – in this case, too far.

Neldon was, of course, immediately distraught by this unexpected outcome. But he became ever so much more distraught when he realized whose window it was he had just decimated. Indeed, he was now downright terror-stricken.

Abruptly, the clanging of the village bell ceased, and Rannion turned and looked at the broken window, his mouth agape. Corim too looked at it, with his mouth likewise as wide as a that of a great, blubby fish.

He was greatly disappointed the snowball hadn't struck Rannion in the head, but this sentiment was almost instantly swallowed up by fear – mostly for Neldon's life.

Breaking the ominous silence, there was the sound of hurried footsteps from within the structure with the shattered window. Abruptly, a contorted, tight-lipped, elderly female face appeared in the newly-formed opening, quivering with rage, and then the owner of the face swiftly extended a long, accusatory finger through the window, straight toward Neldon. And at that moment, he felt by far the coldest he had the entire day.

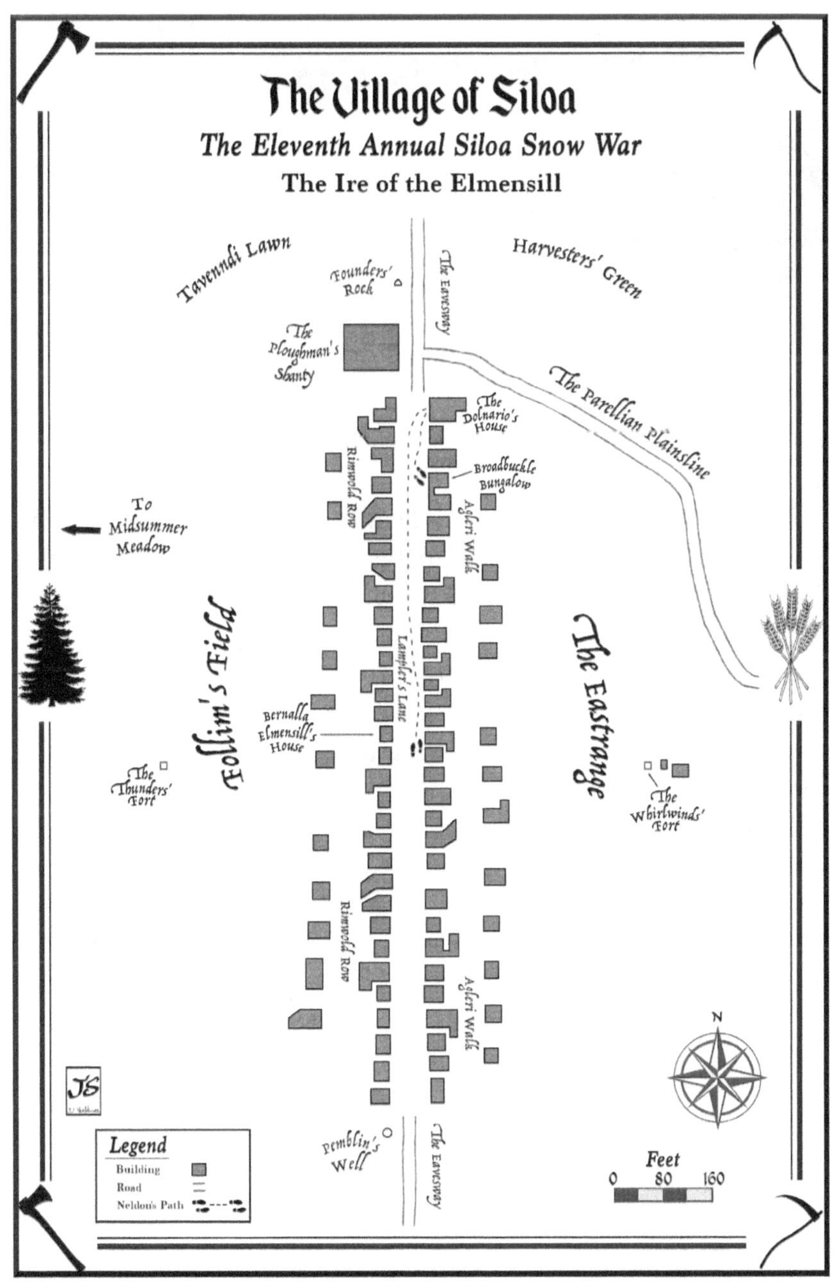
The Village of Siloa
The Eleventh Annual Siloa Snow War
The Ire of the Elmensill
Tavenndi Lawn
Founders' Rock
Harvesters' Green
The Eavesway
The Ploughman's Shanty
The Dolnario's House
The Parellian Plainsline
Broadbuckle Bungalow
Rimwold Row
Asleri Walk
To Midsummer Meadow
Follim's Field
Lampler's Lane
The Eastrange
Bernalla Elmensill's House
The Thunders' Fort
The Whirlwinds' Fort
Rimwold Row
Asleri Walk
Pemblin's Well
The Eavesway
N
Feet
0   80   160
Legend
Building
Road
Neldon's Path

The Ire of the Elmensill

eldon could hardly have been more terrified than he was at that moment. Bernalla Elmensill was the stuff his nightmares were made of; indeed, he had actually had a number of exceedingly unpleasant dreams about her. And now every last drop of her ire was directed at him. Now, the old woman's eyes flashed violently, looking as if they were about to pop out of her head. So infuriated was she that her pointed finger shook as it aimed at his dumbstruck face, and it was all Neldon could do to keep from passing out.

Just then, when Neldon thought he had reached the very limit of his terror, his situation became more frightening still. Miss Elmensill's face disappeared from the window, which could only mean she was coming out to get him.

An instant later, the front door of Bernalla Elmensill's house burst open, and out stormed the old woman herself. Neldon would have run like a harried hare had he not been so petrified. As it was, he could do nothing but pant and shake.

Corim quickly backed away from Neldon, strongly desiring to create some distance between himself and the epicenter of the Elmensill's wrath. Rannion, who was desperately hoping Miss Elmensill had not noticed he was near the front of her house when her window had broken (especially since he had already aroused her great displeasure earlier that day), sidled off to the north to join some of his fellow Thunders who were watching with great dismay the unfolding of Neldon's impending doom.

Other children, both Thunders and Whirlwinds, including Neldon's friend Tallis, were off to the south, and they likewise regarded this grim scene with great angst. Aradis and his siblings were also among these, and they, having seen the whole thing transpire from the fateful shower of glass to the issuing of the dreaded Elmensill from her lair, almost choked on the lumps in their throats as events hurtled toward what would likely be the utter ruin of their friend Neldon. Even those who normally found Neldon rather objectionable were so distraught at the young Broadbuckle's plight that they wished, though in vain, that there was something they could do to help him without endangering themselves. Indeed, Neldon had likely never been more poignantly pitied by the children of Siloa than he was at that moment.

Steaming and sizzling, red-faced and rage-ridden, Bernalla Elmensill stomped across Main Lane to the trembling Neldon. And, just as she reached him, she seized him by the ear and cried triumphantly, "Aha! Neldonicus Broadbuckle! I've got you, you unholy little knave! There'll be no escape now, you beastly baker boy!" She pulled sharply on his ear, shaking his head forcefully as she went on yelling. "I might have known you'd do something ghastly like this before the day was through. In fact, I wouldn't be a bit surprised if you were the one that ran through my turnip patch not long ago."

"It was just an accident, really it was," Neldon squeaked, cringing at the severe berating that was sure to follow.

"So it *was* you!" roared Miss Elmensill, her eyes narrowing to black slits. "Now you're *really* going to get it. I've always told your mother – that Neldonicus is a rotten little tarmin cake if ever I've seen one. A shameful, shiftless slob of a dunce and an unprincipled, pot-bellied scamp besides! Well, this time you've gone too far. It's off to the Dolnario with you! And I can assure you, boy: if I have my way, there'll be punishment enough meted out to you that ten generations from now, the people of Siloa will still fear to speak of it in aught but a whisper. Now, come along, you degenerate, brainless butterball!"

And with that, she began dragging poor Neldon along by the ear north up the street.

"Ow! Ah! Ooh! Ow!" Neldon cried out, as she towed him along, muttering further insults and threats all the while.

Corim watched Neldon being hauled off to his doom with a great deal of remorse but certainly nothing close to what it would have taken for him to accept proper blame in what had just happened. "That's too bad," he said to himself. "It really is. But better him than me. I do hope he makes it out of this all right though."

Although the Thunders should have been reveling in jubilation and the Whirlwinds venting their collective anger at having lost the Turnip at the very last moment, everyone who had seen what had happened had been struck numb. Even adults who were witnessing the affair felt naught but the utmost concern for the Broadbuckle boy, for the wrath of Bernalla Elmensill was legend.

As Bernalla was pulling Neldon past his mother's bakery, his cries became much more pitiful and strident, and he called out, "Mums, please save me! She's going to have me executed!"

"Hush up, you deplorable defiler," snapped his captor. "You've trespassed in my turnip patch and vandalized my property, and now you've got to face your due punishment just like any other criminal. And don't think your mother or anyone else can help you get off any easier. At this point, even the Ruphani couldn't stop me from seeing that you receive your just desserts."

In short order, Bernalla had towed her apprehended convict all the way to the Dolnario's door and was banging loudly upon it. "Mister Barleycroft, I demand a hearing immediately!" she yelled. "Vandalism! Trespassing! Malicious and impudent conduct! Siloa is turning into a pigsty of unprincipled, wayward and villainous youth right before our – "

Not wishing for Miss Elmensill to publicly carry on with her tirade any longer than she already had, Fennadris Barleycroft hurried to the door and let both her and her hostage in. Neldon's mother was not far behind them, for she had heard her son's cries of distress and rushed out of the bakery to see what was afoot.

⸎

In the next few minutes, Mister Barleycroft, as well as a good portion of the citizenry within a significant radius, got a roaring earful about the sinister deeds and contemptible character of Neldon Broadbuckle. Neldon knew better than to interject at any point during this Elmensillic tempest, and so did his mother. And so did the Dolnario, for that matter.

However, once Mister Barleycroft had let Bernalla enumerate and rant about every single one of Neldon's heinous transgressions two times over, he finally cut her off and asked if she would like to formally commence the hearing she had demanded. (Hearings were normally reserved for infractions of a much more serious nature, but Mister Barleycroft knew that Miss Elmensill simply wouldn't settle for anything less than a hearing or at least something having the semblance of one.) She replied in the affirmative, and the Dolnario told her that she would have to hold her tongue, then, while he, Neldon or Neldon's mother were speaking. To this condition, she reluctantly complied.

To officially initiate the hearing, Mister Barleycroft inquired of whether Neldon was indeed guilty of the charges Miss Elmensill had leveled against him. He answered that he was, partially because it was simply the truth, but mostly because he didn't wish to risk being strangled by the Elmensill. In this admission, he disavowed any ill intent, claiming that his offenses were accidental and merely resulted from him fleeing wildly from the Thunders in the one case and trying to hit Rannion Rillspan with a snowball in the other. But he nonetheless made it abundantly clear that he had indeed run through Miss Elmensill's turnip patch and broken her window.

When Miss Elmensill was allowed to speak in response to Neldon's confession, she contested that his motives were almost certainly debased and malicious and that his "explanations" were nothing but a heap of putrid, makeshift lies. Neldon's mother and the Dolnario, knowing the boy, tried to persuade her that this was almost certainly not the case, but to no avail; for in her eyes, he was naught but the most black-hearted, dastardly criminal to ever roam the streets of Siloa.

Unleashing yet another tirade, Miss Elmensill insisted that, as retribution for Neldon's wicked deeds, he ought to be hung upside down outside the Dolnario's house for an hour while the entire village threw snowballs at him and beat him with sticks. Mister Barleycroft firmly rejected this punishment, as well as the next one she proposed, which was that he be publicly flogged and spat upon.

Finally, Neldon's mother, who had gotten a better feel for what had actually happened as the hearing went on, presented her own proposal for her son's consequences. She was adamant that Neldon would pay for the replacement of the broken window out of the coinage that he had saved. Also, she advanced the idea that he should assist Garridan Glazenkiln, the town glazier, in putting the new window in. This, she said, should set right the matter of the window. And for all of his other crimes – turnip-defiling, carelessness, etc. – she thought that Neldon's reparations should involve further assistance to Miss Elmensill in some regard but wasn't sure in what manner. And although Neldon felt rather betrayed at this point, as though his mother was siding with Miss Elmensill in proposing such heavy consequences for him, she really did have his best interests at heart and wanted him to understand that he must make things right if he erred, even if it were only an accident.

Seizing upon Mrs. Broadbuckle's plan, Miss Elmensill herself was quick to suggest that Neldon be compelled to present himself to her every morning for the following year to see to any tasks she needed done around her house and that he also undergo some "moral education," courtesy of her good self, that would consist of stories and lectures about the proper way a child ought to behave. Both Neldon's mother and Mister Barleycroft believed this to be a rather disproportionate consequence considering what Neldon had done. And so, with much effort, they finally convinced her to shorten his sentence so that it would only last until the beginning of spring (or, more precisely, the beginning of what was known as Commoners' Spring, which fell about four weeks earlier than the more formal Sages' Spring). And they also insisted that Neldon only have to present himself for five days a week instead of all seven. They still thought this was somewhat extreme but were so worn down from arguing with the old woman that neither of them felt like lobbying for a further reduction at this point. So they conceded to her terms for his consequence, and she conceded to the duration and weekly reduction they had proposed. As for Neldon himself, he was just glad that his punishment wasn't any worse than this.

Before Mister Barleycroft was able to adjourn the hearing, Miss Elmensill tried to get him to outlaw the Siloa Snow War entirely, since she felt that the event itself was largely to blame for what had happened. However, this he would not do despite her vehement insistence, although he did make a single concession regarding the matter. He promised that the following year, Cobbanick Wrastlebuck, the Denossa (a position rather like a deputy or enforcer), would patrol around her house during the Snow War so that no mischief came to it. He figured that Mister Wrastlebuck wouldn't mind being volunteered for this, since he rather liked to be assigned tasks that had the appearance of great importance, regardless of whether they were genuinely consequential or not.

After this, Miss Elmensill was still not satisfied but knew she would get no further cooperation from the Dolnario. So she menacingly reminded Neldon that he would be expected to be at her place the following morning to see what tasks she had waiting for him and also to receive his first lesson in "moral education." Then, tossing her head disdainfully, she marched out the door and back down the street to her abode.

————•◦•————

In the dim twilight, bathed in the sounds of jollity issuing from the Ploughman's Shanty, Neldon's mother ushered him home. As soon as he got there, he went and laid on the floor just outside his room, staring blankly at the ceiling. Here, at Broadbuckle Bungalow, there was nothing of the merriment in Orinn Berthaway's bright establishment, for Neldon was utterly beyond solace. Indeed, now that he had escaped from the direct forges of Bernalla Elmensill's wrath, he could properly contemplate all that had transpired within the last hour or so. He, Neldon Broadbuckle, had won the Turnip from the Thunders, and he, Neldon Broadbuckle, had been responsible for losing it to them just before the bell rang. And thus the Whirlwinds' three-year streak of losses was now one of four. Besides all this, he was facing several months of an almost daily dose of the Elmensill, and he imagined she would be more unpleasant to him now than she had ever been before. And all this misfortune was without him even considering his mishaps from earlier in the day.

Neldon's mother, realizing that her son had been stricken almost as sore a blow as could be imagined from his perspective, sought to console him about his fate. His father, who had been out north of town assisting a friend that evening, learned some of what had happened as soon as he returned home, and he attempted to lift Neldon's spirits as well, though reminding him that he must be particularly mindful when throwing snowballs in the future.

Several of Neldon's friends came by that evening and offered their condolences as well. Corim, Aradis, Tallis and Darmon came as a group and sat and talked with him for a while, and they learned then exactly what consequences had been apportioned him in the meeting with the Dolnario. Corim and Tallis had half a mind to light into Neldon about losing the Turnip for the Whirlwinds at the last minute, but they knew this was simply not the time. In truth, they really did care about Neldon and were sorry for his sake that things had turned out as they had.

Eventually, after much coaxing from both his parents and comrades, Neldon was roused enough to eat dinner, although he did so with much less gusto than was typical for him. His friends stayed and supped with him for a bit and then went off to their respective residences for the night or else to converse with their fellow Thunders or Whirlwinds.

As for Neldon, as soon as he was finished with dinner, he plodded off to bed and crawled under his covers.

"Well, things went rather poorly today, Yankaboo," Neldon sighed. "Not at all the way I envisioned. In fact, believe it or not, things are even worse than when we talked earlier."

"Surely not!" Neldon answered in his high, wobbly Yankaboo voice.

"Yes, I'm afraid so."

At that moment, there was a quick knock on Neldon's door. A second later, the door was pushed open, and Quinty walked slowly into the room.

"Oh, hello, Quinty," said Neldon. "I was just telling Yankaboo about how the Snow War – err, about how I ..." He sighed deeply, then went on, "Um, you remember how you told me I could change how the Snow War would end? Well, I sure did."

"No need to elaborate," said Quinty, as he sat on his brother's bed. "I ran into Aradis Kingblade out in Main Lane just a bit ago, and he told me the gist of how things ended up. I would imagine you're feeling pretty low right now, eh?"

"Very," Neldon replied mournfully.

"That's understandable," Quinty sighed. "I think anyone would feel that way if all those things had happened to him. And I'm not going to say that you didn't exhibit some poor judgment in some of the things you did. There's no good pretending otherwise. But I am going to tell you essentially the same thing I told you earlier. You can't change what's done, but you can do things to change. Put another way, the past is ice, but the future is water."

"Huh?" Neldon scrunched up his face.

"Never mind," Quinty laughed. "I'll explain it some other time." Then his tone became more sober. "It sounds like some of the mistakes you made this year may be remembered and scorned for years to come. So be it. But from this moment forward, you can keep making choices, venture what you will and see what comes of it. Just keep trying to do what good you can. There's a possibility things still won't work out for you. On the other hand, they might turn out splendidly. Don't fret about that, since you can't control it anyway. The important thing is this, Neldon; at least you tried to make a difference for good, even if it didn't turn out that way. In my humble opinion, it's better to try and fail at something than not to try or care at all. And there are a great many people who fall in that latter category. I'm just thankful you're not one of them."

Standing, Quinty rustled his brother's hair and said, "Have a good night, Nelders. And don't let the Elmensill push you around too much tomorrow. She's only a grumpy old lady, after all." Grinning, he exited the room and closed the door quietly behind him.

Neldon sat and thought for a few moments, then turned his head to Yankaboo and said, "You know, maybe today wasn't so bad after all. Even though I lost the Turnip twice, I helped get it twice too. And there's always next year."

"That there is," he answered in his Yankaboo voice, then blew out the candle that his mother had left burning on his nightstand. A few minutes later, he was fast asleep.

The Village of Siloa
The Eleventh Annual Siloa Snow War
The Distribution of Just Desserts
Tavenndi Lawn
Founders' Rock
Harvesters' Green
The Eavesway
The Ploughman's Shanty
The Parellian Plainsline
Broadbuckle Bungalow
Rimwold Row
Asleri Walk
To Midsummer Meadow
Tollim's Field
Lampfet's Lane
The Eastrange
Bernalla Elmensill's House
Glazenkiln's Glass Shop
Corim's House
Rimwold Row
Asleri Walk
JS
Legend
Building
Road
Pemblin's Well
The Eavesway
N
Feet
0   80   160

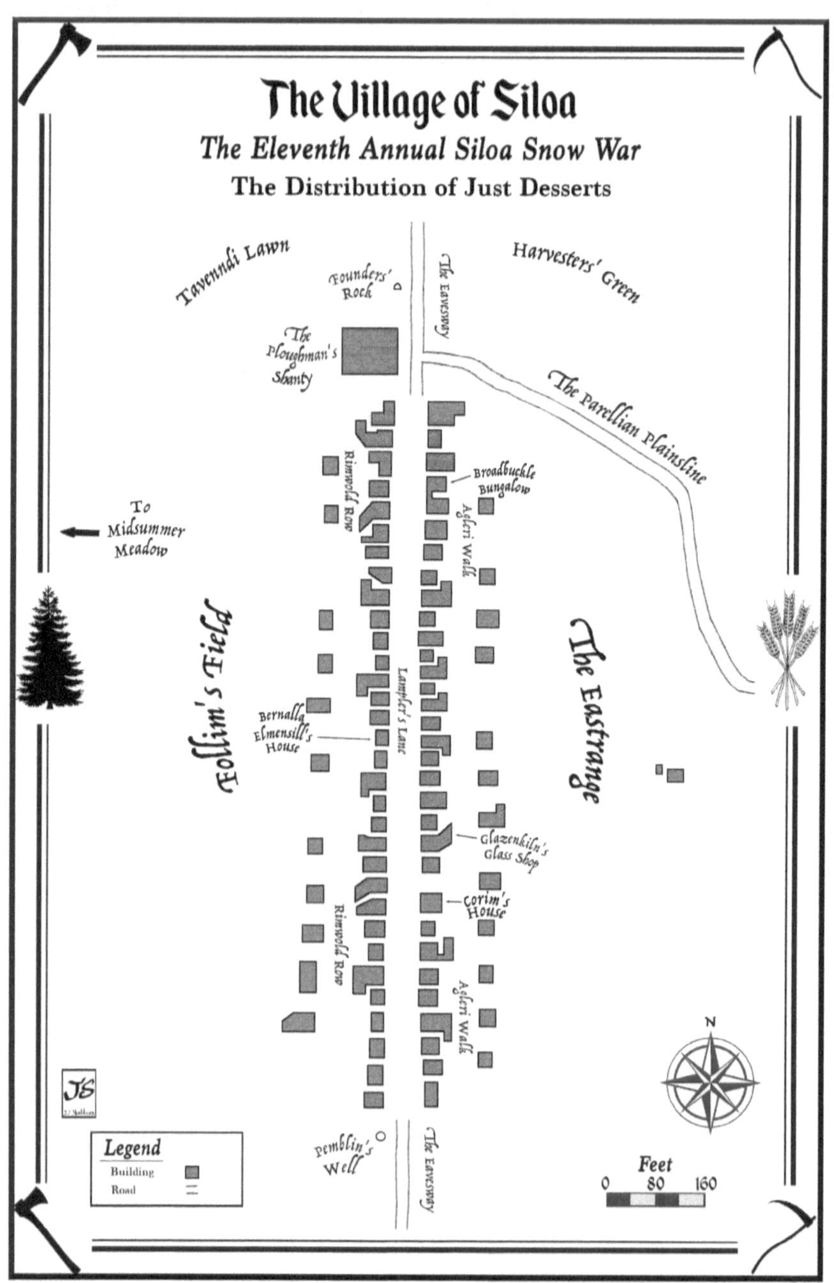

116

CHAPTER FIFTEEN

The Distribution of Just Desserts

he following morning, Neldon paid a visit to Miss Elmensill, knowing this was an obligation he simply couldn't shirk from. And as soon as he crossed her threshold, she took full advantage of the fact that he was compelled to do everything she told him. That entire morning, she took an almost sadistic delight in bossing him around and assigning him all sorts of tedious and meaningless things to do. This bout of trivial tasks culminated in a half-hour long instructional session during which Neldon had to sit on the floor while Miss Elmensill harangued from her chair by the fire about the present delinquency of Siloan youth.

When Miss Elmensill had finally finished with Neldon, she dismissed him, and he immediately went over to see Garridan Glazenkiln about the broken window. Miss Elmensill had nailed a blanket over the opening the previous night, but Garridan, with her permission, removed it long enough to take all the necessary measurements. He then gave Neldon the sum of what the work and materials would cost him. Neldon procured the necessary amount from his accumulated coinage, and, though it essentially left him destitute, he had just enough to finance the project.

During the following weeks, Neldon daily (with the exception of his two days off per week) underwent the drudgery of being Miss Elmensill's lackey. During that time, he suffered hours upon hours of dusting and re-arranging knickknacks, untangling skeins of yarn, polishing various pieces of wooden furniture, straightening and restraightening pictures, fluffing pillows and other likewise mind-numbing assignments. It was a nightmare he feared would never come to an end.

And to make matters worse, during this same time frame, other Whirl-winds let him know in no uncertain terms how greatly displeased they were about how he had so badly botched their efforts both to acquire and to retain the Topaz Turnip. And when word spread (via Corim) that Neldon had been the architect of the Trip Maze of Peddlepot Alley, the amount of Whirlwind vitriol directed at him increased even more, since all Neldon's hidden rocks had managed to do was injure two Whirlwinds so badly that they were homebound for most of the Snow War and then cause Corim to stumble so that Rannion was able to take the Turnip from him right before the bell rang. Indeed, a definite majority of the Whirlwinds made a point of personally berating Neldon on multiple occasions for his many blunders and errors. In fact, even his Stickytub cousins had a grievance to raise against him.

Toward the end of the Snow War, you may recall, they were nowhere to be found. As a matter of fact, they had gone to the Ploughman's Shanty not long after Neldon had gotten the Turnip from Quinnia Greyloam, since they were more worried that the Shanty's snacks would soon be unavailable (due to the arrival of adults for the evening celebration) than they were about protecting the Turnip. And not long after they had emerged, they were terrorized and pelted with snowballs by five Thunders and then prodded all over for the Turnip. Based on what the Thunders had said, the Stickytubs had figured out that Neldon had claimed they had the Turnip, and they were none too happy that he had betrayed them in this way.

Since Neldon had had a good while to reflect on some of the things Quinty had told him, he sincerely apologized to the Stickytubs and accepted all the rest of the criticisms leveled against him graciously, although he was also quick to point out that, even though he had lost the Turnip twice, he had also essentially gained it twice. It was just that the second loss came last. However, this response only elicited further annoyance from the aggrieved parties.

However, it should be noted that contempt was not the only sentiment that the youth of Siloa expressed toward Neldon in the days following the Snow War. Indeed, many Thunders warmly congratulated him on his fine work in the recent Snow War, and Neldon was happy to receive these assessments because at least they were positive in nature. Although if he had been rather more analytical, it would have dawned on him why the Thunders unanimously felt he had done an excellent job, and this would have led him to dread their compliments rather than welcome them. But let us not expect a level of analysis from dear Neldon that we are not likely to get.

There was also a great hubbub and considerable intrigue – found among Whirlwinds and Thunders alike – that arose surrounding the fact that he had thrown a snowball hard enough to break a window all the way across Main Lane, a remarkable feat indeed. Of course, Corim had told a select few about his role in the affair but had asked them to keep the information to themselves so he wouldn't get punished for his part in the matter. Among the rest, various theories were developed to explain the window shattering, with some even adhering to Neldon's conclusion on the matter, which was simply that he was actually quite a powerful thrower.

Now, Miss Elmensill, of course, knew that the snowball had a rock at the heart of it, and that was why the window had shattered, but she hardly ever spoke to anyone in the village (except perhaps the Seedbuckets) unless she was berating them about something or other, so this news did not spread. She had actually not discovered the rock until after returning home from her condemnation of Neldon at the Dolnario's house. Being one to never let a grudge go if she could hold on to it, she kept the rock on her mantle to remind her how much she detested Neldon.

———•◦•———

In the days and weeks that followed, Neldon continued to endure harsh servitude to Miss Elmensill, although it became less burdensome for him as time went on, since Miss Elmensill's attitude toward him began to soften slightly. This trend only became more pronounced after the replacement of her window (a task in which Neldon provided as much aid as Mister Glazenkiln would let him, which wasn't much). Indeed, as winter waned and spring drew nigh, the old woman acted increasingly with something rather resembling fondness toward the boy; it was almost as if her heart were warming with the weather.

Also, Neldon enjoyed getting to know all the nooks and crannies of her house, which was to him, and to the other children of Siloa, like the forbidden and well-guarded dominion of some fabled Witch of old that hardly any had entered and none had come out of alive. Indeed, he came to view his knowledge of her abode's interior as qualifying him as the foremost loremaster of the secrets of the Elmensill, and he began to proudly lord this title over the other children of Siloa. Of course, like any true loremaster, he only shared his knowledge sparingly, and even with those who were both exceedingly curious and worthy, he shared but a fraction of all that he knew.

Extraordinarily, as Neldon's appointed release date drew nearer and nearer, he began to actually take a liking to Miss Elmensill's lessons and stories. That fact alone should make almost anyone feel sorry for him. Of course, morality is by no means a bad thing, but the same cannot be said for Miss Elmensill's reservoir of moralizing tales. In fact, these tales were so abysmal, they're hardly worth describing even in general to the reader, much less relating. The most that should probably be said is that they featured very obviously naughty little boys and girls committing minor infractions of some sort and then receiving horrendous consequences. These were juxtaposed alongside very upright (according to Bernalla Elmensill's conception of the ideal) boys and girls observing some trivial demand of proper manners and receiving excessive, even obnoxious amounts of praise, treats and favors for their behavior. Some of her stories featured animals as characters and others household implements such as mops, balls of twine, forks and pickle jars. Neldon half-suspected she was making them up on the spot, although she claimed they came from the lips of her great-grandmother, Hygrellia Nozzlesnatch.

⸻ ◆ ⸻

At last, the official commencement of Commoners' Spring, the glorious first day of Ferenos, arrived, and, according to what the Dolnario had decreed, Neldon was freed from the shackles of the Elmensill. He would no longer have to do a single odd job for her nor listen to another one of her ridiculous stories ever again.

But Neldon had been changed over the course of the winter to such a degree that he actually enjoyed Miss Elmensill's company. The morning of his release, he decided to go over to her house anyway.

The old woman was quite surprised when he showed up at her door. "What are you doing here?" she asked, bristling with suspicion.

"Oh, I just thought I'd come see if you needed anything," Neldon replied genially.

Miss Elmensill looked absolutely shocked. "Why, yes, as a matter of fact I do." Instantly, her face became less lined and something vaguely resembling a smile crossed it. Gently, she cleared her throat and inquired, "But won't you have a cup of tea and some cakes first?"

"Don't mind if I do." Neldon hummed, as he happily entered the Elmensill estate.

Bernalla was so impressed that Neldon had returned to assist her without being under any compulsion that, after they had finished their tea and cakes, she invited him to work with her in her turnip patch.

"This isn't a trick, is it?" asked Neldon,

"No, indeed," Miss Elmensill replied. "To be sure, I wouldn't let another soul set foot there, but I – well, I trust you'll now give my turnips the respect they deserve."

Dizzy with the prospect of actually entering the turnip patch, not only without being harmed, but at Miss Elmensill's request, Neldon agreed to assist her.

As he worked alongside her among the turnips that morning, he felt as if he had been admitted into some kind of ancient sanctum that was protected by all sorts of curses, except the warden of that sanctum had given him some sort of strange immunity against all of its magical hazards. To him, the whole experience was rather otherworldly. Neldon Broadbuckle knew precious little about the stars or the Skyworlds, but he was certain visiting them must be rather like working with Bernalla Elmensill in her turnip patch.

A number of Siloans that were walking down Rimwold Row saw Neldon and Miss Elmensill working together in her turnip patch, and a fair number of them wondered if they were hallucinating. Almost no one in the village got along with the old woman (excepting perhaps, as we have already intimated, the Seedbucket family), and it was by now extremely well-known how severely Neldon had crossed her several months ago. Indeed, the unexpected camaraderie the two of them exhibited while caring for the turnips was so bizarre that it was actually the main topic of conversation at the Ploughman's Shanty that evening.

———◆———

As spring progressed, Neldon didn't go over to Miss Elmensill's as much as he did initially, but he nonetheless stopped by rather frequently. Also, the boy overcame his natural laziness for once and made an attempt to recoup some of his losses in paying for Miss Elmensill's new window. He, along with his friends Aradis, Corim, Tallis and Darmon, hired themselves out for a modest daily sum to work for Randalig Furrowmead, who lived northeast of town, to aid him in planting his barley fields.

One sunny spring afternoon, when the boys were out sowing barley, Neldon came across a rock in one of the furrows. Picking it up, he said boastfully, "I bet you fellows I can throw this rock all the way to Farmer Furrowmead's house." Presently, the house was quite a few yards away from where they were working.

"Please, Neldon. Don't be ridiculous," Aradis laughed. "Realistically, you probably couldn't even throw it a quarter of the way there."

"I most certainly could," Neldon insisted. "I threw a snowball so hard it broke dear old Miss Elmensill's window. Remember?"

"Ha!" Corim snorted. "First off, will you cut it out with this absurd 'dear old Miss Elmensill' nonsense? She's about as 'dear' as a poison pie stuffed with hornet heads and drenched with spider sauce. And furthermore, it's time we disposed of your dumb little myth about how you're such a great thrower. I, for one, am sick of hearing about it."

Neldon looked at him, puzzled. The other boys, to whom Corim had already divulged the real story, knew what was coming next.

Digging up a clod of dirt with a hoe, Corim went on, "The only reason the window broke is because I intentionally put a rock at the core of that snowball. *That's* why the window shattered the way it did. I was hoping to teach Rannion a lesson. It was already too late to win since the first bell had already rung, but it wasn't too late to get revenge. I just didn't want to get pounded by him myself or get in trouble with his parents or something, so that's why I had you throw the snowball."

"Ah, I see," said Neldon thoughtfully, though he clearly didn't.

The others looked at Corim, shrugged their shoulders and resumed their labor.

Neldon thought about Corim's explanation for several minutes while the boys went on working. Slowly, he began to fit the pieces together of what had actually happened. At length, he announced to all of them, "You know, Corim, that wasn't very nice of you. Not to me, nor to Rannion, nor to dear old –"

"Well, I'm not a very nice person most of the time," said Corim snippily.

"That's actually kind of true," Tallis said.

"Good thing we're not too picky, eh?" laughed Darmon.

And with that, the boys went back to their sowing and spoke no further of the matter.

Several days later, Neldon was over at Miss Elmensill's having tea and cakes, and he happened to notice a rock on her fireplace mantle.

"Say, what's that rock doing up there?" he asked, as he sipped his tea.

Miss Elmensill looked over her shoulder at it and said, "Oh, I'd almost forgot I left that up there. That's the rock you threw through my window. I kept it there to remind me to be mad at you, but I suppose I don't need it anymore. After all, there's nothing to be angry about now. In fact, you've turned out to be such a nice young man that it's hard to believe you were once savage enough to throw a rock at my window."

"Well, I was actually trying to hit Rannion Rillspan with it, as I said at my hearing with the Dolnario," explained Neldon. "I know you didn't believe me then, but hopefully you do now. Also, I didn't even know there was a rock in the snowball at the time. That's because Corim Timberfall put – "

Neldon abruptly caught himself and covered his mouth. "Oops," he squeaked, then anxiously swallowed a swig of tea.

Suddenly, there came into Miss Elmensill's eyes that ferocious, flashing fury of hers that Neldon had dreaded for most of his life, and dreaded even now, though a little less so, since he knew her rage was not directed at him.

"Oh, he did, did he?" the old woman said coldly, as she clenched her fists, her knuckles turning white.

Not long afterward, Corim Timberfall became well aware of the fact that he had been ratted out, as he became the recipient of the Elmensill's undiluted rage. The reader will have undoubtedly correctly surmised that extremely disagreeable consequences were forthcoming for the boy and that he had a thing or two to say to Neldon after they fell upon him. Neldon, of course, felt awful about accidentally divulging Corim's secret, but there was nothing to be done to reverse the matter.

When all was said and done, the whole affair became almost as big of a news item as the debacle with Neldon at the end of the Snow War. But if you wish to know any more about the matter, you shall have to ask someone in Siloa for details, for it would be terribly dreary and disheartening for me to relate them here. But don't bother asking Corim Timberfall, as he almost certainly won't oblige you. It seems the memory is rather unpleasant for him.

And now we have come to the conclusion of our tale, save for one matter – that of the following Siloa Snow War. The reader will be pleased to know (provided he is partial to the Whirlwinds) that during the next year's Snow War, the Whirlwinds ended their four-year-long streak of defeats, which was the longest series of losses up to that point in Siloa Snow War history.

It is impossible to be certain, but the Whirlwinds may well have won simply because Neldon was unable to tamper with the results that year. The rest of the Whirlwinds had made a deal with him that he could keep the Topaz Turnip on his mantle (provided they won) until the following year's Snow War as long as he kept himself to their fort. They even said he could be the sole designer of this fort if he promised to work on it all day. Neldon gladly accepted this proposition, using his eight hours or so to simply pile snow into a massive heap, which he dubbed Neldon's Down (after nearby Dorman's Down, one of the highest rises of land Neldon knew of). And, at the summit of this mound, he dug a little crater for his fellow Whirlwinds to take shelter in. This was certainly unconventional, and no fort had ever been constructed like it before, but the Whirlwinds never found out how effective it was, since they never had to use it.

At the conclusion of the Snow War, Corim and Tressy, who were some of the Whirlwinds' leaders again that year, ceremoniously presented the Topaz Turnip to Neldon. Though neither of them were captains, Corim had been delegated this task due to his close association with Neldon, and he had asked Tressy to assist him.

Grandiosely, Corim addressed all his teammates, "Today, my fine Whirlwinds, as every year, we honor Fargalin Chipperchop, the founder of this most excellent Siloa Snow War and the maker of the Topaz Turnip. We do this by carrying on his vision and keeping the Siloa Snow War alive."

"But we have someone else very special that we need to honor today as well," said Tressy, turning to Neldon, who had puffed his chest out just about as far as it would go.

Corim nodded to Tressy, who handed him the much-coveted Topaz Turnip.

As Corim dramatically placed the Turnip in Neldon's open hands, he said, "In gratitude for your fine service of basically just keeping out of everybody's way, we, the Agleri Whirlwinds, your loyal snow warrior companions, present to you the Topaz Turnip. Now, with our blessing, you may display this hallowed artifact in the great and noble hall of Broadbuckle Bungalow until next year, when we shall have need to defend it again from the grasping claws of the vile Rimwold Thunders."

"Thank you, thank you, all," Neldon said, taking the Turnip and bowing to all of his teammates. "I am deeply honored and hope that I may be of equally great service to you in the future."

"Yes, please," muttered Corim.

A victory toast and celebration was held for all the Whirlwinds at the Timberfall house that night, and when this was concluded, Neldon returned home for dessert. Neldon's parents were there, of course, as was Quinty, along with his wife Halinda and their little children Milbert and Kebley.

The dessert just alluded to was a lovely cherry rum cake jointly prepared by Neldon's mother and none other than Bernalla Elmensill. Although Miss Elmensill still fiercely detested the Siloa Snow War, she hoped for Neldon's sake that the Whirlwinds would win. And so certain was she that he would assist in bringing about their triumph that she had approached his mother that morning and asked if they could make a cake at Broadbuckle Bakery to celebrate his inevitable victory. Though quite surprised at this request, his mother assented and invited Miss Elmensill to come for supper and dessert that evening. However, she declined, citing that she didn't want her entanglement with the Snow War to extend any further than assisting with Neldon's cake. After all, if people found out that she had attended a Snow War celebration, however small, they might think she was beginning to change her mind on the matter.

After receiving many hearty congratulations from his family, the beaming Neldon set the treasured Topaz Turnip on the mantle and then sat down at the table.

"Well, I tried to do what good I could, Quinty, just like you've told me," said Neldon, tucking a napkin into his shirt beneath his chin, "and you said things might turn out either well or not so well. So I shouldn't fret about it, and I've tried not to. But for my part, I think things have turned out splendidly."

"So they have," Quinty laughed.

A few moments later, the Broadbuckles began digging into the cake that had been set before them. And outside their warm and lighted bungalow, gleaming snowflakes fell upon the snow-covered, starlit streets of Siloa.

THE END

Captain of the
Koobachinky

CHAPTER ONE

The Conception and Construction of the Camfino

t was a rather hot day toward the end of the month of Tannaril, and Neldon Broadbuckle, Aradis Kingblade, Corim Timberfall, Tallis Pestleman and Darmon Barnwain were huddled in Hemmigan Hideaway, their secret hideout built under the roots of a large hemmigan tree up in Rimwold Forest. All of them were listening quite attentively to their friend Girion Ringmark tell them about the wonders of the sea. None of the lads except Girion had ever seen the ocean. But Girion had moved to Siloa only a few months ago from Aragest, a large port city and the capital of Velaris, where there were ships and sailors and docks and fish markets and all kinds of other things the lads from Siloa had never laid eyes on before.

"The ocean has the most water you've ever seen!" Girion said excitedly.

"More water than Bardlin Creek?" Neldon asked in awe.

"Much more," Girion assured him.

"Where would you get to if you kept going on it?" Darmon asked.

"Other Neathmarda, right?" said Aradis. "Just like the one we live on?"

Girion nodded. "It depends on which way you go. If you go south, there's a place called Fenrost that's full of ice and snow and barren rock and tall pine trees. And if you go east, you'll get to a very queer place called the Eldritch Isles. But if you went north, you'd end up in a land called Xengula. Most folks just call it the Bushbelt, but Xengula's its proper name."

"What's up there?" Corim asked.

"Come now, Corim, you've heard about the Bushbelt before," Tallis chided. "That's the strip of land that divides us from all the people that live up in the northern half of the world."

"Of course I know that," Corim snapped. "And you should pay better attention, Tallis. I didn't ask *what* it was; I want to know what's *in* it."

"Lots of things," Girion said. "There are jungles with all kinds of strange plants and animals and mountains that spew fire. Also, there are lots of monsters and natives that hardly wear any clothes. Most of them are quite hostile, but they know their way through the dense jungle like you know the way to your own front door."

The others were greatly intrigued by these fire-spewing mountains, but Neldon spoke before they had a chance to inquire about them. "The natives don't wear any clothes?" he asked in disbelief. "What do they wear instead?"

"Nothing sometimes," Girion replied. "But other times they just wear something called a loincloth, and they put paint from grass, flowers or dirt on their faces and chests and wear necklaces and other ornaments made out of objects they find around them in nature."

"All that is very odd indeed," said Neldon, scratching his head. "If I ever met a native from that Xengula place, I'd ask him why they behave so queerly."

"Well, you probably wouldn't get an answer," Girion said.

"Why is that? Because as soon as they saw Neldon, they'd run away?" Darmon chuckled.

"No, because they don't speak Daiga, of course," Girion replied. "They speak all kinds of other languages."

"So when they talk, it sounds like 'Mooga wonka sniggin bopple?'" Neldon asked quite sincerely.

"Probably not quite like that," Girion laughed.

Suddenly, Corim had an idea. "Say, Girion, I think it'd be pretty incredible to explore the Bushbelt. Do you think we could get there from right here in Siloa?"

"Oh, it would take a terribly long time to do that, and I don't think we could manage it anyhow," Girion said. "But, theoretically speaking, we could build a little boat and drift down our own Bardlin Creek that runs just north of Siloa, and eventually we'd come to the sea. And once we got to the sea, we could get to the Bushbelt if we knew what we were doing."

"You know some things about boats, Girion," Aradis said. "Could you design one that we could take down Bardlin Creek at least?"

Girion pondered this. "Well," said he, "when I was in Aragest, I did learn a thing or two about watercraft. If I had a few days to do some investigation and planning, I could probably design a raft that would carry us down the creek some miles safely. We may not be able to get to Xengula, but we could do a bit of exploring and have some lovely adventures nonetheless. If conditions were favorable, we could try to take our raft back upstream, and if not, we could always walk back to Siloa."

"Exploring and adventures? That settles it for me. We're building a raft!" Darmon said with great enthusiasm.

"It may take a week or two," Girion said, "and I'd need help gathering materials and constructing it."

"So much the better," said Corim. "That will give us time to gather supplies for our journey too."

"How long will we be gone?" Neldon asked concernedly.

"We've only just begun planning this expedition, but I'd say a day or two," Girion returned. "We don't want to go too far or it may be difficult to get back to Siloa. Besides, for a longer journey, we'd need more supplies than our raft might be able to carry."

"I guess I'll need to tell my parents then," Neldon said, "just in case they wonder where I've gone."

"Uh, I actually don't think any of us should tell our parents about this idea," Tallis said. "They might think it was too dangerous and forbid us to go."

"Tallis is right," Corim chimed in. "You'd better not tell your parents, Neldon, or I'll bonk you on that big, empty head of yours. Let's all swear a solemn oath of secrecy," he said very gravely.

"I don't know that one of your 'solemn oaths of secrecy' is really necessary, Corim," Aradis said with mild annoyance. "Let's just agree to keep quiet about this whole thing. Who's in?"

Corim, Tallis, Darmon and Girion all said, "I."

Neldon looked around at the other five and asked, "Won't our parents be worried about what happened to us if we just disappear for several days?"

"Of course they will," Corim said rather patronizingly, "but we can fix that when we get back and tell them about all the magnificent adventures we've had."

"Also, I'll leave my parents a note or something on the morning we depart telling them what we're up to," Girion said. "And then they can relay the information to the rest of your parents. That way they won't think we've been kidnapped or something."

"Oh, in that case, I'm on board for all of this," Neldon loudly announced. A few moments later, he asked, "So how are we going to trick our parents into letting us go if they catch us sneaking out early in the morning?"

"We'll just tell them we're going to help Old Farmer Berrydore harvest cherries or something," Darmon suggested.

"But how can we be traveling on a raft and picking cherries at the same time?" asked Neldon.

"We're not going to be picking cherries," Corim sighed. "That's a ruse – a trick so our parents won't know what we're actually doing. But don't tell your parents that we're helping harvest cherries until the day we actually leave for our journey, if that will even be necessary then. It's going to take us a few weeks to build the raft, remember?"

"Oh, right," Neldon said, and began munching on a raspberry pastry he had brought with him.

The remainder of the lads' time in Hemmigan Hideaway that day was spent discussing what kinds of things they might take on the raft for supplies and how they were going to smuggle them out of their parent's houses. When they each went their separate ways a while later, they were all giddy with the prospect of taking a fantastic voyage down Bardlin Creek.

⎯⎯◆⎯⎯

Over the next few days, Girion conducted the investigation and planning he had mentioned, and he soon had the other lads gathering the necessary items to build their raft. Corim, with his friends' assistance, was able to make off with a few handsaws, some hatchets and a number of suitable logs from his father's woodstore. (His father, with much ire, discovered that these items were missing but was unable to apprehend a culprit.) The lads found the rest of the materials they needed for the operation and construction of their craft in Rimwold Forest. These included more logs, vines and saplings for lashing these together and poles for steering, which they could, with the aid of a knife, shape to be a little more paddle-like.

As the boys collected all of these things, they stashed them in a spot not far to the south of Bardlin Creek about a half mile west of where the creek flowed eastward out of Rimwold Forest. This "illustrious shipyard," as Girion called it, was surrounded by a number of large bushes and was not easily seen unless one was practically upon it. Thus, it served as an ideal storage depot to make certain their project wasn't discovered.

Once this stage of material scavenging was complete, the lads started work on the actual construction of the raft – under Girion's skillful direction, of course. They spent a great deal of their free time on this endeavor and, in fact, labored with more energy and passion on it than they did their regular work and chores. And in this manner, shortly before the middle of the month of Harasa, they had nearly finished their task.

Also, during the weeks they were engaged in this undertaking, the lads pilfered provisions for their journey from various places, mostly their parent's houses and workshops. These items included knapsacks of food, small casks of water, fishing poles, a few short coils of rope, a metal weight (which they planned to use for an anchor), knives, a tinderbox, flint and steel, a set of tin cups, several cloth bandages and some rags to use as bandanas. These were all deposited in their shipyard as well. And although these items' absence had not gone unnoticed, the victims of these burglaries, just like Corim's father, were unable to discover who had taken them.

On the Crest of Harasa (the 'Crest of Such-and-such' being what folk call the sixteenth day of a given month), the boys met up in their shipyard to actually lash their raft together, for they planned to launch it early the following morning. They carried all the logs and lashing down closer to the bank of the creek and set about their work. With the concerted efforts of all six of them, the job was finished in good time, and they stood back to marvel at their triumph of engineering and labor.

The raft was roughly square, having both a width and length of a little more than eight feet, just big enough to fit the six lads, along with the supplies they planned to take. Its craftsmanship was definitely not refined, but quite adequate for the vessel's purposes.

"Creekworthy at last," Girion sighed with satisfaction.

"Magnificent, isn't she?" Corim oohed.

"Most definitely," Tallis agreed.

"Very much so, but let's cover her up with underbrush before someone comes along and sees her," said Aradis, eyeing the path that ran along the south bank of the stream.

The lads hastily performed this task, then sat down by the creek and skipped a few stones across the water.

"Now that we are on the brink of our maiden voyage, we shall have to name our splendid vessel," Girion announced, after making an especially spectacular throw.

"Name it?" Neldon said, thoroughly puzzled. "Whatever for? And what girls are coming with us? Nobody told me anything about this."

"'Maiden voyage' is just an expression," Girion laughed. "It simply means the first voyage. And as for the naming, it's a thing people do," he explained. "Out here in the Plains of Agleri, people name their horses and donkeys and whatnot, but those who ply the water name their ships and boats."

"I say we name it *Mergatha* after the girl Corim fancies," Darmon cackled.

"You shut your mouth, Darmon. I most definitely *do not* fancy Mergatha Seedbucket and you know it," Corim fumed. "She's as stuck up as they come, a priggish tattletale and ugly besides."

"It's not right to talk about girls that way," Girion said, frowning.

Corim looked slightly abashed after this reproof from Girion – but only slightly.

"How about we name it the *Koobachinky*?" Neldon suggested.

Aradis' face was seized by a look of almost complete disgust. "I think that's one of the worst ideas I've ever heard."

"Why?" Neldon asked, astonished.

"If you want to talk about something that's *truly* ugly, just take a close look at a koobachinky," Aradis said. "It has to be by far the most hideous bird in all Orona. It's got that mop-top hair or whatever that is on top of its head, huge yellow eyes, wings with mangy black feathers, a blue beak that looks like it got smashed with a hammer, a jaundiced body, spindly purple legs and jagged, crusty claws. Plus, its squawk sounds like it's choking on a beakful of mud. Now, tell me, do you really think our raft deserves to be disgraced by association with that mess of a creature?"

"I like koobachinkies," Neldon insisted earnestly. "I think they're neat."

"Somehow, I'm not surprised," Tallis sighed.

"Can we vote on it?" Neldon asked.

"Yes, and I guarantee you we're all going to vote 'no,' right?" Corim said. He looked around at the group and everyone nodded, much to Neldon's disappointment. "Told you," he said smugly.

"Girion's going to be the leader of our expedition, so I think he should name the raft," said Tallis.

"If you all wish for me to take the position of captain and assume the responsibility of naming our craft, then I will do so," Girion said. "And if all are agreeable to it, I would like to name our raft the *Tamfino*. A tamfino is a type of migratory whale, silver in color, that lives offshore from

Velaris in the summer and then journeys north toward the Bushbelt in the winter."

"I'm all for the *Tamfino*," said Corim. "Honestly, I'm for anything but the *Koobachinky*. You could name it the *Dingdong Dungheap* and I would pick that over Neldon's name for it."

"Come on," Neldon protested. "My name wasn't *that* bad."

"Actually, it was," said Darmon.

Girion now felt a little sorry for how much ribbing Neldon was receiving on account of his suggestion. "The *Tamfino* it is, then," he said, hoping to bring an end to this particular point of discussion. "Now, early tomorrow morning, Darmon, you and Tallis are going to borrow your Uncle Fingam's donkeys to help us drag the raft down to the water, correct?"

"Sure are," Darmon confirmed.

"Yep," said Tallis.

"And we'll all meet here by the raft just before sunrise, right?" said Girion.

The lads all nodded.

"And if our parents ask about what we're up to, we're just telling them we're going to assist Old Farmer Berrydore in picking cherries, correct?" Girion checked.

The lads nodded again.

"The important thing is to just make sure that we can have our adventure in the first place," said Girion. "We can worry about the consequences later. And like I said, I'm going to leave a note for my parents tomorrow morning explaining things, so at least our folks will know where we've gone off to. But now, I suppose we ought to be getting on home so we can get a good rest tonight. I'll see you all for our grand expedition tomorrow morning!" he finished heartily.

After this, the lads walked back to the edge of town and went their separate ways.

CHAPTER TWO

A Ludicrous Launch by a Lubber

he next morning, before Marda rose, Girion wrote his note and put it somewhere he didn't expect his parents would discover it until around midday. Then he snuck off to Rimwold Forest. Meanwhile, Darmon and Tallis borrowed the donkeys as promised, deceiving Darmon's uncle into thinking they were using them to briefly assist Old Farmer Berrydore with hauling a wagon to his cherry orchard. Then they led the beasts up to where their raft was hidden and found the other four boys there waiting for them.

Soon, they had hitched up the donkeys to the raft and dragged it down into the water. As Marda was just peeping up over the eastern horizon, they were unhitching the donkeys, tying the raft to a thin tree on the bank with a length of rope and starting to load up their supplies. Darmon and Tallis rushed to bring the donkeys back to Uncle Fingam and returned a little over half an hour later.

"Hm," said Aradis, who was looking intently at the water when Tallis and Darmon arrived. "The current seems to be moving rather more swiftly than normal." And so it was.

"Perhaps it rained upstream," Tallis said, "and the creek is a little swollen."

"Yes, perhaps so," Girion said. "That will be better for us, I think, because we'll be able to cover a greater distance in a shorter amount of time. Now, let's just check up in the underbrush one more time and make sure we didn't miss anything we were supposed to take with us," he advised. "As soon as we've done that, there shouldn't be any more delays. We'll just untie the rope and be on our way."

And so everyone started to follow Girion back up to the spot where they had stashed all of their supplies the previous day. Everyone, that is, except Neldon.

What happened next can perhaps best be explained by the fact that Neldon Broadbuckle was not always the most careful of listeners nor was he terribly observant. In this particular case, he had distinctly heard the latter part of Girion's comment, "untie the rope and be on our way." But that was all he had heard. So, humming quietly and happily to himself, he untied the rope that kept their craft anchored to the bank, then hopped onto the raft, while his friends walked off into the underbrush.

As the raft began to drift away from the bank, Neldon turned and saw that the others were headed into the woods. With considerable alarm, he called, "Hey, where are you lot going? I thought you said to untie the rope and be on our way!"

All the lads swiftly whirled around and gasped.

"Neldon Broadbuckle, what in the name of all that is sane and decent are you doing?" Girion yelled.

"What are *you* doing?" Neldon shouted back. "Why would you say to untie this thing and then walk off into the forest?"

"Quick!" Girion urged the others. "Down to the water!"

The boys raced to the creek and waded in after the raft, which was getting farther and farther from the shore every moment and would soon be in the center of the current, where it would be more quickly carried downstream.

"Neldon, get one of those poles and steer the raft to the bank!" Girion ordered.

Neldon promptly picked up a fishing pole and stuck it in the water.

"Wrong one, dingleflobbin!" Corim shouted. "Get one of the long ones!"

Neldon frantically tossed the fishing pole back on the raft and seized one of the steering poles, which he stuck into the water and began vigorously moving up and down like the handle of a butter churn.

"Unbelievable," muttered Tallis.

"Not like that!" Girion shouted. "Try to paddle with it, and if that's too hard for you, then see if you can jam it into the riverbed or something."

Neldon first attempted the latter suggestion, and cried out in dismay, "It's too deep!" Then, inadvertently, he dropped the pole into the water. "Oops," he said, as he scrambled to get another.

"What an absolute lubber," Girion muttered, as he waded forward with all haste.

"What's a lubber?" asked Darmon.

"A clumsy buffoon who knows no boatcraft whatsoever," Girion hurriedly returned. "I suppose it isn't the nicest thing to call someone but, well … Neldon really is making a mess of things."

Something of critical importance that must be mentioned at this juncture is that Girion was the only one of the boys who could swim. The other four who were wading in the creek had come to a spot where the water was up to their chests, so they stopped for fear that they should be swept away and drowned.

"Do you think you could swim fast enough to catch him, Girion?" asked Aradis, as he watched Neldon drift ever farther away.

"I'll try," said Girion, and he took off after the departing *Tamfino*, using a vigorous front crawl. Meanwhile, the other boys stood there, helpless to do anything further to aid poor Neldon.

"Use the anchor," Girion gasped to Neldon between strokes, as he had just recalled that this was part of the raft's equipment. "Just throw it in the water."

Neldon set the pole he was unsuccessfully wielding back on the deck and then heaved one of the water casks into the creek.

"No, no!" Girion coughed, but it was too late. Furious, he gasped, "The anchor is the – " Splash! Girion had to pause as his mouth had gone into the water. " – metal weight on the rope."

"Ah," said Neldon, as he grabbed this item and tossed it, rope and all, into the water.

"No!" screamed Girion. "You're supposed to – " Splash! "tie it to the raft first!"

"You didn't tell me that," Neldon exclaimed, growing more overwrought every moment.

Girion was gaining on the raft, and, despite Neldon's blundering, he thought there was still a chance he could salvage the situation. However, an unforeseen factor was about to quash all his hopes.

The raft was now nearing the edge of Rimwold Forest, and there were some trees with limbs that dipped down rather low toward Bardlin Creek at this spot. Neldon had grabbed one of the three remaining poles and was trying to get it lodged in the branches above him, supposing, quite mistakenly, that he might halt the raft in this manner.

"What in all Orona – " Splash! "are you doing?" Girion called.

"I'm trying to stop the raft!" Neldon cried back.

Just then, his pole whacked a limb above, and something tumbled from it down into the creek. There was a loud splash, and a moment later, a very angry, furry gray creature emerged from the water.

"Uh-oh," Neldon said, as soon as he saw it.

"What was that?" Girion gasped.

"A herragoot, I think," Neldon gulped, as the creature started swimming toward the raft.

"A what?"

"A herragoot. It's a rather feisty woodland creature. It looks kind of like a mix between a cat and a dog. You probably haven't heard of them because you haven't lived here that long. They're not too bad as long you leave them alone, but if you make one mad, you'd better watch out because they have frightful, pointed teeth and nasty, sharp claws."

These aforementioned claws were just appearing on the corner of the raft as Neldon said this, and so he wildly swiped at the herragoot with his pole, emitting a high-pitched scream as he did so. Just as it was emerging from the water, Neldon's pole hit it full on in the face, knocking it back in the water toward Girion.

"There's no way – " Splash! "I'm staying in the – " Splash! "water with that thing!" Girion promptly diverted his course and swam frantically for the south bank of the creek.

Meanwhile, Neldon was waving his pole about, trying to keep the herragoot from getting on the raft again.

"Thanks for trying to rescue me, Girion," Neldon called to his friend, who had just reached the shore and was dragging himself onto it. "I hope I can do our mission justice and that I see you again someday."

"Ahh!" Neldon squeaked abruptly, as the herragoot popped up at the raft's edge. He stumbled backward over one of the poles, knocking it into the water, but with the pole in his hand, he bopped the herragoot hard on the head. This time the creature swam toward the north bank of the creek, and Neldon hurled his pole at it to strike it once more. However, the pole missed, and the herragoot kept paddling toward the bank, deciding it wasn't worth any more injuries to try to revenge itself on its frenzied foe.

As Neldon drifted on eastward down Bardlin Creek, he looked sadly back at Girion, who was too worn out to continue swimming any farther.

Girion shook his head and then began walking back toward the west, hoping to take council with the other lads about what to do next.

———•◆•———

Now that Neldon was all alone, he sat down to ponder his fate and take stock of his provisions. Unfortunately, practically the only thing Neldon knew what to do with on the raft was the rations; everything else was virtually useless to him, though it would not have been so to Girion and the others. He had six knapsacks of food and one cask of water, along with a single fishing pole and one remaining steering pole, as well as six tin cups, three knives, a tinderbox, flint and steel, one coil of rope, bandages and six old rags.

"Well, if I'm going to be rafting all the way to the Bushbelt, I'd better be careful to make sure these supplies last," he said resignedly.

As he looked around the raft, a realization came to him. "Hm, since I'm the only one on this raft, I'm pretty sure that makes me the captain. And if I'm not quite mistaken, the reason Girion got to name the raft what he wanted was because he was the captain. But now that *I'm* the captain, I can fix the name to what I want."

Standing up, he boldly announced, "Raft, hearken to me! I dub you … the *Koobachinky*." Sitting back down, he voiced the raft's intended response in a low, amiable voice, "Why, thank you very much, Neldon Broadbuckle. That's what I wanted to be named all along."

"You're very welcome," Neldon replied to his raft persona.

He sat there for a few moments more, then asked, "Mr. Koobachinky, where exactly are we going?"

"The ocean, I believe, sir," he answered in his raft voice. "Once we reach there, we'll be charting our course for the Bushbelt."

"Very good. Carry on," Neldon said. "I'm going to partake of some of our foodstuffs to keep my strength up. One of the worst things that can happen on a voyage of this sort is to have your captain go hungry. If he gets too hungry, he'll start to get weak and dizzy and begin making poor decisions."

"We wouldn't want that, would we?" he answered in his raft voice. "But sir, didn't you already eat breakfast this morning?"

"Yes, but there's been a fair amount of toil and excitement since then, so I need to eat again to restore all the energy I spent," Neldon replied.

"Ah, I see," he responded in his raft voice.

Neldon now began to rifle through the various knapsacks to see which foodstuffs he would like the best. Unsurprisingly, he decided the items he had brought were superior to any of the others, so he promptly began devouring a sizable plum cake and a number of cupcakes, cherry tarts and almond cookies he had taken from his mother's bakery that morning.

CHAPTER THREE

A Debate, A Dozer and Dugamar's Decision

s Neldon was enjoying his feast of pastries, there was a rather sober discussion taking place on the south bank of Bardlin Creek among the other five boys.

"This is a very bad situation," said Girion, "for a great many reasons."

"Yep," said Darmon. "One of them being that Neldon can't swim."

"And he's too dumb to know how to get the raft to shore," Corim asserted.

Aradis remarked, "In all likelihood, he'll just sit on that raft, stuffing his face and floating on down to the Brines of Ferassi, oblivious to the fact that he's in a pretty awful fix."

"Are there any villages along Bardlin Creek?" Girion asked. "Won't somebody see him floating by and assist him in getting to shore?"

"There are a few settlements I know of downstream," Tallis said, "but they're rather small. I'm not even sure I would call them villages. I certainly wouldn't call them towns. Besides, they're set back from the creek a bit, so the only way anyone from there might see Neldon is if he happened to be down by the water. And also, depending on how fast the raft travels, Neldon may pass some of them during the night. But I honestly don't know a thing about raft speed, so – "

"And besides, even if he passes them during the day," Corim interrupted, "he may just wave at the townsfolk, and they'll be oblivious to the fact that he actually needs help in getting to the shore."

"As a matter of fact," said Darmon, "Neldon may well think that he ought to just carry on with the voyage as best he can without us, in which case he won't even ask anyone to help him to shore."

"I rather suspect you're right," Girion sighed. "One of the last things he said to me was that he hoped he could 'do our mission justice.' Now that I think about it, that sounds like him planning to take the journey alone as long as he can. And if that really is the case, he'll be most un-likely to ask for aid in returning to Siloa. If anything, he'll want help getting closer to the ocean, since he apparently thinks that's where he's supposed to be going."

"If Neldon's going to get assistance from anyone, I think it will have to be from us," said Aradis grimly.

"Not so," Girion returned suddenly, as he was struck by an epipha-ny. "I know exactly who can help poor Neldon! My father knows more about watercraft than I do, and he's a better swimmer than I am. Howev-er, we'd of course have to go fess up to what we've done to get his aid. But he'd find out about it soon enough anyway from the note I left. Perhaps we can borrow some horses from someone and ride down Bardlin Creek after Neldon. I should certainly think we could beat the speed of his raft if we were on horses."

"It's not going to be pretty when we face your father about all this," Tallis sighed, "but I think your suggestion is the best option we have, Girion."

The others agreed, and so they set out for the Ringmark cottage, which lay around two miles east of Siloa.

———•◦❖◦•———

Meanwhile, back on the raft, Neldon was still chowing on pastries and cakes. When he had eaten his fill, which was more than half of the food in his knapsack, he sat there for a while, watching the scenery go by. He had already passed under Langman's Bridge (sometimes referred to simply as the Bardlin Bridge), which lay just north of Siloa. Past the bridge, the creek bent rather noticeably to the north, abandoning its eastward course, and then headed north by northeastward for a while. Neldon was, in fact, already on this stretch of the creek and would soon be beyond any territory he would readily recognize.

Bardlin Creek grew a little wider as it journeyed across the Plains of Agleri, and tall rushes and bristly shrubs, filled with humming insects, grew along its banks. Marda was getting a little higher overhead, and Neldon shielded his eyes from its bright rays. After a while, he began to feel a little sluggish (as one does after consuming a great many sweets), so he decided to lay down and take a nap, even though it was still relatively early in the day.

"Keep our course, steady, will you?" he yawned, patting the deck of the raft.

"Absolutely, sir. Don't you worry about that," he answered in his raft voice.

Propping his head up on one of the knapsacks and closing his eyes, Neldon was soon fast asleep in the morning sun, snoring loudly and drifting lazily down the current of Bardlin Creek.

———————•⋅◦⋅•———————

As Neldon was snoozing away on the *Koobachinky*, his five accomplices in its construction were at the Ringmark place explaining themselves to Girion's father, Dugamar Ringmark. He was certainly none too pleased about what they'd done, which included stealing, lying and other unscrupulous and foolish acts. He reproved them sternly for not taking into consideration that their plan might turn into a terrible debacle, which, in fact, it had. However, like Girion, Dugamar had a rather even temperament, and so there was no yelling or anything of that sort on his part (This session would have gone quite differently, for instance, with Corim's father). However, he did assure Girion that he would experience severe consequences as a result of what he had done, and he cautioned the other boys that their parents would undoubtedly have similarly steep punishments for them.

Girion asked his father if he would be willing to lead a search party to find Neldon and inquired whether he and the other boys could go along to help, since they felt awful about being the reason this whole incident had occurred in the first place. Dugamar agreed right away to spearheading a search, provided his landlord, Weslin Furrowmead, would let him postpone some of his fieldwork, although he surmised this wouldn't be a problem, since Weslin was a very reasonable man and would surely understand the gravity of Neldon's plight. However, Dugamar was reluctant to allow the boys to come along, since he thought it might turn into a rather lengthy undertaking. Nonetheless, he conceded that if their parents permitted it, he would allow them to accompany him. Since the matter was rather urgent, he hated to delay the search any longer by taking the time to have them get permission from their parents. However, he said that he would at least consider it, since he intended to head back toward town anyway to begin the search and relay the story to Neldon's mother.

After a few minutes more of insistent pleading from the boys, Girion's father said he would consent at least for Girion to go and that he would make preparations as if the others would be going as well, though if their parents forbade it, he would immediately discharge them from the expedition. And so, he began gathering supplies to last the six of them the next two days, just in case. Girion's father, just like his son, had realized that horses could be instrumental in helping them with their search. Consequently, he said he was going to visit his neighbor, Grammick Gleanworthy, and see if he would let them borrow some of his horses so they could ride down Bardlin Creek after Neldon, for on horseback they could make better time. But even with the help of mounts, he thought it might be well into the evening before they returned. And if the search were unfavorable, they might even have to spend the night outdoors and return the following day. However, he was hopeful that they would be able to catch up with Neldon before it got dark.

Together, they went to Weslin Furrowmead's house, and, after Mr. Furrowmead had heard Dugamar's story, he graciously granted him however much time he needed to rescue Neldon. Next, the company went to the Gleanworthy farm, and after Dugamar had explained the situation to Grammick, he readily assented to letting them use three of his horses. So, Girion and his father jumped on one of these, Aradis and Tallis mounted another and Corim and Darmon climbed up on the last one. And then, with all haste, they rode off to Siloa.

Upon arriving, they went straight to Neldon's house, and Dugamar summarily told Neldon's mother about what had happened to her son (His father was presently at work in Hildenrill Mill in Rimwold Forest). She was, of course, quite distraught, but he assured her that he would do everything he could to bring Neldon back safely soon. Then the party went on to the houses of Aradis, Corim, Tallis and Darmon, all of which were in town. Aradis' father and Corim's, Tallis' and Darmon's mothers all gave permission for the lads to go with Dugamar, although they promised that heavy consequences for the boys' shenanigans would be forthcoming upon their return.

At last, after all these regrettable delays, the search party was ready to begin its mission. So the company headed north and west from Siloa to the spot where Girion had lost sight of Neldon and the raft. Although they could have struck the creek farther to the east, Girion's father wanted to make sure that Neldon hadn't come ashore farther upstream before they began searching for him downstream. But unfortunately, if Neldon had wandered off into the Plains of Agleri, although he might be safer, this wouldn't be optimal either. Indeed, either way, time wouldn't particularly be on the search party's side.

CHAPTER FOUR

Ashore at Angalee

ow we must return to our adventurer aboard the *Koobachinky*. Neldon, who had been fast asleep, began to slowly awaken. The first thing he noticed was that the raft didn't seem to be moving. And the second thing was that he felt rather hot and was sweating a great deal. After an obnoxiously lengthy yawn, he rubbed his eyes and sat up. Looking around, he saw that the *Koobachinky* was resting against a bank of tall, flourishing grasses.

"I wonder where I am," Neldon said, scratching his head. "Somewhere very warm, that's for sure."

He looked behind him and saw a sizable body of water. It was, in fact, just a pond, but Neldon had never seen a pond this big before. The pond was actually fed from the south by Bardlin Creek, which also proceeded out the north side of it, but Neldon was not anywhere near observant enough to notice this.

"This must be the ocean!" he gasped. "Girion said it was the most water you've ever seen, and this certainly is the most *I've* ever seen." If he had been thinking more clearly, he might have remembered that Trollig Lake in Rimwold Forest, which he had seen many times, was actually bigger than the pond before him.

He paused and thought about this, then said, "Wait. I'm by the ocean, and it's very hot here." He looked up at the sun, which seemed to him to be brighter than usual. "Does that mean I've actually traveled all the way to the Bushbelt or some faraway tropical place like that?"

"Yes, Captain Neldon," he replied in full raft voice. "We have landed in Xengula, and you are the first Siloan to ever set foot here."

"Wow!" Neldon exclaimed. "Well, that being the case, I'd better hurry up and disguise myself as a native so I don't get attacked."

Now, the reader must understand that it simply did not occur to Neldon how utterly ridiculous the scenario he imagined was. For of course he could not have made it anywhere near the Bushbelt in his little raft, especially during the course of a single nap. But Neldon was far from being a person of great intellectual prowess, and besides that, he knew next to nothing about the Bushbelt or even geography beyond a few miles from Siloa, for that matter. Also, even what he had heard from Girion had passed through a sort of "Neldonization filter" and gotten somewhat garbled in the process. Thus, to him, it was quite plausible that the pond was one and the same as the ocean and that the shore was that of Xengula and even that he had journeyed thither during a few hours of slumber.

He leapt off the raft and began poking through the grasses on the shore. "Let's see," he said to himself. "What did Girion say about the Bushbelt natives? Oh, yes. They hardly wear any clothes, and they wear necklaces and things made of local plants and smear flowers and such on their faces. These will do," he said, as he picked a bunch of bright yellow flowers and rubbed them all over his face, so that his cheeks were soon covered in yellow streaks.

"And I've got to get rid of this," said he, as he pulled off his shirt and threw it on the ground. "And these too," he added, removing his trousers and tossing them on top of his shirt.

Now he stood on the bank in his underpants, his face covered with bold, yellow marks, and he almost *did* look like some wild Barada of the Bushbelt, were it not for his large, round belly and silly, self-congratulatory grin, features which one would hardly expect to find borne by any self-respecting native of Xengula.

"Ah, and this will complete my disguise," Neldon said, as he reached down into the pond water and drew out a string of long, dark green algae, which he draped around his neck.

"Yech! That doesn't feel pleasant at all!" he exclaimed. "However, I'm afraid it will be necessary to just put up with it in order to appear as native as possible."

"Hadn't you better hide me so no one discovers that a foreigner has landed here?" Neldon suggested in his raft voice.

"That's an excellent idea, Koobachinky," Neldon returned. "Here, I'll drag you up and hide you in the rushes."

Neldon attempted to do this but found that the raft was much too heavy for him to move by himself, so he said, "On second thought, I'll put you in that nice little spot that's hidden behind some rushes. I don't think anyone will be able to spy you there."

"What a clever boy you are," he congratulated himself in his Koobachinky voice.

Neldon had great success with this plan, as he was able to simply wade in the pond and push the raft into the aforementioned inlet, where it was shielded from sight unless one were quite close to it. Also, the rushes were growing so thick around it that Neldon was fairly certain it wouldn't float off.

"All right, I'm going to go and establish contact with the natives," Neldon whispered to his raft. "Stay right here, and I'll return when I can."

"As you say, Captain," he assured in his raft voice.

Now Neldon began walking westward from the shore of the pond, into what he imagined was the interior of the Bushbelt. After only a minute or so of trekking, he saw four boys, all of them several years younger than him, dashing toward him, each with a fishing pole in hand. These boys were, in fact, running down to the pond to fish, but Neldon assumed they were coming to attack him. This delusion was solidified by his belief that the fishing poles were weapons of some kind and that the boys were actually adult midgets. They were far enough off and Neldon so poor of an observer that, to him, such an identification seemed quite plausible. Also, they were all shirtless, though this was actually because of the heat and not for the reason that Neldon supposed, which was that they were following native Bushbelt customs.

Neldon instinctively decided that intimidation was his best hope of dealing with these natives, and so he ran toward them, waving his arms and yelling, "Changanoo bigginbop, smockywab hoosnakoosha!"

As soon as the poor boys saw this hefty, practically naked youth running at them, raving like a madman, with his face covered in yellow paint and a string of algae on his neck, they screamed in terror and whirled around, running back in the direction from whence they had come as fast as their legs would carry them.

After the boys had disappeared through a gap between two little hills, Neldon took a deep breath and said, "I wish Koobachinky had been here to see that. I sure showed them. Hopefully they go back and tell their leader how dangerous I am and they decide to make a peace treaty with me to protect themselves."

Resolutely, he followed the route the retreating boys had taken and soon came to the opening between the two hills. Beyond them, he saw a collection of about a dozen wooden buildings. "Ah, a Bushbelt village," he said. "This must be where the warriors were from."

No sooner had he finished saying this than a number of men, women and children began emerging from the buildings. The men were all in farmer's garb and the women in simple work dresses. Neldon was greatly confused by this, since he expected them to be attired rather like himself.

Within a minute or so, some fifty persons were assembled in the open area in the center of the settlement, and among them were the four boys Neldon had seen earlier. These stood at the center of the company, gesturing and babbling frantically.

All of a sudden, one of the men among this group sighted Neldon ambling toward the village. He pointed at him and said something to the others, and they all began moving toward the eastern edge of the settlement. There they halted and stood in a cluster, their faces riddled by both puzzlement and astonishment, as they regarded the approach of this ludicrous stranger. Actually, they looked at him the same way one views a curious animal he has never seen before, particularly an animal that looks to be much more whimsical than dangerous.

Neldon didn't think it appeared as if these villagers were going to assail him, so he marched boldly forward, raised his arms, and called out, "Shtocken mookle. Chinky dee hoppy nop. Moogen pickle bongy dong, pinkachee!"

This resulted in the people of the settlement becoming even more confused and amazed. Their mouths fell open in complete disbelief as the virtually naked, ceremonially-bedecked Neldon Broadbuckle walked ever closer to their village.

"I guess I should try Daiga," he muttered to himself, then loudly announced, "Greetings, natives of Xengula! I have come in peace from the distant village of Siloa in the far-off kingdom of Velaris to explore your territory and establish good will between my people and your own. Please, estimated villagers … I mean, esteemed villagers, will you grant me safe passage through your land and direct me to your ruler?" Neldon supposed that diplomats and ambassadors spoke in this manner and was trying hard to emulate it.

The people of the settlement looked at each other and shook their heads in utter incredulity.

A few moments later, a man among this company stepped forward and said in a rustic accent, "What are you on about, lad, scaring our children like that?" He motioned to the four boys. "And what's your name?"

"Oh, they're children," Neldon said abashedly, looking more closely at the lads. "I thought they were a party of midget warriors, so I tried to frighten them in order to protect myself. And my name is Neldonicus Broadbuckle. I know such a name may be long and strange to your ears, so you can call me Neldon if that's easier for you to remember. That's what nearly everybody where I'm from calls me, anyway. Neld is even shorter, and if that's still too long, you can just call me Nel. Or Chubkins. That's what my friends sometimes call me, especially when they're annoyed with me about something. I think it's supposed to be insulting, but I'm not really sure."

"You're from Siloa, eh?" the man asked.

"That's correct, sir," Neldon replied, as he halted in front of the company. "And what is the name of your wonderful village, this shining gem of the Bushbelt?" he asked, continuing his earnest attempt to employ the jargon of a diplomat.

"The Bushbelt?" the man laughed, and the whole company snickered behind him. "Is that where you think you are?" Then, seeing that Neldon was gravely serious, he said, "Our settlement is called Angalee, and we accept your offer of good will, Neldon Broadbuckle. On my word, none of us will try to harm you."

"Thank you, sir," Neldon returned politely. "I've been told the people of the Bushbelt are quite hostile, but you have proven otherwise. However, I was wondering: why are all of you wearing clothes?"

"Uh …" said the man, "Were you expecting us all to be walking around naked?"

"Of course," replied Neldon. "Natives of the Bushbelt only wear loincloths and ornaments like the ones I'm wearing. Now, why have you abandoned the ways of your fellow Bushbelters?"

"Have you been out in the heat all day, son?" the man asked, ignoring Neldon's query.

"Yep," Neldon replied. "Since dawn. I'm not used to this Bushbelt weather either, so if you could give me some water, it would be much appreciated. I left my water supply on my – " Neldon caught himself. "Oops, I'm not supposed to tell them I have one of those," he chided in his head. "One can never be too careful in foreign lands, and if things turn sour, I may still have to make an escape on the *Koobachinky*."

"Sure, we can get you some water," the man said. "And I'll tell you what: I can get you some food and a place to spend the night too. It sounds like too much Marda and an overactive imagination may have gotten to you. You can rest up, and hopefully you'll be much better in the morning. I've got a wagon and some horses, and I can take you back to Siloa tomorrow."

"However will you cross the sea to get there with just a wagon and horses?" asked Neldon.

"Don't you worry about that," the man returned graciously. "Everything's going to be all right. Now, where in Siloa do you live? In the town proper or outside of it? If you're in town, you can tell me where you live in relation to the Ploughman's Shanty if that's nearby."

"You know about the Ploughman's Shanty?" gasped Neldon. "I had no idea it was that famous. Well, my house is actually just across the street from the Ploughman's Shanty and a few houses to the south."

"Perfect," said the man. "I'm Hendrig Rimwright, by the way. Now, let's get along to my house, and my wife Dorna will get you all settled in."

"I and my country offer you much gratitude, Hendrig," said Neldon.

The crowd of villagers parted to let Hendrig and Neldon through, though they still stared at the lad as if he were a deranged, mythical creature of some sort. Hendrig led Neldon to a building on the far side of the settlement and then ushered him into it through a sturdy wooden door. Inside was a decent-sized room with a fireplace, a table and chairs and some sleeping pallets.

Hendrig's wife was cleaning some fish by the fireplace, and she looked up in astoundment as her husband led Neldon into the house. "I say, Hendrig, whatever are you doing bringing this – "

"Hold, Dorna," Hendrig said. "I need to talk to you privately for a minute." He led her into another room, which Neldon guessed might be their bedroom.

"I hope they're not plotting to betray me," Neldon thought to himself. He could hear them talking in there, but couldn't make out any specific words.

A few minutes later, the husband and wife emerged. Hendrig told Neldon he had business to finish up for the day but that he would be back for supper. He bid Neldon farewell and then left the dwelling. As soon as he had gone, Dorna asked Neldon if he would care to remove his algae necklace and if he would like a pair of trousers and a shirt.

"Oh no, ma'am. I'm trying to be respectful of your native customs," Neldon insisted.

"Well, as you can see, we're violating our own customs by wearing clothes, so you can feel free to do the same."

"Hm. In that case, I suppose it'd be all right," said Neldon.

After this concession, Dorna discarded his algae necklace and helped him wipe the flower paint off his face. Then Neldon pulled on the shirt and trousers she offered. Dorna urged Neldon to sit at the table, as she poured him out a large mug of water. She set some bread on the table too. Neldon guzzled up all the water in practically no time and scarfed down the bread, so Dorna refilled his mug and gave him a sausage, which he also promptly devoured.

Dorna made polite conversation with Neldon until supper, when Hendrig came home, along with his four children, one boy (the oldest) and three girls. All of them were younger than Neldon. The seven of them had a fine dinner with fresh fish and vegetables and some ripe fruit and nuts, as well as some roasted wild game. As they ate, Neldon put forth many inquiries about the Bushbelt, which were mostly answered by Hendrig, who thought that Neldon was still simply delusional from being out in the sun for so long (Indeed, the lad had quite a sunburn to indicate this). He wasn't sure what it would do to him if he found out he weren't actually in the Bushbelt, so he mildly played along with Neldon's suppositions, and his wife and children did the same, for they had been instructed to do so.

After supper, it got dark, and the family invited Neldon to lie down on one of the extra pallets in the main room of their house. They brought him a blanket and some cider to drink and then wished him a pleasant sleep. Neldon was rather tired from his afternoon and would have begun dozing right away had he not one more order of business he thought needed to be taken care of.

He pretended to be asleep until the rest of the family actually went to their respective beds. Then he crept over to the fireplace and grabbed a poker, which he took and hid under his blanket as he lay back down. His thought was that he might need protection during the night if the natives turned on him. "Only trust a Bushbelter as far as they can throw you," he told himself. (This sounded to him like a proverb that people would repeat to each other, but unbeknownst to him, it was purely a product of his own imagining and a very addled one besides.) "They've been mighty kind, but appearances can be deceiving with these native types. It's just better to play it safe."

Only a few minutes later, Neldon fell into slumber and was attended by dreams of his magnificently heralded return to Siloa, wherein Fennadris Barleycroft, the Dolnario of Siloa (A Dolnario is essentially a mayor of sorts.) acclaimed him as the village's greatest explorer of all time and presented him with a medal and a plaque, as well as the privilege of being the honorary Dolnario of Siloa for a day.

Back Down Bardlin Creek

he reader may now be wondering what was transpiring with Dugamar and the boys while Neldon was having all of these adventures. As a matter of fact, they had been having rather a rough time of things. By the time they began their search along Bardlin Creek, it was about an hour and a half before noon and already quite hot. The party journeyed for hour after hour, giving themselves and the horses breaks as necessary, though they all grew stickier and sweatier and more irked as the day went on, and still there was no sign of Neldon or the raft. They thus presumed that Neldon was yet drifting onward, for if some ill fate had befallen the raft, they supposed they would have found pieces of it along the bank. They preferred not to consider the unpleasant possibility that Neldon had fallen off the raft and drowned, though they did not rule it out altogether, especially considering Neldon's general clumsiness.

And so they pressed on, hoping to cover as much ground as they could, for Dugamar repeatedly insisted that, on horseback, they could surely exceed the speed of the current by quite a bit, and thus it was only a matter of time before they overtook Neldon. As a matter of fact, Dugamar was quite correct, but the problem was that by the time they caught up with Neldon, he had already disembarked and hidden the raft.

Indeed, the search party arrived at the east shore of the pond at almost the exact same time as Neldon reached the village of Angalee. Dugamar hadn't lived in the area long, so he didn't know of Angalee's existence. Tallis did, but he saw no reason to mention it, since the settlement was set back some distance from the water, and he didn't think it likely anyone from there had seen Neldon. If he had noted these thoughts to Dugamar, he would have swum across the pond and at least made inquiries, but as it was, the party looked around the shores of the pond, and seeing nothing of the raft or Neldon, moved on.

They traveled on until around sunset, though at a rather slower pace, for they were quite weary and dejected, then halted at a point which was some miles north of a town called Dallyn. They were thoroughly exhausted by now, drenched in sweat and despondent at their failure to locate Neldon. They tied their horses to a tree along the banks of Bardlin Creek and lay down in the grass, hoping to get a decent sleep before they returned to Siloa on the morrow.

Girion's father was positive that they must have passed Neldon at some point, based on a comparison of the speed of the current with the rate they had traveled on their mounts. He was also quite certain that the raft had not wrecked or something of that sort, for they had continued to watch carefully their whole journey for any stray pieces of it and yet had seen none.

"He must have gone ashore somewhere on the far bank," said Dugamar. "I'm sure of it, as our search on the hither side of Bardlin Creek has turned up nothing. In all likelihood, we just didn't spot the raft wherever he stowed it. So I suggest we return to Siloa tomorrow and then search up the opposite bank of the creek the following day. From what I know of Neldon, he won't have walked terribly far, so we should be able to find him without too great of difficulty."

Dugamar had learned from some locals they had encountered that there was a bridge over Bardlin Creek not far from Dallyn, and he would have preferred to have crossed there and searched the far bank of the creek on the way back to Siloa in order to save time. However, to top off the splendid luck they had been having thus far, this bridge had been destroyed in a recent brush fire, and although plans had been made to construct a new one out of stone, this future bridge would do them no good in their task at hand. So, just as Dugamar had said, they would have to hie all the way back to Siloa to cross Bardlin Creek and begin looking for Neldon on the far bank.

The lads agreed to this plan, and then they all attempted to fall asleep. This, however, proved rather difficult, for there were many malicious insects residing in the area they had chosen, and these repeatedly bit them and crawled all over them, tickling them with their tiny feet, so that the search party spent most of the night in misery, itching their bites and swatting the insects away.

Early in the morning, the party began the ride back to Siloa. It took them the better part of the day, but they arrived back in that vicinity several hours before sunset. Since Dugamar's plan was to search up the opposite bank of Bardlin Creek the next day, they needed to make several preparations for this second journey. For one thing, they needed to visit the Gleanworthy farm to request permission to borrow the horses for two additional days. Also, Dugamar wanted to go by his own cottage to get more supplies and tell his wife of their doings. However, he decided to make their first stop Broadbuckle Bakery, for he felt it essential to update Neldon's mother, Flinny, about how the search had gone before they did anything else.

The party thus hastened to the bakery at the north end of town. Since they didn't find Flinny in the bakery proper, they went to check in the Broadbuckles' house, which was connected to it by a short hallway. The group entered the Broadbuckle dining room, hoping to find Neldon's mother there. However, great was their surprise when they found not Neldon's mother, but Neldon himself! The lad was quite alive and well, sitting at the dining table and chowing down on a variety of victuals. These included an assortment of confections, for although Neldon's mother normally tried to curb his sweet tooth, she was so pleased to receive him back safe and sound that she permitted him to have an array of desserts.

"Neldon, how in all Orona did you get back here before we did?" Girion asked in disbelief. "And what became of our raft?"

"Oh, hello, Girion. And everyone else too! And –" he stopped to think. "Our raft!" he exclaimed. "I totally forgot about it when I left the Bushbelt! Well, I suppose it's too late to go back and get it now."

"The Bushbelt? Whatever are you talking about?" asked Aradis.

"Yes, I've been there," said Neldon matter-of-factly. "And it's quite different from what you thought, Girion. The natives are actually very nice and many of them wear clothes too. And the ocean is big, but it's not as big as you made it out to be."

Suddenly, Neldon' mother entered the room and said, "He got off the raft somewhere near the settlement of Angalee, which lies down Bardlin Creek about twenty miles, although poor Neldon is convinced it's in the Bushbelt."

"It *is* in the Bushbelt, Mother. Hendrig said so," Neldon insisted.

"Someone from there was kind enough to bring Neldon home to us in a wagon," said Mrs. Broadbuckle. "That's who Neldon is referring to." Then, addressing her son, she said, "And Mister Hendrig was just playing along because he thought you were batty and wasn't sure what you'd do if he contradicted you, sweetie."

"No, he just told you that because he didn't want you to think he was from the Bushbelt," countered Neldon. "Because if you did, you might follow him back there and learn the secret location of his village. Unfortunately, I fell asleep on the way down the river on the raft and also in the wagon on the way back. That was probably because I was so exhausted from my adventures, even after a decent night's sleep. Anyway, since I was asleep, I actually don't know the secret location of his village either. And I missed a great deal of what was probably really wonderful scenery besides."

"You're not serious," Darmon said, his jaw dropping. "There's no way you actually think you went to the Bushbelt and back in two days."

"He most definitely is," said Tallis. "Look at him."

Neldon's face was as sincere as the elderberry pie he was presently eating.

"You've got your fair share of crazy theories, Neldon Broadbuckle," Corim exclaimed, "but this has got to be one of the craziest."

———•◆•———

Perhaps you are wondering if anyone was able to change Neldon's mind on the matter that afternoon. I am sorry to report that they were not. In fact, so convinced was Neldon of this fancy that, on the day after his return, he tried to get Fennadris Barleycroft to give him a medal and a plaque like he'd received in his dream or, at the very least, a parade in his honor. Much to Neldon's chagrin, the Dolnario categorically refused all of these requests, asserting that his claims about traveling to the Bushbelt were nothing short of ludicrous. And although Neldon continued to insist on the veracity of his account, he did eventually drop his demand for a medal or parade.

For years afterward, no one could disabuse Neldon of the notion that he'd been to the Bushbelt. His friends, his parents and practically everyone else in Siloa tried to make a dent in the idea, but were utterly unsuccessful. The lad stalwartly stuck by his story, though he was rather disappointed that no one believed him – or even pretended to.

However, this disappointment would have been rather offset for the lad if he knew what had become of his beloved *Koobachinky*. On the day after Neldon's departure, some lads from Angalee discovered it in the rushes of the pond where Neldon had left it. This pond, incidentally, is known as Uppiden Pond. The lads promptly appropriated its remaining supplies and actually established the raft itself as a ferry across Uppiden Pond. The raft was thus dubbed the Uppiden Ferry. In fact, it still serves as such to this very day, thus continuing its service to travelers, even though none of them are attempting a journey as ambitious as going to the Bushbelt. For such a journey as that requires a great deal of prowess and fortitude or perhaps just a host of mistaken assumptions and a lively imagination.

THE END

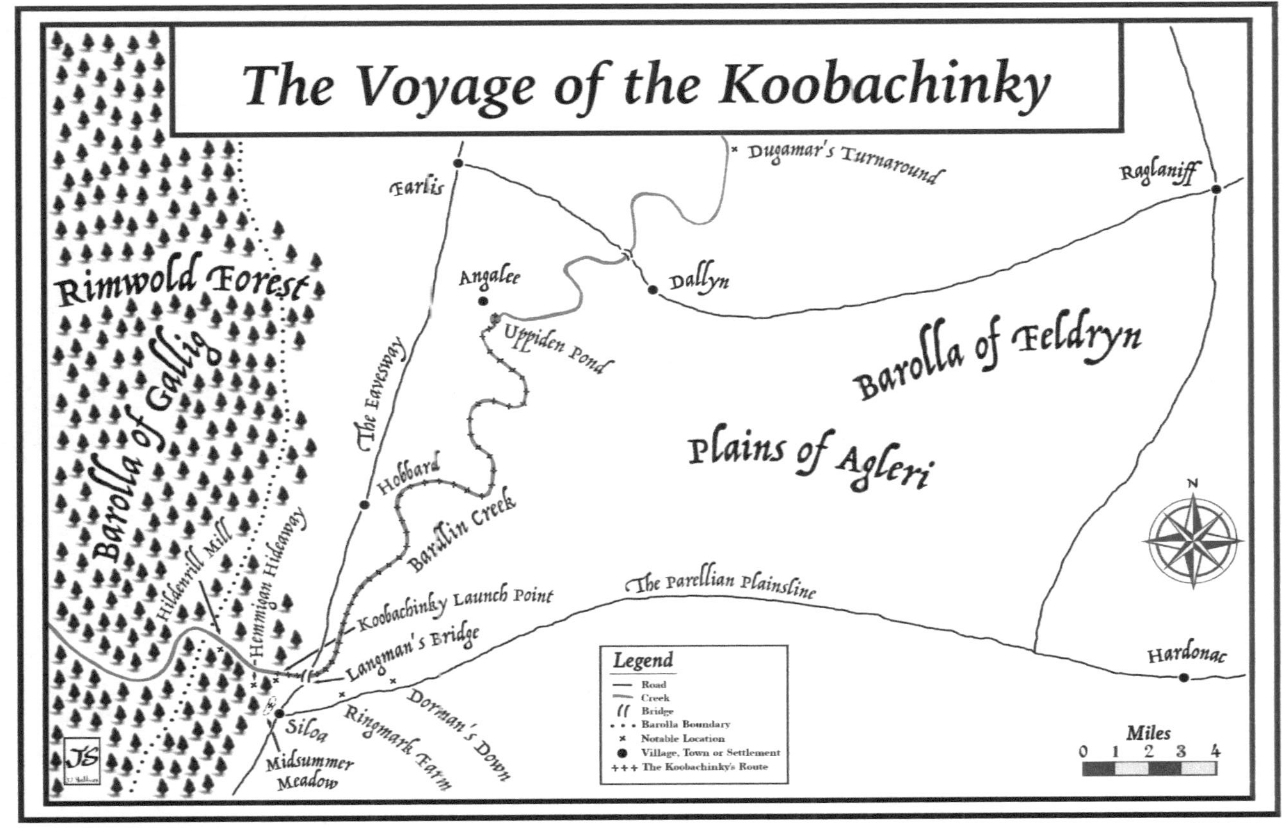

The Voyage of the Koobachinky
Rimwold Forest
Barolla of Gallig
Hildenrill Mill
Hemmigan Hideaway
Siloa
Midsummer Meadow
Ringmark Farm
Dorman's Down
Langman's Bridge
Koobachinky Launch Point
Barellin Creek
Hobbard
The Eavesway
Uppiden Pond
Angalee
Tarlis
Dallyn
Dugamar's Turnaround
Raglaniff
Barolla of Feldryn
Plains of Agleri
The Parellian Plainsline
Hardonac
N
Legend
Road
Creek
Bridge
Barolla Boundary
Notable Location
Village, Town or Settlement
The Koobachinky's Route
Miles
0 1 2 3 4

Pandemonium at the Prandingars' Pageant

CHAPTER ONE

An Account of Auditions in Midsummer Meadow

ll the youth of Siloa were abuzz and astir up in Midsummer Meadow, which lay just to the west of town, for the auditions for the Prandingars' Pageant were about to commence. Fennadris Barleycroft, the Dolnario, the highest (and practically only) government official in Siloa, was leading them, with assistance from his wife, Lannamil, as well as Stammarick Sideboarder and Coribel Tineshine. These latter two had performed major roles in the pageant on multiple occasions when they were younger.

There was a contingent of timid boys and girls among those congregated there who weren't going to audition at all, and thus would be designated either as "Villagers of Sallgart" or "Groddevar's Soldiers," which were just fancy titles for anyone who wasn't selected to play a particular character. However, most present were aiming for one of the prominent roles, particularly the parts of Falderon, the main hero, or Ferlisa, his beloved.

Neldon Broadbuckle was thoroughly convinced he would get one of the main parts this year, and he confidently told his companions so.

"I shall likely be playing Falderon this go round," said Neldon, "so don't be too disappointed if none of you gets the part."

"Ha!" laughed Corim Timberfall. "You wouldn't get the part of Falderon even if you were the only one auditioning."

"There's no way you really think they'd pick you for Falderon," added Tallis Pestleman.

"Yeah, Neldon, I'm not even sure you're a shoo-in for one of the Villagers of Sallgart," cackled Darmon Barnwain.

Neldon frowned. "What makes you so sure I won't get Falderon? And are you really being serious or are you just trying to bring me down so one of you can get the part instead?"

"Listen, Neldon," sighed Aradis Kingblade. "How many years now have you told us that you're going to get the part of Falderon? Every year you've been eligible, right?"

"Yeah," Neldon answered.

"And how many of those years have they just made you a Villager of Sallgart or one of Groddevar's Soldiers?" Aradis asked.

"All of them," Neldon replied, blinking.

"So what makes you think this year's going to be any different?" asked Corim.

"I just have that yumscious feeling in my belly that something magnifulous is going to happen," Neldon returned cheerily.

"That's probably just your breakfast," Tallis muttered.

"Too many turnovers will turn your stomach over, you know," chuckled Darmon.

"I didn't have any turnovers for breakfast today," said Neldon, rather affronted. "Just two blueberry tarts, six tarmin cookies and a small cherry pie."

"All without your mother's permission, we can assume?" said Aradis.

"Well, she let me have one of the blueberry tarts. The rest I just helped myself to, I guess," Neldon admitted. "But anyway, I figured she wouldn't mind – if having a healthy breakfast helped me land the role of Falderon, that is."

"Just objectively speaking," chimed in Girion Ringmark, "I don't think what you just described qualifies as a 'healthy breakfast.'"

"And objectively speaking," said Corim, "Girion has a thousand times better chance than you of getting the part of Falderon, Neldon. After all, he's had training as a thass – thesser – what's that word again?"

"Thespian," Girion supplied.

"Yeah, one of those," Corim said.

"Yes, while I was at Lavrassi Academy in Aragest, thespian courses were mandatory," Girion said modestly. "And when we had performances, I generally got decent parts. But that doesn't necessarily mean I'll get a main part this year."

"Oh, come on. You were one of the three prandingars last year," said Tallis. (The prandingars were the narrators of the pageant.) "This year, they might well choose you for Falderon."

"I doubt it," Girion replied.

"Hoyah, lads and lasses!" called the Dolnario suddenly. "It's time for the auditions to begin. If you don't want to audition, you can just stay where you are. But as for the rest of you: boys, form up a nice and tidy line by Mr. Sideboarder and myself, and young ladies, form up your line by Mrs. Tineshine and my lovely wife. Any squabbles, and you'll be sent straight to the back of the line. Understood?"

"Aye," the youth answered and then moved as Mr. Barleycroft had directed them.

Soon, the auditions were underway, with the youth watching each performance intently. Neldon and his friends were toward the back of their line, so they knew it would be quite a while before the time came for their own auditions. In the meantime, they were mouthing through their lines for the parts they were aiming for, each determined to impress Mr. Sideboarder and Mr. Barleycroft with his own dramatic rendering of dialogue from the ancient legend of Falderon.

Almost no one in Siloa could read, but folk there have excellent memories. Thus, many youth could correctly recall lines from previous years. Also, if there were ever any uncertainties about the pageant's dialogue, they could consult a certain potter in town, Tas Wedgenware, about them. He was one of the only ones in Siloa who could read, and he had purchased a copy of the story of Falderon from a traveling merchant a number of years ago. It was an embellished and altered version of the oldest and most reliable text of the legend, but the Siloa pageant took some liberties of its own anyway, so no one was bothered by this fact.

Of course, though all the lads and lasses who were auditioning were doing so with specific parts in mind, it was up to the directors of the pageant to decide which parts to put them in, so one might get a role either more or less prominent than the one he was auditioning for. Naturally, they all hoped for an upgrade rather than a demotion if they weren't going for one of the biggest parts.

To properly comprehend how intense the stakes were in this audition, it must be noted that the Prandingars' Pageant came only once a year and was attended by virtually everyone in Siloa, so it was an enormous affair in the life of the village. Thus, getting a substantial part in it was the closest thing to fame that a Siloan youth could hope for in a town of not much more than four hundred people in the village proper and only several hundred more outside of it. Besides, it was part of a tradition stretching back several thousand years (though not in Siloa, of course, since that village had only been founded as recently as 463 of the Latter Epoch, a mere 249 years ago).

The Prandingars' Pageant was held every year in Siloa on the 23rd of Tannaril, at the height of summer, for this was the day of the Festival of Falderon. This festival was celebrated throughout Velaris, the kingdom in which Siloa lay, and it was observed in many other places in the world of Orona as well. However, it actually originated in a high mountain range known as the Dargens on the Neathmarda of Tassaru, which lay in northern Orona.

In that place, several thousand years ago, there was said to have been a wicked Elven ruler named Groddevar who oppressed an Elven people known as the Helgonians and even went so far as to feed maidens from a particular village, Sallgart, to a great, hairy, six-legged beast dubbed the Malg. However, a Helgonian lad named Falderon, with the help of a mysterious old woman, a being of Helgonian lore called a drannenfross, slew the Malg with a magical torch and sword. In so doing, he also rescued his beloved Ferlisa, a maiden of Sallgart, who was supposed to have been the Malg's next meal. He is reputed to have done this on the 23rd of Tannaril, which was in the midst of winter in the Dargens. Then, three years later on this very same date, he is said to have killed Groddevar himself, also with the drannenfross' aid.

This story was passed down and ultimately recorded by the prandingars, the bards of the Dargen-Elves, those Elves who inhabited the Dargens. And in later years, the tale was memorialized in an observance of the Festival of Falderon on the date of Falderon's two great victories. Due to the prominence of the Dargen-Elves and their culture in the history of Orona, the celebration of this event spread widely, first throughout northern Orona, and then even to the farther reaches of southern Orona, where Siloa lay.

The village of Siloa had, over the decades, added its own touches, deviations and adaptations to the Festival of Falderon. But for many years now, the Prandingars' Pageant had stood as the great centerpiece among all its other activities, which included eating, singing, dancing, storytelling, crafts and various forms of competition. And even though youths were the only ones who could participate in it, the adults of Siloa were all fully invested in the performances of their children, grandchildren and other relatives, particularly if they were portraying one of the lead characters.

Now, as the auditions for Mr. Barleycroft and Mr. Sideboarder went on, Neldon and his friends eventually reached the front of the line. Darmon went first and recited some lines from Lungrid, one of Falderon's captains. Tallis went next, opting for dialogue from the unambitious role of the Magistrate of Alschendorn, the city where Falderon was put on trial for opposing Groddevar. Then came Corim, with a somewhat obnoxious portrayal of Falderon, followed by Aradis' much better version of the same character. Girion was up next, with a chilling performance as the Malg, as he wanted to try something he thought would be more challenging this year. Neldon was the last of the friend group to go, and he put forward his very best rendition of the hero, Falderon. It was, however, much more like an audition of Falderon for the part of Neldon Broadbuckle in a pageant about Siloa than an audition by Neldon for the part of Falderon in an ancient legend. It was, in a word, hopelessly Neldonish.

After all the youths who wished to audition had done so, Mr. and Mrs. Barleycroft, along with Mr. Sideboarder and Mrs. Tineshine, went and stood a ways off in Midsummer Meadow to confer about the performances. The hopefuls waited nervously during the discussion, talking in low tones about how they thought they and others had done. But at length, the adults came back, and Mr. Barleycroft clapped his hands for attention.

"Good youths of Siloa, we have reached a consensus on all the roles for the Prandingars' Pageant," he announced. "You have all done very well today, but unfortunately, there can only be one person per each part. However, I think the individuals we have selected will do an excellent job in their roles."

Taking a great breath, he said, "Now, I'll just get straight to the names because I know that's what you're all waiting for. First, for the big one – for Falderon himself – we have none other than our very own Rannion Rillspan!"

The crowd cheered, and those standing nearby Rannion clapped him on the back, as he grinned wryly. Rannion was a handsome lad of sixteen with a winsome smile and a great deal of charisma. He was, in fact, the object of a great many Siloan lasses' desire, and even more so presently, as he was not engaged in any sort of relationship.

"I'll bet you he bribed old Barleycroft," Corim muttered. He had an intense dislike for Rannion, as the two of them had something of a negative history.

"I guess you didn't get Falderon, eh?" Darmon chuckled, elbowing Neldon.

"It was probably really close," Neldon whispered back quite sincerely.

Darmon shook his head, laughing.

Fennadris Barleycroft took another great breath and said, "And for our biggest female part, the Drannenfross, we have the extremely talented Fanella Berthaway!"

The youths were equally pleased with this selection, and many immediately congratulated the smiling Fanella.

"For the nefarious Groddevar," Mr. Barleycroft announced, "we've got the fantastic characterization of Crommenblatt Seedbucket."

The Seedbuckets were basically loathed by everyone in Siloa, so all thought this to be an excellent choice. Hence, there was enthusiastic cheering – and a good deal of snickering – for Crommenblatt, who was very proud indeed that he had gotten this part. The irony of his casting, it seemed, had not been perceived by him.

"Now, opposite the handsome and dashing Falderon," said Mr. Barleycroft, "we have the beautiful Ferlisa, who will be performed by Mayvelyn Rushwick."

Mayvelyn Rushwick was Siloa's female counterpart to Rannion and only a year his junior. She was very attractive in both looks and personality, and no small number of Siloan lads sought her affection. There was a great deal of applause on Mayvelyn's behalf, and her friends all earnestly praised her achievement of the coveted role of Ferlisa.

"She completely deserves it," sighed Corim longingly. He had taken a fancy to Mayvelyn several months ago and had been pining after her from afar ever since, but he was too nervous to say anything to her about his feelings.

After the clapping and congratulations for Mayvelyn had died down, Mr. Barleycroft went through the remainder of the cast. Dammorig Tillwater was to be lending his voice to the Malg, and Lissanel Yewlimb, Teric Kingblade and Tedge Timberfall were to be inside the large and unwieldy (and terribly hot and sweaty) Malg costume. The three prandingars, who would be narrating the three major sections of the pageant, were, in order, Callornia Clayspin, Dallis Pestleman and Talaysia Cantlecraft. Lungrid, Falderon's captain, would be portrayed by Belmo Swiftsaw, and Roldina, Falderon's mother, by Sindagil Barnwain. Berridon Greyloam would be taking the part of the Magistrate of Alschendorn and Morillo Puncheonstave that of the Dying Soldier from Urmensdal. Groddevar's Assistant No. 1 would be played by Pannagrin Berrydore and No. 2 by Stecko Wealdwalker. Remarkably and to everyone's great surprise, Neldon had gotten the part of Groddevar's Assistant No. 3.

When the Dolnario had finished announcing all the names, he directed those males who had gotten special parts to meet with Mr. Sideboarder; meanwhile, the females with special parts were to meet with Mrs. Tineshine. Simultaneously, he and his wife would be dividing the remaining youths into the roles of either Villagers of Sallgart or Groddevar's Soldiers.

As things turned out, Aradis, Corim and Girion were assigned to be Groddevar's Soldiers, while Tallis and Darmon ended up as Villagers of Sallgart.

When the adults had concluded all of their meetings with their respective groups, the Dolnario announced that there were no further activities for the day, so the youth were free to go. However, everyone was expected to be at the pageant's first practice in a few days, ready to work hard.

For several minutes after the adults had left for the village, the youths stayed up in Midsummer Meadow talking, mostly standing in little circles in their respective friend groups.

"Girion, I can't believe you didn't get a part," Aradis said incredulously. "Your Malg voice was so good. Plus, you've had training, and Dammorig hasn't had a lick of that."

Girion shrugged. "What can I say? The directors liked Dammorig's performance better, and they're the ones that make the call. I will admit I'm rather disheartened about it, though."

"Don't feel too bad," said Tallis. "None of us got parts either. Guess that shows what Sideboarder and Barleycroft know – ha! It's really –"

"I got a part," Neldon interjected, looking around at his companions rather smugly.

Corim rolled his eyes. "I'm not sure Groddevar's Assistant No. 3 really counts as a *part*, Neldon. It's more like a prop."

"You're just jealous because you didn't get a special role," Neldon returned.

"Trust me," said Corim, "I'm not in the least heartbroken over missing out on playing the dazzling character of Groddevar's Assistant No. 3. I mean, even the name sounds stupid. Plus, let's just stop for a moment and reflect on this fact: for the next few weeks, you have to be an assistant to who? Crommenblatt Seedbuckct. Sounds like an absolute nightmare. It's honestly not something you should be bragging about, Neldon. Really, it's more of a punishment than an achievement."

"I'll tell you what I'm annoyed about," said Darmon. "How did all of our siblings end up getting roles while we didn't?"

"Yeah," said Aradis. "Exactly. I mean, Teric and Tedge are in the Malg costume. Actually, that kind of serves those little ruffians right. I hope they bake in there. And Darmon, your sister got Roldina. And Dallis is one of the prandingars. I just don't get it."

"It's pretty annoying," Corim concurred. "But you know what really steams me?" he asked.

"What?" Tallis queried.

"Rannion getting Falderon, that's what," Corim fumed. "He's such a pompous applehead. Just look at him eating up all this attention."

Rannion was presently surrounded by a number of older boys, who were all laughing and having a grand old time with him and a number of older females who had gathered with them.

"It's pretty rough for you especially," Darmon said, "what with him getting to be with Mayvelyn Rushwick during the pageant and all."

"They're going to be kissing and stuff, you know," Neldon said quite tactlessly.

Corim shook his head disapprovingly. "He'd better not try to get frisky with her or I'll really let him have it. I can almost guarantee he's going to use this as an opportunity to weasel into her affections though."

"If you claim her first, it'll be a lot more difficult for him to do that, won't it?" asked Aradis.

"Hey," Tallis said, nudging Corim. "Mayvelyn's right over there. Why don't you go tell her how you feel about her and see what she says? If she turns you away, you'll be no worse off than you are now, right?"

"I don't know about that," Corim replied skeptically. "I'm not sure if she really knows how much I have to offer yet, so I don't want to blow things prematurely. But still … there is Rannion to consider." He stood there, looking back and forth between Rannion and Mayvelyn, who was chatting with her own group of friends.

"I'm going to do it," Corim suddenly declared. "Wish me luck."

"Good for you," said Darmon, clapping him on the back.

But, to Corim's dismay, as he began walking toward Mayvelyn, Rannion excused himself from his friends and also began walking toward Mayvelyn, although this was not because of Corim approaching, for he hadn't even noticed him. Rannion reached Mayvelyn's vicinity before Corim did and called out to her, "Hey, Mayvelyn! Great job getting Ferlisa. Just wanted to let you know I think you'll be great in that role."

"Thanks, Rannion," Mayvelyn replied bashfully. "And congratulations to you too. I think you'll make a fantastic Falderon."

Corim stopped in his tracks and gulped, his face burning. "He's doing it already, the big sleazebarrel," he stormed to himself.

"We'll have to get to know each other a little better, I reckon," said Rannion, "so we can portray our characters' relationship more effectively."

"I completely agree," laughed Mayvelyn, blushing. "That should help with the romantic scenes for sure."

"Yeah, there are a number of those from what I recall," said Rannion offhandedly. "We've got a couple kisses in there and then, of course, the big one during the wedding at the end."

Corim just about exploded in fury as Rannion was saying this. He couldn't stand even a moment more of this talk, so he turned on his heel and marched back to his friends.

"You just couldn't go through with it after Rannion cut in, eh?" mumbled Tallis, as Corim reached them.

"Tsk, tsk," chided Aradis, shaking his head. "What a sorry suitor you turned out to be."

"It's not funny, Aradis," Corim returned crossly. "Besides, given those circumstances, you wouldn't have said anything to her either. The timing just wasn't ... it wasn't appropriate."

"So what are you going to do now?" asked Darmon.

Corim's eyes narrowed, as he hissed, "Mark my words, lads. I'm going to make that Rannion Rillspan as sorry as a salted slug that he ever started making advances against my girl."

"Um, Corim," said Neldon, "isn't Mayvelyn actually not your girl right now? Doesn't she not even know that you like her?"

"That's beside the point, Neldon," said Corim, with great annoyance. "The fact is that she *ought* to be my girl. And since Rannion is stepping into our relationship uninvited, I'm going to make him pay for it. But I'll need some time to figure out exactly how."

A short while later, the youth up in Midsummer Meadow began to disperse, and Neldon went to Broadbuckle Bakery to tell his mother that he had garnered the role of Groddevar's Assistant No. 3. She was very proud of him and said she couldn't wait to see him perform in the pageant this year.

When Neldon's father got home from Hildenrill Mill in Rimwold Forest that evening, he was equally pleased. In fact, the Broadbuckle family had some extra desserts from their bakery that night to celebrate Neldon's achievement, for as Neldon's parents saw it, he was essentially the star of the pageant, at least in comparison to his usual generic, humdrum roles.

CHAPTER TWO

Bremmingwort, Talgenslip and Zandorgia

The first practice for the pageant came soon enough, and Neldon and his friends, along with the rest of Siloa's youth, spent several hours up in Midsummer Meadow with the four adult directors working through the main outline of the performance. There was a great deal to be discussed and rehearsed, so the time went quickly.

When the practice was over, Neldon and his friends were standing together, with Corim ranting about his hatred for Rannion Rillspan.

"Yes, yes, we all know you loathe Rannion," said Tallis, "but can we carry on the loathing while actually doing something productive?"

"Like what?" asked Corim. "Setting his house on fire?"

"Not exactly what I had in mind," Tallis replied. "I was thinking more along the lines of you fellows helping me and my brother Dallis find some herbs in the forest so it won't take us the rest of the afternoon. Our father needs some bremmingwort and talgenslip for some poultices." Tallis' father, Murraden, was Siloa's resident herbalist and not infrequently would enlist his sons to aid him in finding the necessary plants for his work if he were pressed for time.

"I'd love to go on a botanical expedition," enthused Girion. "There's still a great deal I don't know about the flora of Rimwold Forest, and it sounds like this might be something of an educational excursion."

"I already got all my chores done this morning, so I'm fine with going," said Aradis.

"I don't mind helping out," echoed Darmon.

"I'll go as long as I can still complain about Rannion," said Corim.

"Deal," returned Tallis.

Neldon scratched his head. "I thought we were going to set Rannion's house on fire. Is that still happening? Are we just doing that after we go to the forest?" he asked.

"You know you're not that far yet, Neldon," said Darmon, who could hardly contain his laughter.

"Just so all of you know," Neldon coughed, "I think burning his house down is going too far, so I would suggest doing something a little less extreme."

"We're not actually going to burn Rannion's house down," sighed Aradis. "It was a joke, Neldon."

"Not really," muttered Corim.

Girion nodded toward nearby Rimwold Forest. "Ahem. Shall we get this task underway?"

"Aye," Tallis replied. He motioned to his identical twin brother, Dallis, who joined them, and then the seven of them set off into the pines of Rimwold Forest.

———◦———

"We need to find a number of specimens of those two plants I mentioned," said Tallis, when they had gone some distance in. "Again, they're called bremmingwort and talgenslip."

"What do they look like, and where exactly do they grow?" asked Girion.

Dallis answered, "Bremmingwort grows on a short stalk and has clusters of eight or nine sharp, pointed leaves with rather rough texture. They're a fairly deep green, and the color fades to a dull purple near the edges of the leaves. You can find it near tree roots, but it especially likes to grow by malden trees."

"And what about talgenslip?" asked Aradis.

"That one is a little harder to find, just because it's more scarce," responded Tallis. "Talgenslip is a flower with droopy, little, dark-yellow blossoms. Most often you'll see it growing among patches of ferns. But, you know, once we locate a specimen of each plant, we can just show you exactly what they look like."

"Yeah, that will definitely help," said Darmon.

"Have you ever noticed how Rannion tosses his head like a total worm-bucket every time he says something he thinks is especially clever?" asked Corim. "I just hate it when he does that."

"I think it'd be safe to say that you hate it when Rannion does anything whatsoever," said Tallis, as he bent down to examine a patch of ferns. Sighing, he shook his head. "No talgenslip here. Let's go farther in. Once we find a good spot, we can spread out a bit and hunt separately."

The lads went another five furlongs into the forest, and then Dallis abruptly exclaimed, "Aha! Here's some bremmingwort." He knelt down by a large malden tree and carefully pulled up a short-stalked plant with sharp leaves. He showed it to the rest of the boys and said, "When you pick one of these, try to get as much of the root out as you can. Anyway, this is exactly what bremmingwort looks like. I bet there's some more growing around here."

"Oh, how delightful!" said Tallis. "And here's some talgenslip." He retrieved some from near the edge of a patch of ferns and held it out for his companions to examine. "See, there are the little flowers I was talking about. Now, let's spread out from here and try to find as much of these two plants as we can."

The lads quickly dispersed and began combing the forest for stalks of bremmingwort and talgenslip. Within several minutes, Girion and Darmon had each found some talgenslip and Aradis had located some bremmingwort. Tallis and Dallis, the true masters, had found more of each.

"Ooh," cried Neldon. "There you are!" He bent down and peered at what he suspected to be a healthy stalk of bremmingwort growing at the base of a quarmit tree. Rather clumsily, he extracted it from the soil and held it up triumphantly.

"I've got one! I've got one!" he shouted, running to Tallis, who was not far off.

"Bremmingwort or talgenslip?" Tallis inquired, as the other boys looked up to see what exactly Neldon had found.

Tallis took Neldon's plant in hand, laughing. "This is neither bremmingwort nor talgenslip."

Corim, who was nearby, walked over. "Neldon, that doesn't look anything like the descriptions we were given," he scoffed.

This was quite true. The plant Neldon had plucked was a dark purple with reddish streaks and had six smooth, shiny leaves with wavy edges.

Now, looking at Tallis, Corim asked, "What is this plant anyway?"

"The common name for it is moonweed," said Tallis. "The proper name is zandorgia, and it's actually rather rare to find it in these parts."

"Neldon found some moonweed?" Dallis asked, astonished, as he stood up from the fern patch where he had been poking around.

"Why is it called moonweed?" inquired Girion, who walked over to join Neldon, Tallis and Corim.

"People in olden times said it first grew on Eoreth, our lovely moon," explained Tallis, "and that, at some point, it fell down here to Orona."

"What's it good for?" asked Aradis, who was coming with Darmon to join the others.

"Nothing, really," replied Tallis. "Unless you consider causing insanity something worthwhile."

"It makes people crazy?" asked Corim.

"Essentially," said Tallis. "People – and animals too. And it takes effect quite swiftly too from what I remember hearing my father say. Within a minute or two, I think. Generally manifests as running around, thrashing, twitching and screaming."

"Our father said the effect is only temporary if you consume it once," explained Dallis. "But if you keep taking it, you'll be stuck that way."

"Sounds like a pretty worthless find to me," said Darmon.

"Mostly just a novelty," said Tallis, as he handed Neldon the plant.

"So this isn't bremmingwort?" asked Neldon dejectedly, squinting at his find.

"Nope," answered Tallis. "Just moonweed."

"Since it's kind of rare, do you think I could sell it to the tavenndi or something?" asked Neldon. (The tavenndi were roving traders who came through Siloa on occasion with wagons filled with random merchandise.)

"There's a chance of it," Tallis returned, "since they buy pretty much anything. But then again, even tavenndi, who are better at salesmanship than basically anybody, might have a hard time selling a stalk of moon-weed – which means it's not terribly likely they'll buy it from you."

"I'll take my chances," said Neldon boldly, as he tucked the moonweed in a pocket of his vest. "I think I'll just hold on to it until the next time the tavenndi come through and see what I can get for it."

"Suit yourself," said Tallis. "But don't say I didn't warn you if they turn you down."

After this, the seven lads continued hunting aroundp the forest for more bremmingwort and talgenslip. Sometime later, when they had collected a sufficient quantity of it, they all returned to Siloa, and Tallis and Dallis delivered the herbs to their father.

That evening, back at his house, Neldon put the moonweed he had found under his pillow right before he lay down for the night.

"You're going to make me famous someday," Neldon whispered to the plant. "Hopefully the tavenndi will realize what a treasure you are and give me the huge sum of money you're worth." Then he flopped on his bed, with his head resting soundly on his pillow, and he soon fell asleep.

CHAPTER THREE

The Difficulties of Groddevar's Assistant No. 3

n the next few weeks, there were a number of practices for the pageant, and all of the youths were required to be at every single one of them, though not necessarily to stay for the entire duration. Regardless, this meant a lot of sitting around for the Villagers of Sallgart and Groddevar's Soldiers. This also gave Corim plenty of time to stew over Rannion and Mayvelyn, who had a budding relationship offstage, and Aradis and Girion plenty of time to rib him about the matter. They continued urging him to approach Mayvelyn about his feelings, but he was much too distraught about the situation with Rannion to say anything to her. Darmon and Tallis mostly behaved themselves but did engage in pranks on their fellow Villagers of Sallgart here and there during rehearsals to alleviate their boredom.

While the others were working to stave off the tedium of twiddling their thumbs for hours, Neldon was battling various difficulties with his role. One was forgetting his lines, which was rather unfortunate, since he had so few of them. Another was putting his costume on incorrectly. Groddevar's other two assistants actually had to assist Neldon virtually every single practice with some item or other that had been donned improperly (the most frequent culprits being his bandolier and ascot). Needless to say, this caused them no small amount of annoyance. And this was only fueled further by the fact that Neldon didn't even need to be in his costume at this stage of the rehearsal process; no one else would be using their costumes until the last week before the performance. However, Neldon had received special permission from Mr. Barleycroft to wear his soldier garb this early on, as he insisted that doing so helped him get "more in touch with his character."

Also, as Groddevar's Assistant No. 3, one of Neldon's responsibilities was to escort Groddevar (or rather, Crommenblatt Seedbucket, who was playing Groddevar) pretty much everywhere he went. Pannagrin Berrydore and Stecko Wealdwalker, Groddevar's Assistants Nos 1 and 2, respectively, were to march in front of and to either side of him, and Neldon was to march behind. The only problem was that Neldon didn't pay close enough attention to when Crommenblatt stopped, so on many occasions, he continued marching straight into him. When he did so, Crommenblatt would turn and yell at him for his clumsiness. Neldon would apologize, but then, a short while later, he would forget to pay attention to what he was doing, and it would happen again, with the same results.

The directors actually thought this was a humorous bit that Neldon and Crommenblatt had come up with on their own. They found Neldon's bumbling antics hilarious and thought it really added to the characterization of Groddevar as a mean-spirited maniac if he was constantly yelling at one of his guards, so they asked them to keep the routine. Crommenblatt reluctantly agreed, and Neldon wholeheartedly did so, as he was eager to please the directors. And although he frequently forgot that he was supposed to be running into Crommenblatt, he kept doing it anyway because he got distracted so often. The fact that it happened at random times made it, in the opinion of the directors, that much more comical.

But there was something about Neldon's performance that the directors did not find comical at all – his ineptitude with a particular horse that was featured in one of the main scenes of the pageant. And it was not only the directors who were annoyed with Neldon about his gaffs with this animal: it was everyone because Neldon's incompetence in this regard was an issue at virtually every single practice.

Early on in the pageant's middle section, Groddevar was supposed to lend Falderon a horse for him to ride to the Malg's cave. In the original story, the horse was given as an act of mockery, since it was an old nag, and Groddevar was completely confident that Falderon would be devoured by the Malg. To stay true to this, the pageant committee had asked an elderly chap who lived not far north of town, Camlin Micklemare by name, if they could borrow one of his older horses for this segment of the performance. When they were rehearsing this section, Camlin would show up with his old mare, Delinah, so that Neldon could usher her to Rannion at Crommenblatt's command. But every single time Neldon tried to lead the horse across the meadow, something went awry. Sometimes Delinah would run off. Other times she wouldn't move at all. And still other times she would just keep going round and round in circles. The one thing she wouldn't do was follow Neldon where she was supposed to go, at least not until after the whole rehearsal had come to a screeching halt and Neldon had been publicly berated for his inability to lead Delinah.

Fennadris Barleycroft got more and more fed up with this business, until finally, at one particular practice, when the scene with Delinah was coming up, he asked Neldon, "Shall we just have Stecko lead Rannion's horse today? Since you're having such a difficult time with this, maybe the two of you could just switch parts."

"No, I promise I can do it," Neldon replied earnestly.

"All right, I guess we'll see how today goes," Mr. Barleycroft conceded.

When the time came for Neldon to bring the horse to Rannion, Crommenblatt called out loudly, "Come now, soldier mine, bring me a horse for this poor fool!"

Neldon scuttled off to where Camlin Micklemare was waiting with Delinah.

"Just take the halter and walk straight toward where you need to go," Camlin instructed. "Don't look at Delinah, don't talk to her and don't tug extra hard on the rope. Just take it and walk forward."

Neldon took a deep breath and did exactly as Mr. Micklemare had told him. Almost immediately, he came to an abrupt stop, for the rope had become quite taut. Delinah wasn't moving.

"Uh oh," said Neldon. He yanked hard to urge Delinah forward, but she wouldn't budge.

"So we're back to this again," sighed Mr. Barleycroft, as he watched Neldon struggle with the old mare. "Is there a problem with this particular horse, perhaps?" he called to Camlin Micklemare. "Should we get a different one?"

"No, sir," Camlin replied. "Delinah's docile as can be. No problem with her. I think the problem is with your horse-leader." He looked irritably at Neldon.

Neldon gulped. "Please, Delinah!" he whispered. "You've just got to follow me today."

The horse blinked at him and whinnied, then tossed her head. Still, she didn't budge.

"Go on, Delinah," said Camlin. "Follow the nice young Broadbuckle."

Abruptly, Delinah started moving forward. Neldon, who was tremendously relieved, walked in front of her all the way over to Rannion, who was trying hard not to break character and laugh while watching Neldon's embarrassing struggles with Delinah.

"Ride on, O great prince of the Helgonians!" cried Crommenblatt scathingly, as Rannion mounted Delinah.

"Mark my words, Groddevar. The Malg shall be no more ere dawn!" Rannion called back, as he rode off over the meadow.

Fennadris Barleycroft pulled Neldon aside as Rannion continued with the scene by eating a wafer the Drannenfross had given him and pulling a sword from the ground halfway across the meadow.

"Neldon, I know you really want to lead the horse like you're supposed to for your role," Mr. Barleycroft said, "but it just seems to not be working out. I honestly don't think it would be such a terrible thing if we had Stecko or Pannagrin lead the horse instead. It'd take a huge load off your nerves too if we made that change, I think."

"Oh, please, please, Mr. Barleycroft," Neldon pleaded. "Please let me lead Delinah. I told my parents about this part and everything, and they're really excited to see it. It's my biggest part in the whole show."

Mr. Barleycroft let out a big sigh, then said, "Oh, I suppose you can keep trying anyway. Hopefully it will get worked out by the performance. But that's in less than a fortnight, you know, so we don't have much time. If nothing else, try to play it off in a humorous vein. That seems to be working well with your acting for the rest of the pageant."

"Okay, I'll do whatever you want," Neldon promised, though he wasn't entirely sure what Mr. Barleycroft meant by playing things off in a "humorous vein" and he was even less sure what that had to do the rest of his acting. Indeed, poor Neldon had still not grasped that even his most earnest attempts to be refined and dramatic were seen by the directors as intentional comedy.

— ·◆· —

After practice was over that day, Neldon's friends inquired about his difficulties with the horse.

"What did old Barleycroft say?" asked Darmon. "Did he give your part with the horse to Stecko?"

"Nearly," Neldon replied. "But he said I could keep trying for now."

"What a pushover," muttered Corim.

"I just don't know what to do," Neldon lamented. "If only Delinah could understand People Talk, I bet she would do exactly what I told her."

"Animals don't need to understand People Talk to know what you want them to do," Girion explained. "They're very good at reading body language, emotion, energy and that sort of thing."

"What do you mean?" asked Neldon.

"What Girion is getting at is that Delinah's not following you because you're really nervous around her and clearly lack confidence," Aradis explained. "She can tell that you're uneasy and so she doesn't want to follow you. If you give off a sense of being sure and strong, she'll be more likely to do what you want. But as it is now, anyone could tell from a mile away that you're as jittery as a twippertan every time you try to lead her to Rannion."

Neldon pondered this. "I still think it'd be better if she could understand People Talk. But I guess I'll try your method and see what happens."

The boys went to their separate homes soon after this conversation, and Neldon spent some time wandering around his house, pretending to be confident and leading an imaginary Delinah from one room to another. His imaginary steed responded reasonably well to this technique, and so Neldon was optimistic about trying the same thing with the real Delinah at the next practice.

When the next practice did come around, things went much better, though not perfectly, with Neldon leading Delinah to Rannion. Considerably relieved by this, Neldon felt that as long as he could keep up at least a decent execution of this task, this beloved horse-leading segment of his wouldn't be jeopardized.

On the evening of that practice, a few tavenndi rolled up to Siloa with their wagons full of merchandise and opened them up for business on a grassy area to the northwest of town that was known, quite appropriately, as Tavenndi Lawn. When Neldon heard that the tavenndi were in town, he recalled that he had resolved to sell one of them his moonweed. (A number of them had come through in the preceding weeks, but Neldon had forgotten about his moonweed until just now.) So, he rushed to his bedroom, pulled out the moonweed from under his pillow, and then raced to Tavenndi Lawn to see if he could persuade one of the merchants to purchase it from him. To his great disappointment, they all turned him down, so he dejectedly began walking home without having garnered so much as a single tarion for his attempt.

"I guess I'll just have to find another use for this moonweed," he sighed, looking at the wilted plant in his hand. "I just don't know what. What can you even do with a plant that makes people crazy?"

<hr>

During the following week, the practices for the pageant were longer and more intense, and the youth started running the drama all the way from start to finish at each rehearsal. They also transported the remaining props, costumes, set pieces and so forth up to Midsummer Meadow from a barn known as the Falderon Shed, which was just to the north of Tavenndi Lawn. All of this pageant paraphernalia was stored in this barn during the rest of the year and was only taken up to the meadow in the weeks preceding the 23rd of Tannaril, which is when the Festival of Falderon was held. After the performance, it was returned to the Falderon Shed until the following summer.

Shortly after the auditions for this year's pageant, the youth had begun progressively moving these items to Midsummer Meadow so that they could reconstruct the sets, touch up props and make any necessary adjustments to their costumes. But there were certain things they didn't add until the last few practices. This was for various reasons, such as to avoid these items being damaged by inclement weather or simply because they weren't essential until the performance itself came around. The Malg costume was only brought up for the final dress rehearsal, as children had passed out inside it from the heat in previous years, and Mr. Barleycroft wanted to minimize the risk of this recurring.

Now, before a practice one afternoon just a few days before the 23rd, a number of youths, including Neldon and his friends, were assigned by Mr. Sideboarder to transport one of the final loads of items from the Falderon Shed up to Midsummer Meadow. Neldon and Corim were jointly (and rather awkwardly) carrying a piece of the set for the Malg's cave when Corim remarked, "It looks like your scene with Delinah has been going better ever since we had that discussion about it."

"Yeah, I think it has," Neldon said. "I'm still pretty nervous something will go wrong though, especially at the performance."

"That's totally understandable," returned Corim sympathetically. "I still think your original idea was the best, though," he added nonchalantly.

"Which idea are you talking about?" Neldon asked, struggling to remember that he had any ideas about the matter at all.

"The one about getting Delinah to understand People Talk," Corim replied. "If she could understand what you were saying, things would go just as smooth as a slicked-up sancalla."

"They certainly would," Neldon agreed. "I don't know how to make horses understand People Talk though."

"I do," Corim said matter-of-factly.

"You do?" Neldon asked, excitedly. He was, in fact, so exhilarated at this that he fumbled his end of the set piece, and it dropped with a thud onto the grass.

"Hey, pay attention to what you're doing!" Corim exclaimed, as he almost dropped his own end, which was rather heavy. As Neldon was picking his end up again, Corim warned, "If we break one of these set pieces, Sideboarder'll kill us."

"Oh, right. Now, how do you make horses understand People Talk?" Neldon whispered.

"You still have that moonweed, don't you?" Corim asked.

"Actually, I tried to sell it to the tavenndi," Neldon replied.

"You what?!" Corim returned angrily, nearly losing his grip on his end of the set piece.

"I tried to sell it to the tavenndi," Neldon repeated. "Sadly, none of them were interested. So I still have it under my pillow."

"Oh, that's goo – I mean, oh, that's too bad," Corim sighed. "Although, since you still have it, you may as well use it for something."

"Like what?" Neldon asked.

"Getting that old mare to understand you," Corim slyly returned.

"What old mare?" Neldon inquired.

"Delinah," Corim said irritably. "See, it's like this. If you give that moonweed of yours to Delinah right before the performance, she'll be able to understand when you talk. And what's more, she'll even be able to use People Talk herself. If you don't listen carefully, it will probably just seem like she's making horse sounds. But if you really focus, you'll be able to hear her using words just like you and me."

"Really?" Neldon asked, his jaw dropping in wonderment.

"Honest as torlinberry pie," Corim assured.

"But I thought Tallis said it just made people and animals crazy," said Neldon.

"Ah, he was just saying that because he didn't want you to know what a valuable find your moonweed really was. He was probably hoping you'd think it was worthless, so you'd just give it away to him."

"Huh. I never would've guessed that," said Neldon. "That was awfully sneaky of him. But if this plant's so valuable, why wouldn't any of the tavenndi buy it from me?"

"None of them are herb experts like Tallis is," Corim replied after a slight hesitation. "So I'm sure they didn't know what they were passing up."

"Oh, I see." Neldon nodded knowingly. "So how do I use it on Delinah? Do I have to do anything special with it?"

"Nope, just feed her the whole plant right before you lead her out to Rannion."

"That sounds easy enough," Neldon sighed, relieved. "And you promise it'll work?"

"It'll work all right," Corim said, with an impish smile. "Oh, and by the way, don't say anything to Tallis or the others about all this. Tallis in particular might be mad that I ratted him out, so it's better to just keep it to yourself. Also, make sure you save the entire plant for the performance. Don't waste it on any of the rehearsals."

"Okay," Neldon said. "And I promise I won't tell," he whispered dramatically.

"Solemn oath of secrecy?" Corim asked.

"Solemn oath of secrecy," Neldon returned, as he let go of the set piece to shake Corim's hand. This sudden shift of balance with the set piece caused Corim to drop his own end on his foot.

"Neldon!" he hollered. "Why are you such a dingleflobbin?"

After the boys picked up the heavy set piece again, Neldon said, "I'm sure sorry about that, Corim."

"It's fine, Neldon," Corim replied grudgingly. "Just don't do it again."

Neldon sniffed to blow away a fly that had started buzzing around his head, and then he said, "Hey, Corim, I was just wondering if you ever figured out anything to do to get back at Rannion for stealing your girl Mayvelyn. I know you've been pretty upset about that ever since we started working on the pageant. It has to be really awful to watch them kiss and whatnot multiple times at each practice."

"I actually would appreciate it if you wouldn't remind me of that," Corim said bitterly. "But, as a matter of fact, I do think I've figured out a way to serve Rannion a steaming plate of proper humility."

"Oh, yeah? What is it?" asked Neldon, intrigued.

"You'll see," Corim returned, grinning deviously.

The boys shortly delivered their set piece to Midsummer Meadow, where others were assembling the Malg's cave. A while later, the practice was underway. When the time came for Neldon to lead Delinah, he only barely managed to get her to cooperate. However, he gained no small amount of confidence from knowing that he would be able to use the moonweed at the performance itself.

In the last few practices before the actual performance, Neldon's horse leading started going rather ill again. Thus, Neldon feared greatly that Mr. Barleycroft would still assign the task to either Stecko or Pannagrin. However, this fear was unwarranted, for Mr. Barleycroft had essentially resigned himself to this portion of the pageant being loused up by Neldon, as he simply hadn't the heart to pull the task from the lad.

CHAPTER FOUR

Delinah's Disastrous Debut

inally, the 23rd of Tannaril dawned. It was a beautiful day, with a delightful breeze and rich sunlight and all the brightness and gaiety one could wish for at a festival during high summer. The adults in town had spent the previous day and evening making preparations for the festival by setting up stages in Midsummer Meadow, making food and rehearsing various musical acts. Now the landscape of this greensward next to the eaves of Rimwold Forest was bordered with all the trappings of a great market fair or gala. Colorful buntings of blue, green and red were strung around the edges of the meadow. (These particular hues were employed to represent the Vallensanger, the Festival of Falderon's three main virtues, which are cunning, strength and courage.) And standing on the meadow's eastern border were many long tables covered with bright tablecloths and laden with a great variety of edibles. At the meadow's north end were a number of tents, pavilions and stages, and there were a few of these at the meadow's southern end as well.

In the middle of Midsummer Meadow stood the now fully constructed sets from the Prandingars' Pageant as memorials of ancient times of heraldry, heroism and magic. There was Groddevar's looming fortress of Schardenveld, the forbidding lair of the Malg, the merry village of Sallgart, Groddevar's rustic forest lodge and the polished tribunal of Alschendorn. In the midst of all these was the wedding bower of Falderon and Ferlisa near a large basin filled with water, which was supposed to represent Lake Emmerloss, where the two were married in the ancient legend. Although these sets would be regarded as crude and wholly inadequate by those from larger cities in the Kingdom of Velaris, such as Aragest, Belestro, Rondo and Tarwyn, to the people of Siloa they were absolutely magnificent.

The morning of the Festival of Falderon was filled with all kinds of activities, competitions and games for all ages. Many of the elderly folk sat around and told stories, while younger children chased each other about on the verge of Rimwold Forest. Older children milled about in groups, going from pavilion to pavilion, eating and watching various competitions. Many adults did likewise or else sat in the shade of the tents, catching up with their friends on all the latest happenings in Siloa.

There were multiple races and contests of all kinds: ones for cooking, baking, eating, drinking, throwing, storytelling, music, crafts and many more besides. Girion won (by a significant margin) multiple throwing contests, as well as a musical competition in which he performed on the kindarra, a five-stringed fretted instrument that he had learned to play with great proficiency. Darmon placed first in a juggling contest. Neldon won several eating contests, and Aradis got second in finishing an obstacle course. Rannion, much to Corim's infuriation, beat him in a log-chopping competition, though neither of them actually won. First place went quite deservedly to a strapping lad named Trabbis Woodhew, who lived west of town.

Around the Crown of Marda, when the sun was at its zenith, most of the villagers lay on blankets at Midsummer Meadow's edge for a short nap or else retired to various pavilions to luncheon. And about an hour later, the festival's activities picked up again. Then, as late afternoon (known as the Journey of Marda in Orona) drew nigh, the youth of Siloa withdrew from the merriment and began to prepare for the Prandingars' Pageant.

Fennadris Barleycroft and his wife gave the youth an inspirational talk before they all went to get in their costumes and rehearse any troublesome lines a final time on their own. They also issued reminders about certain parts of the performance that had been problematic throughout the course of their rehearsals. This, of course, included Neldon's segment with the horse. However, Neldon took this reminder without so much as a twinge of anxiety, for he had put the moonweed in his vest pocket that morning and was looking forward to finally being able to execute his part the way it was meant to be done all along.

When the Barleycrofts' speeches were over, the youth moved just inside Rimwold Forest to an area that served as a dressing room of sorts for them. Neldon received aid one last time from Pannagrin and Stecko in fixing his bandolier, and then he made sure to put his moonweed stalk in a pocket of his uniform where it would be readily accessible.

Rannion walked by Neldon on his way to talk to Mayvelyn and asked, "Hey, Neldon, do you think you can handle bringing me my horse today?"

"I sure do," Neldon replied confidently.

"Really? Well, that'll be a first!" Rannion laughed, as he walked off.

Just a few moments later, Corim approached Neldon and asked, "You remember what we talked about? You're going through with it, right?"

"Yep," Neldon answered, briefly showing Corim the stalk of moon-weed.

"Perfect," Corim said, striking his hands together with great satisfaction. "You'll do great, Neldon. I just know it."

Corim now walked off to speak with his older brother, Branko. The two of them withdrew to somewhere they could talk privately for a few minutes, and both came back smiling and laughing. After a parting wink to Branko, who was one of the Villagers of Sallgart, Corim went to join Aradis and Girion, who were standing with the rest of Grod-devar's Soldiers.

"You seem awfully chipper right now," Aradis said, as Corim whistled gleefully.

"Yeah," remarked Girion, "and it seems a little incongruous with the fact that your beloved Mayvelyn and your archenemy Rannion are about to smooch in front of the entire village and then go through a pretend wedding ceremony."

"For all you know, it might not turn out that way," Corim replied cheekily, tossing his head and smoothing his hair with his hands. "You know what they say – any tale can take a tumble or a turn. The pageant's not over until it's over."

"You've got some mischief cooking," said Aradis. "I just know it. Otherwise there's no way you'd be so cheery."

"I guess we'll just have to wait and see if your theory's correct, won't we?" Corim teased.

Girion gave Aradis a knowing look and said, "Oh, he's got something planned. No doubt about it."

A few minutes later, Mr. Sideboarder and Mrs. Tineshine came to the forest to get the youth in their places to enter the meadow for the beginning of the pageant. Meanwhile, Mr. Barleycroft was speaking to all the rest of the people of Siloa, who were sitting on the eastern verge of the meadow, waiting for the performance to commence. Among them were Neldon's father and mother, Drampo and Flinny, as well as his older brother Quinty and his family. All of them were bursting with pride and excitement to see Neldon's portrayal of Groddevar's Assistant No. 3.

Shortly, the official signal to get things underway came from Mrs. Barleycroft, and the cast filed out to begin the opening scene, which was narrated by Callornia Clayspin and consisted of the Villagers of Sallgart migrating to the Dargens, the mountain range where the Legend of Falderon was set. (For the purposes of Siloa's pageant, the Dargens were represented by Midsummer Meadow.) The Villagers of Sallgart then began to tend their new land, until Groddevar and his minions came along and started terrorizing them. Crommenblatt got to go around yelling at and kicking his fellow Siloan youth during this part, and actually seemed to enjoy this segment much more than he should have. This scene also featured the first instance of Neldon bumping into Crommenblatt, which the audience greatly enjoyed.

The pageant proceeded with a pivotal scene in which the Drannenfross, portrayed by Fanella Berthaway, confronted Groddevar in his fortress and made a prophecy against him. After this, Rannion, as Falderon, was introduced talking to his mother Roldina, who was played by Darmon's older sister Sindagil.

Next came a stint at which Corim cringed every single time: Rannion's farewell to Mayvelyn, who was playing Ferlisa. The two pledged their love to each other before Rannion went off to fight against Groddevar's minions. Rannion was then seen roving the countryside attacking Groddevar's Soldiers until he was captured and tried by Berridon Greyloam, who was playing the part of the Magistrate of Alschendorn. Corim always enjoyed this segment because, after the trial, he and some others got to carry Rannion off and lock him in Groddevar's dungeon.

After this was a section in which the Malg arrived in the Dargens and attacked a number of Groddevar's Soldiers, all of whom perished except for Morillo Puncheonstave, who ran and reported the Malg's arrival to Groddevar before dying as well. Subsequently, the Malg took up residence in the cave set at the north end of the meadow, and Crommenblatt schemed in his fortress about how to use this to his advantage, ultimately deciding to feed maidens of Sallgart to the Malg, one each week. And at this point, the first section of the pageant came to an end.

There was a brief intermission, and the audience dispersed to get food and drink before sitting back down. The sun had gotten lower in the sky, so it wasn't quite as hot now, but there were still several hours of daylight left, and a cool breeze was blowing. Ale had made folk merry, as had numerous helpings of wild strawberries, tarmin cakes and torlinberry pie with mint and cream. The audience had tremendously enjoyed the first third of the pageant and was very much looking forward to the next portion. There was a general consensus that the key actors and actresses this year were some of the best they'd had in a long time.

In the second part of the pageant, Dallis Pestleman took over for Callornia Clayspin as the narrator, and his voice rang out over the meadow during a scene in which Falderon was languishing in Groddevar's dungeons. However, the ever-timely Drannenfross showed up to rescue him and give him an enchanted wafer and a magic ring.

The next scene had Falderon confronting Groddevar in his lodge near the Malg's lair. When their conversation had concluded, Crommenblatt called to Neldon the cue line he had been waiting for the entire performance.

"Come now, soldier mine, bring me a horse for this poor fool!" Crommenblatt shouted.

Neldon saluted him and then hurried over to Rimwold Forest, where Camlin Micklemare was waiting for him with Delinah.

"Just lead her straight on like we've rehearsed," Camlin quietly directed. "Then you shouldn't have any problems."

"Don't you worry, Mister Micklemare," Neldon said stoutly. "I'm going to do it *perfectly* this time."

He began leading Delinah toward Crommenblatt and Rannion. Then, when he was a number of feet away from Camlin, he reached into his pocket, took out the moonweed and put it up by Delinah's mouth.

"Here you go. Try this," urged Neldon. "It will help you talk just like people and also understand everything I'm saying."

Delinah quickly licked the plant from Neldon's hand and began chewing it.

"Can you understand me now?" Neldon whispered.

Delinah snorted and let out a little whinny.

"Now, what did Corim say?" Neldon asked aloud. "Oh, yes. In order to understand her, I'm supposed to concentrate."

Delinah made a rather unusual sound, and Neldon scrunched up his face, as he tried to interpret it. "That was 'hello', wasn't it?" he decided. "Well, hello to you too, Delinah! Are you ready to let Rannion ride you to victory against the Malg?"

The old mare made another rather uncharacteristic sound.

"She actually understands me!" Neldon marveled. "And I think she just said she's ready." Looking back at the horse, he remarked, "You've just got to keep following me across the meadow, then, until we get to him."

The horse began coughing after a fashion and started shaking her head.

"Did you just say 'I like?'" asked Neldon. "If so, that's not very good grammar. This is your first time using People Talk though, so that's quite all right. And what do you like? The moonweed? I'm sorry, I don't have any more."

"Hurry up!" hissed Crommenblatt, who was trying to play his annoyance off as part of his character. Rannion likewise looked quite perturbed at Neldon's dallying. The lad had been going extra slow with Delinah so that he had more time to talk with her.

"Just keep going straight ahead," Neldon encouraged, as he guided the horse across the meadow. And for once, he didn't worry one bit about whether she was going to do what he asked.

Shortly, Neldon reached Rannion with the mare and whispered to her, "Thanks, Delinah. You're doing great. We'll talk more later."

Rannion rolled his eyes, as he jumped up on Delinah's back. Proudly, he rode off toward the lair of the Malg, where Lissanel Yewlimb, Teric Kingblade and Tedge Timberfall were waiting for him in a large, hairy costume.

However, as Rannion was crossing the meadow, he noticed that Delinah was starting to get rather jittery, and her head was moving back and forth in weird spasms. He consumed the wafer Fanella had given him, delivered some dialogue and then dismounted to retrieve a sword from the ground. By the time he got back on Delinah, her condition was noticeably worse. He rode forward, then dismounted once more to get a burning torch. This time, when he mounted Delinah, he felt her body twitching every few seconds.

"What in the blazes is going on?" he asked, as he tried to direct Delinah toward the Malg's lair. Sharply, he pulled on the bit in her mouth. However, this proved to be an extremely unwise decision.

Whinnying and braying wildly, Delinah mounted up on her hind legs and then bolted at breakneck speed toward the tables of food on the eastern edge of the meadow, with Rannion clinging desperately to the reins, terrified out of his wits. Right before Delinah bounded into the table area, she got her legs caught on some of the bunting that ran along the border of the meadow and then careened at full speed into a table with a large heap of fruits, iced cakes and nuts that had been carefully arranged around a bowl of ruby-red punch. A great deal of punch and cake ended up on Rannion, who dropped the torch he was holding. The unfortunate cascade of events continued as the torch caught a tablecloth on fire.

Rannion managed to leap from Delinah's back as she stood up. Now rid of her panicked passenger, she turned around and galloped off toward the Malg's lair, shaking the bunting off as she went. Rannion frantically tried to escape from the fire on the tablecloth, but he ended up dragging the burning cloth with him to the bunting, which then caught flame. Then, his predicament worsened still further, as he got some of the bunting wrapped around his legs as well. The audience had by this point all risen to their feet and were rushing to Rannion's aid and also attempting to stamp out the fire. And Camlin Micklemare was running across the meadow, trying to get to Delinah and calm her down.

Meanwhile, Neldon was watching all of this mayhem unfold from afar, horrified. He rather suspected that this was all due to him feeding Delinah the moonweed but wanted to ask Corim first whether insane behavior was a side effect of horses being able to comprehend and produce People Talk.

"I just don't understand. She's never done this before!" Neldon kept saying over and over again, as he shook his head in dismay.

The three children who were inside the Malg costume were dreadfully frightened when Delinah entered the cave set and started thrashing about, so they quickly exited the set via the large opening in its east side that allowed the audience to see into it. Immediately, they took off running across the meadow, still inside their costume. Meanwhile, Corim let out a cry to the rest of Groddevar's Soldiers. He had been waiting for the frenzy to escalate and was now ready to add to it. "Attack!" he yelled, and started running at a full sprint toward the Villagers of Sallgart, who were all clustered in another part of the meadow. Many of the children playing Groddevar's Soldiers were so perplexed, astounded and disturbed by all that had just happened that they just went along with this bizarre order and ran off after Corim. Aradis and Girion were astute enough to guess that Corim was somehow responsible for all of this, but they were rather amused by all this tumult and were quite caught up in the moment, so they ran along behind Corim toward the Villagers of Sallgart, who were actually rushing toward them as well. This was because Corim's older brother Branko, one of the Villagers of Sallgart, had yelled the same order as Corim immediately after him, with the same results – a spontaneous and senseless charge.

Not long afterward, the whole of Midsummer Meadow was embroiled in absolute pandemonium. Rannion was running around screaming, trying to shake burning bunting from his legs, the Villagers of Sallgart and Groddevar's Soldiers were engaged in a full-on brawl, and Mr. and Mrs. Barleycroft were shouting frantically above the crowd for no one to panic, while the crowd was running in wild alarm all over the verge of the meadow. Meanwhile, the three children in the Malg costume were still running to and fro in bewilderment and terror, and Delinah was alternately chasing after the Malg and rolling and spinning on the grass like a lunatic, snorting and squealing all the while. So crazed was she, in fact, that Camlin couldn't even get close to her. And Neldon was trying to find Corim in all this fray.

At last, he located him near the edge of the free-for-all between Groddevar's Soldiers and the Villagers of Sallgart. He grabbed Corim's arm and pulled him out of the battle, loudly asking, "Hey, Corim, do you think Delinah acting up is the moonweed's doing? I thought you said it just would help her to understand me and speak – "

"Of course it was the moonweed's doing," Corim laughed. "Isn't it fantastic?"

"Not at all!" Neldon returned incredulously. "If anyone finds out that I'm responsible, I'm done for. But I'm not the one at fault because you didn't tell me the moonweed would do this."

"How would anyone find out?" Corim asked. "No one saw you give her the moonweed, right?"

"All anyone'd have to do is ask her, and she could tell them exactly what happened," Neldon said worriedly.

"Look, that whole thing about moonweed giving animals the ability to talk and stuff is completely made-up," Corim confessed.

"No it isn't," Neldon insisted. "I *heard* her speaking People Talk."

"You only *think* you heard her using People Talk," Corim retorted.

"Ha!" Neldon laughed. "You may have fooled me once, but not again. I *know* moonweed can make animals talk, because I heard Delinah talking. And I *know* she understood me because she did exactly what I told her to do."

"Don't be ridiculous, Neldon," said Corim, who was growing quite aggravated. "Animals can't talk, no matter what plant you give them. The truth is that moonweed does exactly what Tallis said – it causes temporary insanity. I totally fabricated that business about it making animals talk and whatnot because I wanted you to give Delinah the moonweed and ruin the pageant so I could get back at Rannion."

"You mean you tricked me into causing all this?" Neldon asked, completely stupefied, as he looked around the meadow at all the havoc. "That was really low of you, Corim." Neldon shook his head and frowned.

"How can you be mad about this?" Corim exclaimed, throwing his hands in the air. "This is amazing. Thanks to you, this is officially the best pageant ever."

"Hm, well, I'm not taking the blame for your shenanigans when people get a chance to interview Delinah," Neldon swore, as he walked off. His belief that moonweed could make animals talk had remained utterly unshaken by Corim's assertions.

Corim waved his hand dismissively at the departing Neldon and then returned to the impromptu battle between Groddevar's Soldiers and the Villagers of Sallgart.

"I'll teach that Corim Timberfall," Neldon mumbled, as he walked toward the eastern fringe of the meadow. "Yes, sir, I will. I'm going to tell my father the whole thing, since he'll probably find out very soon anyhow. And then he'll tell Corim's father, and Corim'll get what's coming to him for all this."

Neldon soon found his parents running around by the food tables, trying to stamp out the remainder of the fire there.

"Father, I have something to tell you," Neldon announced loudly, as he reached them.

"Neldon, you've been doing an excellent job in the pageant so far," his father said. "But wow, did things get wild with that horse! Look, she's still running around like a rabid herragoot."

"Um, yes, about that … " Neldon began hesitantly. "That's actually partially because of me."

"What?" asked his father, quite taken aback.

Breathlessly, Neldon proceeded to explain the whole thing to his father, first about how he had found the moonweed and then how Corim had lied about whether it caused insanity or not and how he had fed the moonweed to Delinah so he could talk to her. His father listened patiently all the while.

When Neldon finished, his father said, "I think we need to go find Trambo Timberfall." This was Corim's father.

A minute later, they spotted Trambo dumping a bucket of water on some flaming bunting. Neldon's father went up to him and said, "Hey, Trambo, I'd like to talk to you about something for a minute."

"Sure thing, Drampo," he returned, as he passed the bucket to his wife, Lonnaren, who went to go refill it.

Drampo then proceeded to relate Neldon's tale, and Trambo grew increasingly furious as he explained Corim's involvement in this whole affair.

"Oh, that rascal Corim is really going to get it!" Trambo raged, after he had heard all.

Looking at the continuing battle between Groddevar's Soldiers and the Villagers of Sallgart, he said, "Excuse me, Broadbuckles."

He marched off to the brawl, found Corim, and then dragged him out of the tumult.

"Hey, what's got you so hot and bothered?" Corim asked, as his father continued pulling him by his arm toward Rimwold Forest.

"So moonweed can make horses talk, huh?" Trambo stormed.

"No, who told you that?" Corim asked.

"A horse," Trambo returned sharply.

"Nonsense. Horses can't talk. It had to have been that fink, Neldon," Corim said through gritted teeth.

"So you *did* put him up to this," Trambo said.

Corim gulped.

When they got to Rimwold Forest, Trambo gave Corim a sound whooping and then a stern talking to. Meanwhile, Neldon's father was likewise giving him a firm reprimanding, although there was no whooping to go with it, for as he saw things, Neldon displayed very poor judgment, even outright stupidity, but no intent of either malice or mischief.

Drampo berated Neldon quite harshly for being so gullible, not seeking the counsel of anyone else about the matter and feeding a suspicious plant to someone else's animal. And when he had finished with this upbraiding, he delivered what Neldon viewed as an absolutely crushing consequence: Neldon would not be allowed to eat any sweets for two weeks. The intent of this punishment was that Neldon would be reminded every day for the next fortnight that not carefully weighing what one is told can result in significant loss. Neldon loved sweets so very much that the removal of them was one of the most considerable losses he could experience.

CHAPTER FIVE

Fallout of the Festival Fiasco

ventually, all the pandemonium in Midsummer Meadow died down, and Delinah calmed to the point where Camlin Micklemare could lead her out of the meadow and back to her stable, where she finally recovered her senses. Rannion ultimately was able to disentangle himself from the burning bunting and, to his great relief, he had undergone the whole ordeal with only minor injuries. The various fires that had sprung up were put out by the audience, and the three children in their Malg costume returned to their lair. The impromptu brawl among the rest of the youth died down, and they all went back to their places.

Fennadris Barleycroft was of the opinion that the cast had worked too hard on the pageant for them to just end it there, so he announced that they would be finishing it, starting with the scene where Falderon battled the Malg and removing the conventional subsequent intermission between the pageant's second and third portions. And so the performance went on. However, Neldon's and Corim's parents pulled them out of the pageant and made them sit with the audience as a consequence for what they had done.

Rannion soon triumphed over the Malg after a fierce battle, and Crommenblatt fled to his fortress. Then the third section of the pageant began, narrated by Talaysia Cantlecraft. In this final section, Rannion led an assault on Crommenblatt, and Fanella Berthaway, the Drannenfross, helped Falderon enter the villainous Groddevar's fortress for a final duel with him, which ended in Crommenblatt falling to his character's demise from the ramparts of the fortress set onto a pile of pillows and blankets.

The grand finale of the entire pageant was to be the wedding of Falderon and Ferlisa by the basin that represented Lake Emmerloss, followed by a victory speech by Falderon as he was appointed king over his people. But there was a great surprise in store for those present that day, for Rannion used the opportunity to ask for Mayvelyn's hand in marriage. The only ones who were apprised this would be happening ahead of time were Rannion's and Mayvelyn's parents, for Rannion had requested permission from the aforementioned parties to pursue betrothal to Mayvelyn. As he was already sixteen and she fifteen, with neither of them having been committed to an arranged marriage, it was his privilege to seek such permission. This both sets of parents had gladly granted, thinking it was a splendid match. However, Rannion asked that they not say anything to Mayvelyn about the matter, as he wanted the proposal during the pageant to be a surprise for her.

In any event, when Rannion presented his offer to Mayvelyn, she responded with exuberant affirmation. This was one of the cleverest and most public proposals that Siloa had seen in years, and since both Rannion and Mayvelyn were greatly beloved, this act was received with heartfelt cheering. In fact, it caused many (especially those with a streak of romanticism) to burst into tears of joy. Of course, the reader need hardly be told how Corim Timberfall felt about this whole business.

When the pageant had concluded, which was just shortly before sunset, the audience went to congratulate their young actors and actresses, and Neldon's and Corim's parents, with Neldon and Corim in tow, went to address Fennadris Barleycroft. He was in the midst of receiving glowing praise from several families for his work with the youth, but he stepped aside to speak with the Broadbuckle and Timberfall delegation.

When the Dolnario had heard the full story of what had happened, the four parents present asked him if there was some sort of public punishment he could dispense to their boys for what they had done. Fennadris didn't want to be too hard on them, especially on Neldon, for they were only twelve and thirteen (with Corim being the younger of the two), but he did agree that Neldon should have known better and that Corim was a complete scoundrel for taking advantage of Neldon's gullibility and inciting a fight among the youth during the pageant just for the sheer enjoyment of mayhem.

After a little deliberation, Mr. Barleycroft decided that an appropriate punishment would be for Neldon and Corim to be consigned to forced labor and odd jobs around town for him for a portion of every day, for four days a week, for the next two months, with most of these tasks being either unpleasant or tedious. Neldon's and Corim's parents all thought this to be a quite suitable consequence and assured Mr. Barleycroft that they would see to it that the lads reported to him every morning until their period of discipline had run its course.

Incidentally, it also came out in this conversation that Corim's older brother Branko had been privy to all this mischief-making as well. He had known ahead of time that all this would happen and was thus prepared to lead the Villagers of Sallgart into a needless brawl as soon as Corim gave the signal. However, since Corim was the chief perpetrator in the affair, it was decided that Branko would receive consequences only from his parents, and not from the Dolnario. Trambo made sure that Branko received a whooping that evening and that he had extra drudgery and chores assigned to him for several weeks.

When Mr. Barleycroft had finished disclosing Neldon's and Corim's consequences to them, the two boys walked off and sat dejectedly at the south end of Midsummer Meadow as evening approached, for, as part of their punishment, they had been forbidden by their parents to participate in any of the remaining festivities. However, Aradis, Tallis, Darmon and Girion soon joined them in their place of exile to discuss what had happened.

Hoping to receive consolation of some kind from their companions, Neldon and Corim explained everything to them. The other four lads, however, were only mildly sympathetic. They had certainly enjoyed all the excitement and were grateful for Neldon and Corim inciting it. But they also thought it served Neldon right to receive such heavy consequences for being so naïve as to trust Corim. And they thought it absolutely hilarious that Neldon still believed moonweed could make animals talk. In addition, they regarded it as absolutely grand that Corim was going to be punished for all his scheming for once since he often got away with it.

"Oho! That's how it's going to be, is it?" said Corim, nettled. "Well, just see how sorry I feel for any of you next time you get in trouble."

"I don't think you would find it so funny if it were you that were deprived of sweets for the next two weeks," lamented Neldon, almost at the point of tears.

"Oh, come now, you two," said Tallis. "You've had your fun, and now we're having ours."

"Well said, comrade," Darmon laughed.

"Besides, perhaps these consequences will do you some good," said Aradis. "Maybe you'll learn your lesson this time."

"Knowing Neldon and Corim, I rather doubt it," muttered Girion.

The boys talked for a few minutes more and then Girion, Tallis, Aradis and Darmon went to rejoin the festivities. The Festival of Falderon went on well into the night, and more merriment ensued for the folk of Siloa. Neldon and Corim, who were restricted from participating in any of this, agreed that they wouldn't have done so even if they had been allowed, for they were much too distressed about their upcoming consequences to enjoy themselves. In fact, they could hardly think about anything else but the grim future of affliction and toil that would soon be upon them.

—•◆•—

For the next eight and a half weeks after the Festival, Neldon and Corim had to do tasks that were alternately miserable or boring (or sometimes both), such as picking up rocks out of Siloa's main street, Lampler's Lane, or cleaning up piles of animal dung around town. For a number of days, they were occupied with repairing and replacing various fences and paving stones near Siloa, all the while sweltering in the summer heat. The boys were also lent out to the people of the village to carry buckets of water for hours on end from Pemblin's Well at the south edge of town to individuals' houses. Some of their more pleasant tasks included making deliveries on the Dolnario's behalf, but these were not very frequent, as he tried to make sure they were well supplied with disagreeable things to do.

When the two months were over, one would have thought that both the boys would have reformed their ways, at least somewhat. But unfortunately, Girion's prediction that neither one of them would be straightened out turned out to be quite correct. Corim was just as much of a schemer as ever, and Neldon was still as gullible as they come.

As for Rannion and Mayvelyn (in case the reader is wondering about them), they were happily married, but not until the autumn which fell a year and several months after the pageant, as Rannion had to save up enough to pay Mayvelyn's bridewealth. (The purpose of this age-old custom, of course, was to demonstrate that he could adequately provide for her.) Her father was asking for quite a bit, and so Rannion worked extra hard the next few seasons to earn the necessary amount. Incidentally, neither Neldon nor Corim were permitted to attend the

Rillspan-Rushwick wedding, for Rannion had learned that they were jointly involved in causing the catastrophe at the Prandingars' Pageant, and he didn't want a similar incident to interrupt his marriage ceremony.

Also, when the Prandingars' Pageant came around the year after Neldon and Corim had made such a mess of it, neither was permitted to audition for a part, and the boys were cast as Villagers of Sallgart without any say in the matter. What's more, several other children were asked to keep an eye on them and make sure they weren't up to any antics. Actually, the Dolnario was so concerned about the two of them misbehaving that he imposed the sanction restricting them to the role of Villagers of Sallgart every single year from that point on until they were no longer eligible to be in the pageant. And even with this arrangement, he was still always a little leery about what they were up to during rehearsals and performances.

Yet, though these measures successfully kept Neldon and Corim from creating mayhem at the pageant again, they did nothing to keep them from exulting in their past achievements in that area. As a matter of fact, both of the boys came to view their part in the Prandingars' Pageant that they had created so much chaos in as something of a badge of honor, if nothing else because that particular pageant was remembered for years to come. And sometimes, if one cannot achieve fame, he will settle for infamy. Such was certainly the case with Corim Timberfall, who is far from a model of virtue, and Neldon Broadbuckle, who indisputably holds Siloa's record for the most memorable performance of Groddevar's Assistant No. 3.

THE END

Author's Note on the Appendices

Anyone who has read a Skaddisson book before is well aware of the author's great affinity for lore. Efforts have been made to cull the amount of lore sprinkled into the main text, but conscience did not permit the eliminating of a large amount of it from the book altogether. Consequently, the surplus has been exported here to the appendices. One may safely ignore these appendices altogether if he chooses, and his reading of the main stories will not be substantially affected. However, if the reader wishes to probe deeper into the mines of the lorescape of Orona, he may find various treasures among the following appendices. And, as it is noted in the Sayings of the Sages, "It is the miner, not the jeweler, who knows the gem's true worth."

Sincerely Yours,
Jarrett J. Skaddisson

P.S. For those wishing to access a full rendering of the Legend of Falderon, a tale which figures prominently into the story *Pandemonium at the Prandingars' Pageant*, such a rendering may be found in Appendix 4 of *The Road to Anganor*, Book 2 of the Kingblade Chronicles' Saga 1: *Tarnadins of the Elder Forest*.

Glossary of Useful Terms

The following glossary, which is by no means comprehensive, has been included for three purposes:

1) To act as a quick reference guide for terms which are either used frequently in the text of this book or are of great importance to it.

2) To provide additional information about certain entities which the reader may find to be of interest.

3) To explain, for the sake of completeness, items which are mentioned in entries serving one of the two purposes stated above, even though such items may not appear elsewhere in this book (excepting, naturally, the index in Appendix 6).

Please note that months of the year used in the Manus-Romelliad Calendar, the most common system of Oronic timekeeping, are not included in this glossary, as they are dealt with in Appendix 2.

Agleri – A region in central Velaris which encompasses nine barolli, one of which is Feldryn, wherein lies Siloa. The primary geographical feature of the area is the Plains of Agleri. The regional capital is the city of Temerrin.

Agleri Walk – The easternmost of Siloa's three streets. It runs from north to south.

Agleri Whirlwinds, The – The team in the annual Siloa Snow War that is composed of all Siloan youths in the village proper from ages seven to fifteen who live east of the center of Lampler's Lane.

Apex of Archaea, The – The third age of Orona.

Aradath (adj. Aradathian) – The Southern Moiety of Orona. All those regions of Orona, which lie south of the Bushbelt. It contains the Neathmarda of Byram, Quarana, Fenrost and the Eldritch Isles.

Aragest – The capital city of the Kingdom of Velaris and a port of international significance. It lies on the northeastern shore of Cape Loresso.

Archaea – The central and southern regions of Tassaru.

Balcumberries – Extremely sour, small, purple berries native to central eastern Quarana. They can often be found growing wild in glades in Rimwold Forest.

Barada (sing. Barada; adj. Baradic) – The intelligent inhabitants of Orona, as opposed to the Telnari, the animals. When preceded by the definite article, the word can refer to all Barada as a whole, a group of Barada or an individual; the meaning must be determined by context.

Barolla (pl. Barolli) – One of 27 counties, or districts, of the Kingdom of Velaris.

Bing, Bang, Bongle – A Neldonism. Presumably, it is onomatopoeic and encompasses the idea of a decisive trouncing of a foe or successful completion of a task.

Bogglesnop – A Daigan expression of sharp displeasure. The term is now considered rather old-fashioned and almost comical, although those who still regularly use it generally do so in great earnest.

Bridging of the Tides, The – The fourth age of Orona.

Brines of Ferassi – The great ocean to the east of Quarana. It directly borders the eastern coast of the Kingdom of Velaris.

Bumbadoodle – A word that means precisely what one might think it would mean. Needless to say, it is not a very flattering thing to call someone.

Bushbelt, The – One of the Neathmarda. It separates Huldion and Aradath, circumscribing the entire world of Orona, lying roughly along its equator, which is called Sabakwani's Girdle. It is covered by dense jungle, steep mountains and regions of active volcanism and is several hundred miles wide at all points. The Bushbelt is occupied by savage, aggressive Barada and strange, terrifying beasts; thus, it presents a formidable barrier to movement between the Moieties of Orona. Consequently, almost all travel through the Bushbelt occurs along established routes, which are protected by cooperative garrisons of Barada from various kingdoms in both Huldion and Aradath. This cooperation occurs primarily for the advancement of trade interests.

Cape Loresso – See Loresso, Cape.

Cratchenmanks – A mild Daigan expletive expressing dismay and annoyance. The term was first coined by Gnomish inventors in the Neathmarda of Estereth to refer to particular kinds of mechanical malfunctions. Nowadays, the expression is considered rather antiquated.

Daiga (adj. Daigan) – Historically, the language of the Pine-Elves of Murnia. However, due to the wide geographical and cultural interaction of the Pine-Elves with other Barada, Daiga was used increasingly as a lingua franca throughout Orona in the 2nd-7th centuries of the Latter Epoch. By the opening of the 8th century of the Latter Epoch, it was widely spoken in every Neathmarda, though not by culturally-resistant or isolated populations. Daiga is the daily language used in Velaris.

Dargen-Elves – An ancient Rendaya of Elves who dwelt predominantly in the Dargens throughout the late Apex of Archaea and the early Bridging of the Tides. They had a significant cultural and political influence on many of the Barada of Huldion during the Bridging of the Tides, an influence which continues to the present day.

Dargens, The – A high mountain range in central Tassaru.

Dark Meridian, The – The most southerly point in all Orona.

Dellumberries – Yellow berries, native to Rimwold Forest, that possess a tart, citrusy taste. They are about the size and shape of a Mannish thumb.

Dingleflobbin – A thick-headed, bumbling nitwit. The term as an insult was derived directly from the dingleflobbin, an especially stupid and obnoxious seabird that is native to the Marlassi Coast.

Dolnario – A governmental position in smaller towns and villages in Velaris. The post is somewhat like that of a mayor and includes the responsibility of acting as an officiant in community events, as well as performing duties such as peacekeeping and census-taking.

Druids (adj. Druidic) – One of the Narthanna. Druids are extremely human-like Barada, possessing height within the normal human range of variance and having an average lifespan of around 400 years. Notably, Druids retain a high level of fitness into their fourth century of life.

Dwarves – One of the Narthanna. Dwarves are short, human-like Barada, between 4 and 4 ½ feet tall, with an average lifespan of 130 years. They have thick skin and round noses, and their bodies are stout and muscular.

Eastrange, The – An open field immediately to the east of the village of Siloa.

Elves – One of the Narthanna. Elves are extremely human-like Barada, although they are slightly taller than humans as a general rule, possess an average lifespan of 300 years and have pointed ears.

Fannymash and Fudbuddles – An extremely mild and now mostly obsolete oath of frustration with oneself. The term is of Daigan origin and originally referred to fannymash, a type of porridge made by early Huldionite settlers in eastern Quarana, and fudbuddles, dumplings these settlers ate with holgum broth.

Farga (sing. Farga; adj. Fargese) – One of the Narthanna. Farga are human-like Barada with many bat-like characteristics, possessing height within the normal human range of variance and having a lifespan of around 60 years. They are distinguished from all other Barada by large, leathery wings that protrude from their shoulders. Their ears are like those of a bat, and their noses are a hybrid between bat and human noses. Many parts of their bodies are covered with hair.

Ferassi, Brines of – See 'Brines of Ferassi.'

Follim's Field – An open pasture immediately to the west of the village of Siloa. The spot was named after Follim Micklemare, one of the original settlers of Siloa, who grazed his horses in this field and is also buried there.

Gnomes (adj. Gnomish) – One of the Narthanna. Gnomes are short, human-like Barada, between 3½ and 4 feet tall, with an average lifespan of 150 years. Gnomish morphology varies considerably; Gnomes can have faces ranging from squarish to triangular, and their body frames can either be skinny and nimble or broad and muscular. Their ears can be, variously, indistinguishable from Mannish ears, slightly pointed or shaped almost like a conch shell.

Goblins (adj. Goblin) – One of the Narthanna. Goblins are shortish, human-like Barada, between 4 ½ and 5 feet tall, with an average lifespan of 90 years. They generally have rather gangly, slender frames and possess large, triangular ears. Their noses can be a range of shapes or sizes, and their skin color can vary considerably.

Hemmigan – A very tall hardwood tree native to the forests of central eastern Quarana. Its bark is dark brown, thick and almost spongy, while its leaves are broad and serrated. Frequently, hemmigan trees have very complex, tangled root systems that grow partially above the ground and partially below it. Hemmigan roots are quite thick, and the trunks have a massive girth. Many trees of this variety grow to be hundreds of years old.

Herragoot – A grayish, furry mammal, about two and a half feet in length, that is native to Rimwold Forest. It has four legs, sharp claws, whiskers and a head shaped like that of a dog. It can both swim and climb trees and has a prehensile tail. Herragoots are mostly solitary creatures and generally make their burrows beneath thick clumps of bushes. They often mate for life, and although the male does not live with the female and the young ones, he frequently brings them various plants, small animals and insects to eat. These creatures are known for eating almost anything, although their favorite foods are butterflies and a pungent woodland wort called semmengilly.

Hidewash – A Siloan surname, notably belonging to Gandrian Hidewash, the village tanner.

Hobnoggets – A term expressing dismissal of whatever has just been said as nonsense. Originally, the word referred to a type of coarse, mealy cake eaten by early explorers from Huldion during their voyages in Aradath.

Hody Hody Hoo – A Neldonism. Presumably, it means something along the lines of "Ah ha!"

Holgum – A tall, full-headed grain native to the plains of eastern Quarana. Its kernels are yellowish and oblong, and its flavor has a marked nuttiness mixed with just a tinge of sweetness.

Hoyah – A Daigan exclamation used to attract attention.

Huldion (adj. Huldionite) – The Northern Moiety of Orona, all those regions of Orona, which lie north of the Bushbelt. It contains the Neathmarda of Tassaru, Estereth, Murnia and Jassuna.

Ingans (sing. Ingan; adj. Ingan) – One of the Narthanna. Ingans are tree-like Barada, generally between 7 and 7 ½ feet tall, with an average lifespan of 250 years. Their morphology is essentially that of a tree with human-like features: eyes, ears, nose and a mouth, along with jointed, bark-covered legs and arms.

Lampler's Lane – Siloa's main street, which lies in the center of the village and runs from north to south.

Latter Epoch, The – The fifth age of Orona, in which the tales in this book are set. Its commencement was launched by a highly significant journey, as it began the year after the Elven explorer Vastia the Pathfinder returned to Huldion from his fabled expedition into Aradath. Before Vastia's journey, the peoples of the two Moieties of Orona had been almost entirely cut off from each other for several thousand years.

Leprechauns (adj. Leprechaun) – One of the Narthanna. Leprechauns are short, human-like Barada, between 3 and 3 ½ feet tall, with an average lifespan of 200 years. They have a generally slender build, and their faces are characterized by slightly pointed ears and sharp chins.

Loresso, Cape – A prominent cape on the northeastern coast of Velaris. The term also refers to a region of Velaris which encompasses six barolli on the cape.

Maena (pl. Maenas) – A term designating a female individual who is one of the Menfolk.

Magnifulous – A Neldonism. It refers to something which is tremendously, overwhelmingly excellent.

Main Lane – A colloquial name for Lampler's Lane.

Malden – A variety of spreading hardwood tree, usually between forty and eighty feet in height, native to the forests of central eastern Quarana. Its leaves are flat and egg-shaped, with golden spots flecked among the leaves' predominant hue of green.

Malg, The – A legendary, centuries-old, enormous, six-legged, hairy monster with incredible senses of both hearing and smell, that is said to have made its lair in a cave in the Dargens, early in the Bridging of the Tides. The Malg was reputedly terrorizing a mountain village of the Dargen-Elves when the young Elven hero, Falderon, volunteered to go and slay it, a feat which he accomplished using only a sword and a burning brand.

Marda – The sun of Orona.

Marlassi Coast, The – A region in southeast Velaris which encompasses four barolli. The Marlassi Coast, which stretches from the southern end of Cape Loresso to the southern border of the Kingdom of Velaris, is the primary geographical feature of the area.

Menfolk (masc. sing. Manfellow; masc. pl. Manfellows; fem. sing. Maena; fem. pl. Maenas; adj. Mannish) – One of the Narthanna. Menfolk are human Barada, possessing height within the normal range of human variance and having an average lifespan of 70 years.

Midsummer Meadow – A flowering meadow directly to the west of Siloa and just east of the eastern edge of Rimwold Forest. It is the site of several Siloan festivals throughout the year but is most notable for hosting celebrations in the midst of summer.

Moieties of Orona, The – The northern and southern hemispheres of Orona: Huldion and Aradath.

Narthanna (sing. Narthaya) – In the singular, the term for one of the distinct varieties of Barada, such as Menfolk, Druids, Elves, Dwarves, Gnomes, Ingans, etc. The plural refers to several or all of the varieties of Barada.

Neathmarda (pl. Neathmarda) – A translation of the Daigan term 'dhar-marda', which literally means 'situated under Marda'. The Neathmarda are the nine most populated landmasses of Orona. Technically, one of them is actually a collection of landmasses rather than a single landmass, as it is a group of islands. The nine Neathmarda are Tassaru, Murnia, Estereth, Byram, Quarana, Jassuna, the Eldritch Isles, Fenrost and the Bushbelt.

Neldonism – A word or phrase coined, usually spontaneously, by Neldon Broadbuckle. The meanings of various Neldonisms can often be deduced by the context in which he employs them, although this is not always the case since Neldon himself is not always the most competent handler of language. Neldon frequently attempts to promote the usage of Neldonisms throughout Siloa, although he is rarely successful in this endeavor.

Noddington, Yawnbury and Dozedale – The three villages of Slumberdrift Wood, which feature prominently in the pan-Elven fairy tale, The Three Princes of Sundial Island, a mythical land having different regions perpetually fixed in particular times of day. The three villages are often referred to in the expression, "So-and-so fell asleep faster than you could say Noddington, Yawnbury and Dozedale."

Northern Moiety of Orona, The – The northern hemisphere of Orona, another name for Huldion.

Orona (adj. Oronic) – The world of the Kingblade Chronicles.

Pan-Elven – An adjective applied to an entity (an item of culture, language, food, etc.) that is now common throughout Orona, having spread far and wide in the last few centuries of the Latter Epoch, although such things initially were associated with or originated from certain Elven peoples from Huldion.

Parlaedia – A region in far western Velaris, which encompasses two large barolli. The Parlaedian Mountains are the primary geographical feature of the area.

Parlaedian Mountains – A mountain range, rich in mineral deposits, in the far western reaches of the Kingdom of Velaris.

Pinglies (sing. Pingly) – Small disks used in the game pinglybop. In the game, these pinglies must be bopped (i.e. flipped) into a small bowl called a kibber.

Pinglybop – A pan-Elven children's game somewhat akin to tiddlywinks, wherein one uses a larger disk called a tinky to bop (i.e. flip or strike) smaller disks called pinglies into a kibber. However, even though the game disseminated throughout Orona via pan-Elven culture, it originated with the Brunnigs, the Bay-Leprechauns of western Murnia.

Plains of Agleri – Vast prairielands that cover much of eastern Velaris. Siloa lies near their western edge.

Ploughman's Shanty, The – The village tavern and inn in Siloa.

Quarana – One of the Neathmarda. It lies in Aradath, to the east of Byram and to the north of Fenrost. The Kingdom of Velaris lies on the eastern shores of Quarana.

Quarmit – A knobby, gray-barked hardwood tree native to the forests of central eastern Quarana. It is usually around thirty feet in height and has long, lobed leaves. Quarmit trunks are often partially covered in lichen and moss.

Rendanna (sing. Rendaya) – In the singular, a subdivision of one of the Narthanna; that is, a particular variety of a particular Narthaya. E.g., Plains-Elves are a Rendaya of Elves.

Rimwold – A region in western Velaris, which encompasses six barolli. The primary geographical feature of the area is Rimwold Forest.

Rimwold Forest – A large forest that covers much of western Velaris. Its eastern edge lies just to the west of Siloa.

Rimwold Row – The westernmost of Siloa's three streets. It runs from north to south.

Rimwold Thunders, The – The team in the annual Siloa Snow War that is composed of all Siloan youths in the village proper from ages seven to fifteen who live west of the center of Lampler's Lane.

Ruphani, The – The official title of the ruler of the Kingdom of Velaris. The Ruphani lives in the city of Aragest.

Sancalla (pl. Sancalli) – A species of large seabird, in appearance very much like a seagull, only somewhat larger, that frequents the shores of eastern Quarana, especially regions farther to the north. Sancalli have glossy white plumage and a six-foot wingspan. Feeding primarily on fish, they are quite amiable toward Barada. In fact, they can be domesticated and are sometimes used to deliver objects or messages along coastal routes.

Sardolia, The – A government organization of the Kingdom of Velaris. The agents of the Sardolia act as tax collectors, constables and a standing army. The Sardolia has barracks in the capital of every barolla in Velaris.

Sayings of the Sages, The – An ancient collection of Mannish proverbs.

Shanty, The – See 'Ploughman's Shanty, The.'

Siloa – A small farming village in the Agleri region of the Kingdom of Velaris. It is the home of Neldon Broadbuckle.

Siloa Snow War – An annual snowball fight held in the village of Siloa proper between two teams, the Agleri Whirlwinds and the Rimwold Thunders.

Skyworlds, The – Ten luminaries in the heavens over Orona. Their wandering paths set them apart from stars, and some believe they are other worlds like Orona. They feature heavily in the lore systems of many Oronic people groups.

Southern Moiety of Orona, The – The southern hemisphere of Orona; another name for Aradath.

Tarion – The smallest division of coin in the monetary system of Velaris.

Tarmin Cakes – Cakes employing extract from tarmins as a primary flavoring ingredient. These cakes are traditionally eaten around Midsummer in Aradath, due to the tarmin harvest occurring early in the month of Tannaril.

Tarmins – Largish, tear-shaped nuts that have a flavor comparable to that of almonds. The variety of tree which bears them originated in central western Quarana, but this variety is now cultivated in accommodating climates all over Orona.

Tavenndi (sing. Tavenndo) – Roaming traders in the Kingdom of Velaris. In their wagons, they carry merchandise from larger cities, which they bargain with or sell in more remote towns and villages where such commodities are not available.

Telnari (sing. Telnara; adj. Telnaric) – Refers to the animals of Orona, as opposed to the Barada, the intelligent beings of Orona. The word applies specifically to animals with blood and bones and thus includes mammals, birds, reptiles, amphibians and fish.

Thunders, The – See 'Rimwold Thunders, The.'

Topaz Turnip, The – A turnip-shaped, turnip-sized piece of yellowish wood. It is the prized artifact both teams are competing for in the Siloa Snow War.

Torlinberries – Sweet, juicy, reddish berries about the size of cherries.

Torlinberry Pie – A traditional midsummer dish of Velaris made from torlinberries.

Trolls (adj. Trollish) – One of the Narthanna. Trolls are large, human-like Barada, between 8 ½ and 9 ½ feet tall, with an average lifespan of 50 years. Some aspects of Trollish morphology vary considerably; they can have faces ranging from oblong to triangular, their ears and noses can either be round or pointed and the skin colors of different Trollish Rendanna can be quite diverse. However, Trolls' body frames are generally more slender than stocky, and they are consistently muscular.

Turnip, The – See 'Topaz Turnip, The.'

Twippertan – A small songbird native to the forests of eastern Quarana. Its breast is whiteish, its throat black and its back a bright blue. The bird's name comes from its morning call, which sounds rather like "Twippertan, ta-twippertan!"

Velaris, Kingdom of (adj. Velarisian) – An Elven kingdom in eastern Quarana, having substantial populations of Elves and Menfolk, as well as pockets of Gnomes, Dwarves and Druids. Velaris is divided into five regions: Cape Loresso, the Marlassi Coast, Agleri, Rimwold and Parlaedia.

Whirlwinds, The – See 'Agleri Whirlwinds, The.'

Wiggy-wagging – A Neldonism. It refers to causing or engaging in needless delay.

Xengula – The proper name for the Bushbelt.

Yumscious – A Neldonism. It refers to something which is exceedingly delectable or favorable.

The Months of the
Manus-Romelliad Calendar

The Manus-Romelliad Calendar is the timekeeping system used in a great many places
in Orona, including in the Kingdom of Velaris, within which lies the village of Siloa. It
contains unique designations for the five ages of Orona and the numbering of their years,
the twelve months of the year, the seven days of the week and also the various times
of day. However, this appendix will only examine the months of the year in detail, as
designations from the other divisions (e.g. the times of day) are only mentioned sparingly
in this volume.

The Manus-Romelliad Calendar is both lunar and solar, using twelve months consisting
of 30 days each and a special set of five days called the Middings (also called Pelarond),
which are placed in-between the first two months of Huldion's summer (Aradath's
winter) in order to complete a 365-day solar year. (Huldion is the name for Orona's
northern hemisphere and Aradath that of its southern one.) The Middings is celebrated
all over Orona as a five-day holiday with festivities, parades and joyous feasting.
The Manus-Romelliad year begins in the springtime, and the first month is roughly
equivalent to our month of March. Though to be entirely precise, it begins in the last
few days of our February – February 21st to be exact. Very minor adjustments have
been made to the calendar periodically throughout the centuries in order to maintain
astronomical integrity, much like the case of our own calendar, but in Oronic reckoning,
the extra days have always been added to the Middings. Customarily, every eight
years, two days are added to the Middings for a total of seven days for Pelarond on the
eighth year. Such years are called Years of the Middings. The names of the generally
correspondent months are as follows:

Bellin (March) – 30 days

Serona (April) – 30 days

Alareth (May) – 30 days

Landrenna (June) – 30 days

Pelarond [also known as 'The Middings'] (end of June) – 5 days

Ularos (July) – 30 days

Galrim (August) – 30 days

Ferenos (September) – 30 days

Derrig (October) – 30 days

Elaya (November) – 30 days

Tannaril (December) – 30 days

Harasa (January) – 30 days

Ildurion (February) – 30 days

NB: as the Manus-Romelliad Calendar originated in Orona's northern hemisphere, it should be noted that for Siloa, which is in the southern hemisphere, the year begins in the fall, not the spring. Thus, Pelarond falls in the middle of Siloa's winter and Harasa in the midst of its summer.

The History and Rules of the Siloa Snow War

A Condensed History of the Siloa Snow War

The Siloa Snow War was born spontaneously as a village tradition on the first winter snowfall of the year 701 of the Latter Epoch. The first snow was particularly notable that year, for it had come rather early and somewhat unexpectedly, giving the children much delight. The youths of Siloa had hurried out to play in it, and, as children are wont to do, they commenced a friendly, informal snowball fight. And it just so happened that this fight took place between those living on opposing sides of Siloa's main street, Lampler's Lane. However, several creative youths who were part of the battle decided to add some extra dimensions to it as the fight progressed.

Each side constructed snow forts and bulwarks and designated particular objects as "treasures" that they were determined to guard from being captured by the other side. Partway through the day, those living on the west side of Lampler's Lane, which was closest to nearby Rimwold Forest, began calling themselves the Rimwold Thunders, and in response, those living on the east side of the street, which was nearest to the Plains of Agleri, dubbed themselves the Agleri Whirlwinds.

However, the real spark that transformed this first Snow War into something truly unique was an elderly, ill-tempered woman named Bernalla Elmensill. Miss Elmensill, who was (and is) ferociously protective of her turnip patch behind her house and hated nothing more than children setting foot in it, spied several youths desecrating this beloved plot of ground by racing through it. (However, to this very day, these individuals would deny that they were doing so maliciously; they were merely trying to avoid getting hit by snowballs). Furious, Miss Elmensill decided to go out in the street and demand that the children cease their snowball fight at once or else she would get the Dolnario, Fennadris Barleycroft, to force them to stop. (The Dolnario is the chief government official in Siloa, so if anyone could declare a snowball fight unauthorized, it would be him).

The children did not take Miss Elmensill's threats kindly, and so, while she went to issue her grievance to Mr. Barleycroft, a lad named Fargalin Chipperchop, a Rimwold Thunder, pulled one of her turnips from her garden and declared it to be the greatest treasure of all, for as he jokingly (or semi-jokingly) said, he had risked his life by taking it. He dared the Agleri Whirlwinds to come get it from him and his companions, but he told them there would be no way for them to discover who had it except by hitting them with snowballs, which would force them to freeze so they could be searched for the turnip. However, he also decreed that if any of the Agleri Whirlwinds were hit by a snowball, they would have to return to their main snow fort before crossing over to look for the turnip again. Furthermore, according to his proclamation, any of the Rimwold

Thunders could unfreeze their companions by touching them. And thus, the main outline of the Siloa Snow War was formulated by Fargalin Chipperchop then and there.

Once Bernalla Elmensill's turnip was brought into play, both teams were fully invested in the event, and the turnip passed from one side to the other several times, with the teams reversing roles in each instance so that the turnip-defenders became the turnip-seekers and vice versa. It was determined during the afternoon that whoever possessed the turnip when the sun set would be declared the winner. To make things fair, they asked Pappy Greengrove, who lived just to the north of town and was (and still is) a favorite of all the children, to ring the village bell outside the Dolnario's house to signal when sunset had officially arrived. Of course, he obliged, and as things turned out, the Agleri Whirlwinds had the turnip when the bell was rung.

All the children had enjoyed themselves so much during this event that they decided to hold it again the following year, also on the first snow, with the stipulation that it had to be the first snow with enough accumulation to facilitate a grand snowball fight. And since they wanted to avoid the hazard of stealing a turnip from Bernalla Elmensill a second time, Fargalin Chipperchop volunteered to whittle a small block of wood to look just like a turnip. This would serve as what would henceforth be called the Topaz Turnip, due to the yellowish hue of the wood from which it had been made. (Incidentally, Fargalin Chipperchop is now a highly-regarded carpenter in Siloa.)

Bernalla Elmensill never actually found out that Fargalin had taken one of her turnips or that it became the prize the two teams were seeking. Nor did she realize that the Topaz Turnip was made in honor of her when she heard folk talking about it. And none of the adults in the village thought it wise to help her make the connection. They did feel a little sorry for her in that she was the unwitting object of the children's lampooning, so they discouraged any open jesting against her. Nonetheless, they were unable to alter the children's veneration of the Topaz Turnip, for they were quite unwilling to change either the object or its title.

The second year of the Siloa Snow War, the event had a few more formal regulations instituted, which the children had vigorously discussed throughout the year. They resolved that only children who actually lived in Siloa proper could participate, so as to ensure that the number of participants on each team remained roughly equivalent (for there were far more living east of town than west of it). They also decided that only youths from ages seven to fifteen should take part in the official battle, since youths of sixteen were on the cusp of adulthood and because they didn't want children younger than seven to get injured in any rough play that occurred. With regard to what counted as a strike with a snowball, only those that hit at the waist or above were considered valid. Furthermore, they concurred that whichever side had the Topaz Turnip at Marda's Farewell (that is, at sunset) would retain it for the opening of the following year's fight. And Pappy Greengrove graciously agreed to ring the bell annually at sunset for the event.

For boundaries of the Snow War, the children established that no one would go beyond the base of the slope that rose up to Midsummer Meadow, just west of town, and likewise, no one would pass beyond the north-south line that ran along the back of Hanbro Hemptwist's shed east of town. The marker for the southern border for both teams would be Pemblin's Well just past the south end of the village. And the northern boundary would be Founders' Rock, which stood not far from the edge of Siloa along the road leading north out of town.

Also, those defending the Topaz Turnip would not be allowed to go beyond the street front on their side of Siloa's main street, but those on offense, who were trying to get the Topaz Turnip, could go anywhere within the established boundaries for the Snow War. Additionally, the Rimwold Thunders' fort had to be built at the base of the slope leading up to Midsummer Meadow, and the Agleri Whirlwinds' fort was required to be constructed close to Hanbro Hemptwist's shed.

Another addition to the second annual Siloa Snow War was a sponsorship of sorts by the village tavern, the Ploughman's Shanty. Orinn Berthaway, the proprietor, offered to provide free cider and snacks all day for the warring youth, who were invited to use the Ploughman's Shanty as a rest station and a retreat from the cold. Mr. Berthaway also promoted the idea of holding an event for adults at the tavern in the evening, a grand get-together for them to drink and dance and sing to celebrate the first snow with as much merriment as the children did. Many adults were amenable to this idea, and attendance that year was excellent.

Since that time, the Siloa Snow War has continued, year after year, to be an event cherished by all (or most, since Bernalla Elmensill and a few others still loathe it). Indeed, many parents of participants in the Snow War have become almost as invested in the event as their children. And beyond this, fame of the event has even spread to surrounding settlements, some of which have attempted to replicate it to a degree.

Life in Siloa can often be difficult and laborious. But in the midst of an existence frequently characterized by hardship and wearisome toil, the Snow War is a bright reminder that there is much joy yet to be found in Orona. And such joy is often not found in convenience, comfort or wealth, but in the simple, untarnished pleasures of life, such as getting hit in the face with a snowball, or even better, hitting somebody else's face with one.

Rules of the Siloa Snow War

The following document was taken from the miscellaneous papers of Girion Ringmark, one of Neldon Broadbuckle's close friends. Girion moved to Siloa in the spring of LE 711 (i.e., the year 711 of the Latter Epoch) and first heard about the Siloa Snow War not long after. However, since he resided outside of the village proper, he was ineligible to participate. Nonetheless, he found accounts of the activity fascinating, and, since he was such a dedicated archivist, he decided to make a permanent, written record of its regulations (Although, this was more for his own satisfaction than anyone else's). After consultation of all the most eminent authorities on the subject, including Fargalin Chipperchop, Orinn Berthaway, Pappy Greengrove, Cromnic Barleycroft, Hendra Timberfall and Aradis Kingblade, Girion compiled the following document stating all of the official rules of the Siloa Snow War as they stood in the winter of LE 712.

The Authorized Register of Siloa Snow War Regulations

As recorded by Girion Ringmark

At Ringmark Farm, Village of Siloa and Environs, Barolla of Feldryn, Region of Agleri, Kingdom of Velaris in the Month of Landrenna, LE 712

Section I – Date of the Siloa Snow War

The Siloa Snow War is to be held annually on the first full day of winter on which there is a decent amount of snow. The four team captains (see Section IX) vote if the matter is in question, and in case of a tie, the matter shall be decided by the honorable Pappy Greengrove or his successor or substitute in the post of Grand Bell-Ringer (see Section II).

Section II – Commencement and Termination Points

No player is permitted to start building any fortifications for his or her team until sunrise on the day of the Snow War nor are any attacks permitted until that time. The first attack by the team on offense, conducted either by an individual or a group of any size, officially starts the combat phase of the Snow War.

The honorable Pappy Greengrove (or his successor or substitute) shall be the designated Grand Bell-Ringer for commencement and termination points for the remainder of the day, and it is his sound and impartial judgment that shall determine precisely when the bell is to be rung. Each of his signals will continue for approximately one minute to make sure that everyone is aware of them. However, it is the very first bellstroke of each sequence that marks the official starting and ending points cited below.

The first peal of the village bell outside the Dolnario's house around noon will mark the beginning of lunch and hence the suspension of combat. The bell will then ring again some time later to signal the end of lunch and, correspondingly, the renewal of combat. At sunset, another ringing of the bell officially concludes the Snow War.

Section III – Teams and Participants

The Snow War shall consist of a battle between two teams: the Agleri Whirlwinds and the Rimwold Thunders. The Agleri Whirlwinds will be composed of all Siloan youth in the village proper from ages seven to fifteen who reside east of the center of Lampler's Lane. And the Rimwold Thunders will be composed of all Siloan youth in the village proper and in the same age bracket who reside west of the center of Lampler's Lane.

In the event that the numbers of participants assigned to each team are unequal, the numbers shall stand, since such imbalances are practically inevitable and because it is also likely that advantages and disadvantages in this regard will be reversed in following years. Hence, the matter will be balanced out over time. Furthermore, skillfulness is just as much of a factor, if not a greater one, than numbers, but an attempt to manipulate all factors to be equal would not only prove burdensome, but also dampen the spirit of unity forged between those living on a given side of Lampler's Lane.

Section IV – Objective of the Snow War and Starting Placement of the Topaz Turnip

The goal of the Snow War is to obtain and retain the Topaz Turnip, a wooden, turnip-shaped object (hereafter referred to primarily as "the Turnip") masterfully crafted by the honorable Fargalin Chipperchop. Whichever team has the Topaz Turnip at the first stroke of the bell at sunset will be declared the victor of that year's Snow War. This team will start the coming year's Snow War with the Turnip still in its possession and so will begin on defense (see Section V).

Section V – Offense and Defense

General Discussion

At all times during the Snow War, one team will always be on offense and the other on defense, with the offense being defined as those seeking the Turnip and the defense as those protecting it. Different objectives and rules apply depending on the status of each team in this regard.

At this point, it must be emphasized that honor should be the binding principle for all conduct in the Siloa Snow War, and this is particularly so with regard to the regulations here in Section V, as well as those in Section VIII. Warriors are to be reminded of Siloa's village code: "Noble deeds are a crown to both king and commoner."

Subsection 1 – Offense – The Turnip-Seekers

The goal of the offense is to claim the Turnip from the defense, which is accomplished by throwing snowballs at members of the defense to freeze them and then searching them for the Turnip. If anyone on defense is hit by a snowball, he must freeze and is not permitted to talk (This includes any and all kinds of vocalizations.) or move again until tagged by a fellow member of the defense. Also, it must be specified that the only valid hits with a snowball are those that strike at the waist or above. And if there is a dispute with respect to a hit's validity, both sides are encouraged to do the honorable thing and concede. Whoever concedes first is most honorable.

Those on offense may go anywhere within the Snow War's viable boundaries in their attempt to claim the Turnip (see Section VI for such boundaries). But if a player is hit in a valid manner by a snowball from defense, he must return to and tag his fort (see Section VII) before proceeding and cannot throw any more snowballs until after he has touched it.

Subsection 2 – Defense – The Turnip-Keepers

The goal of the defense is to protect the Turnip, primarily by keeping its whereabouts unknown to the offense. The Turnip may not be concealed on the ground or in, on, under, etc. any other non-human location in the defense area. Rather, it must be hidden on the actual person of one of the players on defense. Furthermore, it must be hidden in an area of his or her clothes that he or she would not mind the opposing team searching. Any violation of this regulation is a severely shameful and dishonorable act, as members of the offense are not permitted to search such areas.

If a member of the defense is hit by a snowball from the offense, he must freeze and remain silent until tagged by another member of his team, as explained in Subsection 1 above.

The defense may attempt to protect the Turnip by hitting members of the offense with snowballs, which, as explained in Subsection 1 above, will force them to go back to their fort before proceeding or throwing any more snowballs. However, those on defense are not permitted to go past the street front of Lampler's Lane on their side of the street. If they do, they are subject to the violations of boundaries by the defense found in Section VI. Also, the same principles outlined in Subsection 1 above must be followed for the validity of hits, as well as for the settling of any arguments about this matter.

Subsection 3 – Reversal of Roles

The instant that the Turnip is claimed by a member of the offense, the identities of the teams are switched, with the defense becoming offense and vice versa. Since it will not always be possible for various members of the teams to be aware that this has occurred, their operations under the prior arrangement of offense and defense will be considered provisionally valid but only until they learn that the situation has reversed, at which point all previous effects are nullified. In such a case, any who were frozen (see Subsection 1), mistakenly assuming they were still on defense, are allowed to move the instant they learn of the new state of affairs. And any who were going toward their fort to tag it under the incorrect supposition that they were still on offense (again, see Subsection 1) need not complete this task before proceeding to throw snowballs at their opponents.

Subsection 4 – Turnip-Snatching

The normal method for the offense to get the Turnip is to freeze a member of the defense and search said player for the Turnip, extracting it as soon as it has been located. However, if this has just been accomplished, the player who has had the Turnip taken from him may simply try to snatch it back from his assailant, since his team has at that point turned to offense. Furthermore, a player need not be frozen to have the Turnip taken from him. If it is in plain sight, such as in a player's hand or on the ground, a member of the offense may simply snatch it if he is able; this is a fully legitimate means of acquiring the Turnip.

Section VI – Boundaries

The permissible combat area for the Snow War is rectangular in shape and is defined as follows:

The eastern boundary of this area shall be the north-south line running through the west side of Hemptwist's Shed. The northern boundary shall be the east-west line running through the north side of Founders' Rock. The southern boundary shall be the east-west line running through the south edge of Pemblin's Well. And the western boundary shall be the north-south line running through the spot where Follim's Field begins sloping up to Midsummer Meadow.

If anyone goes outside these boundaries while in possession of the Turnip, it is forfeited to the other team. And if anyone goes outside these boundaries but does not have the Turnip, the penalties vary according to whether he is on offense or defense. If the player is on offense, he must go tag his fort (see Section VII) before performing any further actions, and if he is on defense, he must return to the nearest point of departure from the boundaries and freeze until tagged by a fellow team member.

Section VII – Forts

Each team must have some kind of fort, although the design and size of this structure need not be strictly regulated. This fort will serve a dual purpose; it is the designated point to which those on offense must return after they are hit, but it also can function as a stronghold for those on defense.

The Whirlwinds' fort must be built by Hemptwist's Shed, and the Thunders' fort must be erected in the spot mirroring this at the west edge of Follim's Field.

Section VIII – Special Regulations Regarding the Ploughman's Shanty and Other Structures

Thanks to the great charity of the honorable Orinn Berthaway, the Ploughman's Shanty (hereafter referred to primarily as "the Shanty") is open to players from both sides as a sanctuary from the cold and as a place to rest, eat and drink. Although the Shanty is technically within the territory of the Rimwold Thunders, the interior of the structure is designated as neutral ground wherein no warfare may occur.

Compromises must be made by both sides to preserve the neutrality of this ground. Rimwold Thunders are not allowed to attack Agleri Whirlwinds who have entered Thunder territory in order to visit the Shanty nor are they permitted to attack them when they are departing. Also, an exception must be made for Agleri Whirlwinds when they are traveling to and from the Shanty while on defense; this will not be considered a trespass of their designated western boundary (see note on boundaries for the defense in Subsection 2 of Section V, as well as the related penalty in Section VI). However, Agleri Whirlwinds must not venture into Rimwold Thunder territory and use a claimed trip to the Ploughman's Shanty as a pretense to keep from being hit when no such trip is really the intent. To minimize such a possibility, Whirlwinds genuinely visiting the Shanty are required to only cross over into Thunder territory near the Shanty itself and to head directly to and from its front door.

Although it is permissible for the Turnip to be taken into the Shanty by a player who is hiding it on his person, trips to the Shanty by any such individual must be infrequent and cannot last for more than a few minutes, and a team as a whole should certainly not make a regular practice of this sort of thing – honor should bind each team not to abuse this privilege.

However, it is not permissible for an individual to take the Turnip into any structure besides the Ploughman's Shanty, such as a home, workshop, shed or the like. If he has cause to enter such a structure, he must give the Turnip to someone else on defense before proceeding.

Players are permitted to enter any structure in Siloa proper if such need should arise, since daily life is complex and obviously not fully set aside on the day of the Snow War. But warfare cannot be conducted in the interior of any building nor can players shamelessly use entry into various structures as an excuse to keep from being hit by enemy snowballs.

However, if there is legitimate cause for such entry, other players should abstain from attacking. In all cases, individuals should exercise good conscience and honor in their doings on the day of the Snow War.

Section IX – Leaders and Captains

There shall be five leaders for each team, selected by popular agreement in the autumn just prior to the Snow War. Two of these leaders from each team will be captains; one shall be a boy and the other a girl. These will have oversight of both their team as a whole and of the other leaders. Among the other three leaders for each team, at least one must be a boy and at least one must be a girl.

Leaders should be selected on the basis of their abilities as both players and strategists. Generally speaking, players with a well-balanced set of skills make the best leaders. Desirable skills include swift running, high agility, sure aim, clear thinking in intense situations, charisma, good interpersonal relations and clever strategizing.

All the leaders, and particularly the captains, are in charge of developing and implementing strategies, as well as making critical decisions, directing charges, etc. However, it is expected that they will not be high-handed or seek to manage too many of the finer details of their team's operation.

Technically speaking, all of the leaders' decisions and orders are only strong suggestions, not binding commands, but the players under their supervision are heavily urged to follow their instructions, since the reason they were elected as leaders in the first place is their ability to guide their team toward victory.

Section X – Lunch

Lunch will be provided by four generous host families, two for each team. Each host house should prepare food to supply slightly more than half of the respective team it is serving that year. Players are permitted to go back and forth between the two houses hosting their own team but are not allowed to enter the host houses of the opposing team, as this would constitute a form of unauthorized espionage. During lunch, this applies likewise to visiting any structure on the opposite side of the street from which a player resides, although players are allowed to visit any structure on the same side of the street as their respective team, as well as the neutral ground of the Ploughman's Shanty.

As noted in Section II, the lunch segment of the Snow War technically starts and concludes with a ringing of the village bell. However, following lunch, players on both sides are encouraged to give a short period of grace to their opponents in which this minor point is set aside, since a few preparations must often be made before starting the latter half of the Snow War.

Team Rosters for the Siloa Snow War of LE 711

Below is a chart listing the members of the two teams of the Eleventh Annual Siloa Snow War: the Agleri Whirlwinds, who live east of Siloa's main street, Lampler's Lane (also known as Main Lane), and the Rimwold Thunders, who live west of that thoroughfare. Please note that the names are listed geographically rather than alphabetically. (This is in accordance with the way Siloans would make such a chart, since they tend to organize information geographically in instances such as this. However, having excellent memories, they have no need for such a chart and almost none of them can read anyhow.)

For the Agleri Whirlwinds, the names are listed from those living at the north end of Lampler's Lane down to those living at the south end, followed by those living on the east side of Agleri Walk (the street just east of Lampler's Lane), also from north to south. For the Rimwold Thunders, the process is mirrored. These are listed from those living at the north end of Lampler's Lane down to those living at the south end, followed by those living on the west side of Rimwold Row (the street just west of Lampler's Lane), also from north to south. In instances where there are siblings, these are listed from oldest to youngest rather than alphabetically. The gender of each individual is indicated by the standard "M" for male and "F" for female. Age is indicated quite mundanely by the corresponding number of years. In the column marked "Notable Features," an asterisk is used to mark persons who are team leaders, with a capital "C" accompanying the two captains of each team. The letter "N" (for 'no good') is used in this column as an ignoble indicator for the Seedbucket children, who every year refuse to partake in the Siloa Snow War.

AGLERI WHIRLWINDS ROSTER			
NAME	GENDER	AGE	NOTABLE FEATURES
Cromnic Barleycroft	M	15	*C
Saneldra Barleycroft	F	12	
Neldon Broadbuckle	M	11	
Tallis Pestleman	M	13	
Dallis Pestleman	M	13	
Edlimar Pestleman	M	11	
Tornigus Pestleman	M	8	
Bingleton Stickytub	M	13	
Hapworth Stickytub	M	10	
Mozzalyn Stickytub	F	8	
Tressy Axleman	F	11	*
Mannidor Axleman	M	9	
Tambris Turnsoil	M	14	
Idaline Heddlehem	F	15	
Ossner Boltsnip	M	14	*
Lempeera Boltsnip	F	8	
Verraliss Peddlepot	F	8	
Crommenblatt Seedbucket	M	13	N
Dretchina Seedbucket	F	12	N
Mergatha Seedbucket	F	10	N
Hendra Timberfall	F	15	*C
Mylis Timberfall	F	14	
Furdie Timberfall	F	13	
Branko Timberfall	M	12	
Corim Timberfall	M	11	*
Tedge Timberfall	M	10	
Leena Timberfall	F	9	
Traysia Timberfall	F	7	
Sharessa Woodhew	F	11	
Egliston Doughbury	M	10	
Sanny Tillwater	F	10	
Daniseth Tillwater	F	7	
Talaysia Cantlecraft	F	14	
Pelania Tarmintree	F	7	
Handora Swiftsaw	F	9	
Ambril Boughpluck	F	9	
Belgo Strapstitch	M	12	
Nemmadib Strapstitch	M	9	
Condrig Brakesnare	M	11	

RIMWOLD THUNDERS ROSTER			
NAME	GENDER	AGE	NOTABLE FEATURES
Fanella Berthaway	F	14	
Donnemig Berthaway	M	11	
Tamyra Berthaway	F	7	
Branlum Harrowdell	M	15	*
Harlia Harrowdell	F	11	
Mallimo Lampler	M	14	
Vahlia Lampler	F	12	
Jalanna Boughpluck	F	14	
Orris Boughpluck	M	12	
Mellinor Rushwick	F	15	
Mayvelyn Rushwick	F	13	
Haldren Wedgenware	M	14	
Rannion Rillspan	M	14	*C
Tallibot Tapertrim	M	7	
Laysaree Lyelather	F	10	
Hobbo Barnwain	M	15	
Sindagil Barnwain	F	13	
Darmon Barnwain	M	11	
Falgren Timberfall	M	10	
Sullaryn Nimbletack	F	8	
Wellis Brackenlay	M	12	
Tombro Brackenlay	M	8	
Nammalyn Bevelbrick	F	12	
Carrayna Nockshaft	F	14	*
Alnasyn Wrastlebuck	F	13	
Damrig Brightcup	M	12	
Erranet Brightcup	F	8	
Farbis Berrydore	M	13	
Faysa Berrydore	F	7	
Aradis Kingblade	M	12	*
Teric Kingblade	M	10	
Mellora Kingblade	F	7	
Quinnia Greyloam	F	9	
Mallany Applecot	F	11	
Pallamen Barleycroft	M	8	
Stecko Wealdwalker	M	9	
Rayela Rushwick	F	9	
Stayla Beamstander	F	15	*C
Ryaleth Beamstander	F	10	
Olligon Furrowmead	M	7	
Rannarom Woodhew	M	7	
Brammiston Lathemaster	M	9	

A Chronology of Significant Dates
in Neldon's Adventures

Ferenos 26, LE 699 – Birth of Neldon Broadbuckle

Alareth 28, LE 711 – The Eleventh Annual Siloa Snow War

Harasa 17, LE 711 – Neldon's Voyage on the Koobachinky

Tannaril 23, LE 712 – Neldon's Performance as Groddevar's Assistant No. 3 in the Prandingars' Pageant

Pronunciation Guide and Index

This final appendix is included for those readers who would like to delve deeper into the lore of Orona, especially its linguistic landscape. Accordingly, it contains an alphabetical listing of all the Oronic entities, along with their proper pronunciations, which appear in the text of this book in the main story and in the appendices. Each entry is immediately followed by a page number reference, set within square brackets, which usually marks either the location of the term's first appearance in the text or the instance in which it is most clearly explained.

Due to its conciseness and suitability for accurately representing various phonemes, the IPA (International Phonetic Alphabet) system of phonetic transcription has been chosen to represent the pronunciation of persons, places, things and events used throughout this volume. Several tables of correspondence between IPA symbols and phonemes in the English language precede the listing of Oronic entities mentioned in this book. There is also a small list identifying grammatical abbreviations that are used in this appendix. Please note that items are generally listed with the singular form as the primary entry unless the plural form is more prevalent in the text, with the exception of the various Narthanna and a few miscellaneous items, which are all listed in the plural. If the plural is irregular, it will often have its own entry, as in the case of the Daigan word 'Narthanna'.

NB: Words or parts of words which are of English origin are not generally provided with IPA representation, as their pronunciation can be readily deduced without it.

NB: A few terms which may seem to be rather mundane are included in this index because they are used in this book in a technical Oronic sense.

Consonants

b – <u>b</u>ook, mo<u>b</u>

c – hear<u>ts</u>, va<u>ts</u>

d – <u>d</u>og, ma<u>d</u>

f – <u>f</u>ire, lau<u>gh</u>

g – <u>g</u>old, fla<u>g</u>

h – <u>h</u>ill, <u>h</u>and

j – <u>y</u>ard, <u>y</u>ore

k – <u>c</u>astle, la<u>ke</u>

l – <u>l</u>oss, ca<u>ll</u>

m – <u>m</u>ark, ra<u>m</u>

n – <u>n</u>ail, bar<u>n</u>

p – <u>p</u>ond, ta<u>p</u>

r – <u>r</u>ow, ba<u>r</u>

s – <u>s</u>oft, pa<u>ss</u>

t – <u>t</u>ale, ra<u>t</u>

v – <u>v</u>ale, ha<u>ve</u>

w – <u>w</u>orld, al<u>w</u>ays

x – as in Scottish lo<u>ch</u> or German Ba<u>ch</u>

z – ma<u>ze</u>, tray<u>s</u>,

θ – <u>th</u>row, ba<u>th</u>

ð – al<u>th</u>ough, fa<u>th</u>er

ţ – be<u>tt</u>er, li<u>tt</u>le

ʃ – <u>sh</u>ore, a<u>sh</u>

ŋ – ri<u>ng</u>, a<u>n</u>ger

t͡ʃ – <u>ch</u>imney, la<u>tch</u>

d͡ʒ – <u>j</u>ar, a<u>ge</u>

ʒ – trea<u>s</u>ure, barra<u>ge</u>

ʔ – glottal stop as in uh(ʔ)oh

Vowels

ɑː – <u>f</u><u>a</u>ther, c<u>o</u>t

ɛ – l<u>e</u>t, h<u>ea</u>d

iː – <u>f</u><u>ee</u>d, l<u>ea</u>f

oʊ – sh<u>ow</u>, m<u>o</u>le

uː – r<u>u</u>de, t<u>oo</u>

æ – s<u>a</u>t, sh<u>a</u>ck

ə – <u>a</u>gree, s<u>u</u>ppose

ɪ – l<u>i</u>d, p<u>i</u>n

ɔː – f<u>a</u>ll, l<u>aw</u>

ʊ – sh<u>ou</u>ld, g<u>oo</u>d

ʌ – d<u>u</u>ck, s<u>u</u>n

aɪ – h<u>i</u>ve, p<u>i</u>le

eɪ – p<u>ay</u>, r<u>a</u>ce

aʊ – n<u>ow</u>, l<u>ou</u>d

ɔɪ – t<u>oy</u>, c<u>oi</u>n

ᵊ – mutt<u>o</u>n, sudd<u>e</u>n

Vowels followed by 'R' sounds

ɑr – f<u>ar</u>, c<u>ar</u>pet

ɛər – b<u>ear</u>, wh<u>ere</u>

ɪər – f<u>ear</u>, ch<u>eer</u>

ɔər – b<u>ore</u>, <u>oar</u>

ɝ – b<u>ur</u>n, w<u>or</u>k

' – This symbol precedes the syllable which is most strongly stressed. (e.g., delectable: dɪ'lɛktəbəl)

Abbreviations

Sing. – singular

Pl. – plural

Adj. – adjective

Masc. – masculine

Fem. – feminine

Disamb. – disambiguation

Agleri [203] – əˈglɛəriː

Agleri Hallockhummers [xxiv] –
əˈglɛəriː ˈhæləkhʌmᵊrz

Agleri, Plains of [208] – əˈglɛəriː

Agleri Walk [203] – əˈglɛəriː

Agleri Whirlwinds, The [203] – əˈglɛəriː

Alareth [211] – ˈælərɛθ

Alnasyn Wrastlebuck [37] – ˈælnəsɪn
ˈræsᵊlbʌk

Alschendorn [166] – ˈɔːlʃɛndɔərn

Ambrick Tarmintree [46] – ˈæmbrɪk
ˈtɑrmᵊntriː

Ambril Boughpluck [68] – ˈæmbrɪl

Anella Ringmark [1] – əˈnɛlə

Angalee [150] – ˈæŋgəliː

Anganor [v] – ˈæŋgənɔər

Apex of Archaea, The [203] – ɑrˈkeɪə

Applecots [xviii] – ˈæpᵊlkɑːts

Applehead [169]

Aradath [203] – ˈɛərədɑːθ

Aradis Kingblade [xlvi] – ˈɛərədɪs

Aragest [203] – ˈɛərəgɛst

Archaea [203] – ɑrˈkeɪə

Balcumberries [203] – ˈbælkʌmbɛəriːz

Ballistic Broadbuckle [85]

Banlogs (sing. Banlog) [xxiii] –
ˈbænlɔːgz (ˈbænlɔːg)

Barada (pl. Barada; adj. Baradic) [204]
– bəˈrɑːdə (bəˈrɑːdɪk)

Bardlin Bridge, The [142] – ˈbɑrdlɪn

Bardlin Creek [129] – ˈbɑrdlɪn

Barleycrofts [xviii]

Barnwain Stead [xlii] – ˈbɑrnweɪn stɛd

Barolla (pl. Barolli) [204] – bəˈroʊlə
(bəˈroʊliː)

Bay-Leprechauns [208]

Beamstanders [xviii]

Belestro [xlviii] – bɛˈlɛstroʊ

Belgo Strapstitch [23] – ˈbɛlgoʊ

Bellin [211] – ˈbɛlɪn

Belmo Swiftsaw [168] – ˈbɛlmoʊ

Bernalla Elmensill [213] – bɝˈnɔːlə
ˈɛlmᵊnsɪl

Berridon Greyloam [168] – ˈbɛərɪdɑːn

Berrydore, Old Farmer [131] –
ˈbɛəriːdɔər

Berrydores [xviii] – ˈbɛəriːdɔərz

Bing, Bang, Bongle [204] – bɪŋ bæŋ
ˈbɑːŋgᵊl

Bingles [56] – ˈbɪŋgᵊlz – see 'Bingleton
Stickytub'

Bingleton Stickytub [19] – ˈbɪŋgᵊltən

Bogglesnop [204] – ˈbɑːgᵊlsnɑːp

Bollicot Pestleman [xli] – ˈbɔːlɪkɑːt
ˈpɛsᵊlmən

Bop [208] – bɑːp

Boughplucks [xviii]

Brammiston Lathemaster [58] –
ˈbræmɪstᵊn ˈleɪðmæstɝ

Branding of Agleri, The [xvii] – əˈglɛəriː

Dark Meridian, The [205]

Darmon Barnwain [xlii] – 'dɑrmᵊn 'bɑrnweɪn

Delinah [178] – dɛ'laɪnə

Dellumberries [205] – 'dɛlʌmbɛəriːz

Demryn [xlix] – 'dɛmrɪn

Denossa [xx] – dɛ'noʊsə

Derrig [211] – 'dɛərɪg

Dhar-Marda [208] – ðɑr 'mɑrdə

Dingleflobbin (disamb. bird) [205] – 'dɪŋᵊlflɑːbɪn

Dingleflobbin (disamb. insult) [205] – 'dɪŋᵊlflɑːbɪn

Dolnario [xix] – doʊl'nɑriːoʊ

Donnemig Berthaway [47] – 'dɑːnɛmɪg 'bɝθəweɪ

Dorman's Down [124] – 'dɔərmᵊnz

Dorna Rimwright [151] – 'dɔərnə

Dozedale [208] – 'doʊzdeɪl

Drampadus Broadbuckle [xxxviii] – 'dræmpədʌs

Drampo Broadbuckle [xxxviii] – 'dræmpoʊ – see 'Drampadus Broadbuckle'

Drannenfross (disamb. type of being) [165] – 'drænɛnfrɑːs

Drannenfross, The (disamb. particular character) [167] – 'drænɛnfrɑːs

Dretchina Seedbucket [25] – drɛ'tʃiːnə

Druids (fem. Druidess; adj. Druidic) [205]

Dugamar Ringmark [l] – 'duːgəmɑr

Dwarves (adj. Dwarven) [205]

Dying Soldier from Urmensdal [168] – 'ɝmᵊnzdɔːl

Eastrange, The [205]

Eavesway, The [xviii] – 'iːvzweɪ

Edlimar Pestleman [xli] – 'ɛdlɪmɑr 'pɛsᵊlmən

Egliston Doughbury [79] – 'ɛglɪstən 'doʊbɝi:

Elaya [211] – ɛ'lɑːjə

Elder Forest, The [xiii]

Eldrasso [xlviii] – ɛl'drɑːsoʊ

Eldritch Isles, The [208]

Eleveners, The [xviii] – ɛ'lɛvɛnɝz

Elmensill, The (adj. Elmensillic) [8] – 'ɛlmᵊnsɪl (ɛlmᵊn'sɪlɪk)

Elves (adj. Elven) [205]

Emmerloss, Lake [186] – 'ɛmɝlɑːs

Eoreth [175] – 'eɪərɛθ

Erdion [xxx] – 'ɛərdiːɑːn

Eribeth Kingblade [xlvi] – 'ɛərɪbɛθ

Erranet Brightcup [55] – 'ɛərənɛt – see 'Netty Brightcup'

Estereth [208] – 'ɛstərɛθ

Falderon [165] – 'fɔːldɝɑːn

Falderon Shed, The [182] – 'fɔːldɝɑːn

Falgren Timberfall [100] – 'fɔːlgrɛn

Fanella Berthaway [167] – fæ'nɛlə 'bɝθəweɪ

Fannymash [205] – 'fæniːmæʃ

Fannymash and Fudbuddles [205] – 'fæniːmæʃ ænd 'fʌdbʌdᵊlz

Farbis Berrydore [72] – 'fɑrbɪs 'bɛəriːdɔər

Farga (sing. Farga; adj. Fargese) [205] – 'fɑrgə (fɑr'giːz)

Fargalin Chipperchop [213] – 'fɑrgəlɪn

Faysa Berrydore [29] – 'feɪsə 'bɛəriːdɔər

Heddlehem, Mrs. [50] – ˈhɛdᵊlhɛm

Helgonians [165] – hɛlˈgouniːənz

Hemmigan [206] – ˈhɛmɪgᵊn

Hemmigan Hideaway [xl] – ˈhɛmɪgᵊn

Hemmigan Hideaway Gang, The [xl] – ˈhɛmɪgᵊn

Hemptwist's Shed [214]

Hendra Timberfall [25] – ˈhɛndrə

Hendrig Rimwright [151] – ˈhɛndrɪg

Herragoot [206] – ˈhɛərəguːʈ

Hidewash [206]

Hildenrill Mill [xxxix] – ˈhɪldɛnrɪl

Hillarnia Peddlepot [xxvi] – hɪˈlarniːə ˈpɛdᵊlpaːt

Hindrogs (sing. Hindrog) [xxiv] – ˈhɪndrɔːgz (ˈhɪndrɔːg)

Hobbalin Broadbuckle [xxxix] – ˈhaːbəlɪn

Hobbo Barnwain [xlii] – ˈhaːbou ˈbarnwɛɪn

Hobbsy [xxxix] – ˈhaːbziː – see 'Hobbalin Broadbuckle'

Hobnoggets (disamb. expression) [206] – ˈhɔːbnɔːgᵊts

Hobnoggets (disamb. food) [206] – ˈhɔːbnɔːgᵊts

Hody Hody Hoo [206] – ˈhoudiː ˈhoudiː huː

Holgum [206] – ˈhoulgʌm

Hoyah [206] – ˈhɔɪjə

Huldion (adj. Huldionite) [206] – ˈhʊldiːaːn (ˈhʊldiːənaɪt)

Hygrellia Nozzlesnatch [120] – haɪˈgrɛliːə ˈnaːzᵊlsnætʃ

Idaline Heddlehem [50] – ˈaɪdᵊlaɪn ˈhɛdᵊlhɛm

Ildurion [211] – ɪlˈdɝiːən

Ingans (sing. Ingan; adj. Ingan) [206] – ˈɪŋᵊnz (ˈɪŋᵊn)

Jacanno [xlix] – d͡ʒəˈkaːnou

Jalanna Boughpluck [47] – d͡ʒəˈlænə

Jassuna [208] – d͡ʒəˈsuːnə

Journey of Marda [187] – ˈmardə

Kebbles [xxxix] – ˈkɛbᵊlz – see 'Kebley Broadbuckle'

Kebley Broadbuckle [xxxix] – ˈkɛbliː

Kibber [208] – ˈkɪbɝ

Kindarra [li] – kɪnˈdarə

Kingblade Cottage [xlvi]

Knucklebuckle [102]

Koobachinky (pl. Koobachinkies) [133] – ˈkuːbətʃɪŋkiː (ˈkuːbətʃɪŋkiːz)

Koobachinky, The [139] – ˈkuːbətʃɪŋkiː

Lake Emmerloss [186] – ˈɛmɝlaːs

Lamplers [xviii] – ˈlæmplɝz

Lampler's Lane [207] – ˈlæmplɝz

Landrenna [211] – lænˈdrɛnə

Langman Lampler [xviii] – ˈlæŋmən ˈlæmplɝ

Langman's Bridge [xviii] – ˈlæŋmənz

Lannamil Barleycroft [162] – ˈlænəmɪl

Latter Epoch, The [207] – ˈiːpaːk

Lavrassi Academy [xlviii] – ləˈvræsiː

Laysaree Lyelather [85] – ˈleɪsariː ˈlaɪlæðɝ

Leddaric Pestleman [xli] – ˈlɛdərɪk ˈpɛsᵊlmən

Leena Timberfall [25] – ˈliːnə

Legend of Falderon, The [202] – ˈfɔːldɝaːn

Stickytub Alley [32]

Stickytub Cheese [xxxix]

Stickytub Sortie [32]

Stickytub Taffy [xxxix]

Storvossi [l] – stɔərˈvoʊsiː

Sullaryn Nimbletack [86] – ˈsʊlərɪn

Talaysia Cantlecraft [55] – təˈleɪsiːə ˈkæntᵊlkræft

Taldryn [xxii] – ˈtɔːldrɪn

Talgenslip [173] – ˈtɔːlgɛnslɪp

Tallibot Tapertrim [85] – ˈtælɪbɑːt

Talliford Stickytub [xxxix] – ˈtælɪfɝd

Tallis Pestleman [xli] – ˈtælɪs ˈpɛsᵊlmən

Tambris Turnsoil [26] – ˈtæmbrɪs

Tamfino [133] – tæmˈfiːnoʊ

Tamfino, The [133] – tæmˈfiːnoʊ

Tamyra Berthaway [103] – təˈmaɪrə ˈbɝθəweɪ

Tannaril [211] – ˈtænərɪl

Tapertrim Chandlery [xlii]

Tarino, River [xlix] – tarˈiːnoʊ

Tarion [xxii] – ˈtɛəriːɑːn (alternatively, ˈtɛərlːᵊn)

Tarmin Cakes [209] – ˈtarmᵊn

Tarmin Cookies [163] – ˈtarmᵊn

Tarmins [209] – ˈtarmᵊnz

Tarnadin [v] – ˈtarnədɪn

Tarwyn [xlix] – ˈtarwɪn

Tassaru [208] – təˈsaruː

Tas Wedgenware [164] – tæs ˈwed͡ʒenweər

Tavenndi (sing. Tavenndo) [xxv] – təˈvɛndiː (təˈvɛndoʊ)

Tavenndi Lawn [xxv] – təˈvɛndiː

Tedge Timberfall [25] – tɛd͡ʒ

Tellig [xx] – ˈtɛlɪg

Telnara (pl. Telnari; adj. Telnaric) [210] – tɛlˈnarə (tɛlˈnariː; tɛlˈnarɪk)

Telzuri [xlix] – tɛlˈzɝi

Temerrin [203] – tɛˈmɛərɪn

Teric Kingblade [xlvi] – ˈtɛərɪk

Tessnah, The [xxix] – ˈtɛsnə

Three Princes of Sundial Island, The [208]

Thunderdunders [72] – ˈθʌndɝdʌndɝz

Thunders, The [210] – see 'Rimwold Thunders, The'

Timberfall Hall [xliv]

Timberfall Principle, The [xlvii]

Tinky [208] – ˈtɪŋkiː

Tombro Brackenlay [72] – ˈtɑːmbroʊ

Topaz Turnip, The [214]

Torlinberries [210] – ˈtɔərlɪnbɛəriːz

Torlinberry Pie [210] – ˈtɔərlɪnbɛəriː

Torlinberry Syrup [xv] – ˈtɔərlɪnbɛəriː

Tornigus Pestleman [xli] – ˈtɔərnɪgʌs ˈpɛsᵊlmən

Trabbis Woodhew [187] – ˈtræbɪs

Trambo Timberfall [xliv] – ˈtræmboʊ

Traysia Timberfall [25] – ˈtreɪsiːə

Tressy Axleman [25] – ˈtrɛsiː ˈæksᵊlmən

Triple Wave Whammer, The [19] – ˈwæmɝ

Trip Maze of Peddlepot Alley, The [16] – ˈpɛdᵊlpɑːt

Trollig Lake [xliii] – ˈtrɔːlɪg

Trolls (adj. Trollish) [210]

Jarrett Skaddisson

Jarrett Skaddisson is a native of the Midwestern US, an accomplished musician and composer and an avid linguist, philosopher, author, researcher, mountain climber, spelunker and tea enthusiast. He lived in the Orient for several years as a child and has traveled to more than 30 countries for mission work, performance tours and good, old-fashioned adventures. His favorite pastimes are reading, writing, making music, learning languages, eating exotic foods, voice acting, doing improv comedy, impressions and engaging in a wide variety of shenanigans. He lives with his wife, Michelle, to whom he has been married for 15 years, their son, Fritz, who is an exceedingly happy, imaginative, energetic and hilarious 4-year-old, and their beautiful and exceptionally cute baby daughter, Nora. Jarrett can be contacted via email at jarrettskaddisson@ gmail.com or through his Facebook page, facebook.com/TheKingblade Chronicles. He also has a website, thekingbladechronicles.com, which features concept art for the series, along with other material not found in the books, and you can follow him on Twitter at @AradisKingblade and on Instagram at @thekingbladechronicles.